Joe,

I consider myself fortunate to have joined the SQN team. It's such a great group of folks who work hard together and know how to laugh together. Everyone has been so supportive.

Thanks for your leadership and more importantly, your friendship.

Paul Steinberg

HURRY MOON

HURRY MOON

Paul Steinberg

This Book is a work of fiction. All names, characters, locations, organizations and events are products of the author's imagination or are used fictitiously

HURRY MOON Copyright © 2013 by Paul Steinberg

All rights reserved

ISBN-13:978-0-9910853-1-6
ISBN-10:0991085310

Dedicated to the Love of my life, Dorrie. You have made every part of my life, even the challenging parts, seem like a dream.

Table of Contents

- Same old same old and then… 5
- Dalton: Things start getting better 23
- Horrible and wonderful at once 32
- New beginnings 45
- Don Hunter: Maybe I am finally figuring this dad thing out 59
- Sienna: Love and loss and love 64
- Dalton: Growing up is… 70
- A Nikon moment 78
- The first temptation 86
- Laurie: Someplace special for two 93
- Heart, mind and body 98
- That's entertainment 107
- Now serving - crossroads for everyone 122
- Sienna: The first move 135
- Father's day 147
- The camera never lies 163
- Amanda: The goddess and the mortal 170
- Bingo! 175
- Birthday presents 191
- Traveler: Pursuing the One 206
- Departure 211
- Sienna: Dalton shares his croissant 222
- Dalton: My life is a dream, and yet 228
- Fashion, detection and conversation 237
- Fishing in the Big Apple 246
- Baiting the hook in designer shoes 260
- Samantha: I have a dream 271
- Sienna: A day at the beach 276
- Heart to heart 281
- Decisions decisions 288
- A recipe for success 296
- Dalton: A taste of real 302
- Day and Night 313
- Bowing the A 325
- Samantha: I raise the baton 338
- Romantic daybreak 345
- Checking in and checking out 359
- Penn Station 374
- Sienna: Once upon a time… 380
- Sealed with a kiss 386

1.

Same old same old and then…

Harris Elementary School stands like some red bricked medieval castle made larger by its mirrored reflection in the rain drenched street. Dalton Hunter stares nervously up at the imposing structure. Large steel doors painted a dark institutional green are the only things that stand between him and the dungeon-like classrooms on the other side. He doesn't have to go through those doors to imagine the polished wood floors or the dark, turning stairways leading to the second floor. He can almost smell the mix of fear, authority and floor wax in the air. At seven years of age, he is already experienced in the art of sizing up new schools. Despite its menacing appearance, this school has some good qualities. It is surrounded by a large playground and tall trees perfect for remaining hidden when the bullies are looking for you. He has seen them all; new ones with sprawling layouts and classroom doors that go directly to the outside, and city schools that mean a ride on public transit and tall chain link fences. The one constant is the kids, all different and still the same.

Looking up at the sky, he remembers walking to one school and hearing a boom so loud, he thought it must be God speaking. He remembers that moment and realizes that, in his eyes, the world is still big and scary and full of things he doesn't understand. It is all too true today. Today there are thick gray clouds, heavy with the remnants of storms the night before. There is the light splashing sound nearby as the rainspouts finish carrying the last of the downpour. Large trees lift wet, black, leafless branches into the early February morning. It is the perfect day for entering yet another new school. Still, the chill in the air is nothing compared to the chill in his heart.

Dalton is grateful for the comforting feel of his mother's hand. It is warm and safe, conveying a gentle authority as she leads him along. He hears the sound of her reassuring words. Though he is more than a little distracted, a few words find their way into his ears, reminders to be thankful for the good things in his life. As he looks at the wet pavement and the shiny street, he realizes something else he can appreciate. Since the rain stopped just before they left their new house, his mother was unable to insist that he wear his bright yellow raincoat. Anything that color is practically an invitation to get beat up; like waving a red cape in a bullring.

Unfortunately, the minuses far outweigh the plusses. He is the new kid again. Again. He'll be invisible unless one of his classmates needs a target for teasing or worse. Dalton tries hard to understand why he is always that second or two late with the quick reply that others do so easily, those magic words that turn the laughter around. Since the school year is well past midterm, he will have to figure out again how the studies in this school compare to the ones in the last, or the one before that. There will be a whole new list of names. He will have to do his best to identify the ones that will make his life miserable. He doesn't even want to think about that first report card. He can already see his father's expression of disappointment.

"Dalton, come on."

Dalton's mother finally breaks through the cloud of gloom. She dresses her face with a hopeful smile. Although he hasn't exactly been pulling back, the weight of his body has stretched his arm to the limit of his reach behind her. Afraid. For a long time Dalton thought of this as almost two words. I am a Fraid. He dresses in a Fraid in the morning and takes a Fraid off every night just before sleep takes over. There are so many things that seem too large and too hard to figure out. What do the faces of all the new kids mean in school after school? Why doesn't his smile work the way he has seen other kid's smiles do?

Soon they are inside. The large steel doors squeal as they open and clang loudly as they shut. The heat inside is a meager, barely noticed comfort as they move through a second set of doors. His mother stops and asks an adult for directions to the main office. For the few moments they are stopped, Dalton wisely maintains a safe distance away from his mother. Now as they are navigating a sea of chattering children, he keeps his head down and tries not to notice the stares of the older boys. What was God thinking when he made sixth graders so big?

They enter a door that leads to a large counter where teachers and secretaries are scurrying before the first bell. Dalton will miss that bell and more before he makes it to his new class. There will be forms for his mother to sign and a talk with the principal. Tomorrow he will ride the noisy bus and have to worry about the first bell like everyone else. A secretary stops momentarily to ask Dalton's mother if she can help and soon directs them to a couple of chairs.

A few minutes later, Dalton and his mother are ushered into the Principal's office. Mr. Fisher is a dark haired man with a friendly face and a voice that sounds like one of those guys on a game show. His blue suit is wrinkled and his tie has wide blue and white stripes. A pair of glasses sits carelessly atop a stack of typed papers.

Dalton glances out the window as Mr. Fisher asks his mother about the previous school. They discuss Dalton's grades. He grabs his glasses and pushes them back on his straight nose as he pulls a folder and a pen from the desk. Outside, the clouds seem to be thinning and there is just a hint of sunshine, a momentary glimpse of sky. Looking around the room, Dalton notices the framed Diploma behind the desk and a banner in scarlet and gray that reads 'Home of the Cardinal'. In the corner is an American flag. In the other corner there is a flag that might have something to do with Ohio. It has stars and stripes with a big "O" on a field of blue. There are gray file cabinets on the opposite wall. On the top of one are a trophy and a picture of a pretty, smiling lady and two smiling children. Next to the cabinets is a book shelf filled with loose leaf binders in an array of flat useful colors.

When the paperwork is completed, Dalton rises with his mother as she gathers him close.

"Be good, pay attention, and Dalton, do your best to make friends okay honey?"

"I'll try Mom," he answers quietly.

"I'm sure he'll do fine, Mrs. Hunter."

Mrs. Hunter bends to stare into her son's eyes. She shares a long look, as if she is trying to impart some secret strength. She has the same wavy, brown hair as her son, but her eyes are hazel while his are blue. They are both slender, but on him it looks youthful, while on her it seems delicate. Dalton watches her departure past the long counter and through the main office door.

Now Dalton follows Mr. Fisher down the long, empty hallway to his classroom. Overhead, long pipes hang one after another, each ending with a glass bowl filled with shabby yellow light that falls onto the wood floor in circles. Mr. Fisher opens a door with a window that sits just above Dalton's eye level and quickly enters, stopping just inside. The teacher is talking to the class when the Principal moves closer, interrupts and whispers a few words. He turns, pats Dalton lightly on the head as he passes, and leaves. The door closes with a final thump.

Dalton looks around the classroom, noticing the red Valentine's hearts and the black silhouettes of George Washington and Abe Lincoln, all made from construction paper. The teacher, whose name he was told and has already forgotten, stands in the front of the room beside her desk. She claps her hands twice to bring the class to attention. The classroom murmur fades.

"All right class. This is Dalton Hunter. He comes to us all the way from Philadelphia, Pennsylvania. Let's give him a warm welcome, shall we? Everyone together..."

The whole class joins her in singsong unison.

"Hello Dalton."

Dalton cannot help but notice two bigger boys in the back as they nudge each other. Their eyes roll up and around and their snickers are low and unfriendly.

The teacher claps her hands again.

"All right now settle down. Dalton, I'm Mrs. Rush. You can take a seat there."

Mrs. Rush is an older teacher with gray hair pulled close to her head. She has dark eyes hidden behind small lensed glasses attached to a golden chain that hangs around her neck. She isn't very tall and has to lean only slightly to meet Dalton with an encouraging smile.

She points to an empty desk near the front. "Do you know what assigned seats are? That will be your desk every day."

Dalton nods and takes his seat. He does his best to hide the disappointment as a desk near the front of class is just one more setback in a day that promises more of the same. The desk has a lid that opens upward with space to store books and pencils. As this is his first day, Dalton leaves the desk alone. Mrs. Rush soon approaches with a book and places it in front of him.

"This is the literature text, Dalton. I will see that you get the other books you need after lunch. We are all fascinated by our new subject, which is 'myths and legends'. Did you study that at your last school?"

Dalton tries to smile, but it only half comes out. She walks back to her spot to continue.

"All right, who can tell me what a genie is?"

Lots of children raise their hands. It has begun.

The clock moves slowly through a talk about genies. Dalton thinks the idea of some big guy living in a little bottle and coming out in a puff of smoke seems a bit silly. The clock moves slower still as they dive into math. The class seems slightly behind the one he left in his last school. They are just starting fractions while Dalton has been doing them since last fall. He is able to answer an easy problem which gathers another smile from Mrs. Rush, but also a dirty look from a girl nearby.

"Know it all," she whispers.

Dalton tries to ignore this, but it is not a sign of a good start. He is happy when the bell rings and it is lunchtime. The children all line up. There is the normal pushing and then they are headed for the cafeteria. Thankfully, his mother remembered to hand him lunch money before they left the house. There was an earlier first day that ended badly when he was left with neither lunch nor money and the teacher had to purchase lunch for him. He smiles at the memory in spite of himself. The class walks down the hall, cinder blocks painted light green halfway up the wall and cream white going on to the ceiling. There are runners high along the wall with the artwork of each class hanging there. The runners are occasionally interrupted by bulletin boards with more detailed displays of projects and class activities. The aroma of hot dogs and pizza indicates they are close to the lunchroom.

After lunch, the children line up again and are led to the playground. As they move outside, the line disintegrates and recess begins in earnest. Mrs. Rush walks over to join the other teachers keeping watch over the students at play. She could not help but notice that the new boy sat alone during lunch. It was clear that he sought out an empty table. What was less clear was whether he wanted to be alone or whether he was hoping someone would join him. In any case, none of his new classmates were interested. A couple of kids finally sat at the other end of the table. Both acted as if he were completely invisible.

Experience has taught Dalton that trying to force his way into established groups is unwise. So he shrugs off the lonely feeling and heads for a nice dry spot near one of the large trees he noticed earlier. With his coat pulled close against the breeze, he nestles against the trunk of the tree. The couple of chocolate chip cookies left from lunch are munched slowly as he scans the sky. The clouds are still prominent, but here and there slashes of blue sky begin to appear.

Girls are running in the schoolyard, playing tag. The boys are playing basketball on the blacktop. There on the damp grass playing soccer, are a few more boys. The still wet play area with its swing sets, slides and monkey bars is deserted. The sound of happily released energy only emphasizes Dalton's quiet situation. He turns to the other direction, where there are houses gathered in a pleasant neighborhood. There are splotches of light on some, turning the grayed whites warmer and golden and the cool blues more like the color of the ocean in summer. He lets the color fill his eyes as he munches the remnant of his last cookie.

Agnes Rush scans the playground keeping an eye on Dalton. She had watched as he found the spot next to a large oak. He seems like a quiet and earnest boy, she thinks, and he has a nice smile. She understands the challenge he faces in making friends with the other children this far into the school year. His reserve will only make things harder. She makes a mental note to put him into one of the reading groups with the kids most likely to give him a chance.

"Agnes, have you heard the latest news from last night's PTA meeting?"

"No Lee, what happened?" Distracted, she lets her thoughts of the new boy fade.

Soon the recess is over. Balls and jump ropes are collected. The children march back to class. Dalton shrugs his way to the end of the line, thankful that the other boys in class had more important things on their minds today than seeking him out. He is pretty certain that they'll be bored enough to think of some torment before too long.

Finally the school day is behind him. Now there is only the dangerous ride on the school bus to survive. By the time he mounts the tall metal stairs there are only a few of the green vinyl seats remaining, each with another child already seated. Two of the three have girls seated which leaves only the last one with a boy who is at least a fourth grader judging by his size. Dalton gets no answer to his quiet 'hi' and spends the next twenty minutes bouncing along the oft-patched suburban roads, trying his best to ignore the playful pokes of his seat mate's elbow. When he finally arrives at his stop, he starts down the aisle and turns back to see the boy's triumphant grin.

The noise and fumes of the departing school bus are replaced by the sounds of the few kids who got off at the same stop and by the aromas of the wet grass in Dalton's front yard. The kids move on quickly with little notice of the new boy. The house sits conveniently at the corner where the bus will appear mornings and afternoons. It is a nice light green cape cod with black shutters and a one car garage. A picket fence that was probably white at some point in the past surrounds the back yard.

Dalton runs into the house and finds his mother seated on the couch in the living room. The sunlight through the window highlights billions of specs of dust like a miniature universe. It is a sign of his mother's efforts to make progress. Still, the boxes are everywhere and the couch is nearly the only clear space in the room. She soon tells him that she spent the day upstairs unpacking things. They look together at the open ones that contain dishes, pots, pans and silverware. It will be a few days before the house takes on some semblance of order.

Dalton reads to his mother from the literature text as she relaxes after the long day's efforts. The assignment is seven pages. He has always been a good reader, so it is completed easily. He returns the book to his worn book bag next to the texts for math and social studies. Each is new, with shiny covers and lots of black and white pictures inside.

"Leave your book bag by the door tonight, honey, so that you can find it easily in the morning. What time does the bus come?"

"The bus driver said to be at the stop at seven thirty."

"We'll get up about twenty minutes before seven then, so you'll have time to dress and have breakfast."

"Okay, Mom."

"Come into the kitchen and keep me company while I make dinner. Do you think you could take the glasses out of the box and stack them neatly in that cabinet?" She points to the place where the glasses will go.

"Sure. What's for dinner?"

"I'm making meatloaf tonight. Dad likes that and I think it will be good to have a nice meal after his first day, don't you?" She smiles hopefully at the thought.

Dalton carries a few glasses at a time to the counter. He carefully peels the newspaper wrapping and then climbs on a kitchen chair to load them into the cabinet. He pulls the door, an aging and slightly stained walnut facing. The kitchen already smells good from the chopped onions that his mother is kneading into the ground beef and the potatoes baking in the oven. It is a warm and comfortable place. The house itself is not particularly large. It is smaller than their last home. Somehow, no matter where they live, these afternoons with his mother are the best parts of his day. They chat about the new school, carefully avoiding the topic of the other children. It seems like no time at all before his father walks in, but the sun has nearly vanished and it won't be long before a nearly full moon hangs in the sky.

Dinner is almost over. Dad settles back in his chair, his tie hanging loosely across his clean white shirt. Don Hunter is not a particularly large man. He is medium height and has just the slightest bulge around the midsection. His hair is curly, but thinning on top, and his sideburns are trimmed to match the lower end of his ears. His eyes are brown and his expression shows the first signs of relaxation after a long day.

"Thanks dear. Dinner was very nice. So Dalton how was your first day?"

"Okay I guess."

Don's expression of ease fades. Dalton's mother sits quietly. She is clearly staying removed from the conversation, her eyes down. She continues eating her dinner.

"What does that mean?"

Dalton does not answer. He knows that his father only wants him to make friends, but doesn't seem to understand the challenge new schools present to seven year olds.

"Dalton, you have to make an effort. You have to make them notice you. It's not so hard to make friends if you'll just try. You have to grow up. There's no place in this world for crybabies. I'll tell you one thing… I don't want to hear any crying from that bedroom of yours tonight. Understand?"

"Yes sir."

"What was that?"

"Yes sir," Dalton repeats with a bit more volume.

"Okay then."

Dalton works up his courage and faces his dad.

"Father?"

Don Hunter stops eating and responds with a look.

"Do you think we can stay here a while?"

Don Hunter looks at his son's hopeful expression, knowing that this job is not the one, but just a stepping stone for the prize he has in sight about six months from now if things go well.

"We'll see."

Dalton leaves the table, his head down.

"Don, he's just a boy."

"Sharon, we've talked about this. The boy has to learn to adapt."

Sharon Hunter picks at the last of her meal, occasionally looking up and hoping to see some opening, some crack in her husband's armor that would enable him to see their son as she does. Don is not a hard man and he honestly thinks the tough approach he believes in will prepare Dalton for the world. Perhaps, she thinks, he is right. Her love for her husband and her dreams for her son are in constant conflict. She hopes that she will be able to make her husband understand the cost of all the moving that neither he nor she has paid. Unfortunately, that hope will have to wait for another day.

Moonlight splashes the walls of Dalton's bedroom. Both of his parents have pulled the covers close around him and wished him 'sweet dreams'. His mother has already laid out a folded shirt and pants on the back of his desk chair for tomorrow's school day, and turned off the light. With his father's threat still in his ears, Dalton has held himself still, longing for the deeper silence of his parents slumber. Shadows of tree branches swaying just outside leave their marks on his bedroom wall and have kept him company during the long wait. His parent's whispers retreated a while ago behind their bedroom door. Then the last words between them, unclear but still audible, were spoken. At last the house is quiet.

Dalton rises from his bed and approaches his own partially open door. He listens there a short while longer, before returning to his bed. The only sound he hears is a restless neighborhood dog barking nearby. He carefully sidesteps the shoes neatly settled on the floor and eases himself beneath the covers again. Only now, when he is certain that his parents are sleeping, does he let the tears he has held back roll silently down his cheeks. He wipes his eyes and relaxes now that his sadness is released. The toll of the long wait finally overtakes him. Soon his eyes are heavy and he sinks into sleep.

"Hey Sleepyhead, wake up."

Dalton lifts his head from his pillow and blinks his eyes as he adjusts to the light. Remembering that his mother turned the lamp off earlier, it's odd that it seems even brighter than before. As he looks around, the corners of the room have deeper shadows that seem strangely fuzzy. For a second he wonders if he should be scared, and quickly realizes that for the first time in a while, he is not. Bending near him is a very pretty girl who seems close to his age with red hair and freckles. Her blue eyes sparkle in the reflected glare.

"Huh, who are you," Dalton asks.

"I'm a friend. My name's Sienna, Sienna Snow."

Dalton is torn in how to react. He has little experience with friendship and is afraid to trust the offer right away. Still, there is something about the girl.

"How did you get here?"

Sienna has a wide-eyed, honest expression. She brushes a stray hair from her face and shrugs as she replies.

"Don't know."

There is something almost magical about the way the shadows seem to rise and fall, swelling and dropping like the surface of the lake he went to with his parents last summer. It's a soft rhythmic movement. The girl seems solid enough.

"Are you an angel?"

Sienna giggles exposing straight white teeth. "No."

Dalton rises from his bed. The floor doesn't quite move beneath his feet, but there is still something odd about it. He rubs his eyes, expecting to find the remains of his tears, but his face is perfectly dry. He looks out the window and it is still dark. At least the stars seem to be normal enough. Now that he feels a bit more awake, he takes a moment to look at the girl more closely. Her hair is parted to one side and looks as if it hasn't been combed in a while. She is wearing a red plaid skirt with pleats, those black and white shoes that the girls like to wear and knee high white socks. Her blouse is white and she has a red scarf around her neck tied to one side. The blouse is a bit wrinkled and there are a couple wet muddy stains on the skirt as if she just came in from a rainy day. Of course, it hasn't rained since earlier in the day. She seems kind of like a tomboy.

"What time is it?"

"This is a dream," Sienna replies. "Dreams don't have clocks. In fact, it really isn't any time at all."

"How do you know that?"

"I just do."

Dalton isn't sure what to make of this girl who appears out of nowhere and seems to know everything. The dream thing explains why the shadows are acting weird and the floor isn't quite solid. Still, it bothers him that she is taking this so calmly, not to mention the way she seems so at home in his room. He decides to react the way so many have done to him.

"I don't think I like some boring, smart-aleck girl showing up in my room, even if it is a dream."

"Don't be mean. I'm not being a smart aleck, and I am hardly boring. Maybe this was a mistake."

Sienna starts to walk away back to the shadows.

"I thought you could use a friend," she continues directing her comment over her shoulder. "Guess I was wrong."

"Wait, I didn't mean it. Don't go. Come back. You're right I do need a friend. I could be your friend, but you might have to teach me how."

Dalton is surprised as the girl turns, her eyes now sparkling and wet. He approaches her slowly. She stands still and lets him come close. He reaches out gently and wipes a tear away. He looks at his fingers with some surprise as the tear feels wet to his touch.

"I'm sorry. I shouldn't have said that. Please don't go."

Sienna is surprised by the boy's quick apology and his gentle touch.

"You were crying earlier. I heard you just before you showed up."

"Yes."

"Why?"

Dalton doesn't understand how she could have heard him, much less where she was exactly when he 'showed up', but talking to this girl seems like the right thing to do. He looks in her eyes and sees that her interest is real.

"We move a lot. It's hard to make friends when nobody knows you and they all have friends already. What's worse is that I never know how long I will be in one place so it just gets harder every time. My father is always moving from job to job and it's always to a new city."

Sienna nods sympathetically.

"Same for you, huh?"

"Sort of," Sienna answers. "It's a little hard to explain."

Dalton worries. Even though Sienna has said that there are no clocks in dreams, he doesn't want to end up falling asleep in class tomorrow.

"Umm, you're nice and all and I want to keep talking to you, but there's school in the morning."

"You don't have to worry about that. Like I said, this is a dream. You'll wake up just like you slept all night. Wait and see."

"I don't get it."

"This is a dream and time stops whenever we're here. When you wake up, it will be just the same as any other dream."

"That's pretty cool."

Sienna smiles and Dalton takes a seat at the end of his bed.

"Yeah, so today was your first one at a new school. How was it?"

"Well the bigger boys made fun of me and all the girls acted like I was from another planet."

Sienna sits down next to Dalton.

"I know what that's like. Where I live, everyone thinks I'm from another planet."

"Where is that?"

"It's far from here. It doesn't matter. I just meant that I know how you feel." Sienna isn't sure why, but is certain that telling Dalton where she lives will only make him less willing to trust her. For some reason, being here feels right and she wants to stay.

"So we were talking about Genies in class today…" Dalton explains to Sienna about the myths and legends session at school. They both agree that the idea of a magic genie is nice, but kind of silly. They both giggle.

2.

Dalton: Things start getting better

Sienna was right about the dreams. In all of the time since she first showed up, I never felt tired in the morning. She's been everything I could have asked for in a friend. She really listens and she always seems to know how to help when I don't know what to do. She makes me laugh. The best thing is that we can sit side by side for the longest times without saying anything at all and it's just fine. One time when I was sick with a fever, she stayed by me and placed a cool cloth on my forehead. I swear that she had more to do with me getting better than any medicine I took.

    I remember that night when we sat together in my empty bedroom talking about the move to Baltimore. That was almost a year ago. The cool breeze from the window in my dream was a nice change from that day's unfair heat. She sat there telling me that it would all be fine, and I sat there trying to be brave; certain it was over. She was right then too. I think that was when I first started to really trust her. During our drive to Baltimore, my parents stopped at a motel in Friendsville, Maryland. As soon as I fell asleep, Sienna was there. The next day I smiled for all one hundred and eighty-three miles.

    The few weeks after we got to our new home, Sienna worked with me to get ready for the school year. This time I wasn't so scared. This time, I felt things would be better. I was still the new kid though, and not everything was easy. There were still bullies to avoid and things to learn. Sienna helped me to stay calm and quiet. She told me that if I could hide my fear and keep to myself, I might not make any friends, but people would leave me alone at least. It was good advice, and I made it through third grade pretty well.

Changing cities and schools continued to be a constant though and before another school year started we were on the move again. The house in Houston was the nicest one we ever had. Dad's new job was the first where we got to sit in an airplane and all of our things were loaded into a big truck. The moving men packed everything up and then unpacked it all when they got to our house. Dad bought a nicer car that was almost new and bought Mom some new dresses. He bought me some new school clothes and a cool video game. Not everything was wonderful though. Dad was working even more hours, and he seemed even more impatient than before that I find some friends. He took the video game away one time when he thought I wasn't trying hard enough. The worst thing happened when I went shopping with Mom. That night, I had to tell Sienna.

"Hurry Moon," I said, even though the clouds were thick and no stars were out. It's funny how I learned about those words. In the beginning I would wait and wait each night to relax and let my eyes get heavy. Then as time passed, I began to notice a huge full moon that was always there in my dream to welcome me. I would see it hanging low and golden over the trees. A few clouds seemed to pass quickly, and the moon always seemed to be racing. The next night I remembered the image and the words came to my mind. "Hurry Moon" I said then and as soon as I did, I fell fast asleep. There was magic in those words, but I was afraid to waste it. I didn't use them every night. Instead, I kept them like an allowance to be used for special or important things. That night, I had news to share.

"Uh oh," Sienna said as she emerged from the dreaming shadows, her face tight with concern as she looked at me.

"Dalton, what's happened? You look terrible." She pushed her red hair behind her ears with both hands as she saw my face. It had grown longer in the time since our first dream and now fell well past her shoulders.

"It's my Mom. I don't know, but I think she's sick or something."

"What makes you say that?" she answered, her blue eyes reaching out to mine and urging me to go on.

"Mom and I went to the supermarket this afternoon. Everything seemed pretty much like always, but about halfway through, she just stopped. She looked pale and so tired all of a sudden. She seemed to be having trouble catching her breath. I asked her if she was okay and after a minute she told me she was, but it scared me."

"Then what happened?"

"Well, I helped her with putting the stuff in the car and unloading it when we got home. Then she went upstairs and took a nap. When she came down she looked better, not so pale anymore, but something she said still bothered me."

Sienna waited for me to continue.

"She said that I shouldn't tell my dad. She said that she had just gotten a little tired and that we shouldn't worry him with something so silly. I didn't want to upset her so I agreed. But as I looked at her, she seemed nervous. All of a sudden she seemed so small and frail."

Sienna pulled me closer that night and hugged me for a long time. I didn't cry, but I was surprised when she pulled away and her face was wet. She wiped her eyes with her sleeve.

"Why are you crying?" I asked.

"I don't know. I guess I feel like I know her sort of, from the way you talk about her. She's so nice. It just made me sad."

That night I realized what a kind person Sienna is. Even though she's a girl and she does things that I don't get, she has always known what to say to make me feel better.

"School will be starting soon," Sienna said, changing the subject. "I brought something with me."

"What is it?"

Sienna held out her hand. At first there was nothing in it and then suddenly a baseball appeared.

"How did you do that?" I ask.

"This is a dream, remember? There's magic in dreams."

She takes a couple of steps back and I stand up. She tosses the ball gently to me and I try to catch it, but it skitters past my hand. I pick it up and toss it back and she catches it easily. Just about anyone I have ever known would have laughed at my clumsiness, but Sienna just smiled gently.

"Try again," she said. After several tries, I catch one and then another.

"Think of this as an experiment," Sienna tells me. "I don't know if it will work, but if you can learn to catch a ball in your dreams, maybe you can remember how to do it during the day."

"Sienna, I'm not athletic."

"No, but if you can play a simple game of catch, you might be able to make the other boys see you as normal."

"But they throw a lot harder than this and we can't exactly do that here."

"Let's go outside." She goes to my doorway and waits for me. "Well?"

I was dressed in my pajamas and didn't see how we could just go outside. I look down and then look back at her.

Sienna senses my confusion and sighs.

"Okay, go ahead and change your clothes."

It seems a bit weird, but I start to unbutton my pajama top.

"Not that way!' Sienna's face looks like she swallowed something horrible. "Look, close your eyes, doofus. Think that you're wearing your jeans and a t-shirt and you will be."

I closed my eyes and when I opened them, I was dressed. We walked through the house and made our way outside. It was still very dark.

"Dalton, how are we gonna throw a ball in the dark?"

"I was just going to ask you that."

"It's your dream, dream sunshine."

Just as quickly, the sun is out and it's just Sienna and me tossing a baseball. She throws the ball like a girl, but she can throw it harder than I can and she knows how to catch. We spent the rest of my dream that night throwing a baseball. By the time she had to leave, I was doing pretty good.

I started to walk toward the front door of the house and Sienna began to giggle.

"What," I asked.

"Dalton, you have to start getting this. In your dreams you don't have to do everything the hard way. Close your eyes and think bedroom and we'll be there."

I shrugged as I did what I was told and there we were, back in my room. When I opened my eyes she was practically nose to nose with me just next to my window.

"We may have to work on that a bit," she said smiling as she took a step back. She turned and walked across the room toward my closet where the shadow was gently moving and flowing. Just before she stepped into the shadow, I stopped her.

"Thanks Sea."

"Sea, I like that." Sienna smiled and faded away.

I don't know whether I learned to throw a baseball that night or not. I do know that when I asked my dad to buy me one, his smile was as big as I can ever remember. The next day he brought a hardball home and he even went in the back yard with me to play catch. It was one of my best days.

When school started, I took the ball with me and tossed it up in the air during recess. Davy Linden saw me and asked me if I wanted to play catch. He seemed okay but I knew there was a chance that he might take the ball and throw it to somebody else or maybe just walk away with it. Sienna had told me not to worry so much. I threw the ball to him and he threw it back. He wasn't quite my first friend, but he talked to me a little after that. The day we left for Detroit, he came by the house and said goodbye.

Our next house was not a house at all. We now live in an apartment in the city. It is almost as nice as the house in Houston. My room looks out on Lake St. Clair from the twelfth floor. It's smaller than my last room, but still pretty nice. There are two large windows and I can keep the blinds up since we are up so high. My bed and desk are side by side on the other side of the room and I sometimes sit on my bed reading and looking out the window as the sun sets. Dad has always done one thing to make the room seem more like a boy's room. He buys a flag of the closest baseball team and hangs it above my bed. The Detroit Tigers are supposed to be my current favorites. I guess it will be okay when I set it in the drawer over the Houston Astros and Baltimore Orioles.

    The school is an older building again, but it is in a clean neighborhood. I don't know why, but the kids here don't look at me like the kids at the other schools had. Maybe they are used to having new kids move in the second week of the term. Sienna says it isn't the other kids who are different; it's me. All I know is, I don't eat alone at lunch anymore and I usually walk the three blocks home with a couple of other boys. One thing Sienna was very clear about. She told me that I must not tell anyone about her, and I didn't really need her to tell me that.

For my tenth birthday, mom asked if I wanted a party. She was pretty surprised when I said no. "I thought you were making friends here," she said, and I told her that I was. I told her that since we probably wouldn't be staying, I didn't want to get too close to these kids either. Her face turned really sad for a minute and then she went to the kitchen to fix dinner. From where I stood in the living room, it was clear that Mom was getting thinner, and her hair had more than a few streaks of gray.

"Do you need any help Mom?"

"You can set the table, honey."

When I told Sienna about the talk with mom, she got it. She said something about being okay with having me all to herself. I didn't know what she meant, so I just sat there and nodded. She looked thoughtful for a moment.

"Your mom's still having days when she gets real tired, huh?"

"Yeah, she says it's nothing. She jokes that she's getting old, but I can see that she worries about it."

"Let's have a catch," she said, picking up the ball from my desk. At first I am surprised by how quickly she changed the subject, but then I guess that she is doing her best to keep me from getting too sad.

"Sienna it's December and I live in the city on the twelfth floor."

"Dalton, you are going to have to use your imagination once in a while. You can close your eyes and we can be back in Houston on that warm summer day."

Without a word, we were back there. It felt so right throwing the ball back and forth. I started thinking about

"Mom! Mom!"

"I'm in here, Dalton." Her voice is soft and drawn. Her pale features are a hard reminder of an illness that is steadily advancing. Dalton, in his excitement, has pushed the thoughts of his mother's condition away for a short while. He calls out as he approaches her bedroom at the back of the house.

"I'm invited! Rebecca McDonald's having a party and she gave me an invitation!"

Dalton stops suddenly, his voice trailing away as he nears her bed. His mother tries to hide her cough, but it is a losing battle. The room is cool and dark with the shades drawn so that she can sleep whenever she needs to.

"That's wonderful honey."

"Well, the truth is that everyone got invited, even that bully Roger. But still…Mom, how're you feelin' today?"

Mrs. Hunter tries to hide her discomfort as she turns toward her son, but Dalton sees the pain. She replies softly.

"I'm very tired dear."

"Well, I'll let you rest. Do you think we can get Rebecca's present tomorrow?"

"I think your father will have to take you. You go along now."

Dalton bends down and delivers a quick peck on the cheek before departing. It is damp with a light sheen of sweat. He does his best to hide his sadness with a smile.

"Okay Mom."

Dalton carries the weight of his book bag as he climbs the steps to his room. He is struggling to be brave, but a few tears escape in spite of the effort. His voice is little more than a whisper as he tries to put his feelings into words.

"I'm losing her Sienna. What am I going to do?"

From his window, Dalton scans the sky, trying to see past the flimsy, stretching clouds into the deeper blue beyond.

"Hurry Moon, I have so much to tell her."

Sighing, he reaches into his book bag and removes Homer's 'The Odyssey', the reading assignment for his Literature class. He flips it on the desk and does his best to fill his mind with Greek heroes. At the height of their powers they seem to be less than an adequate match against the overwhelming sadness that surrounds him.

Don Hunter walks into the house after a long day, shouldering the same heavy burden as his son. The new job is finally settling into a routine and he's been able to get his boss' buy in for some of his ideas. The progress at work would be a lot more satisfying if things at home were not so troubling. He has never felt so powerless. He goes to the kitchen hoping to see his wife preparing the meal as she has done before, knowing in his heart that she won't be there. Then he heads for the bedroom, entering quietly and sitting on the side of the bed. Sharon is obviously weaker today.

Sharon's eye's flutter as her husband walks in.

"How was your day?" she asks, her voice reed thin. The sound when added to the sight of her rips at Don Hunter. He struggles to keep his tone light.

"Not bad. How're you feeling, hon?"

"Not good Don. I'm so tired. I feel like I can hardly move."

"Then just rest. Don't worry; I'm sure you'll feel better soon. Where's Dalton?"

Sharon hesitates. There are things to discuss, but she has never been good at getting her husband to just listen. Perhaps today she will have to find the strength to make him see things as they are. She decides that she will try to urge the conversation along a little at a time.

"He's in his bedroom doing his homework I think."

"His homework? I looked in on him the other day; he was sleeping. At four o'clock in the afternoon he was sleeping. He's about the laziest boy I've ever seen. He needs to get out in the fresh air. He should be out with other boys."

Don's agitation forces him to stand and pace back and forth. His thoughts race as he struggles to understand why his son is nothing like he was at that age. Boys are supposed to run and fight and swear and play baseball, not spend all their time doing homework and waiting for bedtime.

"He's not lazy. And you should have seen how excited he was when he got home from school just now. He's been invited to a classmate's birthday party." Sharon watches her husband for the reaction she knows will come next. It takes a couple seconds for this news to penetrate the building anger. Just as quickly, it subsides.

"Oh?"

"Yes, he's finally making some friends, I think. Don, come sit down. We need to talk."

Don hasn't completely processed the news that his son might finally be learning how to socialize. He stands still a bit longer.

"Come on Don."

Eager to hear any sign that his son has made progress, and conveniently forgetting that Dalton had been doing better at the previous school, he smiles and returns to his wife's side.

"We need to talk about Dalton and there's not much time," Sharon continues.

"Sharon, please."

"Don, I have tried to be a good wife. I've tried to let you be the man and I have done my best, but now you have to listen. I'm not going to get better. It's true and we, you and I, have to face it. I have this thing inside me and it is nearly done. I'm sad to leave you, I'm sad to leave Dalton, but we have to face facts."

Don tries in vain to ignore the meaning of his wife's words. He looks around the room at the furniture made shabby from so many moves. One of the lamps has a torn shade that he has been promising to replace for some time now. He is reduced to pleading.

"Sharon, please," he repeats.

"Don, you have to hold still for a while. You want your boy to have friends. Well, I think he does. I don't know who, but he's been happier lately. He's always going to be a quiet boy. He just has a lot more of me in him."

Don cannot hold back his emotions any longer. The tears flow from guilt and distress.

"It's my fault. I dragged us all over the place like a pack of gypsies. I'm always looking for that better deal, that better job. Look at this place, it's a damn wreck."

"Don. Don, look at me."

Reluctantly, Don faces his wife once more.

"Honey," Sharon goes on, "you've been a good husband and a good provider. You've done your best. Now be a good father. Give your son a stable home. Give him some time."

"You're right, I know you're right."

Pressing the first feeling of compromise that she has received from her husband in a long while, Sharon is insistent.

"Promise me Don. Let me go, knowing you two will be okay."

"I promise. We'll stay put and he'll make friends… Only…"

The chill of worry returns. Sharon closes her eyes and wills her question out.

"What?"

"Well, I heard about this opening up in Chicago. A real ground breaker. I could finally get back on track and give the two of you all the things you deserve…"

Don Hunter looks back at his wife as his own words echo in his ears. He realizes that the time for providing all of those things for his family is coming to a close. Sharon eases back into her bed with a look of defeat. Don is torn between sadness and an ambition that no longer has any purpose. Watching his wife, he decides.

"Sharon."

Tears are threatening and they break Don's heart.

"Sharon, I promise. I'll do my best to stay put. I'll do what I can to be a good father to our son. You say he has a birthday party coming up? I'll take him out tomorrow so he can buy a present. Please Sharon, don't leave us."

Sharon turns back to Don, a small, weak smile returning. She utters words she uses so seldom.

"I love you Don. I love you so much. And there's something else you should know. Your son loves you. Give him your approval. It's all he really wants."

Dalton's bedroom is brightly lit by the lamps on his nightstand and dresser. The shadows at the edges of his room undulate softly. He sits on the edge of his bed turning his baseball in his hands as he awaits Sienna's entrance. When he is not focused on the shadow, he is counting the stitches on the ball. Finally, she seeps into the room from the shadow as she has done so many times before.

"Sienna, God, I thought the night would never get here! I have so much to tell you. It's been such an amazing day, wonderful and horrible all together."

Dalton tries to maintain the smile he found on Sienna's arrival, but his next thoughts stall the effort. "Have I told you my mother's dying?"

"You said she's sick."

"This is the first time I've said it out loud. Well…out loud in my sleep. Um…you know what I…"

"I get it. Do you want to talk?"

Dalton is touched by the look of concern on his friend's face. She pulls his desk chair closer so that they can continue to talk face to face.

"I don't know what to say. She's my Mom and all I had until you. You know what's strange? It never occurred to me; not once; that he really loves her. Sometimes I think he kind of forgot, but now he's remembering."

The boy collects his thoughts as images of his parents at the dinner table and on so many family outings run through his mind.

"It's not that he's cruel. He's just used to being in charge. She knows how he is and though it's not always been easy, she gives in to make him happy."

"You have a great mom," Sienna responds softly.

"Oh Sienna," Dalton cries out, "she's leaving…she's dying."

Sienna reaches out to her friend as he hangs his head and begins to cry. Sienna touches Dalton's shoulder, a comfort and he starts.

"Wow!" He rubs his shoulder as if stung by an electric shock.

"What?" Sienna asks, surprised by the intense reaction.

"I felt that. I mean, I really felt that. You never did that before. It's as if you're here, really here. Did you feel it too?"

"Yes, I did. I do every time."

Dalton looks directly at the girl through wet eyes. Sitting so close, he catches a whiff of her perfume with its sweet hints of flowers and vanilla.

"You're the only friend I've ever had, you know that? You know, during the day, well, I hate to say it, but sometimes I wonder if you're real. I worry that maybe I'm…"

"Crazy?"

Dalton feels badly about the feelings he sometimes gets. His worries about Sienna being some imaginary friend seem like a betrayal of all she has given him.

"I'm sorry. I shouldn't be saying this. It's not fair. All you ever do is make things better for me."

"What was the other thing?" Sienna asks, trying hard not to show the hurt she feels at his continuing doubt.

"Huh?"

"You said wonderful and horrible. What was the good thing?"

The change of subject lightens Dalton's heart at once.

"Oh, I was so excited today. I got invited to a birthday party."

"Dalton, that's so awesome."

Thoughts of that moment earlier in the day as he jumped off the bus run through his mind and bring his smile back.

"I ran in from the bus shouting about it. Mom looked happy, I think."

As he runs through the memory to the time when he sees his mother in her frail health, he is just as quickly returned to sadness. Sienna touches Dalton's shoulder again. This time he is not surprised so the contact remains.

"It's okay Dalton. I'm sure she's excited for you. When is it?"

"This Saturday."

Dalton watches as Sienna rises from the desk chair. She runs a hand carelessly through her red hair, brushing it back off her shoulders. He knows how soon it is and can see from the look of concentration on her face that she is mentally calculating the work ahead of them. As he watches Sienna, Dalton notices how much she has changed in the years since that first dream. The pretty rounded cheeks have begun to show more definition and that in turn has helped make her large eyes appear brighter. There is a hint of pink gloss on a lower lip that is a bit fuller than Dalton had noticed before. Her clothing has changed as well. She still has a tomboy's careless approach to her clothing, disheveled and wrinkled, but now the schoolgirl outfits have been replaced by jeans and rock and roll tee-shirts.

She walks a little and then stops and then walks again. Her expression changes by stages, slowly indicating that she has solved one problem and then another. Finally, she calmly sits back in the desk chair and arranges herself.

"Tell me about the girl whose birthday it is. Do you know what you're gonna give her?"

"How did you know it's a girl?"

"Seriously Dalton, boys stop havin' birthday parties when they're about, I don't know…five?"

As much as he has come to depend on her friendship and advice, there are times when she comes across as a bit of a know-it-all. He rolls his eyes and shakes his head at this, and she giggles.

"All right, all right, I know I can get carried away. So tell me about her."

"Rebecca McDonald, that's her name. Her parents have lots of money. She always dresses nice and all the girls follow her around."

Sienna has already made a list of all the things they have to do in the next few days. First, they have to decide on a gift, then what Dalton will wear, and then they have to discuss a few things about the party itself.

"Is she pretty?"

Dalton shrugs and Sienna continues.

"Okay, does she like music? Do you know what she listens to?"

"She has a very cool CD player but I don't know what she plays in it." Just having to think about Rebecca McDonald seems akin to punishment, but he focuses instead on the party.

"Music is out unless we know the right group which we don't. It can't be clothing or jewelry or perfume; too personal. What else?" There is a look of concentration on her face that seems to make her freckles stand out even more.

"It can't be too expensive..." As the conversation has gone on, Sienna has moved closer and closer. Her face is mere inches away now. Like a sunburst through the clouds, she smiles and jumps up.

"I've got it! You remember that movie last year? It was an animated one with live actors. It's funny and it just came out on videotape. Not too expensive or personal, but a nice little gift. It's perfect."

Dalton can't remember the name of the movie, but he knows the one she means. He agrees, nodding and stands up to be closer to Sienna. He wants to give her a hug but hesitates. Sienna senses this and draws him close for a quick embrace. They pull apart gently with his eyes on her.

"You're really good at this."

"Thanks, but we're not done yet."

Dalton returns to the end of his bed like an eager student ready to continue his lesson. He asks what's next.

"Are some of the kids in your class together, like boyfriend and girlfriend?"

"Yeah, there's Bobby Wheeler and Kathy Duncan and…"

Sienna wants to move on so she stops him there.

"Right, so there's a good chance that there will be dancing. At least the girls will and maybe some of the ones who are paired off."

The idea of having to dance at this party has obviously not occurred to Dalton. It is a frightening concept.

"Get up. You'll see; it's not so bad." Sienna pulls him to his feet. Then she goes over to the stereo and turns on some music.

"Not too loud, I don't want to wake…" He stops, realizing his mistake.

"That's the great thing about dreams," Sienna replies. "You can play your music as loud as you want." Sienna demonstrates some dance moves and gets Dalton to copy. He is stiff at first.

"Loosen up, Dalton. Close your eyes and feel the rhythm." She watches as he begins to relax. "That's better."

"A friend of mine was fond of Chinese proverbs. I always liked this one: 'It does not matter how slowly you go, so long as you do not stop."

Dalton laughs at the thought.

"In that case, we should really take our time."

"You'll need to wear some nice jeans and a cool shirt. Do you have anything like that?"

Dalton stops dancing and Sienna does right after.

"Can you take a look at my stuff?"

"Tomorrow night. I should go now. We have a couple more nights to get you ready. Bye Dalton."

The toughest moments of each night are the inevitable goodbyes. Sienna fades into the shadow and disappears.

"Bye Sienna."

4.

New beginnings

Pushing the door in a near panic, Dalton finds the surprise inside to be quite different than the one he had feared just seconds before. Seeing his father's car in the driveway at this time of day was far from normal and triggered a series of dreadful images. Instantly he had raced inside. The sight of his mother lying comfortably on the couch with his father seated beside her was nearly as shocking as anything he might have considered. His father chuckles a little at his son's amazement, while his mother seems more concerned at her son's brief distress.

During the previous night's dinner conversation, Dalton had made no mention of the party invitation, and a look had passed between the two parents that it should remain that way. Sharon had eaten a small amount; a couple of bites of spaghetti from the nearby takeout Italian place along with a few sips of tea. Don took her hand briefly and shared a smile before carrying her back to the bedroom. When he returned, the rest of the meal was finished quietly.

Now Don broke the silence, motioning his son closer.

"Your mother tells me that you have a party coming up this weekend. I came home a bit early so that we can pick up a present for your friend and then get some dinner. What do you think?"

"That's great Dad."

"Do you have any idea what you want to get?"

"There's a movie that just came out; a VHS tape. It's the one with the cartoons and the live actors together. I don't think it should cost too much."

"That's good thinking son," Don replied, "so let's get going. Sharon, we'll be back in a little while."

Don kisses his wife gently, and she smiles. Dalton is pleased, but not quite sure what to make of his father's change in behavior. He goes to his mother and gives her a kiss; she looks a little better today, not quite so tired.

"Bye Mom, we'll see you later."

"Have fun."

The shopping trip is enjoyable. The department store clerk found the movie easily and Dad led Dalton to the gift-wrap area to finish the gift properly. Afterwards, they head to a Chinese restaurant and order take-out. In the car as they travel home, a brief conversation takes place. Dalton is able to tell his father about his day without any questions about friends. It is a solid first step.

"Good night son," Mr. Hunter says after the two had cleared the table and cleaned up the few items in the kitchen. Mother had decided to pass on the Chinese, and Don had prepared a small bowl of soup for her instead. They returned to the living room as Don turned off the kitchen light.

"I hope your friend likes her present."

Dalton is surprised by the warmth in his father's voice, and without thinking he turns to his father and gives him a brief hug. The bag with the present is sitting by the stairs. Dalton grabs it as he starts up.

"Thanks Dad. Thanks for the gift… and everything." He rewards his father with a quick smile and climbs the steps to his room to finish his homework.

The present, wrapped in shiny silver foil with a large floral pattern sits on Dalton's desk in plain sight. He opens his eyes once he has fallen asleep and it looks even larger and more impressive. Sienna appears in an instant and they go through his closet to see what he might wear on Saturday. He is confident that he will remember what they have chosen once he wakes up. Sienna quickly locates a pair of jeans that are a little faded but nice. She gets him to try them on by imagining he is wearing them and gives him an approving smile when he does. He uses the same technique to model a few shirts until she is satisfied that they have the right one. As always, a full moon glows through the window. Sienna turns on the music and the dance lessons continue.

"So now you know what to wear." she says. "Keep dancing; you're getting better at this. Next we have to figure out who you can dance with."

"How do I do that?"

"First we figure out who you can't ask. Then we can figure out who is left. You can't ask any of the girls who are paired. Does Rebecca have a boyfriend?"

Dalton rolls his eyes and smiles. The idea of Rebecca McDonald with a boyfriend seems comical. "No," he responds and moves his hand to his mouth to hide a snicker.

Sienna sees Dalton's reaction and realizes that the Birthday girl is not someone he likes very much, but she ignores his reaction and goes on.

"That's okay, she's too popular anyway. About how many girls would you say are left?"
Dalton pauses to consider, counting half out loud.
"Maybe eight."
"Who's the prettiest one?"
"I don't know, Amber I guess."
"Who's after that?"
"There's Caitlyn Harris. Why?" All of these questions are making his head hurt so he stops dancing.
"You don't want to ask the prettiest girl because that can cause problems. Is Caitlyn nice?"
"Yeah, I think so. She was at the same table at lunch with me last week and I think I saw her smile when I looked at her."
Sienna tries to choose her next words carefully. She is not sure how prepared her friend is for the realities of boys and girls.
"Dalton, there are two kinds of boys, nice ones and bad ones. Lots of girls like the bad ones and you are never going to be that. You're not bad looking and if you act like you know what's going on, even when you don't, if you act confident, then being nice will be fine."
There seems to be a lot to think over in what Sienna has just said. Maybe some other time he will do it.
"So I should ask Caitlyn?"
"Yes," she replies, more than a little amused by his tone.
"She might say no. Who do I ask then?"
"Then you ask the next prettiest girl, but if she is as nice as you say, I don't think she will. So when the music starts and some kids are dancing you go over and talk to

her. Make sure no other boy is there first. You ask her things like: what did she get Rebecca. If she answers and seems interested then you keep talking. Talk about the classes you're taking or some music you like, anything you can think of. The main thing about talking to a girl is that whatever you say, it should come from the heart.

"Another thing that is just as important and maybe a little more is that when the girl speaks you can't just pretend to listen. You have to show that you're interested in what she has to say. She will see that you are paying attention and that will mean a lot." Then, if the music is like this, you can ask her to dance."

"What if the music is slower? Sienna, I don't know how to dance to slow songs."

Sienna smiles and walks toward the shadow.

"There's still one more night. We can try slow dancing tomorrow. Good night Dalton."

A few cars drive by the little Colonial the next night, their windshield wipers pushing the sheets of rain out of the way. Their drivers are too busy to notice the corner home late at night with all of its windows dark. Inside, Dalton is dreaming and the room is light. He is looking out the window. The moon is shining and the sky is clear. His expression is confused as he examines the dry road.

"I thought it was raining."

"You're so silly," Sienna chuckles. "Don't you know it never rains in dreams?"

Sienna starts the music. This time it is a slow number. Sienna motions Dalton toward her and indicates a spot. She takes his hands and places them, one on her waist, and one in her hand.

"This is a box step. I will lead, but tomorrow you'll have to, okay?"

Dalton nods nervously.

Sienna demonstrates the steps pulling the boy one way and pushing another.

"Is this right?"

"You're a natural," she says smiling. She covers a wince as he steps on her toe. "Don't look down. Look at me. Look in my eyes."

Dalton complies and they dance quietly for a few minutes.

"Dalton, if things are going well, if the girl really likes you, you will feel her moving closer, like this."

Sienna slides into Dalton's arms. She rests her head on his shoulder as he places his hands gently at her waist. They move to the music.

"This is nice."

"Shhh, just dance."

On the day of the party, Dalton is sitting in his father's car. He is going over all of the things Sienna has taught him, not realizing that he is saying things aloud.

"…ask Caitlyn what classes she likes…"

They pull up in front of a very pleasant, upper middle class home in a fairly affluent neighborhood. There are balloons on the mailbox to assure that this is indeed the right location. Other children are approaching the house, walking up the drive and across the walk to the doorway. The door is open and Rebecca, a slightly overweight young lady stands there with arms crossed. Dalton's father is about to ask what Dalton has been saying, but before he can get a word out, Dalton is bolting from the car.

"Bye Dad!"

Don Hunter shakes his head, but smiles as he thinks of his son finally starting to show signs of life. The car drives away. Dalton approaches the door behind a couple of laughing children, carrying the small, nicely wrapped present. At the door, he offers it to Rebecca, who accepts it with a look of suspicion and quickly passes it to her mother standing just behind her. Cold blue eyes stare out from beneath her short blonde bangs and curls.

"Hi Dalton," Rebecca says coolly.

Dalton ignores the girl's tone.

"Hi, happy birthday Rebecca, thanks for inviting me," he continues sincerely.

The girl seems surprised and almost touched by his tone. She smiles as he walks in the house. Dalton walks in through the entrance hall. The children are guided toward a large family room that is decorated for the occasion and is situated next to a large kitchen. The furniture has been removed and there are strobe lights and large speakers. Next to the family room is the eat-in kitchen. Tables with punch and snacks sit next to the island counter holding a very large cake. Another table sits further back with a growing stack of presents. In the corner of the kitchen there is a shadow. In the shadow, there is a hint of someone standing there not clearly visible at this moment. Dalton heads for the snack table and is helped to a soft drink by one of the parents acting as chaperone.

There were more than a few of his classmates already at the party when Dalton arrived, many bunched in groups talking about their classes or the latest music videos on MTV. There are shouts and girlish screaming from time to time as some of the more popular kids arrive. Dalton is more than a little surprised when Caitlyn walks past and smiles right into his eyes. It lasts just a second, but it is real. He takes a sip of pop and tries desperately to still the nervous shaking of his hands.

When the partiers are mostly accounted for, the parents urge the kids to fill their plates and enjoy the sandwiches, burgers and snacks that fill the tables. Dalton sits quietly at a table and Caitlyn chooses a seat nearby, but spends most of the time talking to a couple of girls that she hangs out with at school.

Soon after the eating has ended, Rebecca is seated in front of the table with the gifts. The guests form a semi-circle in the area between the kitchen and family room. She opens each present and calls out the names of the classmate who has brought it. Rebecca's reactions are followed more closely than the presents, with the other children recording who has done well and who has not. She rips into a medium sized box.

"This one's from Troy," she says in a matter of fact tone. She rolls her eyes and tosses it aside without revealing the contents. It lands in a pile with a few other items that are clearly marked 'loser'.

"Thanks Troy," Rebecca continues coolly. Rebecca's parents are standing nearby and they both chuckle at their daughter's behavior.

The next package is from her best friend Julie and receives the attention and respect it deserves.

"Oh Julie, It's just what I wanted."

Rebecca holds up a very pricey charm bracelet that draws oohs and aahs. She moves on to the present from Dalton. She removes the wrapping from the gift and lifts the video cassette for everyone to see. There are looks that pass between the girls in the room. Rebecca's face is neither smiling nor disapproving.

"Thank you Dalton, this is very thoughtful."
She places it gently in the approved pile. Rebecca moves on to the next gift. Dalton is aware that more than a couple of the partiers are looking at him in a new way.

Now the music is playing and a few couples are dancing along with some of the girls who are dancing together. The boys are mostly huddled in the family room near the music, while the girls are talking together in the kitchen. Dalton fidgets as he tries to decide when to make his move. Caitlyn is still sitting with her friends. He starts to approach when another boy goes over to her. The girls remain and soon the boy leaves. Dalton gathers his courage and crosses the room. This time the girls depart with a few words. Dalton takes a seat that one of the two girls just left. He tries to look as confident as he can and follow Sienna's advice.

"Umm, hi Caitlyn. Nice party."
"Hi Dalton, yes it is."
Dalton can hear Sienna's voice in his memory, pushing him to keep going. Caitlyn watches Dalton, waiting to see what he will come up with next. She is not surprised when he takes a while to get started. Just as she is starting to lose interest and turns to watch the others on the dance floor, he decides he had better speak.

"You gave Rebecca that Rolling Stones T-shirt. I thought it was very cool."

"Thanks. Rebecca has a thing for the Stones. I don't know why, but she told me that once."

Caitlyn pauses for a minute. Her eyes still appraising Dalton. She is surprised when he continues more easily.

"Have you known Rebecca for a long time?"

"We've been friends since second grade."

Dalton thinks about the many schools that he has attended. He wonders what it must be like to stay in one place long enough to make friends that way.

"That must be nice."

"Why do you say that?" Caitlyn responds, thinking that Dalton's reply is about Rebecca and not about having friends in general. She looks at him with a questioning glance.

Dalton turns away.

"We move around a lot. I haven't known too many people for more than a year."

"That must have been hard," Caitlyn replies, sympathetically, remembering his recent arrival. Caitlyn pauses for a minute. Her eyes still appraising Dalton. Dalton watches the dancers silently.

"She seemed to like your present. That tape was a good idea. What made you think of it?"

Dalton tries to come up with a believable answer. A new song begins with a strong rhythm and he is saved.

"Hey Caitlyn, what do you think? Do ya want to dance?"

Caitlyn is surprised but in a good way. She looks around the room to see what the reaction is from the other girls. Their looks seem to be neutral. There doesn't appear to be any reason to say no.

"Sure, let's go."

She follows him to where the others are dancing and watches as he moves easily to the rhythm. Once they begin Caitlyn smiles. The looks from some of the other girls confirm her feeling. She had pretty much decided that she would dance with Dalton if he was interested, and she was happy to see that the signals she had been sending earlier had not been missed. Still, it was never a good idea to ignore the reaction of the girls who count. Even more important was the reaction Brad was showing. Caitlyn looked in his direction just long enough to make sure that he was noticing the two of them dancing and then quickly turned away as if she had seen nothing at all. She smiled brightly at Dalton.

"You're a pretty good dancer."

Dalton figures it won't hurt to return the compliment.

"Thanks, so are you."

Dalton tries to appear nonchalant as more than a few kids are watching him, including some of the girls who are dancing with other boys. Immersed in the music, Caitlyn and Dalton shout to each other above the music. They laugh together easily.

From the corner in the kitchen another pair of eyes is watching the couple. The shadow now reveals Sienna. It is clear that she is not physically in attendance. Her expression changes back and forth from pride in her friend's victory to sadness that someone else is sharing this moment with him.

They dance together for a couple of songs before a slow one begins. Caitlyn surprises Dalton by taking his hands much the way Sienna did and places them to start a slow dance. Dalton leads and Caitlyn is satisfied that he seems to know what to do. Before long, she moves closer and they dance.

"Dalton, I think we look pretty good together. Do you think, I mean, would you like to be my boyfriend?"

Dalton smiles and looks at Caitlyn with confidence.

"I think that would be nice."

The rest of the party passes as in a dream. Dalton is content to dance with Caitlyn and she feels kind of nice during the slow ones. They no longer feel the need to talk much, which suits perfectly him since he pretty much used up all of the things he had to say. Just as Dalton turns to leave, Caitlyn smiles enticingly at a boy sitting nearby. When his father arrives, the girl walks out with him and blows him a quick kiss as he drives away.

"Did you have a good time, son?" Father asks with a smile. He did not miss the cute brown haired girl who accompanied Dalton out of the house. Perhaps, Dalton has made even more of a stride forward than he had guessed.

"Yes sir, I did." Dalton's smile brings one to his father.

The dream picks up later that night. Dalton and Sienna are dancing very close, listening to the same slow song that Dalton danced to with Caitlyn.

"So, now you have a girlfriend. I guess you're a big man now, huh?" Sienna's eyes latch on to his with an elfin grin.

"Cut it out. I like Caitlyn. I think she likes me too. But you know this stuff better than anyone. If a girl doesn't have a boyfriend in seventh grade, the other girls think there's something wrong with her. I happened to be just good enough."

Sienna punches Dalton playfully

"It's a good thing you get that."

"Owww! Cut it out."

Dalton pulls away for a minute. "You know that it could not have happened without your help. Caitlyn isn't bad, but she's not you. You're my best friend and…"

"And what?"

Dalton turns away, not wanting Sienna to realize how pretty she seems to him at this moment. Sienna knows what her friend is feeling.

"Someone I once knew asked me to tell you something. Can I tell you now?"

Dalton is puzzled by the idea that someone might have told Sienna to tell him something, but curiosity overcomes his bewilderment. He nods for her to continue.

"She said that you should call me 'Meng Zhong Ging Ren'. It's Chinese for the girl of his dreams. She thought you might want to know that we have a connection."

Dalton looks uncomfortable. Sienna worries that she has chosen the wrong time and she works to change the mood instantly.

"Come on big shot, we have a lot of work to do. Caitlyn is going to expect you to be an even better dancer. We also need to see if you can have a conversation that lasts more than three sentences."

They both laugh and Sienna holds Dalton tightly.

"Hey, Sienna, I was watching this show on TV tonight. It was all about photography. It looked like fun. Think I'd be any good at that?"

Dalton Hunter contentedly smiles and rolls under the covers in his darkened room at his dream girl's reply.

5.

Don Hunter: Maybe I am finally figuring this dad thing out

My son has grown up a lot these past several months. He has a girlfriend of all things. Coming home from work has been a very different experience, seeing the two of them sitting in folding chairs on the front lawn, talking and laughing. Their little picnics lightened the mood around the house, especially for Sharon. Of course, now the summer has ended and the new school year has begun, it will be interesting to see how things go.

The promise I made to stay in one place has already been rewarded in more ways than one. I had casually mentioned to one of my coworkers that I was planning to stick around. Apparently, news travels fast. Just a few days later, Mr. Rosings, the Regional VP of Sales called me and asked me to come see him. As I followed his secretary into his office, I was a bit nervous, worrying what he might have in mind. I stood in front of his cluttered desk in the otherwise spare office and did my best to appear relaxed. It wouldn't do to lose this job now. Thankfully, he got straight to the point.

"Don, take a seat. Would you like some coffee?"

When I declined, Charlie nodded and the secretary departed closing the door behind her.

"Word around here has it that you're planning on staying with us. Is that true?"

"Yes sir, it is."

"I have to tell you that I am a bit surprised, but also pleased. When you first came to us, I knew your reputation and I figured you would stay with us until something better came along. We didn't have anything to lose and folks in sales can be a bit, um, transient shall we say? Nevertheless, your performance has been everything I was hoping for and more."

Charlie took a moment to catch his breath and to give me a chance to respond if I wanted. Not knowing where he was headed with this, I stayed silent though it seemed clear that I was not being fired. I relaxed a little as he went on.

"The reason I called you in here is that I am going to be moving to the Corporate VP of Sales slot and management has asked me for a recommendation on my replacement. I want you to know that the job is yours if you want it. I would never have considered you, but if you are truly committed to staying, I think we can offer you a nice challenge along with an increase in pay."

My smile widened slowly as I processed what I had just heard. I didn't hesitate but accepted immediately.

Mr. Rosings chuckled. "Don't you even want to discuss compensation, do a little haggling?"

"Charlie, sometimes life makes you an offer that not only you can't refuse, but one that is so clearly too good to hesitate over for even a second. I know you will be fair and I am happy to count on that."

Charlie rose and offered his hand. "Thanks Don. Welcome aboard."

I shook his hand gratefully and went back to work with a quick call home. I was hardly prepared for such an obvious reward just for doing the right thing. There was another immediate benefit. When I told her of my good fortune, Sharon perked up at once. The doctor would not use the word 'remission', but her energy returned and she is up and around and smiling. With the new salary, I am able to afford a part time housekeeper.

The new job came with a lot more challenge as promised. That is, if you spell challenge W – O – R – K. My hours have increased, and I have several days a month travelling as well. On the other hand, I have become closer to a number of the people I work with, not the least of whom is Mr. Rosings. As I confided in him more and more about my personal life, he has made it clear that while there will always be a lot of work priorities, I have to make some time for my family. I even found time to take Dalton to a Cardinals game. Sharon was right. All the boy needed was a little stability and some approval from me to blossom. I wish I could take the credit. Whoever that first friend was, the one that urged him out of his shell, they made it happen. Otherwise I might never have recognized my son's potential.

Dalton answers the door each night when I come home, no matter how late. We sit and talk for a few minutes. My son has a quiet wit and expresses himself better than I ever expected. He has found an interest, and I haven't seen any harm in being supportive. He asked me to buy a camera and some film for him. The camera was a little pricey, and once in a while I have to spring for getting the film developed. It's worth it. I'm no expert, but the stuff looks okay to me. I think he gets the creative thing from his mother. He sure didn't get it from me. Still, it is hard to miss the way he notices things. There are times when you can just tell that he is seeing something in a way that is different from other people. He wants to take a photography class when he enters high school next year. Certainly there's no harm for now. There will be plenty of time later on to push him toward a more realistic profession. Meanwhile, we get to sort through batch after batch of snapshots from family outings. I especially like the ones he has taken of his mother. There are pictures of birds in the sky, trees in the park, and of course, more than a few of his little girlfriend. All in all, the best part is the pleasure it has given Sharon. I would have happily spent twice as much to see her so happy.

    The trip to work and back on the Metrolink is no longer just filled with the day's work plans. I think about my wife and son, as I never have before. The click of the rails on the way to work is punctuated with images of dinner conversation. The dishes are scattered around the table after the meal with no hurry to clean up. Instead we sit together as we never have and share bits of our day. Sometimes we just sit together quietly. There are other times filled with laughter. That's perhaps the sweetest and most unexpected reward. The new job demands a lot of attention and I am enjoying the added responsibilities. Still, I can't help but think about the changes at home and especially the changes in my son. Going home is filled with anticipation. With each mile, I feel like I am mentally pushing the train along, my eagerness to get there is so strong.

    Tonight as I navigate the parking lot on my way to the car, I feel the first chill of autumn when the breeze picks up. The clouds on the horizon are turning a darkened pink. It won't be too long before my arrival at the station takes place in evening darkness. As I have this thought the lights in the parking lot begin to glow. There is a merging of taillights from the many cars making their way home with the glow that spills out of the sky. Even with all of the other cars nearby, I can still enjoy the ride to the house with my windows open.

    I make a quick stop at the grocery on the way home to pick up my wife's favorite ice cream. I notice people going about their daily routines in a way that seems happier somehow. A smile from the cashier matches my own. Getting closer now, I practically run out of the store.

    Finally I am home. I pull the key from the ignition and grab my briefcase. The light at the front door is off and the walk is bathed in darkness. A minor annoyance, but I'm in such a good mood that this little disappointment barely registers. The front door opens to the sounds of the local television news. The picture scatters dancing lights across the wall in the otherwise darkened room. The volume is loud enough that it masks anything else. I drop my things and turn the volume down. The words 'I'm home' never escape my lips as I hear the heartbreaking sound of my son's tears. The sack with the ice cream slips from my hands as I rush back to our bedroom. Dalton is sprawled over my wife's inert form. I go to him and do my best to provide comfort as my own silent tears begin to flow.

6.

Sienna: Love and loss and love

Inside the world of Dalton's dreams I am alive as I am nowhere else. Our bond is so intense that nothing else seems to matter. Dalton often speaks of how my arrival ended his loneliness, but it was just as important and powerful for me. It brought me to life. In the instant I stepped out of the shadows and into the light, his sweetness was a nearly tangible thing. I have stopped trying to understand the mystery that connected me to him. However it happened, I am more grateful than I can say to be part of his life.

There is a strange feeling to our dreaming that clashes with what you might expect in a dream. It is as if our senses are on fire. Everything we see, every sound seems magnified or charged with electricity. While the edges are velvet soft, the place at the center, our little bubble is so alive. It started with the time we spent together there; the friendship we shared. Then I began to understand the magic. In his dreams, we can do anything. We can go anywhere in an instant and we share everything down to the smallest detail. It's so awesome.

I have to tell you about those early days. It seemed like my life was defined as a series of dreamtimes with short periods of nothingness to mark the end of one from the beginning of the next. Each encounter was so incredible that there was no choice but to hold on and then go back. As time went on, I began to sense how the connection worked. It wasn't so much that I understood the path as that I could feel how to get there. The dreams were only the first step. Later, I learned how to go to him from inside my own dreams. I began to realize that I could sense things that he did during his daytime, like that afternoon at Rebecca's birthday party.

How can I describe what I see through Dalton's eyes? Well, it's different than what I see in his dreams. As I said, when Dalton is asleep, the connection is so vivid but we still have this clear feeling of ourselves. I feel like I know who I am and who he is and there is a line that identifies each of us. During his day, the line disappears or maybe you could say it blurs more than a little. I see what he sees, but in a way that feels as if I am off to the side or not quite there. It's hard to explain. As soon as I figured out that I could share even more of his life when he was awake, I did whatever I could to be there with him. It took some pretty hard lessons to convince me that I could not stay connected all day long.

The years have just flown. It's hard to believe that Dalton is twelve already. More than five years have passed since I first found my way to him. I smile when I think of the children we were. There was so much laughter and fun. Now that we're nearing our teens, it is still lots of fun, but it has become different in a way that's hard to explain. First, there's the fact that we have both grown. I have begun to notice things about the shape of Dalton's face or the way his voice has begun to grow deeper and I can tell that he seems aware of some changes in me. Dalton used to look me right into my eyes. If anything, I might even have been a bit taller. Now I have to look up to see into those eyes. Somehow, looking up seems right, but now the eye contact has become more random. Simple things like the way we look at each other or a simple touch can sometimes feel, I don't know, awkward maybe. Certainly it has become more serious, and that was before. Now with his mom's passing, it's much more intense.

Dalton has taken his mother's death really hard. The past couple nights he's been so quiet. He hasn't spoken a word and all I can do is hold him, leaning my head against his back. The other night I tried to rock him to sleep. At first he was reluctant to let me and he had the look of someone lost. Eventually though, he gave in. Other times, he just stares at the walls. He was so close to his mother. I think he is beginning to realize that his father has changed, but he still isn't sure if he can really trust that change to last.

The morning of the funeral is draped in a fitting shade of gray. There is just the slightest mist of rain falling at intervals like a mourner's tears. Dalton goes to his closet and pulls out his one suit, fittingly black. He dresses slowly and carefully. He combs his thick brown hair and brushes his teeth. He answers a call from his father and goes downstairs to get help with his tie. There is a silence between the two, but now it is the silence of shared loss instead of the deep gulf that was there before.

"You look good," Don Hunter says patting his son's shoulder. "Let's go."

The service in church is very quiet. Large stands of flowers bracket the casket along with a small adorning bouquet on the lid. There is a somber light through the stained glass that mixes sadly with the light falling from overhead. Since the Hunters have not lived in this area very long, there aren't too many people among the congregation who knew Dalton's mother. At least, that is the best explanation I can come up with for the rows and rows of empty pews. The minister completes a very compassionate eulogy and praises the father and son on their love and care for Sharon. Once the service is completed, the few neighbors who did attend stop by to express their sympathy including one of the nurses who had become fond of Sharon during her visits to the hospital.

    The trip to the cemetery is long, nearly an hour, and both Dalton and his father have their moments of grief during the ride. The traffic parts as the short funeral procession makes its way there. Finally, the limousine slows and Don Hunter pats the hand of his son before he departs. Dalton takes an extra minute to get ready and then follows. I find a spot nearby where I can watch and hear the service.

    Father and son approach the gravesite just as the sun peaks out from behind the clouds. It looks like a spotlight casting a focused glow; as if Sharon is trying to let her men know that she is okay. Dalton looks up into the brightness. The moisture on the nearby trees reflects the light. Their leaves have just the very first faint tinge of autumnal color. Even the smell of the damp grass is comforting.

    The kindness of those few who came to the church is extended as one by one, they arrive at the cemetery. They gather closely around father and son, bringing comfort by their attendance and their genuine sympathy.

"The community of man is a shifting tide," the minister begins, "with a thousand loves delivered and a thousand loves conveyed. Father, we ask for your continued love and care for our departed sister, Sharon Hunter. Take unto you her gentle spirit. Spare also, if you will, a moment to heal the hearts of her husband Don and her son Dalton." The minister is obviously a well-meaning man with a poetic bent.

As the minister finishes the final rites, the casket is gently lowered. My world goes black for a short time as Dalton closes his eyes. I can feel him willing himself to reopen them, to face this loss. There is a huge gap in his heart now, an open space where his mother's love used to live. As the mourners disperse, father and son share a few brief words with the minister, thanking him for his prayers. Finally alone, Don Hunter pulls his son closer and then they are hugging. The hole that was there so recently, begins to fill with his father's love. In that moment, Dalton begins to feel that everything can be alright between them. Perhaps for the first time, he can finally feel what it is like to have the love of both his parents.

On the way back to the car, I feel the early fall breeze against my face cooling while the sun warms me. Even though I know that these sensations are really Dalton's, they feel so much a part of me that I claim them as my own. I feel Dalton's hunger and when his father asks if he could eat something, I am sorry when he says no. I try to urge him to reconsider, but he can't hear me during the day. I sense it as his idea of honor that tells him that eating so soon after the funeral is wrong. Apparently, Don has become more attuned to his son, because after a few minutes, he is telling his son that his mother would expect him to take care of himself. With that encouragement, my friend agrees to a meal and the two set off in search of lunch.

As connected as I am to Dalton, I understand the boundaries of our friendship. I recognize that this is a moment that a father and a son should be able to share alone. Respecting their privacy, I say a silent goodbye and fade back to the shadows.

7.

Dalton: Growing up is…

Two steaks are sizzling in the pan surrounded by onions and peppers. The aroma charges out of the kitchen and through the house. I'll have everything ready to go when Dad gets home and then he'll make his way to the table. The potatoes are nearly done baking in the oven. The canned vegetables are sitting in a pot on the back burner ready for heating. Tonight I am trying something new as I pull four doughy dinner rolls from a round refrigerator can. Following the instructions, I buttered the flat pan and set the round, white slabs of dough in place. I can't wait to see dad's face. Cooking dinner for the two of us is one of the chores that I knew I could do. While the results at first were not exactly restaurant quality, he managed to finish those meals without complaint. Now he smiles and tells me that I seem to have found my mother's touch in the kitchen. As to the housework, we've kept the housekeeper a couple of days a week as neither of us is the neatest person. Our lives have settled into a comfortable routine as we mark almost a year and a half since we lost mom.

    I have developed a few dishes now for our dinner routine. I can prepare a reasonable spaghetti dinner as long as I use a decent sauce from a jar. Mom left a few recipes and I can manage the tuna casserole and a better than average meat loaf. At least this way, we aren't dependent on take out and fast food every night. Since dad has to travel several days a month, it only seems right that there be something like home cooking waiting for him when he is here.

Lunches are a different matter. Now that I'm in tenth grade, carrying a bag is out of the question. Dad is careful to make sure I have cash for the week, and in return, I do my best to see that I am eating healthy stuff; that is if whatever they serve in the school cafeteria can be considered healthy. The other guys give me some good natured kidding about the occasional salad, but we all laugh and it's fine.

Caitlyn and I have lasted a lot longer than I thought we would. We lasted long enough that Dad sat me down and started a very serious birds and bees talk. It was kinda funny, though I didn't dare let a smile show. He hit all of the high points, making sure I knew about things like responsibility and life choices and I did a lot of yes sirring and no sirring. I had plenty of time to notice the dust on the sofa tables, and a few dishes that needed to be taken to the kitchen and the number of stains on the carpet. When it was over, he asked me if I had any questions, and I thanked him and told him I would come back if I thought of anything, and then beat a hasty retreat. I know my dad didn't have a lot of communication with his dad, and certainly nothing on this subject. Dad's father's generation didn't talk about stuff like that.

If I could have gotten the words out, I would have told dad that he didn't have anything to worry about. Caitlyn and I only got past the hand holding stage recently and even that wasn't anything huge. We were rolling around on the floor in my room, just playing around. My hands began to wander a little and I tried to kiss her, but she turned away quickly. Then she got to her feet and for the rest of the afternoon, she acted like nothing had happened. At first I thought she was shy, but I found out I was wrong when I saw her flirting with Brad Parker a few days later. Of course, he's still going with Suzie Ramis, so Caitlyn is biding her time with me.

Don't get the wrong idea, I really like Caitlyn. Caitlyn is good company at the movies. She's pretty and funny and we have a great time together. We laugh a lot, but the boundaries are very clear. The other morning we were walking to the park and she summed things up perfectly.

"You're a great guy Dalton, and I could give you the names of at least three girls that would be happy to take my place in a minute. In fact, I'd write them down for you if you asked me to."

I shook my head and she smiled beautifully. Her eyes brushed against mine and then she turned forward, her chin lifted to catch the light. I love the way little smile lines appeared around her mouth as she went on.

"There's someone else for me," she continued, "and I think you know who it is, but you've never said anything and you have stayed with me and been so great. Remember that day at Rebecca's party; you were so determined not to look scared. I told my friends not to leave for anyone else but you. To tell you the truth, they thought I was nuts, but something told me that you would be a safe choice. My guess is that we're both in some kind of holding pattern, like planes at the airport waiting to land. I have that nameless guy and you're holding out for…well whatever it is or whoever, I hope they're worth it. I'm kinda sorry it can't be me, but I'm glad you're here."

She squeezed my hand tight for a second, and then she laughed and took off running. I chased her and everything was just fine. It would be impossible to watch her running that way, so smooth and easy, and ignore the motion of her hips or the long lines of her legs in motion. We arrived at the park gasping for breath and giggling like little kids. When she grabbed a swing, she looked so wonderfully alive.

"Come and give me a push."

I take my place behind her and her face glows as she turns and follows me with her eyes. A little bit of morning mist remains and the sunlight bounces off it and lands squarely on her shoulders. In the sky, long streaks of thin, golden, swirling clouds appear to be dancing above. Grabbing her waist gently I tug her back and then push her forward. The feel of her is soft and feminine. As she kicks out the first time her hair is caught in the sky and each strand seems for a moment to be flying but still like I've hit the pause button on the VCR. There are tiny strands of ruby red and gold among the lush chestnut cords. Then she's moving again away and then toward me and I position my hands between her shoulders and set her flying again. Her laughter fades and grows. When she is in the air, she leans back and I see her deep brown eyes and her soft pink lips inverted like some new-age Picasso or something.

Finally, she has had enough and brings the swing to a stop. I walk away trying not to show how much I have enjoyed this moment. It's been friendlier, almost uncomfortably close. She sheds the swing and runs to catch me, pulling to turn me around.

"Dalton, I'm deeply in like with you. I wish it could be more, but I want you to know that I will never forget our time together." With that, she stood on her tip toes and brushed her lips quickly against mine. A second later the moment was gone.

"Walk me home," she said softly. I did, though neither of us said another word right up to the time when her front door closed behind her.

When I told Sienna about it, she looked at me carefully for a while.

"You're in love with her, aren't you?"

"No, I'm not. Even if I was, it would be pointless since there's no way she could ever see me as more than second best to Brad. I'm not though," I said trying to will her to believe me. "She said that thing about the airplanes and I think…"

"Do you think she's right? Are you in a holding pattern?"

I finally have an imaginative idea all my own. Suddenly we are back at the park. Sea gasps in surprise when we appear as if by magic, the sun turning her hair to flames.

"Take a seat."

Sienna looks at me as if I am a complete stranger. Her body feels very different from Caitlyn's, but I can't be sure if it is our dream life that explains it. The first push is easy, but pushes her impossibly high and she lets out a whoop. She settles into a nice rhythm and returns to her question. "Well, are you in a holding pattern?"

In my dream, I can actually stop the motion and see the way her hair is arrayed away from her face and inspect the pattern of her freckles along her cheeks and down her neck. I can allow the motion to go forward slowly and appreciate the rise and fall of her chest as she breathes. In my dream I can take all the time I want to see the lovely friend who shares my nights.

"What do I know, Sea? I'm having enough trouble with basic algebra and you want me to figure out this love stuff?"

"Seriously, you're growing up Dalton. I know you have hormones like everybody else. Are you really satisfied just to pretend to be in a relationship? I'm surprised you didn't at least ask who the others were. Don't you want more?"

"She didn't want me to ask. That would have hurt her. The truth is I have more… I have… you."

"Me?" Sienna stammered for a moment, something I never expected, but instead of turning away she looked right into me with those blue eyes. She drank me in and waited for more. It was so beautiful at that very second that my heart literally hurt.

Looking up at the sky, the clouds have the very same dancing pattern I noticed earlier with Caitlyn.

"I have one more surprise for you. Try this." I launch myself from the ground and begin to fly in circles above her in a way that I have never done before. The breeze kisses my face while I whisper an invitation to Sienna from a new height. I swoop towards her just as she launches herself from the swing. There is a sound of absolute delight that tumbles from her lips that is matched by a glow that seems to emanate from inside her and makes the rest of the daylight feel dull. We flow over the ground and the playground is suddenly a field filled with daisies, then with tulips, then with tiger lilies.

Sienna floats toward me and takes my hand and we dance on the tip of a cloud. Somehow she feels exactly as she is supposed to in my arms. There is music with guitars and keyboards and graceful strings that paints the aire in broad, sweet strokes. When the tempo slows, Sienna folds herself into me and then we settle down like a feather and gently touch the floor back in my room. She starts to pull away, but I hold her close to me. Once again, I have surprised my friend.

"I don't know about hormones or how other guys are, and maybe it's different because we meet in my dreams. I have a girlfriend who might as well be on the other side of the world. It doesn't matter because she fills the spaces in my waking time and you own my nights."

"What about sex or making out at least? Don't you have needs?"

"I'm guessing that's a question and not an offer." Sienna grimaces and rolls her eyes like only she can. "The answer is of course I have needs. The answer is also that I am fourteen and in no hurry."

"You do think about it."

"Can we please talk about something else? Actually, there is one thing I need."

Sienna looks at me expectantly. I bring my lips very close to her ear and let just a little breath escape. She shivers expectantly as I whisper in her ear. I hold back as long as I can to allow the tension to build.

"I'm thirsty," I tell her in my deepening voice, "let's go get something to drink."

"You!" Sienna pulls away from me and picks up a pillow, unleashing a torrent of blows to my head and shoulders which I make few efforts to repel. I can tell that Sea wonders how I can possibly be patient; what I am waiting for. Someday, if she doesn't know already, she'll realize that these moments are all I need. As we both fall over in hysterics, I know I could kiss her now and she would happily kiss me back. The thought crosses my mind and I push it away. When I kiss Sienna for real, when I kiss her for the first time, it won't be at the end of a discussion that began with describing my feelings for another girl. I get up and offer my hand and she takes it. The soda pops in my dreams are colder, sweeter and more satisfying than the ones during the day.

8.

A Nikon moment

'There,' Dalton thinks as he places the last hanger in the closet and shuts the door before taking a seat on his bed. The last chores of moving in have finally been completed. He looks around at the other changes that have become part of his life. It's a bigger room for starters. A small TV sits in the corner and a stereo inside one of his bookshelves. Another shelf is filled with cameras and lenses. The recently purchased computer monitor dominates his desk while the attached tower sits alongside.

With the improvement in his dad's career, a larger, nicer house was a natural next step, but this time the move has kept them in the same city. The new neighborhood is situated close to his school. All of the material possessions have made a difference, but not nearly so much as the change in his father's attitude towards him. Dalton smiles as he thinks of how much more relaxed his dad has gotten. 'Dad is happier, but it is more than that', Dalton realizes. 'Now that he has stopped chasing success, he has the time to appreciate what he has accomplished and he has time to get to know me'.

Dalton calls out as he heads to the bathroom to brush his teeth. His father's door is down the hall and the door is open.

"Goodnight dad."

"Did you lock up and shut off all the lights?" Don Hunters tone is mellow now, and the question is more habit than inquiry. Dalton turns around and leans through the doorway.

"Yessir and I set the thermostat like you told me."

"Thanks son, sleep well."

Later as he edges into sleep, he waits for Sienna's arrival. He grabs a stack of prints that he has taken for his photography class; he watches the shadows for her arrival. The images are ones that he developed earlier today. He also has a surprise for Sienna. He is impatient and says the words he has said so often.

"Hurry moon." Dalton laughs to himself as he realizes that he is already asleep and the magic won't make his friend arrive any sooner. Still, maybe there is some magic as Sienna appears from the shadow as if on cue.

"Hey you, what's new?"

Sienna's expression is the same mix of impish delight and warming charm that he comes back for every night. Her hair now reaches halfway down her back. She's wearing a little makeup with eye shadow and liner and a soft, peachy shine on her lips. It's not a glamour look, more like a healthy, prettier than the girl next door style that is carried through her white t-shirt and jeans.

They don't fly in the air as much as they did a while ago. It's still fun, but they agree that now that they're grown up, it's time to cut back on the kid stuff. Sienna plops down next to her friend and puts her arm around him, giving a light squeeze as she looks to see the pictures he is thumbing through.

"I just got my new prints finished; want to see them?"

"Sure," she says as he passes them to her.

"Dalton, these are really good. I'm no expert but I think you have a gift."

"My photography teacher Mr. Kirchner says that I can probably get into a good school with these if I keep working hard. Close your eyes, I want to show you something."

Sienna hesitates with a slightly suspicious expression. Finally she agrees with a cautious "okay."

"Oh get your mind out of the gutter," he teases. "It's nothing bad. My Dad got me a new camera. He's been doing pretty well lately and he's decided to encourage me taking pictures."

Sienna ignores the kidding and looks at the new camera. Her expression indicates that she doesn't understand the reason her friend is so excited. It looks pretty much like any other camera to her. Dalton sees her reaction and explains.

"It's a digital camera. You can take the pictures and see them right away. Dad gave me a new computer and printer so that I can print the good ones."

Sienna still doesn't see what the big deal is but wants to show her support.

"This is great," she says, still looking for any clue of the significance of a 'digital' camera.

"I haven't told you the best part. Before I could only show you pictures after I took them into the darkroom and developed them. With this thing, I can take a picture and you can see it right away. Watch…"

Dalton focuses on a book sitting on his desk. The camera flashes. He shows the display screen to Sienna.

Captured in the small two by three inch screen is the book on the desk.

"Wow, I can see it." Sienna is starting to see the value of a camera that you can take pictures with and see the results immediately.

Dalton focuses on the new stereo on his bookshelf. Again he shares the result. He begins shooting other objects in the room. An idea starts to form in Sienna's head as he continues.

"Dalton, why don't you take some of me?" she asks shyly.

He hesitates for a second, but quickly realizes just how much he wants to do as she asks.

"Okay, why don't you stand over there where the light is better and we'll try it out?"

Sienna walks toward the spot Dalton indicates with her face lit by a mischievous grin. She waits for a moment as he focuses his camera and then strikes a silly pose and sticks out her tongue.

"C'mon, get serious." Dalton smiles at her antics. It's a smile that widens as she sticks out her chest as she stands at attention and salutes.

"Yes sir."

Dalton is looking through the viewfinder and lets the camera stray a bit to the south. Suddenly, he lowers the camera. His expression is one of surprise and a little like awe.

"When did you get those?"

"Ummm, these?" Sienna replies with feigned confusion.

Sienna makes a show of following Dalton's eyes locked on her chest. Her intention to chastise him is broken though as she starts laughing in spite of herself.

"I don't know, one day they just sort of showed up. Seriously Dalton, I've had these for a while. You know, for a photographer, you're not all that observant."

Dalton gets back to work and begins shooting. The girl's expression is both comical and yet appreciative. She stops laughing and tries to sit without looking posed, less like a fashion model, more just herself.

Dalton shakes his head and mumbles. "I had no idea."

"What?"

"You've been there with me for so long. All of a sudden, you're grown up. Grown up and…" Dalton stops, wondering if he could really complete the thought.

"And…" Sienna says, encouraging him to continue.

"Grown up and beautiful," he replies nervously.

His friend is genuinely touched. She can barely push a word from her lips. Finally she manages a soft, querulous "Dalton?"

Dalton gets quiet as he focuses on his work. Sienna stands and moves gracefully. Dalton is sad that these photos won't really be on the camera when he wakes up, but knows that they will share them for a little while before he awakens. Sienna talks as Dalton moves and shoots.

"Do you ever hear from Caitlyn?"

Dalton thinks back to that day a few weeks back. They had sat on his front step as they'd done at the very beginning. Caitlyn looked strangely sad.

"Brad broke up with Suzie last week," Caitlyn began. "He asked me if I want to go out on Friday."
"It's about time," Dalton answers carefully. "I hope you will be very happy."

"Honestly, I don't know how I feel. I've had this thing for Brad for so long. You know what they say about being careful what you wish for. I know one thing for sure. I am going to miss you."

They exchanged one last hug more brotherly than intimate and Caitlyn walked away without a backward look. Dalton shakes off the memory and answers Sienna.

"No. It was inevitable once we broke up. I see her at school from time to time, but she keeps her distance so that Brad won't think he has competition, which he doesn't. Then there was the move. Now that I live in a different neighborhood, we have that much less chance to see each other.

Once the shooting is done, Dalton sits on the end of his bed and motions Sienna over saying "Come take a look."

Sienna sits on Dalton's right as they examine the shots in the little screen.

"Dalton, these are really good. I'm sorry I teased you before. You have a good eye."

He scans to one in particular and nudges her.

"Take a look at this; I think the light is really interesting."

Dalton raises his right hand to point to something specific in the display. As he does, he accidentally brushes against Sienna's arm. As before, the sensation is so real and powerful. A little overcome, he acts on impulse, landing a quick kiss on Sienna's cheek. Sienna turns away, blushing. Conflicted, she blurts out her first reaction.

"I…I've wanted you to do that for so long. I have. But…"

"But what?"

Sienna turns back to him but her eyes are turned to the floor.

"You are the only real friend I've ever had. With things as they are, I know we can be friends for a long time; maybe for a lifetime. I don't want you to think of me like I'm just a body…"

"I don't. I won't."

"Dalton, you say that now, and it seems easy enough."

"I don't understand. It was just a kiss on the cheek." Dalton looks for some explanation that he can comprehend. Sienna turns to him and fixes him with an expression of gentle affection.

"I know and it was very nice. But a kiss on the cheek can easily lead to a kiss on the lips. Dalton, once that starts, where does it end?"

Now it is Dalton's turn to think their situation through. He doesn't feel like he has done anything wrong, but he is starting to see how complicated their relationship could become if they stray into the places where their bodies would lead.

"You're right. God, I know you're right. Why do you always know everything before I do?"

Sienna shoves Dalton playfully. "Well, we could start with the old 'Girls mature faster than boys' stuff. Of course the truth is a lot simpler. I'm just a bit smarter than you."

Dalton returns the shove. The two continue looking at pictures in Dalton's new camera as well as a few prints. Dalton casually drapes his arm around Sienna. She notices but lets it remain. Soon it is time to leave. She gets up and heads for her shadow.

"Good night Dalton. See you tomorrow."

Dalton stares at the spot where Sienna was standing just a moment before. He thinks out loud. 'Night after night you come here. I brush against you and it feels like electricity. You tell me things that I don't know, and things that make me feel better. You must be real. You have to be real.'

9.

The first temptation

Bare trees and a sky full of cold, lonely clouds fill the viewfinder. It is the next afternoon and Dalton is walking on the school grounds after classes have ended. He is unaware as he walks, that he is being watched. Laurie Greene, a senior over a year older than Dalton, has decided that the good looking boy with a camera could be interesting. As he stares intently, focusing his manual camera to capture the interlaced branches, Laurie decides that she could be the perfect distraction. She sneaks closer and just as Dalton prepares to click the shutter, she jumps in front of him, blocking the shot.

"Hey!" Dalton cries out, startled.

"Hey, yourself," the girl replies with a calm, straight expression. Oops, did I get in the way?" She brushes back a strand of strawberry blond hair from her face as she chuckles, her innocence leaking away.

Dalton eases the camera down and lets it dangle from the strap around his neck. When he looks up, he realizes that the intruder is standing very close. Little plumes of breath escape as she stares at him, green eyes gleaming. The aroma of her perfume mixed with the warmth of her breath is quite inviting.

"I hope I didn't mess up your shot. I really didn't mean to make you stop. My name's Laurie, Laurie Greene."

"I'm Dalton."

Dalton backs up a step but Laurie moves quickly to close the gap. Her eyes continue to be locked on his.

"That's okay; I was pretty much done for the day." He places his camera back in its case and backs up again. This time Laurie stays put. With the advantage of the added distance between them, Dalton is able to get a better look at his new friend. Besides the green eyes and light red hair, her skin is smooth and her nose is straight and just the littlest bit upturned. Her lips are full and they part just a bit in a smile as his glance goes by. The leather jacket she is wearing is stylish and swells in a very appealing way. Dalton tries not to continue but cannot help himself, and as his stare moves on, Laurie twirls with a little giggle. Her jeans look so tight that she must have attached a vacuum cleaner to her waistband to suck out every bit of air from them.

Laurie ends her spin and Dalton forces his eyes back to hers. For her part, Laurie is quite happy with the display of admiration. With no appearance of disapproval from the girl, Dalton's embarrassment is short lived. Laurie fights back the urge to make some kind of snide comment about his wandering eyes, and just falls in next to the boy. She begins walking next to him, guiding him while trying to appear that she had no particular destination in mind.

"I've seen you around. You taking Mr. Kirschner's photography class?"

"Yes." Dalton is surprised by the girl's forward approach, but somehow it only makes her more intriguing.

"I hope you weren't working on an assignment. I'd hate to think I kept you from your schoolwork."

Even the girl's tone, which is softly mocking, only seems to make her more attractive, and her looks are equally enticing. He can't seem to pull away from those deep green eyes.

"No this is pretty much just for fun. At least it was…"

Laurie checks Dalton's expression and is delighted to see that he is returning her teasing. Her instincts have been rewarded as the boy she has been watching for some time has a bit of charm after all.

"What do you do when you don't have your eyeballs glued to your camera?"

"Not much. These days I seem to spend almost all my time with glued eyeballs."

Sienna is hiding in the shadows behind a tree. She is smiling in spite of herself. She finds Laurie refreshing and different; someone who would be fun to know for herself as well as Dalton. She senses that his response to this girl is very different from anything he's had in the past. In the back of her mind, she wonders if she should be worried, but pushes the thought away quickly.

Laurie continues her advances by moving on to the next stage of her plan. "Could you use a break?" she asks innocently.

"What did you have in mind?"

"Well, I thought we could stop by the pizza place near the mall and get a slice? Do you have a car?" Laurie already knows that the boy walks to school. She has been making inquiries and watching him for a few weeks.

"Not at school. My dad lets me borrow his sometimes."

"Great, we can go there in mine." After the short walk, the parking lot is in sight and her car is not far off. "That is, if I haven't scared you off or anything."

Dalton is more than a little surprised at how quickly things are moving, but he likes the feeling and sees no reason to stop yet.

"I guess we can chance it."

Laurie leads him towards her car. She moves closer and wraps her arm around his, encouraging the closeness. "Come on, it's this way."

Unlocking the door of her Mustang, and then hitting the release for his door, Dalton gets in and buckles his seat belt. He soon sees that Laurie drives much the way she has done everything else so far; a bit fast and with a definite sense of purpose. Green lights at intersections are prized and yellow lights barely acknowledged. They soon round the corner where the shop is located. The neon sign blinks red in the window.

Once out of the car, Laurie grabs Dalton by the arm and pulls him into Tony's pizza. She smiles as they arrive at the counter and order a couple slices and cokes as the music blares in the background. There is a noticeable reaction as several classmates turn to see the new 'couple'. The volume of the conversation starts to compete with the rock music blaring in the background. Dalton leads the way to a table, but this is mostly because Laurie has a plan and has allowed him to go first. When Dalton takes a seat in a booth, Laurie ignores the seat opposite and pushes Dalton so that she can sit beside him. He slides over and again she continues until he stops. She wants him to feel her nearness, for it to become second nature to him.

"I've seen you around a few times you know. You're always taking pictures. Is it just a hobby, or what?"

"I haven't decided. Mr. Kirchner thinks I could do something with it, but I'm not sure. I know there aren't too many things I like as much."

"Maybe I can help you with that," Laurie replies impishly. Dalton does not miss her meaning. "Do you think I could see some of your shots sometime?" She continues as she picks up her slice and begins to nibble at the edges. "Maybe I could go around with you and watch you work."

"Well maybe, but you'd have to promise to stop jumping in front of the lens."

Laurie giggles a little at Dalton's reply. The boy has some life in him! She puts the pizza down, wipes her hand quickly on a napkin and extends it to him.

"Deal. How about if I just stay glued to your side? Seriously, tomorrow's Saturday, do you want to go for a walk?"

"Sounds like fun. Where would we go?"

"We could start downtown. You could take pictures of street life. Then we could head over to Miller's Park and see the geese in the pond. I go there sometimes. The afternoon light on the pond is amazing."

Dalton responds without thinking. "It's a date."

Laurie's eyes widen just a bit. She really hadn't expected it to go this easily.

"Great, I'll drive you home after this and then meet you at your place about ten thirty." Just then she starts looking around, noticing all the other kids trying to act as if they aren't watching.

"God, look at all the busybodies with nothing better to do than watch us."

"Should we leave? I'm almost done…" Dalton realizes that his companion has hardly touched her pizza.

"No. Let 'em all stare. In fact, we should give them something to stare at."

Before Dalton has a chance to react or speak, Laurie turns and pulls his face to hers. Her lips are on his quickly and she holds him in place for several seconds before letting go. She turns back and picks up her slice as if nothing has happened but with a huge, smug smile on her face. Dalton is speechless and decides that in the absence of something witty to say, silence will do. Around the shop, the reaction is quite the opposite as several of the customers clap and whistle. Laurie acts as if nothing at all has happened.

"Dalton, I told you that I have seen you a few times. That's true, but it isn't everything. I like the way you look when you're taking pictures. I like the way you move. I'd love us to spend lots of time together. People say that I am kind of pushy, and I guess it's true. I don't have time for holding back; never saw the point. I'm not very patient. Do you think you could handle it, being with me?"

In her mind, Laurie sees Dalton respond not with words but with a kiss. Dalton turns to Laurie, considering just such a response, but he is not as bold as she is. Her face is very close.

"I like you just the way you are. I can't think of anything I'd enjoy more than spending time with you." Dalton is amazed as he realizes how much he means it. The two stay very close. Dalton gets another whiff of

Laurie's cologne. It seems to hold him in place and sends little unmistakable signals deep into his brain. Finally, Laurie seems satisfied. She turns, pops one more bite of pizza in her mouth and jumps to her feet breaking the trance.

"Good, that's settled. Let's go."

10.

Laurie: Someplace special for two

Millers Park is one of my favorite places. Mom says I spend way too much time here, but she doesn't understand and since I don't do anything else that she objects to, she doesn't make a big issue of it. It has a large pond, full of small fish and frogs. It even has a couple of geese and two white swans. There are trees everywhere and a few large rocks perfect for sunbathing when the weather is warm. Not today of course, as October has already made it clear that summer is behind us. There was a crystalline chill cutting the air in my bedroom that urged me into a heavier wool sweater this morning. Now the woods have started to unveil their autumn magic with the leaves having already warmed to a buttery yellow and just a few hints of rose and orange. Their reflections are mirrored beautifully in the water where the surface is practically glass smooth with only the very rare ripple to break the perfect inverted image. The afternoon sunshine bounces star-like bursts of light off them when the wind or a moving fowl troubles the water.

    Lots of families come to the park on the weekends when it's warmer, their children running and splashing and having a great time. I love the sound of their shouted joy and infectious laughter. The picnic tables are everywhere and there are open fields perfect for spreading out a well-worn blanket. The best part though is along with the many open spaces, there are more than a few hidden ones. Whenever I need to think things through, I go to my secret place, lay on my rock in the sunshine, and before long everything is clear. No one has ever bothered me here and today I have reason to be thankful for the concealment.

    I waited a long time to share this place with anyone. Lots of guys would have been happy to spend time with me here, and I had to really fight the urge once or twice as I considered sharing my secret place. It wasn't so much that they were unattractive or anything, and heaven knows they would have been thrilled with the plans I had in mind for them once we got here. Still, I always held back. It was just that after the festivities were over, I worried whether there would be a repeat performance or worse yet, whether I might find one of them squatting on my space, my place, with someone else. I could live with the idea of getting a reputation, at least I think I could, but not if it meant finding some lecherous moron and his next diversion here.

    Today is different. Today I have finally found someone who will understand what this place means to me. He will know without me even having to explain that everything I share with him here, my lips, at some point my body, and most certainly this place are not things to take lightly. Dalton will understand. Even now, as he kneels, almost prayerfully, getting just the right angle for his photo; I can tell that he gets it. I sit staring at him, his nice shoulders and lean torso warming me up enough to consider shedding this sweater after all. As if he caught a whiff of my thoughts, he turned just now and shot me that soft hearted smile. God, he can make me melt.

    I'm in no hurry. I can tell that he doesn't have a lot of experience if any at all. The best part of that is that neither of us will have anything to compare things to, and we can learn as we go, together. I do wish he'd finish with that camera now.

It has been a pleasant morning. We did just as I suggested. I came by his house and we made our way downtown. I carried his camera case and a picnic lunch so he could concentrate on his work. He often took digital shots and then repeated them with his film camera, telling me about light metering and f stops as we went. I hope I showed enough interest as boys can get funny if they think you don't care about their hobbies. I have to say that the shots of the people on the street seemed incredible to me though I barely know which end of the camera faces forward.

We ate the sandwiches and drinks that I packed and talked about the pictures he took. I am not sure, but he seemed genuinely interested in my opinion, treating me as if I knew something about photography. I pointed to the pictures I liked and he even asked me to tell him some things about the ones I liked less. All the time, his eyes were locked on mine, absolutely interested in me.

Even from this distance, I can hear the repeated click of his shutter as he points in every conceivable direction. Finally, he is easing the camera into its case. He zips the bag and sets the whole thing carefully on the grass beside us. He sits next to me, close though not touching, and I am content to stay as we are for a little while.

"It's beautiful here," Dalton says as he continues to take the place in with a slow turning gaze. I'm hoping that his attention on me will soon be as intense. Whenever he turns to look at me, it is everything I have ever wanted from a boy. I don't want to waste another minute.

"This is my favorite place in the world. Nobody ever comes here but me, at least as far as I can tell. I've never brought anyone with me either."

"Thanks for sharing it with me."

"You're never going to guess what I spent last night doing."

"What?"

I swallow his gaze, warming to his intense interest.

"I spent the whole evening drawing little hearts with felt tip pens in a bunch of crazy colors and wrote your name a thousand times in all kinds of scripts and letters. I felt like I was twelve all over again."

I thought he would laugh at me or worse, but all he said was, "A thousand times, huh?"

The time is right and I know that I will have to encourage him just a little. I lock my eyes on his and lean forward just enough that he can feel how close I am. The rest is like a slow motion avalanche. He reaches out and touches my face as I wrap my hands around his waist. The beginnings of the kiss are soft and tentative; nothing like the quick pushy one I laid on him in the pizza place. The feel of his lips send little flashes of lightening right down my spine and I can't help but let a small responsive sound out. Parting my lips just a little is not quite enough to get him to the next step, so I gently urge my tongue past his. His response is so sweet and good and the kissing goes on and on. He's a natural kisser and just the littlest bit wet. I wish I had followed through with that idea to remove my sweater as it might have given him some ideas as far as my button down blouse. It's too late now and I don't feel bad as the mouth to mouth is quite satisfying.

When I finally pull away, I reward him with the most appreciative smile I can offer and he pays me back with change to spare.

"We should get going," he says, and I shake my head in agreement. We have plenty of time. He reaches out for my hand but I need to be closer to him and I wrap my arm around his back and walk as near as any person can. His arm quickly closes around me and my day is complete.

11.

Heart, mind and body

Heavy gray clouds fill the warm summer-like day with a sticky gloom as Dalton slowly approaches his mother's grave stone. He lays a bunch of flowers on the plot and closes his eyes for a moment. As Sunday Services concluded he was suddenly filled with a longing for his mother's comforting presence. Sienna stands by the trunk of a large oak, feeling the sadness radiating from her friend and watching him from a slight distance as she has so many times before. The grass beneath her feet is damp, but she is only vaguely aware that it is there at all. Today is different from those other days in at least one way. Normally, Dalton's thoughts would be open to her and she would sense everything as he did. Today there is a distance to his feelings as he focuses on his Mother's memory.

"Hi Mom, I just got here. I was at church with Dad. I know it's been a while since I came to see you. I'm sorry but everything has been going so fast lately and now it seems faster than ever. I wish I knew what to ask you. I feel so selfish always coming to you just to talk about me, but I don't know what else to say. I know you're in heaven and I know that you are happy. There's some comfort in that at least.

Anyway, I've told you about Sienna. God Mom, I wish you could see. I know you see me, but can you see someone that I only see in my dreams? Anyway, she's gotten so pretty and so grown up. She always knows what to say to make me feel better when I'm down. She's smart and special and sweet. She's the kind of girl I know you would love."

A little smile pulls at the edges of Sienna's lips. Dalton's feelings for her have been clear for some time, but this is the closest she has come to hearing them from him. A chuckle seems to come unbidden. It's funny to her how so many things that seem obvious to her are such a mystery to him.

"Dalton, of course your mom can see me."

"Sienna makes me feel like I can do anything. She helps me with my photographs, and all kinds of things. She has always been there. When she talks to me, it almost always seems like something you would say. The problem is; the feelings I have for her are so hard to describe. Even though it's only in my dreams, when she touches me, the sensation is so strong; so real. Don't worry Mom, even in my dreams, we don't misbehave. Sienna is a lady and she makes me want to be a gentleman; someone you'd be proud of. If she was a real girl it would be so easy to say 'I Love you' to her."

Sienna's smile brightens a little more, but is quickly dimmed as Dalton's thoughts stray in another direction. He pauses briefly, trying to find the right words to describe his day with Laurie.

"I did something yesterday that might not make you so proud." He looks around quickly even though he's very sure nobody is nearby. "To start with, I have to tell you something. I've met someone. Actually, it might be more accurate to say that she met me. Her name is Laurie and she is wonderful and funny and quirky and very real. She isn't quite as pretty as Sienna, but she has this cute upturned nose, short strawberry blonde hair and lovely green eyes. She has this way of standing so close to me face to face that's challenging and exciting. It's so different than with Sienna. To tell you the truth, Mom, she kind of scares me a little, but mostly in a good way. She's like this human roller coaster. She leads me around some time and I don't know what she'll do next."

Sienna whispers from her spot nearby as if she is worried Dalton might hear.

"Laurie is amazing. I wish I didn't, but I like her too. I like what I see in you when you're with her. You seem so alive."

"Mom, I have to tell you about yesterday. We walked around the city, you know? I've always wished I could do something like this with Sienna and not have it be a dream. It was just great. She has a good eye, even better than she realizes and she made several suggestions that led to great shots. Did I tell you about the new camera Dad got me? By the way, he and I are doing much better. Anyway, after we were done downtown, we went to Miller's Park. The pond there was full of light and reflections and there were these geese and a couple swans. We sat and had a picnic. Laurie brought it and carried it all over the place and even helped me with some of my stuff. She wouldn't let me carry anything at all. She said I had to concentrate on my pictures. Well, she took me to this spot that's kind of private. I took some really good shots there and when I finished I saw her smiling at me and the next thing I know we were kissing. Mom, I'd be lying if I said it wasn't nice. She doesn't hold back, and I think she cares for me a lot. It's just…I felt like I'm cheating Sienna. Also, I just have this feeling that she is so anxious to do things, and I don't know if what she wants is about me or about her."

Dalton catches his breath and feels the wind pick up around him.

"Mom, am I making any sense? I'm sure that I'm saying this all wrong. I feel pretty certain that you wouldn't be ashamed of me for what happened at the park. We only kissed for a while and then we came home. The problem is what happened later after I went to sleep. I know that I should have told Sienna about the picnic and everything, but I couldn't. I couldn't tell her about making out with Laurie any more than I could tell Laurie about this girl that visits my dreams every night. I feel guilty about both. When Sienna showed up, it almost seemed like she knew something, but she never said a word. I tried to tell her, but I didn't know what to say. My feelings for both of them are so different and so powerful. It's so confusing and I don't know what to do."

Sienna watches her friend with real sympathy. Her feelings about Laurie are nearly as confused as his. On the one hand, she understands her friend's dilemma, especially because she has been the one advising him about girls up till now. On the other hand, it has been a while since Dalton was this distracted.

"Dalton, this is hard for both of us. What we have is fascinating and powerful, but I understand how conflicted you must be. I could see last night that you were troubled. If you need to keep your feelings for Laurie to yourself, it's all right. You should know what you mean to me. Only you can decide what you need and I won't stand in your way if Laurie is the one."

"Mom, I know that this is one decision you can't help me with," he goes on, "but it feels good to talk to you. I'm going out with Laurie again. Guess the only way to decide is to go on. Laurie is real. I have to find out if I am."

Dalton hesitates for a second, not completely ready to end his visit. The polished marker reflects a broken image back to him. Closing his eyes, he sees his mother's warm smile in his mind, lending support and grace. For a little while he is content to have what he feels is her blessing.

"I'll try to get back here soon. I have to go now."

Dalton starts to walk away and then turns back. "Mom, I wish with all my heart that Sienna was real. I wish that she was here right now. Bye."

"I am here Dalton. I'm right here," she responds with a hint of desperation.

Later as Dalton awakens to find Sienna waiting in his dream, he knows what he has to do.

"Sit down, Sea. I have something to tell you that I should have told you last night."

"What is it?"

"Yesterday, I spent the morning and afternoon with Laurie, the girl I've been telling you about."

"I know," Sienna replied, trying to keep her emotions steady.

"Well, what I didn't tell you is that we spent about half an hour kissing when we finished the picnic at Miller's Park. I'm sorry I kept it from you; that was wrong."

Sienna sits quietly wondering if there is more when Dalton continues.

"I can't imagine how you must feel about this. I'm not sure I know how I feel or how I should feel…"

Sienna smiles as she realizes that her friend is still there, still hoping for her help and advice.

"Dalton, we're friends. We started with that and whatever happens, I hope we will end with that. I'm glad you trusted me enough to share this with me. I don't think I can help you too much as far as your relationship with Laurie, but I will continue to be your friend as long as you want me to. If the day comes when you decide that she is the one, I will stand aside and be happy for you."

The look of surprise on Dalton's face lasts only a second before he is rushing to his friend and wrapping her up in his arms.

The rest of the weekend passes in a blur and then it is Monday morning and Dalton is driving to school in his father's car. The plan to take things to the next level with Laurie is bouncing around in his brain. He knows there's no reason for the nerves he is feeling as she has made her interest so clear and her answer is in no doubt. Only Sienna's place in his life as things go forward can explain his jumbled thoughts.

He makes his escape from the conflicting emotions by diverting his attention towards the upcoming day's classwork. A quiz is looming in American Literature. Thankfully, 'Catcher in the Rye' is more than enough to offset anything else lobbying for his attention. By the time he pulls into the school parking lot, he is completely focused and ready for class. Pulling his jacket close, Dalton scoops up his books and joins the crowd of arriving students.

Laurie sets her tray down in the lunch room and waits for her friends to arrive. It's a typical Monday and classes have been long and more boring than usual. The bad part of having a separate lunch from Dalton is that she misses the chance to talk with him and share a bit of his day. The good part is that she can spend the next 42 minutes sharing the juicy details with her friends Candy and Heidi who have just arrived and are already giving her a hard time. "So what's he like? Can he kiss or what?" Candy is the typical blonde bombshell, although Laurie is pretty sure that Mother Nature had a little help from Dr. Implant in town.

Heidi is quick to join in. "Yeah, let's go. We know he's fine looking, but spill…" Heidi is a brunette, as lithe as her friend is buxom, but she has a smile that can melt a boy from a hundred paces. The two girls met at cheerleading practice and have been close ever since. Laurie is not sure how she hooked up with them, but one day they were all sitting and laughing, and it kept going.

Laurie is enjoying the back and forth and replies in a singsong voice full of mischief, "I'll never tell."

"Come on, we tell you…" the two girls whine in unison.

"All right, there's one thing that I'll say. When we went to the pond last Saturday, I didn't give him much time to take pictures." The girls light up with conspiratorial glee. They start giggling and Laurie soon joins them.

Heidi goes back to work as their laughter fades. "You're so bad…I knew it. You like him. So what's next?"

"Well, I saw him in the hall between first and second period. He was so cute and a little nervous when he asked me out to the movies. Okay, so you know I have that thing with my folks this weekend. He was a little disappointed when I told him I couldn't go with him until I explained. I promised that I'd be spending a lot of time with him in the meantime, but we won't have that first serious date until a week from Saturday night. We're going to the movies, then back to Miller's Park."

Candy jumps back in, goading, "Then what?"

"Then I attack of course. Actually, I plan to see if Mr. Hunter can live up to his name. If he's smart, he will bring some ammo and I will be his prey." This brings an even louder round of laughter to the girls; so much so that some of the kids nearby turn to see what's so funny. When they turn away again, Laurie continues.

"Okay, for real now. Dalton is a real sweet guy. I don't think I've met anyone quite like him. He's quiet, but all of a sudden he can be funny. He really doesn't mind that I take the lead; he's not threatened like some guys."

Laurie's voice trails away as she thinks of something.

"Why do I think I hear a "but" coming?" asks Heidi. "What's wrong with Mr. Awesome?"

"I can't quite put my finger on it. There's something I can't understand. We are there; the two of us. It's on and it's right there. He's really with me. Then all of a sudden he's pulling back. Any other guy would never have stopped the way he did; at least I don't think they would. If I didn't know for sure, I'd swear that he has somebody else, but he doesn't. Believe me, I checked this guy out for a while before I made my move."

The two girls chime in again, this time very sympathetically. "We know. You were very thorough."

"Not only that, but he is so sweet, so honest. He is the furthest thing from a player."

Laurie stops to think about everything, but all she can remember is the feel of his lips on hers. She tries to shrug it off by presenting a cool attitude.

"It really doesn't matter, I suppose. He's good looking, he's fun and as long as he keeps me entertained, he's all mine. If he isn't everything, he'll do for now."

12.

That's entertainment

Old fashioned neon lights festoon the marquee of the Lane Theater. They sparkle in patterned processions that draw the eyes into the crowning features above the entrance. The outdoor ticket booth is centered between two sets of doors. It is brightly lit and ready for business. Colored bulbs also glow around the sign where the features are listed. As Dalton and Laurie approach the theatre from the convenient parking space just a block away, they can see the young, smiling cashier through the narrow window. Dalton purchases tickets for himself and Laurie, and they enter the building. The ride here was a bit longer than he expected, but it was pleasant enough as his dad let him borrow the car. Laurie made sure to sit nice and close all the way.

  Dalton offers to buy his date some popcorn and she asks for a coke as well. With snacks in hand, they give their tickets to the usher. He is an older man who has laid his silly usher's hat on the podium in front of him. He smiles appreciatively at them and punches each ticket with a flourish. They smile back and pass him before pushing through the double doors into the theater. The Lane is an older "palace" type movie theater with a balcony, but to Laurie's dismay, the balcony is closed. The aroma of warm salty butter hangs in the air as it can only do in a theater such as this. They head towards the faded red, crushed velour seats, with Laurie choosing ones in the back and to the right of the screen. The theater is warm enough, so they both shed their coats and flip them to nearby seats. Laurie has additional motives for wanting her wrap removed. Dalton is a gentleman and holds the snacks until Laurie is settled in her seat before handing them to her and settling next to her.

"What made you decide on this movie? I mean the drive was fine, but hasn't 'After the Fall' been out for a while?"

"Well, there were a couple of things. Want to hear?" Laurie is in a teasing mood and thinks that making a game of the conversation will break the ice quite nicely.

Dalton is up for it. "Sure, fire away."

"First, there's the title. No mystery there. It's almost November, we're together, and just in case you haven't noticed, it's how I feel about you. I have so fallen." Laurie bats her eyes just to make the point.

"Second…" the boy urges, stifling a laugh.

"Second, you might not think this of me, but I'm kind of a sucker for romance films. Besides, I love this old theater. It's so much nicer than those multiplexes that show a hundred films and have no character."

"Why do I think there's more?"

"No, I can't tell you," Laurie replies, a trace of embarrassment creeping into her tone.

"Come on, what is it?"

"No, I couldn't possibly," she continues, positively elated at the back and forth. Dalton is surprised at the effect his date's smile is having on him. It occurs to him that he has never been this excited by anyone other than Sienna. The words just seem to be coming to him with no effort at all.

"You better tell me or I'll have to tickle it out of you."

Laurie looks around. She sees that the theater is still mostly empty. There is enough light to see by, and the screen is showing a slide show with ads for local merchants and easy film trivia questions. The other patrons are mostly couples looking for a similar amount of privacy.

"That would almost be worth it," she answers with a look of defiance, but when Dalton brings his fingers up in preparation for a tickle attack, her resolve crumbles. Still, it's a second too late and he goes in with both hands.

"Okay, okay, here goes," she says breathlessly and he retreats. "The sorry truth is that I used to have a crush on the star, Clive Jackson. I have since the movie 'Not Another Birthday Party'.

"Are you kidding? I mean… the guy was a real geek in that one. Oh, there's only one thing we can do about that."

"What?"

Before she can defend herself, Dalton has brought his fingers to Laurie's midsection, and her initial scream and subsequent laughter bring more than a couple amused looks from the seats nearby. Thankfully, the theater darkens and the projector lights up with a loud soundtrack.

The girl catches her breath and whispers, "Saved by the previews."

"You are a very lucky young woman."

Laurie responds with an air of mystery. "I guess time will tell."

Dalton turns to Laurie who smiles but keeps her face locked on the screen. The previews end and the film starts. She tries to keep her eyes and mind on the film, but it's becoming increasing difficult as she is anxious for some indication of interest from her new boyfriend. After the day at the park, it only seems natural that he would be more than ready to take up where they left off, especially since that was nearly two weeks ago. As the movie continues, Dalton is not unaware of his date's expectations. Two things are holding him back. He still wants to be a "nice" boy, and he has not resolved his sense of betrayal where Sienna is concerned.

Laurie is starting to fume just a bit. 'Don't they pack hormones into boys anymore?' she wonders. Finally, unwilling to allow the whole movie to go by, she turns, grabs Daltons arm and pulls it around her.

"I hope you don't mind, but I'm getting just a little chilly."

Dalton thinks this is strange as the theater seems comfortable to him. The real meaning shows up soon as Laurie tucks herself very close and guides Dalton's hand under her arm and just below her breast. There can be no mistaking her interest or desires now, but Dalton still holds back. Laurie, caught up in the romantic action of the film and unwilling to wait longer, finally takes her hand and urges the cautious boy's fingers upward. Unable to fight off his girlfriend's clear intentions or his own feelings of attraction, he completes the movement himself, allowing his fingers to wrap around her shapely endowment.

Laurie turns to Dalton and smiles adoringly.

"You're so sweet. I knew I would Love you."

She then turns her head into Dalton's neck and nibbles lightly. Afterwards, she rests her head on his shoulder and watches the film. Dalton leaves his hand where it is, not only because she obviously wants it there, but for a much more natural and selfish reason; the pleasure is undeniable. As minutes pass it becomes clear that just leaving his hand in place is not quite enough. Laurie glows with naughty satisfaction as her boyfriend's attentions become more intense. As the movie becomes sadder, he brings his hand back to her shoulder and turns her for some serious kissing. Laurie is more than ready. Later, as the credits roll and the lights come up, Dalton helps Laurie with her coat before donning his own.

"Why thank you sir," she offers with a sincere, luminous smile. 'It may take a while to get the feeling back in my right boob,' she thinks to herself, 'but at least we're starting to get somewhere.'

The two exit the theater. Immediately, they feel the night's chill and they smile as their breath escapes in steamy bursts. A few cars pass by and they turn away from the noise and the bright lights to decide what comes next. They huddle close together and Laurie stamps her feet a little to emphasize that it is cold out.

"It's still pretty early; do you want to go somewhere?" Dalton already knows the answer, but it seems like the easiest way to start the conversation.

"Did you have any place in mind?" Laurie asks pointedly. She is pretty sure that he knows where she would like their date to go next.

"Not really; are you hungry?" Even though Miller's Park is clearly the next stop, Dalton is unwilling to voice the suggestion. In spite of his date's obvious inclination, he does not want to appear too anxious.

"No, the popcorn filled me up, how about you?"

Dalton looks up at the sky searching for the moon, but it is hidden behind a heavy layer of cloud. A silent apology dies in his mind. Laurie's eyes follow into the sky, but she doesn't understand what it means.

"I'm not hungry either, but I'm not ready to see this night end yet."

Laurie spends a moment, trying to appear as though she's giving the matter some thought so that her next words appear casual and not premeditated.

"There's always the park."

Laurie reaches out her hand and Dalton takes it. They make their way to his father's car. Dalton opens the passenger door for Laurie and she smiles. Soon they are driving away. The drive to the park is quiet. Laurie is filled with anticipation for things to move forward from the pleasures at the theater. Dalton is trying to accept the decision he's made that he needs to take the next step with a real, live girl.

Sienna sits in the back seat feeling conflicted and sad. Watching the two make out in the movie house was akin to torture. She feels a little responsible as she wonders if the concerns she expressed about kissing have encouraged Dalton to find physical affection with someone else. At the same time, she can't help but like Laurie and other than wishing she was the one in the passenger seat, she has no ill will or jealousy towards the girl. She doesn't even think of her as a rival. They are nearly there but Sienna's curiosity will not allow her to leave just yet. She wonders just how far Laurie is planning to lead and how willing Dalton will be to follow.

Finally, with the car settled in the privacy of the Millers Park lot and the engine off, Laurie begins her appeal, facing straight ahead and more serious than Dalton has yet seen her. She chooses her words carefully.

"I have a question for you. Do you think I'm bad, like a slut or something because of some of the stuff we did at the movies? Tell me the truth, not what you think I want to hear."

"Of course not," he says, more than a little surprised. "You seem very natural. You really know who you are and what you want. I wish I was more like you."

"It's just that I find you…very attractive, and I feel ready to show someone, to show *you* what that means to me." Laurie curses herself for the slip, but is hopeful that he will be too polite to notice.

For his part, Dalton does not want to give a quick, easy answer. As always, when he is unsure, he stays quiet. Unfortunately, this is less that his date had hoped for, and she is disappointed that she has to work so hard to get to his feelings.

"Dalton, am I pretty? I mean, do you think I'm attractive?" Laurie is almost holding her breath as she awaits his answer. The wait does not last long. Dalton turns to Laurie and for once, he is the aggressor. Pulling her close, he begins kissing her gently, but with obvious enthusiasm.

Sienna watches sadly from the back seat. There are no tears, and her eyes are glued as the couple's kissing becomes more intense. It is clear that her friendship for

Dalton is stronger than the hurt she feels. She realizes that the two deserve their privacy and is just about to depart the shadow when…

Dalton is kissing Laurie and her mouth is warm and pleasant. Her tongue is sending powerful jolts of pleasure through his whole body and is making it very clear that she is ready for him. Soon his hands have come alive and are making modest ventures over her opening terrain. His eyes open for just a second, and what he sees makes him stop quickly. The face he sees is not Laurie's but Sienna's and the shock and guilt are overwhelming.

"Is something wrong? Did I do…"

"No, it's just…"

The tears well up as she waits for an explanation.

"Laurie, you're so beautiful and it would be so easy to let myself go. I have never felt anything like this. You're amazing. I could get lost very quickly. The thing is that I do care for you. As much as you want to and I want to, I think you deserve better than this." Dalton stops and indicates the car with a simple quick turn of his head. "I'm not going anywhere. We should take it slow and be sure; don't you think?"

Laurie is not really sure how far she was prepared to go, though she was hardly ready to stop this quickly. Trying to be honest with herself, she realizes that stopping now was probably the last chance before things escalated past the point of no return. With that in mind, she decides that Dalton is sweet and considerate and still worth the effort. She wipes a tear and tries to straighten out her clothing before she replies.

"One of the reasons I like you is that you seem so different from other boys. Most guys would not have stopped for anything. If you think that we should take it slow, then I am happy to go that way. Just remember what I told you before. I know what I want and I am not very patient."

Just because she has reasoned that stopping now was a good idea, Laurie still wants Dalton to know that he should plan on delivering as much or more pretty soon.

"I understand. Maybe I should take you home now."

For his part, Dalton is relieved that his girlfriend has taken his decision so well, although her warning was also very clear. He starts the car and it slowly exits the park. Sienna in the back seat is thoughtful. She is not gloating over the turn of events, but feels satisfied with Dalton's decision.

Dalton climbs the steps to his room remembering everything that happened this evening. His physical attraction to Laurie is undeniable, but his feelings for Sienna would be more than a match, if Sienna was a flesh and blood girl. He enters the room and tosses his clothing as he prepares for sleep. His eyes are barely shut as he falls into a deep sleep.

"Hurry Moon."

Dalton trails off as he realizes he is already asleep and Sienna is standing over him.

"A little late for that tonight, I think." Sienna says, chuckling.

Dalton sits up in bed, propping himself against the headboard with his pillow. Sienna sits down next to him. For the first time he notices something, Sienna is wearing perfume, a fragrance both subtle and unmistakable. He thinks to ask her about it but decides against it. Instead he simply takes in the enticing aroma.

"How was your date?"

"It was nice," he replies quietly, not looking at her.

"Why don't I believe you? You don't sound very happy."

"No, it's true. Laurie's amazing. She's full of life, full of... surprises."

Dalton stops as he thinks again about the evening's activities. Those thoughts soon head in directions he'd rather not spend too much time on like the taste of Laurie's lips or the way she felt in his arms. He starts to get so wrapped up in his thoughts that he misses the beginning of Sienna's next question.

"So, if she's so great, how come you're not still out with her? It is Saturday night, right?"

Dalton emerges from the fog of his thoughts. "I'm sorry, what?"

"I said, it's pretty early, how come you're home so soon?" Sienna's expression is a mix of curiosity and sarcasm but Dalton turns away, shaking his head. He can't tell Sienna what he's feeling; especially since they have agreed to maintain their relationship as it is. Sienna senses his dilemma and decides to let him off the hook.

"Okay, then at least tell me about the movie. 'After The Fall' was it? I haven't seen it."

Dalton is drawn back to Sienna's gaze and her comment sparks a curiosity of his own. He knows so very little of her life, wherever and whatever that life is.

"We never talk about you. Are there no movies where you are?"

"Of course there are, I don't live on Mars you know." Sienna is amused, but she is also aware that he has so many questions.

"Sometimes I wonder," he answers. "We spend so much time together. I can't imagine falling asleep and not finding you here. But that's so selfish. I take your time, but what do you get? Is it better than anything else you might be doing?"

Sienna is impressed as always with his concern for her, his hope that she is gaining something from this.

"It's hard to explain. I don't really know exactly what brought me to you. Ever since I found my way here the first time, it has gotten easier and easier to come back. There's so much I want to tell you about where I am, where I go when I leave you, but I can't. I don't know what it all means. There's one thing I can tell you. No matter where I go when I leave, my home is here; in your dreams; in your dream of me."

Sienna knows that this is not the answer he has waited for or deserves and she is hoping the subject will change, but feels compelled to add one thing.

"Someday I promise, I'll tell you everything, but not tonight."

Dalton gets up from the bed as he weighs Sienna's words. His trust in her is so strong because she has always led him towards better things and clearer answers. He knows that whatever she is withholding, she must have good reasons. Still, he hopes that the day when she can finally open up is not too far off. At the same time Sienna feels bad keeping the few scant details of that first trip here from him. Her deepest worry has less to do with those details. How would Dalton feel, she wonders, if he knew how much I am able to watch during his waking hours? Would he feel threatened? Would he think she has been spying on him?

"So, 'After the Fall', was it?" Her transparent effort to change the subject brings a laugh to them both and the spell is broken. Dalton makes a mental note to pursue it again sometime.

"Yeah, it was all right. The main character, the one played by Dinah James; she reminded me a lot of Laurie. She was spunky and full of fire."

"She's really beautiful."

"Who?"

"I was thinking about Dinah, but I guess you could say that about both." Sienna wonders if her friend thinks the two are close to comparable. Laurie is cute but hardly movie star gorgeous.

"There was one part that was really funny."

"The leading man, played by Clive makes this speech near the end when he thinks everything is over. It cracked me up." Dalton strikes a pose as he saw the leading man do in the movie and then continues. "He goes...The woman turned me upside down. I changed my clothes, shaved my beard, anything I could think of; anything she said. I thought she meant to make me over. I thought the idea was to help her find me more attractive. That wasn't it at all. The only thing that bitch wanted was to turn me into one huge, reeking pile of crap. And the best part was…it worked. I've never made anyone happier. Of course, I've also never ended up more alone."

Dalton can't help but laugh as he thinks about the scene.

"That's terrible," says Sienna though she is quite obviously amused. She rises from her seat on the bed and approaches Dalton.

"Yeah well, right after that, the girl he's talking about comes in and reveals a deep, dark secret that she's never told anyone and then she apologizes for the way she treated him. They end up in one of those end-of-the-movie kisses and then the credits roll." Dalton rolls his eyes.

Sienna finds his reaction incredibly sweet and charming. Suddenly, she realizes how close Dalton is. The feeling is overwhelming. She pulls him closer, their lips meet, and their kiss is natural and quickly turns very passionate. After a few minutes, she pulls back.

"Sea, you kissed me." Dalton's face is full of astonishment and affection.

Sienna leads him back to the bed, taking her place next to him. She rests her head on his shoulder and allows her eyes to close. Dalton happily spends the rest of his dreamtime watching her lovely face and stroking her long radiant red hair.

A few weeks have gone by. Dalton and Laurie are walking in Miller's Park in the late afternoon. His girlfriend is very quiet. Dalton knows he doesn't have to be a rocket scientist to realize that something is wrong.

"Who is she Dalton?" Laurie cries out abruptly.

"What are you talking about?" Dalton knows what is coming but he is clueless on how to make things right.

"There's something here I can't quite figure out. I don't know who it could be, you're with me all of the time and everything, but it feels wrong."

Laurie starts to walk faster. She pulls away from him as he tries to pull her back.

"You know the other night when we were in my room and my folks were out? I made a decision before you came over. I wanted to give myself to you. I spent the whole day getting everything ready for you. I tried on all these different outfits and almost went crazy trying to choose just the right perfume. I went to the mall and bought some things just for you and even made a trip to the drugstore to buy a box of things that I thought we might need. Wasn't that a wasted trip?

I really thought that you and I had something and I wanted to give everything I have to you to let you know that I felt that strongly about you. Either you don't love me or there's someone else because you still kept talking about waiting for the right time and all."

Dalton catches up to her and turns her around.

"I'm crazy about you."

"You know, that's the part I want to believe, but it doesn't help. In my heart, you're not all there. Dalton, I've known nice guys, but it's like you're too nice. I don't know what else I could have done to let you know, and it's like… nothing."

Laurie starts to cry as she begins running away.

Dalton calls after her "Laurie, I'm trying to do the right thing!"

"Don't you get it? I don't want you to do the right thing; especially if it is not for the right reason. I told you I wasn't patient. God, I don't know what I'm saying. I can't do this." Her cries tear at him as she reaches her car. "Goodbye Dalton."

Dalton lets the girl go. In his heart, he knows that he has been unfair. He doesn't blame Laurie for her anger. He knows that he's guilty. 'What happened to the idea of exploring my options with a real girl', he wonders? 'Did I keep my distance with Laurie because I was unwilling to risk the safety of my dreams?' He turns up his jacket collar and heads for home.

13.

Now serving - crossroads for everyone

Accepting the diploma from the smiling assistant principal seems like the singular moment of graduation to Dalton. But then, as he squints looking into the crowd to find his father's face, the expression of pride he finds there makes the previous moment seem ordinary. He is surprised as he hears applause and cheers from a couple of his classmates, so much so, that he has to work to keep his balance as he begins to navigate the steps down from the podium. Caitlyn Harris is in the row just in front of him, and she turns and smiles briefly as he retakes his seat.

"Graceful as ever, I see," Caitlyn jokes.

"Well, I work at it," Dalton replies with a smile.

"Talk to me after this is over, okay?" Caitlyn says and then turns around as if nothing has happened.

The names continue endlessly. It's a warm June day, and more than a few fathers have shed their suit jackets, though Don Hunter continues to wear his like a badge of honor. It's a large class with almost 700 students and once the kids have all picked up their papers; there are still the closing remarks before the tassel move and the grand headgear toss can be performed. On cue, all of those mortarboards are in the air like a black fireworks display and somehow it is still an image of celebration. Finally though, the cheering and hugging is over and kids are milling everywhere. As Dalton makes his way along past the families and friends posing for pictures or discussing the evening's party plans, a couple friends from the school newspaper stop him and ask if he'll sign their yearbooks. He obliges and feels bad that he didn't think to bring his own.

"Dalton," a voice calls from behind him. It is Caitlyn. "You haven't forgotten me already have you?"

"How could I ever?" he replies, ignoring the fact that her request to chat once the ceremony was over had escaped him.

Surprisingly, Caitlyn comes right up to him and delivers a very friendly hug before stepping back and appraising him. The feel of her is familiar and lingers a while after her release.

"You look good," she says as they both continue moving along with a sea of black robed graduates and smartly dressed attendees. She pauses, trying to decide which thing to say next. "I want to thank you," she decides finally.

Dalton reacts as if his old girlfriend has spoken in some foreign tongue. His look of surprise mixed with confusion brings a smile to Caitlyn's lips.

"For what?" he asks finally.

"You let me go, and made it very easy for me to get together with Brad. You never made me feel bad, although I have to tell you that I had some guilt of my own. More important, you made yourself kind of disappear so that Brad never felt that you were hanging around. He told me to tell you thanks for that."

"Where is he, by the way?"

"He's gone to get his pickup. I think he loves that car more than me, but lucky for him, I'm not the jealous type." Caitlyn delivers this last bit with a twinkle in her eye that reminds Dalton of how sweet their time together was.

"I have some news." Caitlyn says and lifts her left hand to display the modest sparkler that adorns her ring finger.

"Congratulations, I'm very happy for you." Dalton meets her eyes with a look that is completely sincere. "When's the big day?"

"Next weekend," she answers. "I would have invited you…" She trails off.

"Understood, just be happy okay?"

"I'll try. God," she keeps going, "I hope I know what I'm doing. He's a good guy and I know he loves me. You know what he told me?" Caitlyn carries on without awaiting an answer. "He told me that he dated all of those other girls so that he would have it all figured out when he got started with me."

"So how'd he do?" Dalton asks for fun. It's a leading question and he pretty much knows how she'll respond.

"He still needs work, but I'm doing the best I can." Her smile shows that they have reached a nice place as friends. "By the time I'm done I should qualify for a certification in reconstruction or something."

"I'm sure you'll do a great…"

"Laurie's a mess," Caitlyn blurts before he can finish.

"I didn't know that you knew her."

"Well, she came to see me a few months ago. She's heard about the two of us and had some questions for me.

She wanted to know if you ever saw anyone else while we were together. I told her that you hadn't."

"And now you're wondering if that was the truth."

Caitlyn looks down at the grass, not wanting to give her thoughts away.

"I never dated, or asked anyone else out while we were together." Dalton answers truthfully. "I never lied to you, or pretended. Remember what you told me that time about the planes at the airport?"

"I remember, and I never really thought you had cheated," she says a little defensively.

"I'll just say this. You have finally landed, Caitlyn, while I am still circling the runway hoping that I don't run out of fuel."

"You were always funny, Dalton. I will miss that." In a swift, singular movement, she brings her lips to his, and kisses him softly. "I never forgot your kiss," she says and starts to walk away, and then turns back. Their walk has taken them outside the high school stadium and near the road.

"Go talk to Laurie."

Just then a shiny, new, red Toyota pickup approaches. Brad hangs out the window and shouts to them.

"Hey, Dalton. Come on Cait, we have to get going. We have a million things to do before next weekend." Brad announces this with an unmistakable gusto, underlining the news she has just delivered. From Brad's expression, it seems clear that he is not as completely comfortable with Dalton's friendship with Caitlyn as she had indicated.

"I'm coming, I'm coming," the girl replies teasingly. It is a sweet remembrance as Dalton watches that effortless stride. She shrugs a goodbye at Dalton as she climbs in. There is a slight cloud of dust as the vehicle disappears quickly out of sight. Dalton walks away, shaking his head just a little. His father is nowhere to be seen, probably waiting by the car.

As he starts to make his way toward the parking lot, it isn't long before he hears another familiar voice. This one brings a small jolt of pain and a pang of guilt.

"Hello Dalton," Laurie says softly.

Dalton had heard that Laurie started sleeping around quite a bit after their failed romance. There was even a rumor that she had recently become pregnant, though there was no sign yet, Dalton thought, as he looked at her. Her hair is the same short strawberry blond cut that she had worn then, but her eyes have lost their shine, and some of the attitude has faded as well.

"Hi Laurie." There is a silence as each looks the other one over. Dalton stands still and faces his last girlfriend when she starts to speak.

"I saw you talking to Caitlyn. I guess the two of you are still friends."

"She just wanted to tell me her news. She showed me her diamond. And yes, I would like to think we're still friends, though her life is going in a very different direction from mine. Now that I think of it, I'm pretty sure she was just telling me goodbye."

"We talked about you. She still has some feelings for you I think." Laurie watches his eyes looking for any sign of disagreement and finds none.

"If that's true, then I can tell you that she's made her choice and is very happy with it. Enough about me though, how are you doing?" Dalton doesn't see the point of talking endlessly about Caitlyn, and he's pretty sure that isn't why Laurie came over.

"I came to tell you that I'm sorry and that I don't hate you anymore." Laurie's eyes get back a little challenge as she says this. "Maybe hate is too strong," she says, "I know I blamed you for a lot of things I did after we split up that were not your fault. I'm pretty sure you've heard the stuff about me that's going around. I'm not pregnant, though I was late enough a couple of months ago that I thought I could be. This is what happens when you confide something to the wrong people."

Dalton is a little uncomfortable, and decides against a casual 'I'm sorry', choosing instead to show support by meeting her gaze.

"You were right about waiting for the right time. After we broke up, I went kind of crazy trying to prove otherwise. I lost my virginity, my common sense, my reputation, and a couple of worthless friends in the process. I wish I could say it was worth it, but you know better already."

Dalton can see the tears beginning to form and doesn't know what to do, but when the girl takes a step toward him, it seems only natural to comfort her. He puts his arms around her and she shakes a little as the sobs begin. When she has calmed a bit, he lets her go and she smiles through wet red eyes.

"Thanks. I seem to do that a lot lately."

"I never meant to hurt you Laurie. I did, but it was never what you thought. I never cheated."

Dalton feels bad because this is only technically true, but he can't explain the rest.

"Caitlyn told me something and told me that I shouldn't repeat it. The way she said it though, I really don't think she cares if I do." Laurie wipes her eyes on the sleeve of her graduation gown. The motion pulls the gown tight across a very flat stomach. Dalton sees the girl pull herself together as if she is bracing for a strong wind.

"Are you gay?" Laurie asks pointedly.

"Am I what?" he explodes. His eyes bounce off a couple of clouds as he tries to find his normal calm. Dalton does his best to meet Laurie's eyes without laughing.

"Caitlyn said that it occurred to her after you two broke up that the reason you had made so little effort to make out with her was because you were dealing with issues. She told me the airport analogy, and it almost made sense. If you are coming to terms with your sexuality, it would really help if you could let me know."

Dalton doesn't need any time to think of an answer. "Laurie, I never felt anything more powerful than the feelings I had when we were together. Physically and emotionally, you know I was right there with you. Think about those nights. I wish I could make you understand why I held back, but I'm not sure I know myself. Even if I could, I doubt that it would help you very much."

"So you're gay."

"Feel free to believe whatever you want. If it makes you feel better, if it will help you to get back to the carefree person I remember, then I will happily let my wrists go as limp as dishrags." Dalton finishes with a playful flourish.

"I think I'll just try to get on with it and not worry about you so much," she replies, finally smiling her old smile.

"This is what I will think about when I remember you," Dalton says quietly as he pulls her close for a last quick hug.

"Goodbye Dalton." Laurie takes a last deep look into his eyes.

"Take care," he answers as their paths diverge.

The walk to his father's car seemed very long and instantaneous at once. The mid-afternoon sun and the heavy black gown are less responsible for his sweat than the two startling encounters, though now that he thinks about it, he realizes that shedding the graduation gear is overdue. Looking around, he sees that the crowd has long since departed and the street is mostly empty now. The long winded version of the walk involves all of the thoughts he is trying to process around the two girls he has just spoken with, and the very different results. Dalton tries to convince himself that both conversations have come to acceptable endings, though he is more hoping than certain where Laurie is concerned. The shorter version is that lost in his thoughts as he is, he comes to his father's car before he realizes how long his approach has been noticed.

"Ready?" his father asks simply.

"Yes. Sorry, have you been waiting long?"

Before Dalton can completely grasp what is happening, his dad pulls him into a tight bear hug. Dalton releases his breath slowly, and for just a second he is completely at peace.

Driving home doesn't stay quiet for long.

"I saw you talking to a couple girls. It was Caitlyn and Laurie, wasn't it?" Dad's look is one of curiosity mixed with a little amusement.

"Caitlyn wanted me to see her engagement ring. She and Brad are getting married next week."

"How do you feel about that?"

"I'm happy for her, Dad. She always loved him, even when we were together." Dalton smiles even though he feels more certain than ever that he won't see Caitlyn again. He looks out the window at the blur of trees passing and the impatient cars that seem to fly by. He looks back at his father, who is a little older, a little grayer, but still very much alert and alive.

"So what about Laurie, what did she want?" Don Hunter is really curious about this one as he felt certain that Laurie was a really good match for his son. "I have to tell you that I never understood what happened between you two. She was such a sweet girl."

"Dad, it's hard to explain. The truth is that she wanted things to move faster than I did. She wasn't willing to take things slowly and I didn't want to rush. Heck, I was only sixteen. What did she expect?"

Don takes a minute to digest this information. It isn't a complete surprise, but it confirms what he has begun to suspect for a while. If this is even half true, his son has a lot more sense than he ever gave the boy credit for.

"You did the right thing, Dalton. There's still something I don't understand though. You broke up with that girl almost two years ago. Haven't you wanted to date anybody else?"

Don's son has wondered when his father would ask the question. He's had an answer ready for a while and recites it from memory.

"The thing with Laurie was very difficult for me. I really cared about her and when it ended, I just wasn't ready to try again. Then with my classes and applying to college and working on the school newspaper, I just figured I needed to focus on my studies. There will be plenty of time for the other stuff when I get to college."

Don stares out at the road ahead as he asks the father's question.

"Dalton, are you gay? If you are, you can tell me and know that I will love you just as much."

Dalton breaks out into nearly hysterical laughter. Don turns and smiles, but as if he has heard a joke that he doesn't understand.

"Sorry Dad, it's just that someone else asked me that today. Apparently, the idea is making the rounds. In a word, No, I am not gay. Can't I have a plan for my life that doesn't include girls twenty four seven?"

"All right, I have to say that I didn't really think you were, but I thought I should ask, like a show of support or something." Don Hunter's face betrays a bit more relief at the answer than he meant to show, but Dalton understands and doesn't hold it against his dad.

Don pulls the car into their driveway and shuts off the engine. Sitting there ahead of them is a shiny, blue

Mustang with new plates. The red bow on top makes it clear that this is a graduation gift. Dalton turns to his father with a look of disbelief and awe.

"I hope you don't mind," Don says with a hint of sarcasm, "I traded in your old clunker for this thing. I had the boys at the dealership take that one and bring this while we were out. If you don't like it, we can always get the other one back."

"Dad, it's amazing! I can't believe it!"

The two sit quietly for a minute, just looking at the new car. Dalton jumps out to get a closer look and Don trails him at a safe distance. The car has all kinds of sporty touches, including shiny rims and dual exhaust pipes. Glancing through the driver side window, Dalton spots the manual shift and a sweet stereo with a 5 disc CD changer.

"Well come on, let's take her for a spin." Don pulls a set of keys from his pocket and tosses them easily to his son. After he moves his own car out of the way, they are on the road again. Dalton is driving his new chariot and breathing in the new leather aroma.

"So what are your plans this evening?" Don asks, breaking his son's trancelike meditations.

"Well, I told you that I wanted to get on the road tonight. I have to get settled into my new apartment and start summer classes at Middle Western U. By the way, where should we go?"

"Let's head over to that Italian place on Fairview Avenue."

There is someone waiting at the restaurant, and Don wants to tell his son about it, but is building up the nerve, so he decides to talk about something else.

"I heard some of the kids talking about this huge party tonight. Don't you want to go?"
Dalton sets his response beautifully.
"Oh Dad, that's Rick Johnson's thing. That's the biggest sex and drugs party ever."
Now it's the son's turn to stare though the windshield stifling his emotions as he navigates towards their dinner destination.
"Are you serious?" Don is shocked.
"No Dad," Dalton answers laughing uncontrollably. He has to work hard to focus on his driving as tears soon appear.
"Okay wise guy, you get that one. But it still doesn't answer my question."
"If I had someone to take, and if nobody I knew was going to be…"
"I get it," Dad answers without waiting. "Dalton, there's something I have to tell you before we get to the restaurant. We aren't going to be dining alone.
Dalton turns briefly to look at his father's face, but soon has to get his eyes back to the road.
"There's a woman at work. We started out having lunch once in a while. Then we became friends. I thought tonight might be a good chance for you to meet her, especially if you are heading out for school like you said."
Dalton considers this in silence, a silence that stretches uncomfortably for his father.
"Are you upset?" he finally asks. 'Sherry is very nice and I think you'll like her. Do you think I'm wrong…?"

Dalton interrupts his father. "No Dad, it's great. I don't think Mom would want you to be alone, especially now that I'll be heading off to college. Is she pretty?"

"Well, she's not your mother, but she's not bad." Don turns to his son with a conspiratorial look. "Don't tell Sherry I said that, all right?"

"Your secret is safe with me."

Once the car is parked, father and son approach a very attractive woman who is clearly a few years younger than his father standing just outside the entrance. Dalton leans toward his father as they approach. "She's a knockout."

"Sherry," Don announces, "this is my son Dalton."

14.

Sienna: The first move

Picking through the scattered boxes, I've already banged my knee twice. This room is so dark tonight. It took me a second to remember that Dalton was no longer living at home. It makes me realize again that whatever brings me to him is not directed by any conscious thought of mine. Wherever he is, there is something that draws me to him like a magnet.

Dalton's sleep is so deep that I can barely squeeze into his dreams. I hate to wake him up; he's had such a long day. He looks almost childlike with his white, woolen blanket wrapped around him as he lies on the floor. I opened his bedroom door and walked just far enough into the living room to see the blurry contours of furniture still stacked in a clutter; just another detail he didn't want to mess with. He couldn't even be bothered to lay his mattress out.

The new apartment is nice enough for campus living, at least as far as I can tell. The bedroom seems pretty large. I can't tell what color the walls are and the carpet feels funky enough that I'm pretty sure I don't want to know too much about it. The room I am standing in seems strange until I realize that there are no windows anywhere. I can see a sliding door in the living room. I think that's because Dalton was so tired when he arrived that most of the details haven't quite stuck yet.

Leaning against the wall, I am happy enough watching the rise and fall of his chest and listening to his soft, steady breathing. Even on nights when his sleep is not so deep, there have been times when I have come back after one of our conversations just to watch him there. It gives me such peace. I can even hear his heartbeat, slow and regular and surprisingly quiet.

I don't know what to make of the two conversations my friend had with his old girlfriends. Caitlyn's announcement came as no surprise, but it seemed a little showy with the way she jumped into the pickup and the two of them drove off so happily. I couldn't tell if she wanted to let Dalton know that she was going to be all right or wanted him to be sorry for what he was missing. He took it in stride just the way I would have expected. Laurie was a bit harder to watch. Dalton isn't the only one who feels guilty where she's concerned.

"Hi." The sound of his voice is dry and muffled.

"Hi yourself, how're you feeling?"

"Tired, but otherwise I'm okay."

Is there anything sweeter than the sound of a man's voice when he looks at you in that certain way with a smile that goes further than his words ever could? I smile back and for a couple of minutes there is no need to speak. Finally the silence stretches a bit long.

"Tell me about the graduation ceremony. How did it go?" I ask.

Dalton scrambles from the floor and stretches, never taking his eyes off me. As he wakens in the dream, the windows show up in his room.

"It was nice. Dad was very proud. He bought me a new car; a mustang."

"New, new?"

"Yes, right off the showroom floor new. It's a very cool shade of dark blue. It came fully loaded and I think you're going to love the leather seats. We could take her for a spin."

"That's a great idea, but not tonight. There's something I want to talk to you about, but I want to hear all about your day first." It's hard sometimes to ask about things that I already have seen without giving it away that I was, in a sense, right there when it happened. Still, it would be worse, like an admission that I already knew or worse than that, that I didn't care if I never asked at all.

"I ran into Caitlyn and Laurie after it was over, not together, but in that order."

"How is Caitlyn? Is she still with what's his name?" Dalton smiles at me. He knows that I know Brad's name.

"They're getting married. They're all set for two point five kids all hanging off the back of his shiny red pickup. If I sound a little jealous or something, I'm not; they're nice people and I wish them well." Dalton's expression suggests there is a bit more here. I sense that he also felt that something was staged for his benefit, but doesn't want to say so since he's no more certain than I was.

"What about Laurie? How is she doing?"

"I think we had a good conversation. She told me that she didn't blame me anymore which I thought was good even though I still blame myself a lot. I know I'm still young and nothing prepared me for this, for us. She was great when we were together and I think we could have had something if the time had been right." Dalton turns away as he says this, worrying about how I might respond to this admission. I tug on his shoulder and he turns and pulls me close.

"I liked her too," I say, "and she brought out a side of you that I never could. I would have gladly stepped aside for her if that was what you wanted."

"I know," he replies and kisses my cheek. "She was good for me, but I loved you; I love you." He holds me even tighter to make the point before he continues. "I'm pretty sure she felt better after we talked though. She got a little of the sparkle back in her eyes."

The feeling of our bodies touching is as magical as always. The pleasure I am feeling reminds me of what we still need to talk about, but not yet; not yet.

"Let's go to your old bedroom. At least there we can sit. My shins are about black and blue from knocking into things and there's nowhere to sit."

Instantly, we are back in the bedroom in his father's house. It looks just the way it always has with all of his things and even a little of the typical boyish messiness. I smile at the two balled up socks lying beside his hamper; he's such a guy. We both take a seat on the bed side by side.

"Ahhh, that's better," I sigh leaning against him as we both relax.

"Something else happened today and I don't know exactly how I feel about it." Dalton's expression is not exactly one of concern, more like a pensive consideration.

"What?"

"Well, after Dad gave me the car, he said we should take a drive and soon after that we were heading to a restaurant for dinner. Just before we got there, he told me that someone would be joining us for dinner; a woman. Dad's got a girlfriend. Her name's Sherry."

Dalton's eyes bore into mine to gauge my reaction. I offer him my supportive smile in return, but it's not enough. So I ask the obvious question, hoping it will help him to talk about it.

"What's she like?"

"She's a little bit younger than Dad for starters. She's thirty-seven and Dad will be fifty this year. She's attractive with dark brown hair and brown eyes. She smiles a lot."

"Oh, I can see how that could be a real problem," I joke, trying to lighten the mood.

"She has a nice sense of humor too. She tells these great stories. Dad and I could hardly stop laughing. From the time we sat down till it was time to go, she never stopped touching him, holding his hand or leaning close."

I brush a loose strand of hair behind my ears. I can see that Dalton wants to be all right with this. "You should be happy for him," I say, knowing that it is much easier for me with nothing at stake.

"I know, I know, I am happy for Dad, but it isn't so simple. She was married before, and while she had all these wonderful qualities, I couldn't help but worry about that."

"Did she talk about it?"

Dalton smiles as he remembers the conversation.

"She was very open. She talked about how they had both been too young and how hard it had been on her husband when they learned that she couldn't have kids. One of her funnier stories was about all the different things they had done to try to have a baby. She said that they had parted ways on good terms and while it had been a tough adjustment, she knew it was for the best."

"How long ago did she get divorced?"

"She said it was about three years ago. She said that she was trying to take her time before she got involved with anyone and when dad showed some interest, it seemed like the time was right."

"She sounds very practical. Did you have any reason not to believe her?" I wait for an answer and he shakes his head 'no'.

"I don't want him to be alone. Mom wouldn't want him to be alone." Dalton stands suddenly, fighting his confusion and not wanting to show how conflicted he is about all this. I stand up and reach out to him, offering as much comfort and support as I can.

"Listen my friend; you say the words because you know they're the right words to say. That's always the easier part. The hard part is listening to the voice inside you that knows the truth."

"I'm listening."

"I don't mean me, silly. Look, you miss your mom. There's a part of you that feels that being supportive of your dad as he moves on with his life is a betrayal of her in some way. The grown up part of you, the part of you that knows the right thing to say, also knows that your mom really wouldn't want him to be alone. You're going off to college; you're there. He's done everything he promised. He gave you a stable home and spent the time he told your mom he would. He's a good person. He's your dad. What does your heart say?"

Dalton takes a moment to consider my words. It is the thing that I love about him so much. He doesn't just jump to a conclusion, he works it out. When the smile comes, I know it will be okay.

"I think Sherry will be good for him and I'm pretty sure Mom would have liked her as a friend."

He turns and gives me a sweet kiss on the cheek and follows with a more passionate one on the lips.

"What was that for?" I ask when we both come up for air.

"That's for showing me how to figure things out, like you always do." Just as quickly, he is back at it; gratitude and eagerness combined in the contact of his mouth with mine. It is easy to give in to him for a while and I do, but then the thoughts come back, the other thing I know we have to talk about.

"Hold that thought," I tell him with a promising smile, my lips still tingling.

"I'd rather hold *you*."

"Down boy, take a seat there." He follows my pointing finger back to the bed and covers his disappointment as he satisfies my request.

"We have to talk about this," I say as I watch him from a safe distance. "We've been avoiding this problem for a long time and we have to deal with it."

The closeness and familiar feel of these surroundings comforts me. On Dalton's dresser are pictures of his mom and dad and of Caitlyn at Rebecca's party and Laurie during their picnic at the park. I don't doubt that there would be pictures of me if the circumstances were different. His camera case hangs in its usual spot over the back of his desk chair. The room smells like…me; at least what Dalton thinks of as my smell. He has integrated me so much into his idea of his room, that both smell the same to him. In my mind it's a generous thought. As I pace back and forth, I know how much of this dilemma is my fault. I just hope he can accept my solution.

"We have to talk about Sex," I say, hoping that launching into it so forcefully will give me the momentum to get through.

"Ooh goody, my favorite subject," Dalton responds playfully, until I shoot him my serious look. He sits up straighter and places his hands on the bed as if to brace himself, which only serves to crack me up. Once I get back in control, I start again.

"You know I love you, right?" I don't wait for his answer. "It would be the easiest thing in the world to give in to the feelings we're both having. I think about it more than you know; probably as much as you."

He shoots me his 'get serious' look but is nice enough not to interrupt.

"In any case, I've given this a lot of thought. There are lots of reasons to go ahead and give in to what we both want. That would be the easy answer. After all, the sex would only be in your head. We wouldn't need any contraceptives and we both know that the pleasure we'd experience would only be enhanced by our close connection."

"Good, that's settled, let's get to it." He starts to stand, but I push him back.

"Not so fast Mister, I have one concern that I want you to think about. You're my friend; you've been my friend for a very long time. Once we do this, everything will change, not necessarily for the worse, but it will change. I have been holding back because your respect means a lot to me. You're a good guy and that allowed you to accept my wishes back when we first kissed and ever since. If we give in to this now, I am afraid that I will only end up as your fantasy partner with just one purpose."

"I would never…"

"That's good since if you ever thought of me that way, I would have to kill you. Still, are you so sure that this wouldn't just become an easy recreational activity?"

Dalton looks up at me while he considers what I just said. I know he doesn't believe that he would treat me that way, but he is careful enough of my feelings that he is willing to yield to his doubts. He looks up at me with longing.

"What's the answer, Sienna? I get what you're saying, but you have to give me a little break. I don't see anyone because of how I feel about you. I can't go out and take advantage of some other girl since that would be complicated, and I don't think you would like me very much. Maybe it doesn't seem like it in this little mental world of ours, but I am a physical person with physical needs."

"I know and I think I have come up with an answer. Will you trust me?"

He answers "Yes" with a look of curiosity and expectation.

"Take your shirt off and lay down on the bed."

His covers his surprised expression and complies quickly. I remove my blouse and move slowly around to the other side.

"Close your eyes."

Once again he obeys although he can't resist the impulse to peek at me a couple of times. I take my place next to him on the bed, him on the right and me to his left. He looks very relaxed with his eyes closed and his arms at each side. The blankets are still in place beneath us. I place my right hand on his chest over his heart.

"How does that feel?"

His answer is cautious. "It's nice."

"This is kind of like an electrical thing. You have to complete the connection. Place your hand over my heart."

Dalton smiles into my eyes as he lifts his left hand and moves it to my bra covered right breast. He gently pushes the fabric out of the way and wraps his fingers around it with a light squeeze.

"Umm, I'm pretty sure that's not my heart," I tease, but he shows no inclination to let go and I shrug as his smile widens.

"All right, I suppose that's close enough, but you have to keep your eyes closed."

When he closes them once more, I close mine and feel the connection between us. Soon a sensation of warmth runs down my arm, through my fingers and into his chest. His surprise forces his eyes open just for a moment, but he quickly closes them again as the warmth begins to spread in every direction. He shudders as it makes its way north to his brain and south to more sensitive areas. The warmth starts to bounce back along his arm, through his fingers and makes its way, eventually, to my heart where the pleasure begins to spread.

    A slow, heartfelt sound begins beside me, deep and low. I reach for a little bit more magic as I begin to infuse our surroundings with scent, a combination of vanilla and just a tiny bit of cinnamon spice. My body begins to vibrate as the pleasure pulses.

    "Turn out the light sweetheart," I beg breathlessly, and once more my eyes are closed and I can focus on the first tidings of ecstasy moving back and forth between Dalton and me. My hand and his stay just where they started, heart to almost heart. There is no need to undress further or touch in a more intimate fashion. A rhythm begins that we soon find sweet and then dizzying and finally overwhelming.

I watch Dalton as he awakens on the floor, now that the morning has come. He untangles himself from the blanket and rises stiffly, rubbing his aching muscles and stretching his knotted limbs. The sun is breaking through the low hanging mist now and his stomach growls as he looks out the bedroom window. With his face drenched in early morning glow, it's impossible to miss the satisfied smile that stretches nearly from ear to ear. Proxy sex obviously agreed with him.

    He goes to work in earnest, opening boxes and unpacking their contents like a demon possessed. It is not long before the hangers are set in the closet and the drawers are given an initial stocking. The computer is set up though not completely plugged in and with great care, his camera gear is stowed.

Now that he is up, I can see that my suspicions about the place were at least partially right. There are more than a couple stains on the living room carpet that indicate the apartment as the scene of some rather intense college partying. But as I look around the rest of the place, it is surprisingly clean and attractive. The kitchen is larger than I would have expected.

Dalton does a little unpacking in the living room before he returns to the bedroom with the box spring and then again with the mattress. He sets both on the metal frame that had been leaning against the far wall. He finds the linens and his pillows and sets them on the bed as well.

"I'll finish with you later," he says to the mattress with a wicked grin. He straightens his clothing as he walks away to find his keys and his wallet where he'd left them the night before, on the white laminate countertop between the kitchen and the living room. The door makes a happy sound as he closes it behind him in search of breakfast, or maybe that's just how it sounds to me.

15.

Father's day

Strains of 'Here Comes the Bride' begin to rush from the church organ as father and son stand at the altar, awaiting the procession. The wedding is taking place on a perfect, sun drenched day in June. Dalton finds it hard to believe that a whole year has passed since that first dinner with Dad and Sherry. They had both been kind enough to agree to postpone the ceremony until he could attend in the break before continuing his summer course work. He was also pleased by his father's insistence that he be the best man at the ceremony, and had done his best to perform the role satisfactorily. The church is filled with people, mostly his father's coworkers and their families on the one side and Sherry's larger family contingent on the other. Sherry's older brother and sister each have children near his age and two of the nieces are bridesmaids. The room has the hushed buzz of conversations being conducted in shorthand, expecting at any moment to be interrupted by the main event. For his part, Dalton has three guests, though he is only aware of the two who are physically present. Sienna has taken a position by a door in the back where she can see everything easily. She is wearing a lovely burgundy dress that fits her perfectly. The invited guests include Jonny "Skip" Randall, who is both his friend and mentor at Middle Western University and Skip's latest girlfriend, a young lady who very much fills out the standards that Jonny sets for his companions.

Actually, Sienna thinks, Skip's girlfriend may be doing a bit more overflowing than filling out any of his standards.

Seeing Skip, Dalton takes a moment to think back over the past year. Classes have been fine and his nights with Sienna have been very satisfying. He met Jonny at a coffee house near the campus on a night when there was live music. Jonny struck up the conversation, of course, making a point of announcing his ongoing relationship with the pretty blonde guitarist on stage at that time. She had a sweet voice, perfect for ballads, and even then, Dalton suspected that Skip would give her some material for ones as yet unwritten. He had been right, as the singer was at least four girlfriends ago, but try as he might, he couldn't find it in his heart to think badly about the guy. The girls all seem to know what they're buying, he thinks, and Jonny is very lovable.

Other aspects of school have been equally enjoyable. The course on dark room practices added to Dalton's understanding of the basics of his craft, and he breezed through the freshman English and Math requirements. Outside the classroom, he developed a group of friends who share his interest in photography. Some of the sessions with them were as valuable and educational as anything he heard in class. He has learned so much about digital photo editing from them. Photoshop has become his other new best friend.

A few last notes from the organ and the crowd starts to quiet. Dad looks good in his charcoal colored tux, Dalton thinks, as he shares a brief smile with his father. They are both quickly drawn to the sight of the approaching procession. A co-worker's young daughter has been enlisted as the flower girl, and she is enthusiastically tossing petals in every direction as she approaches. They burst from her hands like little white and red fireworks before settling on the polished wooden floor. A friend of Sherry's has the maid of honor's position and makes her way to a spot on the opposite side of the altar. Sherry's two nieces follow, each wearing the same lovely burgundy gown as Sienna, but neither as perfectly fitted. One of the girls is escorted by the flower girl's father, the other by Sherry's brother. Dalton can't help but notice the smile directed at him by the second of the two and he politely smiles back. Finally Sherry makes her appearance and she is truly radiant. Her smile is a laser directed so singularly at Don that Dalton can't help but think fondly of her. Her gown is a warm creamy color with a delicate, beaded bodice. It flows easily from the pleated waist with just the slightest swaying motion as she moves. Sherry's dark brown hair has been pulled back and a crown of small flowers sits atop in a way that seems so appealing and right.

    If the past year has been one of satisfying growth for the son, it has been one of happiness and healing for the father. Sherry moved in with Don a few months after that graduation night dinner, but not before getting Dalton's blessing. For his part, Don had taken the lessons learned about priorities and commitment that had come from his efforts to fulfill his promise to Sharon, and wrapped Sherry in the warmth of the real, loving home that he had built from those efforts. As she took the last step toward the altar, the happiness on her face radiated back to the man whose hands she now took in hers, and whose smile met hers.

The vows echoed over the assembly, not as some perfect mystical expression of love, Dalton thought, but more as a sincere promise made by two imperfect people. They had overcome their frailties and survived to try again. As the ceremony ended in the traditional kiss, and nothing particularly shy there he observed, a sense of calm satisfaction took hold of him; it was good.

Sienna smiles from her shadow as people begin to make their way outside. Dalton followed the happy couple out the door and he was quickly followed by the rest of those in attendance. She had not missed that moment of serenity that occurred for him just as the ceremony ended. A thought appears briefly in her mind that she could be very content with him wearing a similar expression following rites in some dreaming or real world church that might be found for the two of them.

The reception begins at a nearby inn with the typical open bar and a generous buffet full of hors d'oeuvres. Skip and his date waste no time in taking advantage of the liquor selections, while Dalton selects a few items from the buffet. Sherry's niece never seems to be far away, though whether this is intentional or by chance seems unclear at first. Her smile finds its way to him more than a few times over the next several minutes and he begins to sense her interest. When he settles on a soft drink, he is not surprised when she makes a similar choice soon after. As people begin to mingle, Dalton goes around to greet as many of his father's coworkers as he can. Finally it is time to sit down for dinner. The niece has suddenly disappeared which he finds strangely disappointing.

    The distress is only momentary. Sliding into a chair next to Skip, Dalton is quite surprised to see that Sherry's niece has appeared almost by magic to take the seat next to him. The original plan had Dalton seated at the head table next to his father, but Don had resisted indicating that sitting with his friends and other 'young people his age' might 'help him find someone for himself'. The girl's smile is brighter now than before and the invitation is becoming very clear. As she says 'Hi', he responds. Then he taps Jonny's shoulder so that his friend will untangle his lips from those of his date. Jonny stops long enough to at least say hello and proceeds with the introduction.

    "Hey buddy, this is Dana," Skip says without missing a beat.

    The two nod hello as introductions continue around the table. Two of Sherry's friends are there with their husbands. As conversation begins, waiters appear with trays filled with salads and dressings. Soon they return holding bottles of champagne, and every glass is filled. With the reception in full swing, the musicians arrive and start out playing soothing background music that is easy on the ears, and no impediment to conversation.

    Dalton has a few brief words with the niece and a little back and forth with Skip as the salads are consumed. Then it is on to the main course where the guests are treated to a choice of prime rib or lobster tail. The smells of the food are enough to keep the gathering focused on the meal and conversation to a minimum. Dalton can hardly help but notice the sparkle in Sherry's niece's eyes as they both grab for the same warm roll.

When the meal is nearly consumed, Dana takes her leave before heading off to the ladies lounge to adjust her makeup. Sherry's niece excuses herself as well and walks along with the girl making small talk as they go. It is an interesting contrast; Dana is blonde, buxom and curvy, while the as yet unnamed niece is a bit taller with brown hair similar to Sherry's and very willowy.

"Wow, that Courtney is gorgeous," Skip offers.

"I thought you said her name was Dana," Dalton replies vaguely.

"Not my date, you idiot, the other one," Skip answers quickly. "I'd throw Dana out the door right now if I thought Courtney would give me a look. Unfortunately, she seems to have set her sights on you, ya lucky dog. She's your cousin now, though only by marriage thankfully."

"What are you talking about? What sights?"

"Dalton, I think there's an optical store at the mall nearby. If we hurry we might be able to get your eyes checked and be back in time for the cake. The girl is sending out signals strong enough to be picked up by the Hubble telescope. Ask her to dance if you think I'm wrong. She'll be out on the floor with you before the 'ce' in dance has stopped vibrating."

Dalton shoves his friend playfully, "This one's going to cost you."

"Go ahead and ask her if you think I'm wrong. I'm betting you'll be buying the drinks next week." Skip's expression is playful and challenging.

"You're on."

Courtney turns out to be a very good dancer and feels splendid in his arms when the slow song arrives.

"This is turning out to be one of the more expensive dances I've ever had," Dalton confides.

"Oh, why is that?" Courtney asks with an expression of innocence, doing her best to conceal the pleasure she feels at a plan well executed.

"My friend Skip bet me that you would agree to dance and I foolishly accepted. We have a running wager that involves the loser buying the beer and liquor for the next party." Her laughter is sweet and musical when it joins his.

"You shouldn't pay," she says with a semi-serious tone.

"Oh I could never go back on a bet."

"You can on this one. I talked to your friend Skip beforehand and suggested the whole thing."

"Why would you do that?" he asked. Her brown eyes looked straight into his, and the effect is nearly overpowering. Even in the darker lighting on the dance floor, her expression is intense and easy to see.

"Because you are the most attractive guy here, with or without a date and lucky for me, you don't appear to have one. I intend to make you an offer later on, that you won't be able to refuse."

Dalton tries to think of something clever to say, but is stopped before the first idea arrives by the touch of Courtney's fingers on his lips.

"No need to say anything now," she added. "Just give it some thought."

Sienna watches again from the shadow. Her thoughts are in turmoil as Dalton dances by with his pretty partner. Once more her friend is dancing and yet again it is with someone else. The jealousy she is trying to overcome is heightened by the look in this girl's eyes. This is a leaner, more experienced version of Laurie. It's very clear that the girl is only looking for an evening's entertainment, rather than for any kind of lasting relationship. Sienna is not certain that she should mind that kind of arrangement or if she even has the right to mind it. The evenings she shares with Dalton continue to provide so much closeness and communication, though he no longer depends on her counsel the way he once did. The sexual alternative that she has come up with has eased his physical needs, but is not the complete intimacy that either of them craves. Try as she might, Sienna is just not ready to give herself fully.

Being here tonight was a mistake, Sienna realizes, taking a long last look. No matter how much I want to be part of his life, this isn't sharing in even the broadest sense of the word. There has to be more than this for both of us, she thinks, though how they can get to that more is something she is struggling to work out. Her mascara just begins to moisten as she moves more deeply into the shadow and disappears.

Dalton's breath hitches for a second, but he continues dancing and soon shakes off the strange feeling.

"Are you all right?" Courtney asks, concerned. "For a second there, you looked like you just saw a ghost."

"Sometimes I get this strange feeling that someone is watching me, even though I know that nobody is there."

"Well," she replies, "it's not so strange this time. Somebody is watching you; it's me." The spell is broken and the two continue moving to the slow music. Courtney pulls herself even closer as they go. She whispers into his ear "I think there's a bit of magic in you Dalton." She takes it a step further as her tongue quickly traces the lobe and then retreats. "You're not like any of the guys I know at Florida State."

Courtney figures that this piece of information should seal the deal. Obviously, with her going to school more than a thousand miles away, she isn't looking for anything permanent. And what's the point of going to a wedding if you can't have a short, sweet fling? By the time the newlyweds head out to the airport on their way to the honeymoon, she thinks, I should have him properly amped. As if to encourage just such a state she presses herself even more firmly against him.

The evening continues nicely for the couple. They spend most of their time on the dance floor, and Dalton gets a big 'thumbs-up' and a huge smile from his father. It occurs to him that his father worries about his apparent single and lonely status. He wishes there was some way to let his father know that his life is not like that, but what could he say? Of more immediate concern is the very clinging young woman who is making her desires so obvious. Dancing with Courtney is exciting and sensual, and it would be so easy to let things go forward. Her announcement of her current college location has left no doubt about what she has in mind.

"So Dalton, what are you majoring in?" Courtney asks with a grin. Dalton's eyes have been unable to resist the exploration she had been doing her best to encourage. He manages to bring his focus back to her face as he answers.

"I am actually doing a double major in Photography and design. It will add a year and a half to my coursework, but I think it will be worth it."

Courtney takes in this information and decides that it dovetails perfectly with her plans to extend the evening. "Do you have your camera with you? Maybe you could take some shots of me after the reception ends. I would love to get some in this dress." 'And out of it,' she thinks.

"I have my camera in my car and I would be happy to take some shots."

"Great." Courtney's smile widens as the evening gets more and more promising.

Soon the cake is cut. Don carefully avoids any silliness as he gently feeds a little bit of cake to Sherry. She on the other hand wants to play to the crowd, and manages to smush just a bit of cake into her new husband's face at the very last second. There is gentle laughter and scattered applause as the couple completes the tradition with a kiss. Once the slices are served and the cake is consumed, Skip is entranced by Courtney's very subtle and very sexy movements as she carefully licks a little bit of icing from her fingers. Dana is not amused and pulls Skip up for another dance.

"I think I may have gotten your friend in a little trouble, quite unintentionally of course." Courtney's expression is one of utter feminine innocence, and Dalton can't help himself. He leans close and responds.

"I doubt that anything with you is unintentional, but I'll take your word for it." Her lips are soft and responsive as he continues in for the kiss. Her mouth tastes of white iced yellow cake.

"Nice," she says as they separate. She pulls the napkin from her lap and wipes a little lipstick smudge from his mouth.

"You'll have to excuse me," Dalton says.

"Not for that I won't..."

Dalton laughs and Courtney smiles coyly.

"No, I have to go say goodbye to my Dad. They're getting ready to leave."

"Oh, I see." Now it's her turn to laugh. Once more, it's a lovely, almost sparkling kind of sound.

Crossing the room to the head table, he turns suddenly, to find Courtney watching him. Her reaction is quizzical.

"The answer is yes by the way," he says grinning.

"Yes?"

"You know, the offer I can't refuse?"

"Ahhh. Go on then and talk to your dad."

Courtney's smile widens as he turns away. She follows him with her eyes until her concentration is broken by the ring of the cell phone in her clutch purse.

"You guys all set?" Dalton asks as the newlyweds gather their things.

"Talk to your father for a minute. I have to powder my nose before the photographers get their last shots in."

As Sherry walks away, Dalton notices that the flowers on the tables seem to already be fading. The wait staff is just beginning to remove the last signs of the evening's festivities.

"She's terrific Dad. Are you happy?"

"There's only one thing I need to be absolutely content," Don replies. "When you can tell me that you have found someone, then I can be happy."

"I'm working on it."

"Well, in the meantime, I hope you'll spend some time with that Courtney. She's gorgeous."

Sherry has straightened herself and is making her way back from the ladies room when her cell phone rings. A moment later she closes the phone and shakes her head.

Dalton goes back to his table and grabs the jacket that he left over the back of his chair. Courtney is nowhere to be seen. He scans the room, but in the movement of the crowd, all following the departing couple outside, it is difficult to find her. Perhaps she is already ahead and waiting for him there. Curious but not concerned, he follows the last of the party outside and makes his way past the throng as his father and bride pose at the door of their limo. The shiny windows reflect the closest faces of those in attendance, but the face he is searching for is not among them. Flicking the distracted thinking from his mind, he awaits the last flash and then embraces his father. Sherry's expression is warm, but Dalton sees something else there as well. When she comes closer to accept his farewell hug, her whisper is nervous and apologetic.

"Courtney left. She told me to say goodbye to you and to thank you for a lovely evening. She said some other things, but the important thing is this. She got a call from the guy who broke up with her last week. He just arrived at the airport full of apologies and asking for a second chance. I don't think she meant you any harm, but she couldn't say no to him."

Dalton takes a second to digest this before responding as he pulls back.

"Tell her I enjoyed her company and that I wish her all the best. Now you two get going and I'll see you when you get back. Have a great time."

Don Hunter's face is full of questions and Sherry responds with a look that says don't ask, I'll tell you later.

The limo pulls away to shouts of good luck and goodbye and a stray "be careful". Dalton watches the vehicle and is torn between disappointment and relief. Skip and Dana come over showing all the signs of two people anxious to get to their hotel room.

"Hate to eat and run buddy, but you know how it is…" Skip's face is lit from the alcohol and the anticipation. "By the way, what happened to Courtney?"

Dana gives Jonny a playful shove and then hugs Dalton goodbye.

"It was nice meeting you," she says and Dalton thinks for a second that she has more that she might say, but has decided against it. Her eyes flash and then she grabs on to Jonny and they are gone.

Saying his goodbyes, Dalton is soon on the road. His conflict is resolved with relief having won the day and he wonders what he can possibly tell Sienna. He determines that there's no point in hiding something especially with the way it ended and so he clears his mind as he makes his way back to his father's house. He will stay there and look after the place for a couple of days before going back to campus.

Once the house is locked up, Dalton makes his way to his bedroom. He is touched by the way his father has kept it for him. There is comfort in knowing that even though he doubts that he will be returning home after college, the room is waiting should fate have other ideas. Tossing his wedding finery on the floor, the light is extinguished; the pillow punched into a comfortable shape and Dalton's sleep is coincident with his head coming to rest.

Sienna is naked, lying on the bed as he arrives in their dream. She is on her side, facing away, with her rich, red hair offering glints of reflected light from the full moon outside. Her breathing is deep though she is clearly awake.

"How was the wedding?" she asks softly.

"I wish you could have seen it. Sherry was luminous and Dad has never looked happier or more content. The ceremony was beautiful and the reception was everything they could have wished for."

"Did you have fun?" Sienna struggles to keep her tone even. She knows it isn't his fault that they can't share these events. She knows too, that the jealousy she feels is misplaced, and seeing what time he has come home, there is little to worry about.

"We need to talk," Dalton answers. He practiced the speech to come from just about the first moment he started home. No point in changing it now.

"You know about the deus ex machina?"

"I've heard of it," Sienna replies, wondering where this strange opening might lead.

"In Greek mythology, whenever the playwright didn't know how to save the hero, a God machine would come in and deliver him to safety."

"And are you driving the God machine these days?" Sienna turns to Dalton with a look of interest, showing no sign of the concern she is feeling.

"Kind of, well no, not exactly, I mean…this is what I meant to say. With the Greeks, it is the hero who is whisked away from the danger. Tonight, it was the danger that was whisked away at the last possible moment, saving the hero from doing something he might otherwise have done. There was this girl, Courtney, one of Sherry's nieces. She came on to me and I was very definitely tempted. I don't know if I should even be telling you this, but the bottom line is that nothing happened."

"You're saying that you might have?"

Dalton thinks hard before staying with his decision to be completely honest. He knows the risk, but can't find it within himself to shade the truth.

"I'm saying that I would have. Just before the reception ended, and just before Courtney would have undoubtedly gone anywhere I wanted, I walked over to chat with my dad. While I was gone Courtney got a phone call from her ex-boyfriend and she left. She had just been through a breakup, and he had come to his senses apparently. The fact that nothing happened doesn't excuse me from what I was planning, but I hope you will accept this as true. I am telling you everything because, when Courtney ran off, the thing I felt most, the thing that fills me right now is relief that I have nothing more than a wayward thought to feel guilty about."

Sienna looks at Dalton calmly. She could page through his mind and see the events that happened earlier, but his complete honesty makes that unnecessary. Instead she simply moves closer to him and lays her hand on his chest. As her left breast is crushed into his side, her mouth joins his fiercely. He carefully places his hand on her heart and the spreading warmth soon fills them both.

16.

The camera never lies

Dreams, dark and floating, full of promise and mystery, shimmer at the edge of Dalton's wakeful mind. He's had so many years consumed and enriched by a singular, beautiful dream. The world revolves, spinning each nighttime delight as a spider might spin a lustrous web. Waking is a ceaseless drive to understand why the luxury of his lovely companion is held captive inside his sleeping brain.

     Dreams have been on his mind a lot this year, and he's decided to see how those feelings might express themselves in his photography. From his nightly forays, he wants to capture the slightly different gravity; the floating, undulating edges and of course; the unending magic awaiting him there. From his waking life he's gathered ideas from mythology, psychology and art and fashion. The glow of the safelight in the art building's dark room seems like the perfect atmosphere to let his mind play with the idea. As he hangs each dripping print on the line, he smiles at the progress in his work.

     His inspiration comes from the moment when Sienna stands in that luminous shadow, either on arrival or just before departure. Since he has no means of capturing Sienna as he would love to, he has had to settle for the real girls who pose for him at the studio. He has done his best to create the effect with smoke and lighting and movement. The girls have been very enthusiastic and helpful and he has varied the poses to augment the initial concept. He has not limited himself to girls his age. He was able to find a couple of Moms willing to bring their daughters to his studio when he explained the project, and the youngsters were both beautiful and thrilled to be photographed. So he has now a large set of images in black and white that he has developed and printed himself, along with even more color images captured with his latest digital camera. The camera, a recent gift from his father and Sherry, has made a huge difference in the kinds of photos he can now produce.

Hanging the last shot, Dalton smiles as he thinks about the night before last when he showed Sienna all but these most recent pics. They sat together in his apartment living room, with the work in two piles on the coffee table; the color shots in one stack, and the black and white ones in the other. Each stack was arranged so that the younger models came first and the older ones later. Dalton was careful to see that Sienna progressed through each stack concurrently so that she could see the progression in both formats. She realized without any help from him what the images represented.

"This is me, isn't it?" she said happily. "They're me. I mean, they don't look like me, but somehow, this is the me you see when I come to you or when I go."

Dalton didn't have to say anything. The look on Sienna's face showed how clearly she loved the idea. For a while there was only the sound of the ruffling of paper as she paged carefully through each print. He loved the way she spent more than a few seconds on each, taking in the whole image and occasionally making a comment or asking a question to get a better understanding of what she was seeing. There was only the slightest sideways glance when she passed the last shots of the younger girls and came to the first of the college models posing nude. "Hmm," she thought out loud, but did not stop her progress. "I do see a bit of resemblance, and...Hold on. I don't think this girl looks like me at all." Sienna lifted the latest shot so that Dalton could see. The image was almost completely black with just the thinnest line of light tracing the outline of the model's head and body. The silhouette accented her rather impressive bust like an exclamation point. Sienna's expression was one of lighthearted disdain.

"Oh, I don't know," Dalton answered; the soul of innocence. "Don't you remember the night you first posed for me? You stuck out your chest and I noticed things for the first...ouch!" The sofa pillow had landed quite squarely in his face and the conversation stopped as Dalton rose and swooped in for a counterattack of tickling and kissing. When they both came up, gasping for air, the look in Sienna's eyes was both grateful and sad.

"I love that you did this."

"Shhh," Dalton answered. "You know I wish all of these were you."

The memory of Sienna's body beneath him on the couch in that dream is so complete; he can almost feel her there right now. The remaining pictures in Sienna's hand fell quickly to the floor as other pursuits took precedence. The review of the work eventually resumed after a very sweet interlude. Shaking his head to clear away some very powerful memories, Dalton grabs the stack of prints that are now dry and carries them out to the studio. The sunshine outside brings a little tearing as his eyes adjust. It's a lovely morning full of cool winter light.

Three plus years have flown by. There have been days filled with friendship and learning, nights filled with parties and all the usual college stuff plus Sienna. With the aid of summer classes, the end of college life is approaching. The bare trees shiver against white cotton clouds as he makes his way through the studio and quickly presents his work to Professor Purcell who has become Dalton's primary advisor for his photographic efforts.

Amanda Purcell is a shapely forty-something brunette whose attraction to Dalton is obvious. Her large, hazel hued eyes are on him immediately, hungrily wandering all over. Her admiration for his work however, is sincere. She sits at her desk and admires the prints as he stands by.

"These are wonderful, Dalton. Your sense of mood and light are remarkable. You are developing a very original voice. Take this one for instance; the curve of the hip is quite seductive. "

"Thanks Professor." He tries to remain untouched by his teacher's clear personal interest, while staying focused on her critique. It's not that he finds her unattractive, quite the opposite, but that just makes it all the more difficult. Of all the women he might consider as a potential romantic partner, the very last would be someone whose unbiased opinion is critical in making him the best photographer he can be.

"Can you tell me what influenced you? The lighting is so…dreamlike. It's dark and confined, but somehow comforting and warm." Amanda lifts her gaze to the student, thinking how much she could teach him about life if he were open to it, but his response is guarded. He's not shy; she thinks, perhaps he only needs a little encouragement, a little persuasion to make things happen. She makes a mental note to pursue these thoughts in more detail at some later date.

"I wish I could tell you. I...the truth is I don't really know myself," Dalton says with the straightest expression he can muster. He feels a little badly that he can't be more honest, but knows that his reality is not something he can share.

In spite of his protestations to the contrary, Amanda Purcell can see very clearly that the inspiration is no mystery to her student and that he is simply unwilling to reveal it; perhaps he will change his mind if they become closer. Actually, it's more the closeness that she is after. Details about his creative inspirations would be interesting but hardly critical.

"That's okay Dalton; the best photographers always keep a few tricks for themselves. What kind of camera are you using for these?"

Dalton tells her about the Nikon body he is working with for the black and white shots and their discussion becomes technical for a few minutes.

"Just remember, photography, like every art form doesn't start with the lens of the camera, but with the eye and brains behind that lens. You have good equipment and that always helps, but it's nothing without the vision and the inspiration. I think you have a gift and if you keep working, you can do some great things."

"Thanks Professor, that means a lot." Dalton blushes a bit at her praise hoping that it is sincere and not driven by her personal attraction.

"Listen, I have an idea. You are going to graduate soon, right? Any idea what you're going to do after that?" She looks up at Dalton again and consciously leans just a little forward to give him a better view of her scooped neckline.

Her student does his best to ignore her flagrant invitation and finally looks away.

"No."

"Have you ever thought about Fashion photography? The lifestyle isn't bad and there are all these beautiful women and men and gorgeous locations. The money is better than most jobs you could get and unlike a lot of other things you can do, it seriously rewards talent." Amanda lets her imagination go for a second, as sand and sea form a romantic backdrop for the young man standing so close. It is easy to use the highlights and shadows of his shirt to form a very clear image of the nicely muscled young man with the shirt no longer blocking the view.

"I really have my sights set on art," Dalton answers, breaking Amanda's near trance as he backs up a step from her intense stare.

The professor stands, facing Dalton.

"I see you there in time, I do. But art is a tough one to crack. You could lose a few pounds waiting for that first show even with your talent. Why not keep developing your craft and make a few dollars while you are at it?"

Looking out the window, he pretends that he can't smell the subtle floral and spice, obviously expensive perfume emanating from such a nearby source. Amanda smiles and brushes by him as she walks toward the door.

"I suppose. Yes actually that sounds good." Dalton stands where he is as she turns back to him. Actually, he thinks, 'that would be a great idea', one that he had discarded as not very likely. Something in the way his professor has suggested it makes Dalton think she might have the means or contacts needed to open the door.

'I overheard a friend of yours the other day. Is it true you have a birthday coming up?"

"Yes," he answers, "it's next week."

"If you'll let me, I will call a friend of mine who might have a job for you. Perhaps I will have a very nice present for you. How would that be?" 'And maybe I'll get you the job too,' she thinks.

Dalton's excitement at the possibility temporarily overwhelms his judgment. He jokes: "Professor Purcell, if you weren't my teacher, I swear I could kiss you right now." Realizing what he has just said, he avoids eye contact as he pulls his work together, grabs his jacket and books and rushes off.

Amanda Purcell finds his awkward retreat more than charming; she finds it strangely arousing. She watches as he moves with a determined effort, disappearing down the hall.

"For Christmas sake, don't let that stop you."

17.

Amanda: The goddess and the mortal

Greek Goddesses striking fear into the hearts of mere mortals; I love the idea of these women, motivated by justice or vengeance or even caprice. Amazons and huntresses, whether mythic or real, who take no prisoners and give as good as they get. I have used them as a source of inspiration in my creative life as well as the model for my real one. I am nobody's little girl. That attitude has fueled the successes in my career and whatever love life I have allowed. All this tough talk may seem a bit overdone in light of my role as an art professor in a University setting, but this current gig is almost like a vacation. I can sleepwalk through the mindless lectures and endless parade of mediocre undergrads who take my class looking for a few easy credits. I certainly had my share of fun in helping a few of them to regret that choice. Never mind. I'll get back in the game after the spring semester. New York is calling out to me and Paris of course. Artemis the huntress will be setting the terms soon enough.

 There has been one reward for my time here in Middle America. I have unearthed a singular talent who also happens to be a very attractive; you might even say hunky young man. I am going to see what I can do to give him a start, and perhaps I will show him a few other things as well. What a view he offered when he left a little while ago. I could watch him walk away for hours.

 I wonder why Dalton is so shy. Not shy exactly, just reserved. He is easygoing with his classmates. He is open and charming right up to the point that anyone approaches with clear interest. I have seen the same response more than once as a couple of his pretty female classmates tried their luck. There's no sign that he's gay. I overheard a couple of the girls talking. He does not seem to be involved with anyone. He seems a bit young to be looking for some special *one*. Maybe he's just looking for something a little out of the ordinary. He hasn't been any more open with me than his classmates, but perhaps it's just the whole teacher student thing. I'll just have to see if I can show him that our relationship can only be enhanced by some interest on his side.

    The first step will be to secure a job for Dalton and I know just the person that can help me. I spent the time since his hasty departure assembling an email with the best pieces from Dalton's portfolio. Paris is about 7 hours ahead of us. That makes it about five in the evening now. Marcel should be done work and having his first glass of wine. I'd better catch him right away. Heaven knows, his activities later will make him virtually unreachable. His company would make a very nice first step. Beneath all his flamboyance and attitude, there's a decent man who would give my student everything a talented newcomer would need to make a go of things there.

    "Pick up the phone you fruit sal…Marcel! How are you darling? It's Amanda Purcell."

    "Mandy darling, whatever can I do for you?"

    The tone comes out sweetly. Anyone might reasonably think that Marcel was really happy to hear from me. But much like the wines he loves, he has a body that is very complex with lots of layers. I can taste the peeved notes very clearly. Obviously something has delayed that first glass. Oh well, no time like the present.

"Marcel, it's what I can do for you that matters. In fact it is the purpose of my call, and for that question I have a very interesting answer."

I count to four as I await my old buddy's response.

"Ah Mandy, whenever anyone tells me that they can do something for me, I get very tight in areas that you and I never discuss. What are you selling dear?"

This is not going as well as I hoped, but I can turn on a bit of venom too if needed.

"Now don't take that jaded tone with me, my friend, or you'll miss out. I have a student I want you to employ and he's simply delicious." Funny how telling a gay man that there's a delicious male student available will change the whole tenor of things.

"Delicious, you say? Okay, but can he hold a camera?"

"Down boy, that's not what I meant. This one's straighter than the proverbial arrow. To answer your question, not only can he hold a camera, but you will adore the work that comes out of it." Now things will begin.

"Let me see if I get this, you want me to take on some virgin shooter that I can't even romance?"

The edge is back, but it's more for fun now. Knowing Marcel, the rest is more dancing than negotiating; time to pick up the rhythm.

"In a word, yes."

"In a word, no."

"Honey, your lips say non, non, but there's a 'oui oui' in your voice. Marcel, don't make me beg."

"Beg, plead, do whatever. I don't need another shooter."

"This guy is hardly just another shooter. If he was, I wouldn't have wasted the energy to pick up the phone. Look, remember that time you spent all night crying in your beer over what's his name; the one with the curly blonde hair? Who got you home, and fixed you tea and biscuits in the morning? All I want to do is send you a few shots. If he doesn't ring your chimes, I will personally come to Paris and get you laid. On the other hand, if you like this kid as I am certain you will, you can fly me to Paris and spring for a two week holiday. Do we have a deal?

The laughter on the other end is a sweet surrender. The last notes of the dance have arrived much faster than I could ever have imagined possible.

"Okay honey, you know that I can't resist a bet. You know the email. Bye sweets."

That was fun. Just the reminder I needed to motivate me to get back in the game. Not with Marcel necessarily, but the two week vacation that I will most certainly cash in will put me back with a few friends. One who will be very happy to see me and another who won't like it one bit. Meanwhile, I'll hit send and get this email out.

Once I have the good news for Dalton, I will see whether the boy has any life in him at all. I am positive he will find exquisite pleasure at the hands of a certain Greek Goddess. Unlike so many others whose contacts with the tenants of Olympus have experienced tragic outcomes, my talented student will find nothing but satisfaction in our odyssey. It is easy to imagine a very Maxfield Parrish-like scene atop a mountaintop in the cool, clear morning. I am wearing a long white gown sitting on a comfortable bench with Dalton reclining, his head in my lap as I feed him grapes one at a time.

    Looking out the window at the brilliant morning sky pointing east to Paris, I see my reflection. My expression is one any cat chomping on a canary would appreciate.

18.

Bingo!

Birthdays should be met with thoughts of parties and gifts and relaxation, thinks Dalton as he stands in front of his mirror. With only a couple of weeks remaining and semester exams staring back at him, the festivities will need to be modest at best. Splashing a little water on his face after shaving, it's time to get going. A photography assignment will keep him busy for most of the day. Still, even though he has a lot to do before he can relax, he has already dressed with a little extra flair. Then he will meet Skip for dinner and then grab a few beers at a local pub.

The windows are coated with a frosted pattern. Dalton notices their castle-like elegant shapes as he reaches for his coat and gloves. He can't help himself. He runs for his camera to get a quick shot and is rewarded with a ray of sunshine just as he finds his focus.

The snow crunches beneath his shoes as he walks toward the campus. It's a pitiful remnant of the storm that happened over a week ago, dirty and dripping. He hitches the strap of his camera gear further up his shoulder as he exchanges glances with a couple of freshmen girls who appear quite friendly. One of them shares a quick wave along with a generous smile that is visible despite the fact that the sun has just begun to make an appearance. There is just the slightest glow in the east turning the buildings from black hardened shapes to softer violet. As he continues walking, he spots a friend from the photo crew who shouts a birthday greeting. Dalton marvels at how different his life is from earlier in his childhood. Photography has filled out his confidence as the years have filled out his body and improved his looks.

He pulls his cell phone and calls his friend Jonny knowing that it is way too early for the guy to be awake. 'Hell,' he thinks, 'if you can't have a little fun on your birthday…' The call is connected interrupting his devilish thoughts.

"Hey Skip, what's up?"

"What time is it?" Jonny's voice is rough from a lack of sleep and a full night of maneuvers with his latest someone special. Dalton waits for his buddy's head to clear. He doesn't have to wait long.

"Hey D Man, Happy Birthday, what are you up to?" Skip takes the interruption of his sleep as he takes almost everything, with easy good humor.

"Heading out to shoot some local color and then back to the dark room."

"You should see the local color I'm looking at right now. She's amazing."

"I can imagine, I'm sure," Dalton answers laughing. "Be careful with that my friend. One of these days, that local color or one just like her will snap you up and your carefree days will be over."

"Yeah, yeah, don't worry about me. So are we on for tonight?"

Dalton stops for a minute as he navigates crossing the road that leads to the campus. As he returns the cell to his ear he does his best to ignore the background noises that indicate that local color has been awakened by the call and is ready to start the morning where she left off the night before.

"Yeah, for sure, first we get some dinner and then the pub. It's called Bingo's right?"

Jonny continues unaware that his lady friend's activities are not quite as secret as he might think.

"Absolutely, and I've had an idea. What do you say I wake local color here and get her to call her girlfriend?" Jonny takes on a singsong voice. "I've seen her, she's gorgeous, and she's available."

Knowing that he should end the call as quickly as possible, but unable to ignore his friend's meddling, he answers tersely.

"Jonny... come on man, don't start."

"Dalton, *you* have to start sometime. What are you waiting for? You won't be this young forever."
Dalton thinks for a minute, looking for a way to change the conversation or end it on a good note.

"Look, is it so terrible that I just want to spend my birthday with my best friend?"

Jonny's voice is starting to show signs of his companion's attentions, so he willingly capitulates.

"Okay, okay, it's your b-day. We'll do it up right and see that you're home in time for late night TV. Bye."

Dalton shakes his head at the abrupt end of the call, flipping the cell's top and stashing it in his coat pocket. It's a shame that Skip and Sienna can't meet. He feels certain that she would find him as charming and irresistible as he does. He heads for Main Street, looking to see if he can bring some of the same moody feeling to some urban landscapes that he has found in his portraits.

Later, as he enters the photography lab, he is greeted by Professor Purcell who is busy working on her laptop, doing some Photoshop editing. She looks up as he enters the studio and flashes a quick smile. The room is empty. Between preparation for finals and the fact that it is the weekend, Dalton felt certain that he would have the place to himself.

For her part, Amanda would not have put in an appearance on a Saturday for any amount of money. Only by the slenderest good fortune had she heard Dalton telling a classmate of his plans for today in answer to a question the other had asked about his birthday. Time to put operation Greek Goddess into effect.

"Happy Birthday Dalton, it's today, isn't it?"

He smiles his reply, having convinced himself that the interest the professor showed a couple weeks earlier was nothing more than his overactive imagination. She had certainly done nothing else since to make him think otherwise.

"It is."

"Have a good one. Would it be inappropriate of me to ask what the number is this year?" Amanda continues to play demure for all it's worth. A little polite conversation should make the boy relax.

"The big two - two."

"Any plans? If I were you, I'd be out with dark intentions tonight." She watches him carefully to see how he reacts.

"I plan to, well, maybe not dark intentions; more like dusky. I have to take it easy. Exams are coming up, you know."

Rising from her desk, the professor heads to the dark room. Keeping her expression as neutral as possible, she carefully launches the first step of her plan. She turns back to Dalton. He's busy setting his camera case down and removing his coat which gives her the chance to enjoy the view without his noticing. He makes a very tasty silhouette against the late morning sky shining through the window.

"Before you get started, could you give me a hand in here? There are a couple heavy boxes that I could use some help with."

"I'd be happy to."

Amanda switches on the safelight as she waits for Dalton to catch up, before opening the door to the darkroom. He follows closely and closes the door behind him. His head is turned as he makes sure that the door shuts completely, so he is startled when Professor Purcell pulls him back, grabs his face and starts kissing him. She skips the preliminaries and launches a full, invasive attack before Dalton is able to pull away.

"Professor, what are you doing?"

"Consider this my birthday present, and please, call me Amanda."

She reaches for Dalton again. Dalton is so surprised, that he has trouble escaping her clutches before she has resumed a forceful mouth to mouth. Finally, he pushes her away and puts some distance between them.

"Please professor, I can't do this." He is amazed at the hungry intensity in her eyes. It's like nothing he has seen from this woman before. Her breathing is almost animal and the scent of her perfume is like a cloud around them.

"I asked around, Dalton. As far as anyone knows, there's nobody in your life." Amanda makes one more attempt to urge her body closer and sees that her estimates of the young man's strength were not in error. A brief, delicious image of Dalton in her bedroom making sexual noises with her flashes behind her eyes. He holds her back long enough for her to see that he is serious. His lack of interest is disappointing, but she accepts it as gracefully as she can as the image quickly fades. "Don't you find me attractive?"

"Of course I do. You are amazing; beautiful and very sexy. The truth is there is someone in my life. But that isn't even the whole thing."

Amanda closes the distance between them, encouraging him to continue.

"I have a habit of hurting women no matter how hard I try not to. I would never forgive myself if I repaid all that you have given me with anything like that."

"I hope you don't think I was looking for a long-term deal. Never mind, tell me about this girl; a long distance relationship, is it?"

There really are boxes to be moved, and Amanda gestures towards them as the conversation continues.

"You could call it that. She is this incredible girl and all I do is hurt her."

Sienna stands in the shadows. She watches as Dalton makes quick work of the items he is asked to handle and responds sadly as she hears his last comment.

"Oh, Dalton, the one thing you never do is hurt me."

Amanda sees the sincerity in his expression and her heart melts even more for him.

"You know Dalton; I think I can tell you one thing with authority. Whoever this girl is, the last thing she feels is hurt by you. I'm betting she feels like the luckiest woman alive."

Dalton is surprised by the rapid change in his professor's tone.

"You aren't upset? For a minute, I thought I'd lost..."

Amanda can't help but tease him a bit.

"What, a very valuable professional contact?"

"No, I thought I lost a friend; a really good friend."

Amanda is disappointed in the very final tone that ends any thoughts of further pursuit, but can't help but smile at the knowledge that at least there is someone in his life that is keeping him from her clutches.

Dalton turns back and gives the professor a friendly hug and then leaves the dark room.

Sienna is not sure how she knew that this would be an important moment today. She had seen some indications of the professor's increasing interest. She whispers to no one in particular as she sinks into the shadow.

'Every time I think I have catalogued everything I love about you,' Sienna thinks to herself, 'you add something else. You turn an uncomfortable moment into something relaxed and easy.'

The professor follows discreetly and shuts off the light. Dalton has already gotten his coat and camera and is heading out into the cold. The work he had planned for today will have to wait for a less challenging moment. Taking a few minutes to gather her own things, she discreetly follows him out and locks the door.

Later, Dalton and his friend Jonny approach the campus watering hole having already finished dinner. Bingo's is the favorite place for not only students, but for some of the faculty and a few of the locals as well. It sits on the corner of Main Street and First with large double doors in the center and a large window to each side. The windows normally each feature a neon sign. With the approaching Christmas holiday, there are a full set of lights twinkling. It is a charming place, and the street it occupies is equally decked with wreaths and lighting. Through the windows, the two can see lots of well-dressed customers and more Christmas décor. The winter air has a sharp bite to it so the two friends hurry inside. Skip looks around.

"Jeez, Bingo's is crowded tonight."

He starts heading to the opposite end of the long horseshoe shaped bar. Dalton follows knowing that Skip has a talent for finding seats in the most crowded places; a piece of luck that Dalton envies.

"I think I see a spot," Jonny says, shouting on the move.

"Great work Skip."

Dalton waits till Skip locates the last 2 empty barstools in the place. They begin shedding their coats, hanging them on some nearby hooks before settling in.

"You know Skip; I doubt you've ever had to wait for a seat your whole life," he remarks chuckling.

Jonny can't resist, and he brings his best smart-aleck tone as he reacts with eyes twinkling. "Well there was this one time…"

"Oh don't tell me, let me guess: Blonde, five foot eleven, green eyes and enough attitude to last you for a week or so."

Jonny winces a bit at how accurate his friend's guess is to the truth.

"Pretty close, but she managed to keep me going for almost two months."

A barmaid arrives wearing a white scoop-necked top and a tight black skirt that comes to a screeching halt well before her knees. She takes their drink orders and turns with a deliberate sway that Jonny finds mesmerizing as Dalton scans the crowd for a couple minutes. When she returns with the beers, Jonny rewards her with a tip and a smile.

"So, other than getting a bit longer in the tooth as they say, what's new?"

"Hold on a sec," Dalton says, catching the attention of the barmaid. He pushes the mug back towards the girl. "Excuse me, I've changed my mind. Can you bring me a scotch on the rocks?"

Skip makes things easy with a smile and a quick interruption.

"You can leave that with me."

The barmaid nods and soon returns with the Dalton's drink. Jonny is more than a little surprised as this is hardly Dalton's usual beverage. Dalton thanks the girl and she sends another smile to his buddy before turning away.

"Wow, I didn't think you'd take the age thing so seriously," Skip says between eyeing the new glassful and looking back at his buddy. "What's up?"

"It's nothing, really. In fact, I got some very good news recently. I haven't had the chance to tell you but Professor Purcell thinks she can get me a job in fashion photography. She sent my portfolio to a friend of hers." Dalton is smiling and seems happy, but it doesn't explain the hard liquor that has just been delivered. Skip decides to see where the conversation goes.

"Purcell? Is she the one with the rockin' body and the eyes to match?"

Dalton puts a big dent in his drink and shakes his head laughing. "Skip, do you ever use the brain above your waistline?"

"Not if I can help it buddy, but that is great news about the job stuff. You gonna pack me in your suitcase when you fly to those exotic locations with all those supermodels?" Skip works his eyebrows and the two share a hearty laugh before Dalton puts a serious dent in his drink.

"Absolutely, that's just what the fashion world needs, a bunch of gorgeous women; each and every one in the family way."

Jonny feigns looking wounded as he replies. "Hey man, I use protection."

Dalton finishes his drink and signals for another. He is distracted, watching as a couple heads out the door, looking very cozy together. Suddenly the crowd comes alive…

"BINGO!"

Dalton looks around, a little mystified.

"What's that all about?"

"That's right," Jonny replies, "you haven't been here before have you?"

Dalton smiles at the barmaid and starts right in on the new drink while Jonny is still working his first beer. The scotch seems even stronger this time, and he looks at the glass as his head begins to buzz just a little.

"Nope, so what gives?"

Skip notices his friend's atypical drinking and gives him a little shove.

"Hey, slow down man. The night is still young."

Dalton continues working on his scotch. Jonny drains his beer and grabs for the one that was meant for Dalton. The barmaid is extraordinarily attracted to the guy sipping the beers and hovers nearby whenever she can. She takes away the empty mug with a smile. Dalton has almost drained his drink and his smile alerts the barmaid that he is ready for yet another refill.

"I see, so it's that kind of night is it?" Skip loves telling a good story, especially to someone who hasn't heard it before. "To answer your question, this place used to be called Frank's Place or Joe's or something. Several years ago, the story goes, some dude noticed a friend who was heading out the door looking very much like he was about to score. As the couple left, he shouted out "BINGO!" and everyone chimed in. At least, that's the way the story goes. It became such a tradition here that they went out and changed the name of the place."

Jonny is sipping his beer and Dalton's glass is nearly empty once more. Another cozy couple departs.

"BINGO!"

Skip chuckles at the guy whose meager hopes with the lean, dark haired girl he was accompanying may have just vanished. He watches as they part just outside the door. When he turns back to his friend, the empty glass has been replaced yet again. Dalton is starting to look just the slightest bit glassy eyed.

"You know, I think I'd better go slow. One of us will have to be vertical enough to get the other one home. You've done it for me more than once. So what was her name?"

"Nope, no names tonight," Dalton slurs, "but I can tell you that I was prepositioned by a very beautiful woman this morning."

"I think you mean propositioned. So what's the problem?"

"Yeah, she made a pass, but I had to say, thanks but I'll pass." Dalton chuckles a little at his pun. "It's Sienna, you see."

Jonny can tell that the alcohol is beginning to take its toll.

"What's sienna got to do with it? Isn't that like a shade of brown or something?"

Dalton continues his attack on his drink, downing yet another. His signal to the barmaid is a little comic. The hand signal causes Dalton to lose his balance. Jonny moves quickly to steady his friend. He gives the barmaid a look that says no more and she smiles her understanding. She adds a little extra to the end of that smile that Jonny has no problem deciphering. He mouths 'Some other time' and the girl's smile brightens a bit more.

"Sienna is a shade of beautiful," Dalton replies dreamily. His eyes glaze as he thinks of her. "She lives in my heart; she invades my soul and visits me nightly in my dreams."

"So Sienna is an old girlfriend? How is it I've never heard of her before? More important, why is she still such a big deal?"

Skip knows that the time is fast approaching when he will have to get his buddy home. This is not the same guy he's used to.

"Sienna isn't old. She's young and beautiful and always with me. She's in here…" Dalton points to his head. "And she's very much in here." Dalton points to his heart.

Skip decides that the alcohol is fogging his buddy's brain, so he decides to go back to the earlier topic.

"So what happened with the woman, the one who made the pass?"

"Nothing, nothing at all; we're still friends," Dalton answers very matter of fact.

Jonny can only shake his head. "Of course you're friends. Why wouldn't you be?"

After settling their tab including an overly generous tip, Jonny stands up. He gives the barmaid a last once over; which earns him another glowing response. He starts to help Dalton off his stool. He grabs their coats from the hooks, donning his own before assisting his buddy.

"Come on champ, let's get you home."

They make their way toward the door, with Dalton hanging on to Jonny to keep from collapsing.

Several of the patrons notice the two guys staggering out and a thought occurs to them at once. "BINGO!" The shout is greeted by cheers and laughter. Skip turns back to the crowd and offers up his middle digit.

"You guys are a riot," he calls as they depart carefully.

He notices that even the barmaid can't help but laugh. It doesn't keep him from making a mental note to check back with her sometime soon.

Jonny gets his friend home. Luckily the first floor apartment involves no steps, just a small lift at the doorway. With a little more effort, he gets Dalton to his room and helps him into bed. He throws the covers over the still fully dressed form and pats his shoulder.

"Happy Birthday, my friend. Sweet dreams and no Sienna tonight, okay?"

Dalton mumbles something unintelligible and rolls over. Jonny watches his buddy's easy breathing, satisfied that nothing more is needed, and makes his way out of the apartment. 'It's not all that late,' he thinks. 'Perhaps I should go back to Bingo's. After all, it would be cruel to make the poor girl wait.'

Dalton awakens in his dream to sounds of Happy Birthday. He is still very drunk. He tries to clear his head, but nothing works. Somehow the alcohol is limiting his ability to do some of the magic he normally does. Thankfully, it does not appear to limit his dreaming vision. Sienna flows out of the shadow. Her movements are calculated to entice. Her face is glowing with a little extra make-up and a lot of excitement. Her skirt is fluid and her legs move as if to a slow ballad.

"Hey there sleepyhead, I know you were going out tonight, but still, I thought you'd be here sooner." Sienna stops as she realizes that something is different. Slowly it dawns on her that Dalton's partying went a bit further than he expected. Meanwhile, Dalton is noticing through hazy eyes how Sienna is dressed. There is something feminine and just a little provocative about the extra button undone on her blouse or the way her hair is pulled to the side.

"You look…different." The slurred words tumble awkwardly from his lips.

Slowly Sienna comes to a stop. She is realizing that all of her preparations for the evening have been for nothing. She continues a little sadly.

"I wanted tonight to be just perfect. I spent some extra time getting ready. Now I wish I had kept a little eye on you." Sienna stops, worrying that she has given away something.

Dalton's head clears just a little at her words.

"A little eye on me; what do you mean?"

Sienna looks away and tries to act nonchalant. "Nothing, never mind, I just wish I hadn't spent so much time getting ready."

Dalton motions Sienna nearer. He is trying so hard to get his eyes to focus.

"Sienna, you look so beautiful. I don't think I've ever seen you like this. You're like an angel. What a day. What a mess I made. I think I drank a little too much…"

"You think so, huh?" Sienna chuckles just loud enough to be heard. "What was your first clue?" She hesitates as his face clouds a bit. "That's okay my darling. I'm just sad because I wanted to give you your present."

Dalton is starting to give in to the alcohol. His memory starts to play back the offending events of the day.

"Professor Purcell, no I can't, it's not right. Oh Sienna, what a day. I made such a mess, and all I want, all I ever wanted is you."

Sienna answers quietly letting Dalton give in to the alcohol at last.

"Oh my darling, I know that."

Her love's mumbling gets quieter and less coherent as he drifts away.

"Beautiful Sienna, lovely Sienna, the one in my heart and my soul and my dreams…"

Sienna pulls the covers around Dalton's shoulders and kisses him on the cheek. Her eyes well up but she manages to keep herself from breaking down. She whispers as he begins to snore.

"Good night my love and Happy Birthday; I promise that your present will be waiting when you are ready."

Sienna starts to walk toward the shadows and then stops. She turns back and sits in the armchair near the bed. It feels right that she should keep watch over him.

"Sweet dreams my darling."

19.

Birthday presents

Sunlight streaks past the curtains, bounces off the wall and straight into Dalton's eyes. He lifts his arms to block the white remorseless light, tightens his eyelids and moans. The first effort to sit up is unsuccessful owing in no small part to the way the room has suddenly become his own personal gyroscope, so he concentrates instead on unsticking his tongue from the roof of his mouth. Payment due for the previous night's activities arrives in various forms, from the vulgar taste of too much scotch, to the generally achy feeling and of course, the jackhammer doing double-time in his brain. After several tries he manages to make it to the side of the bed. Eventually there is enough energy and his head is clear enough to stagger toward the bathroom. He only slightly bangs into the door frame as he enters. The shower starts, and above the white noise are a series of long, pitiful whines. Dalton is confused at first until he realizes the sound is coming from him.

    Getting ready for the day is a slower process than usual and involves a singular focus on each task in turn. There will be plenty of time for guilt and recrimination later. Right now each step of pouring water into the coffee maker, adding the filter and the coffee grounds, and turning the damn thing on seem herculean. Dropping the bread in the toaster is not too bad, but gathering the butter and the butter knife and a dish for the toast seem every bit as daunting. Finally, the hard work is behind him.

Watching the drip, drip, drip of the coffee as it brews into the pot is a little too much like the Chinese water torture pulse of pain that continues even after Dalton's shower has started him on the way to recovery. He only spills a couple drops when he fills his cup and determines that he will forego the cream and sugar in favor or whatever hangover reducing efforts black coffee can make. Any other day and he would have easily handled the task of catching the single runaway slice of toast ejected from the toaster instead of missing it and watching it head with evil intent toward the floor. Grabbing the wayward slice, he pushes the butter knife quickly over the surface only to bobble it and see it land on the floor again, butter side down. He shakes his head, smiling in spite of it all as he retrieves the toast once more.

As he gingerly slouches into his chair, a plate with the slightly soiled buttered toast in one hand and the cup of coffee in the other, humanity is beginning to seep back into place. The black coffee flavor is a little rougher than he expected, but he takes a couple sips; further payment rendered. The comfort of the gray flannel robe and black cord slippers start to reduce the pounding between his ears. Pounding that returns in full when his cell rings. If there is one person he is unprepared to speak with, it is Professor Purcell, so of course, hers is the name he sees on the phone's id display.

"Hello?"

"Dalton, this is Amanda Purcell. Do you have a minute?" Her voice through the cell oozes syrupy sweet, with no trace of their abortive tryst. Putting thoughts of those uncomfortable minutes aside, he tries to affect a casual tone.

"Sure professor, what can I do for you?" Dalton winces mentally at his poor choice of words. Amanda Purcell smiles on the other end, thinking of several responses she would love to give if this call was less important. She foregoes her flippant responses and stays with the speech she practiced earlier.

"I wanted to start by apologizing for my behavior yesterday. I certainly didn't mean to upset you, and I would hate to think that you found my actions… unprofessional." 'Not,' she thinks to herself, 'that it matters much to me one way or the other'.

"Professor, there's nothing to apologize for; I just hope you understand."

"Certainly I do. I only called because I have some very good news. You will be hearing from a colleague of mine; someone I worked with a long time ago. His name is Marcel Ardan and he has a job for you. I don't know all the details, but I know he will be looking for you to join his team pretty much immediately. I think you should grab this and not look back." Amanda toys with the phone cord as she awaits a response.

"Professor, that's wonderful, but there are still classes and exams and graduation."

Amanda moves back smoothly to her role as teacher and mentor.

"Dalton, I have spoken with your other professors and the dean of the school. You were going to graduate at the end of this semester, right? Your grades are exceptional and your talent is obvious. Everyone is willing to grant exemptions from finals except that old grouch Mr. Appleby and I persuaded him to let you slide with a final grade of B. You can take the little hit to your GPA, am I right?"

Battling the throbbing in his brain, and struggling with the idea that this could be any more real than his nights with Sienna; the seconds stretch on before he realizes that he has yet to respond. When his wits return, he asks the only question he can think of.

"Sorry for the delay Professor, I may have partied a bit harder than I planned last night. I can certainly handle the hit as you call it, but are you convinced that I am getting the job?"

"Well Dalton, before this morning is over, I guarantee that you will have reason to party even harder. Your phone should ring very soon. Good luck honey… and Dalton…"

"Yes?"

"Thanks for Paris. By the way, if Marcel tries to start you at anything less than 100 K, you tell him I will personally flambé his lower extremities."

The connection ends instantly. Dalton looks at his phone as if it is made of something sticky.

'Thanks for Paris? What is she talking about? One hundred thousand dollars, is she kidding?'

It is amazing how a job offer, especially a job offer involving a salary of this magnitude can aid the recovery process. Achy body? Painless! Pounding head? Suddenly still and remarkably clear.

Dalton ignores the slight pounding in his chest that might indicate any doubt about his readiness for this next step. He stands easily, makes his way back to his bedroom and prepares to finish dressing. Until a few minutes ago, he had no specific plans for the day. Now, throwing on some rough jeans and a Rams jersey seem less than adequate. He settles for his nicer jeans and a shirt he might wear to visit family. If the promised call comes, and if the job is real, a trip to his Dad's house will be in order. Just as he is starting to doubt that his conversation with the professor was anything more than a drink induced delusion, the phone rings again. The display shows an unrecognizable number with a foreign exchange.

Knowing that the person on the other end could be his future employer, Dalton replaces his customary hello with something a bit more professional. "This is Dalton, can I help you?"

"Dalton, my friend, today is your lucky day. I have just finished looking at your portfolio and I am excited to say that I want to offer you a job. Mandy did not exaggerate your talent. "

Dalton takes a second to process Mandy to Amanda to Professor Purcell. Everything is happening so fast that he worries that the room could begin to spin again at any time.

"That's great Monsieur Ardan. I can't wait to start." He smiles to himself at the brilliance of having included the French honorific.

"No, actually you can't, and please it must be Marcel. I need you in Paris by Wednesday at the latest. That means having your tush on an airplane Tuesday morning. Can you settle things where you are and get here that quickly? I'll get you the ticket."

It is obvious that his new boss is used to getting things pretty much as he wants them and very quickly at that. There are other questions to be asked, but since he is astonished by the idea that he has more than a job, he now has a career; Dalton tries to buy time for his reeling brain.

"Can you tell me about the assignment?"

"We can discuss all of that when you arrive, but I need an answer right now." A slight edge of impatience tinges Mr. Ardan's tone.

"Um, Marcel, I hate to bring this up, but could we talk about compensation?"

The silence from the other end of the line has Dalton convinced that he may regret having listened to Professor Purcell; an opinion that seems even more worrisome as he hears Marcel thinking out loud.

"This is the chance of a lifetime, I'm gambling everything on an untested shooter, and he's worried about money."

From somewhere in the greedy recesses of his brain, the young photographer remembers some saying about fortune favoring the bold. 'It sure would be a shame to lose this job on the same day that I get it,' Dalton thinks, 'Ah, what the hell.'

"Right, so how much?" he says with a slightly ironic tone.

"Well, since you asked, I have very good news. I am prepared to start you at seventy five thousand per year."

The astonished silence on the other end of the line is even more pronounced as Dalton makes no reply.

"Dalton?"

"Marcel, I don't want you to think that I am unappreciative of your very fine offer…"

"Okay, okay, how much did Mandy tell you to rob me for?"

Amazingly enough, there is a bit of a chuckle attached to the end of Marcel's question. The job is his and the salary to match. "You have already been so generous; I am hesitant to name a figure."

"How much?"

Dalton sits holding his cell, waiting for the next word from his new employer.

"All right, I am guessing she told you to hold out for six figures. Just remember one thing, lose your edge for a single second and I will not only cut you from my firm, I'll take your manhood as well."

Dalton laughs in spite of himself.

"Understood, I will see you on Tuesday."

"The ticket will be at the airport, first class of course. Dalton, I like your style. I think you will do well. Have a good flight. We will have some fun, you'll see."

Dalton hits the end button and the call is finished. Looking at himself in the bedroom mirror, he is more than a little surprised by the triumphant face grinning back at him. It felt so good and he believes that he could take on anything now. He can't wait to share the news with Sienna. Meanwhile there are others to contact beginning with his dad. As he listens to the ring and the call goes through, his father's voice is pleasantly surprised and he quickly begins to share the good news. It might be the best conversation he has ever had with Dad, who can't completely hide his amazement that Dalton is going to make a living taking pictures. Sherry is equally pleased if less shocked.

The day passes pleasantly. Dalton shares a good laugh with Skip when his friend jokingly suggests that they go out again to celebrate his job offer. There are several words of gratitude added for the way the guy had taken care of him the previous night. He stops short of promising to introduce his buddy to any supermodels despite Skip's insistence that he was owed at least that much.

With the remaining calls and congratulations behind him, he heads over for a nice meal with his family. When he gets back, he can't wait to voice the words that still are still saved for special occasions.

"Hurry Moon."

Dalton settles into the most comfortable sleep he has had in months. It has been a busy day. With his future on track and full of exciting possibilities, Dalton awakes in his dream ready to spend an evening relaxing in his dreams with Sienna. There is some vague, slightly exciting recollection of her behavior from the previous night, but it isn't completely clear. Dalton starts immediately to prepare a celebration. A large bouquet of flowers appears in an expensive vase, candles in a pair of brass stands and dinner is instantly settled on his kitchen table with a table cloth and as much splendor as he can imagine. Sienna appears from the mist and immediately notices the ambience.

"Wow, look at all this," she says impressed.

"There you are, come on in and sit down. Dinner is nearly ready."

Upon her arrival, he gets the stereo started, playing a variety of instrumental new age jazz and classic rock ballads. The mood is soothing.

"Mmmm, smells wonderful. I had no idea you were such a good cook." Sea walks over and offers a friendly kiss on the cheek which soon turns to something a bit more passionate. Once their lips are separated, he has the time to notice her dress, which is dark blue and very fitted but not nearly as provocative as the one she was wearing the night before.

"Truth be told, I'm a much better cook in my imagination than I am in real life. Thankfully, that is all the talent I need for us here. By the way, you look very pretty tonight."

"Thank you," she says as she takes her seat at the table. He quickly joins her and waits for her to start. The candlelight sparkles in her eyes and glows on her cheeks. Sienna begins with the filet mignon, cutting a piece and sampling it. She closes her eyes with delight.

"This is the best steak I have ever had. Maybe you should try this during the day. You'd have a thousand proposals before the week is out if you could cook like this when you're awake…Um, what am I saying? Better keep the cooking just for me."

"That's a deal. Would you care for some wine?"

"Yes please, but not too much. I may need my head clear for later."

Dalton considers the possible meanings of these words. First might be a reference to his excessive consumption the previous night. Second and more pleasant might refer to the open-ended possibilities that might be entertained with just a slight bit of fermented influence. Refusing to indulge in either meaning, he opens the bottle of red wine and pours a glass for each of them. The candle lit wine sparkles extravagantly as it fills the glass.

"How is that?"

Sienna sniffs and samples the wine. "Just right, I think. Yes it's very nice, not too sweet and not too dry with a very rich body."

Dalton's eyes wander over Sienna's very rich body. She is a beautiful woman and even more so tonight as he contemplates the beginning of the next stage of his life. Sea appears to be responding to the music on the stereo, gently swaying in her seat to the slow new-age rhythms.

Sienna watches him devouring her visually. His excitement is obvious and she is trying not to be so connected to his mind that she spoils whatever surprise he has for her. She has tried to put aside her thoughts about what happened the night before, or more accurately, what did not happen. It seems clear that while he has some recollection of things being different in her mode of dressing, he was not sober enough to decipher her intentions. She is not sure what to expect and does not want to seem too eager.

"You must be wondering why I have gone to all this trouble," he begins, with a gesture aimed at the food, the candles and the flowers. He starts laughing as he finishes the thought. "I have some news and it felt like we needed to celebrate it in a way that we've never done before."

Sienna is suddenly still, worrying about how she will fit into this great news. Her hopes that the dinner might be an extension of his birthday celebration seem dimmed.

"Drum roll please. I hereby announce the imminent employment and departure to foreign lands of one Dalton Hunter. I start my career this week with a very nice salary and wide open opportunities. I have been recruited by Marcel Ardan to be one of his shooters as he calls his photographers."

"Dalton, he's like, world famous in Fashion."

Sienna jumps up from the table and flings herself into Dalton's arms. Her elation is real as is her pride in his success. They hug for several minutes before Sienna starts to worry. Her voice is quiet and her smile subdued when she goes on.

"I am so happy. I couldn't dream of anything I'd rather see for you. I know how much you've wanted this."

Dalton can see her concern as well as her happiness, and wants to end it immediately. He takes her face in his hands.

"Sea, you don't think I'd go anywhere and not take you with me do you? You're in here," he says pointing to his head, "and here," he adds pointing to his heart. "That is not going to change."

Sienna pulls away and turns toward the shadow.

"This is going to be different though. You will be so busy and you will need all of your concentration. There will be a whole lot of people to meet, and yes, lots of beautiful women; live women who will see your talent and want to be part of your life. Maybe this would be the best time to let you go so that you will be free to find your success; your life." Her shoulders tremble and her tears flow freely as she tries to deal with the inevitable loss.

Dalton goes to Sienna and pulls her back from the shadow into the light. His voice is sincere and his kiss gentle as he tries to assuage her doubt.

"Sienna, I don't know what the future will bring. I don't want to make promises now that I may not be able to keep. The only thing I know for sure is that you are so much a part of me, so much a part of everything I have become. Leaving you now would be like removing an arm or leg. I can't even imagine it. Stay with me and let's try to make this life, this love under the moon, as real and as lasting as anything I could find when I'm awake."

Sienna pulls him closer, holding on as if her very life is at stake.

"Oh Dalton, I want that. I want it with all my heart."

Sienna looks up at him expectantly and their lips join. It is a lover's kiss. When they end it, Dalton is aware of their closeness. He is afraid of what might or might not come next. They are not kids anymore, he knows, but the promise he has been keeping for so many years still holds him back. He decides to lighten the mood.

"All right then, let's finish dinner."

The great thing about having a large meal in your dreams, Dalton thinks, is that you never have that full feeling. Bite after bite of perfectly prepared filet disappears, filling his mouth with flavor, but leaving his stomach feeling only the comfort of a hunger nearly satisfied. The potatoes au gratin and the asparagus spears in the sauce béarnaise are perfect compliments, as is the Australian Malbec wine he has chosen. There is a very nice banana cream cheesecake standing by on his kitchen counter, but dessert is not high on his list of after dinner priorities. The couple works through the meal with only the music in the background and the occasional shared smile.

Once the meal is ended, the dishes disappear, and the couple moves to the living room, satisfied to continue listening to the music. The loveseat is perfectly cozy. The line of physical contact stretches the length of both their bodies. The room is dark and warm. Sienna turns to Dalton with a special song in mind to get things going.

"Is it okay if I select a song?" she asks.

"Sure."

With nothing more than a slight nod, Sienna changes the music to Sade's *'Haunt Me'*. The gentle and slightly sad guitar work plays as Dalton wonders if the song has special significance. When the soulful and ethereal voice begins singing, the question is answered with the first words.

"Hold me in my dreams…"

Dalton still hesitates and Sienna realizes that his respect for the wishes she expressed so long ago, trump any thoughts he might otherwise entertain. It is also clear that her worries about the future have not made things easier for him. Sienna decides the time has come to reverse course. She rests her head on Dalton's shoulder.

"So when do you leave?" Sienna's voice is quiet, her face expectant looking into his eyes.

"I have to be on a plane Tuesday morning. Good thing I've kept my passport ready. If only you knew how many times I've been kidded about that one, I…"

"If it's help that you need, never dare to doubt me..."

Sienna's expression turns from interest to concern. "That soon? I thought you'd have to finish the semester."

"Professor Purcell arranged it so I can earn my credits and get my degree and still leave a bit early. She was very persuasive."

Sienna's eyes lock on Dalton's. "She has a thing for you, you know." She knows that the moment between them that happened the day before was resolved, but is still curious to see how he will respond.

"Maybe she had a thing, but that's all been worked out. I told her about you."

Dalton turns and catches a whiff of Sienna's hair and the scent of her perfume. His arm is already around her and his fingers stroke her shoulder lightly.

"You smell very nice."

Sienna is hoping that this is the beginning of an overture she can answer with a passionate affirmative.

"Thanks. "

Dalton keeps looking at Sienna. His longing is almost painful; caught between his desire to be a good guy and his need for that next step. He looks at her with a little hesitation.

"I'll be quiet, like an angel..."

"Sea, do you ever wonder what…

Sienna now has all she has waited for, any indication that what will happen is a mutual decision. She pulls him closer and begins a deep, satisfying kiss. She does not need any more words from him. His eagerness is powerful and very real. They stand and Dalton immediately begins to help

Sienna out of her clothing. She is just as eager to help him, so they take turns.

"Never dare to doubt me…"

Dalton's dream is so urgent, he can no longer think in terms of walking to the bedroom. Instead, they (magically) appear there. The lamp is on and he reaches for it to resume the darkness. The covers rustle and the lovers intertwine.

20.

Traveler: Pursuing the One

This diary will need to be replaced soon. The pages are almost completely filled and the lock sticks from time to time. So let's see, the date is December 9 and oh God, it's almost nine thirty, Mom will be calling soon. Better try to at least get started with this entry before the inquisition begins. The hotel pen on the desk is handy and remarkably full of ink.

The Hotel Xavier in downtown Chicago is one of your standard shiny glass jewelry boxes. The room is comfortable enough and I can see the Sears tower from my window. The early morning light is a bit harsh as I sit here in the plush, white bathrobe provided by the hotel with a towel wrapped around my head. Looking in the mirror, I hardly recognize myself. The shower was helpful, but it hasn't completely broken through the fog.

Last night was amazing; definitely worth the wait.

Damn, there's the phone already. I better get to the bed and answer it. Her majesty hates to be kept waiting. I think I'll hit the speaker button so that I can leave the towel where it is. Then I can settle back on my pillows and brace myself.

"Hello Mother, how is everything in the empire these days? No I am not being flippant. All right, maybe just a little." 'Unbelievable,' I think. 'Who says flippant anymore?'

"Sweetheart, how soon will you be coming home? There's a lot that I need you to do around here." Mother's voice could make nails scraping across a blackboard sound like a choir of angels by comparison.

"Mother, I told you that I don't know how soon I can get back. I think he's nearby, but he won't be for long and I don't know exactly where he's headed next." I would tell her about last night, but daughters can hardly be expected to tell their mothers everything, can they?

"Honey, are you sure this is a good idea?"
There is a tone of almost sincere concern there. Mother doesn't resort to that one very often, so I offer a little genuine angst of my own.

"Mom, I wish you would try to understand. To you this seems like some wild goose chase or silly, childish crush. This is my life. I have to do this." Of course, if you had any idea about the way the previous evening went, there's no way you'd understand. I hope my tension isn't too obvious. I did go to bed last night, but there was almost no sleep involved.

Mother's quiet Mother-Daughter tone is just as quickly replaced by the more imperious one.

"I don't know why you have to do this. You have lots of nice friends and a home and parents who love you. Can't you just find some nice boy here and get started? Your father and I were married and building our business by your age. It's a business that we'd like you to take over one day; preferably one day very soon."

Okay, the gloves are off.

"Mother, why is this so hard for you? If you were me, and this was the only way you could have found Daddy, what would you have done?"

"Believe me, if your father was this difficult to find, I would have found someone else. That very nice James Kinston would have been a very acceptable alternative."

Not Jimmy Kinston again! You have to be kidding me. The guy's the size of a humpback whale without the brain capacity. Oh sure, he has the money, but I can't believe that she would have given him the time of day, no matter how many trips around the world he could have offered. Talking to him is like sensory deprivation without the tank.

"Mother, we have been over this again and again. I'm not like you. I want something different. I really think you should stop waiting for me to join the business. I have other dreams. I don't need lots of money or fancy things…" Uh oh, might have gone a bit far with that last bit. She'll probably go for the credit card threat after that one.

"I could cancel your credit card. That would put a stop to your travels very quickly." Nice one Mom. The judges are giving it a solid nine point seven; just the smallest deduction for the little knife twist at the end.

Wonder how long she will wait this time. Silence after the credit card threat has been a reliable tool since I first discovered it a couple of years ago. One…Two…Three…

"Sweetheart…"

Eleven…Twelve…Thirteen…

"Okay Sweetheart, you win. You are highly educated and I will have to count on that intelligence of yours kicking in at some point."

"Thanks Mom," I answer with my sparkly voice

"Sure, sure, as long as you get what you want." Her tone is a piquant blend of amusement and frustration with just the slightest dash of affection. It has an amazing body with a sharp tangy finish.

"I love you Mom. Tell Dad I think he was a much better pick than that stupid Jimmy Kinston. Besides, haven't you noticed how fat that man has gotten? Tell Dad I love him too."

I have to give it to Mom. She is a gracious loser. Her laughter comes through the speaker and reminds me that however different we are and whatever we disagree on; it is hard not to love her.

"Stop, you're such a little devil. Take care of yourself and call soon."

Ending the call on such a pleasant note is rare enough that I may just have to add it to this morning's diary entry. Where was I, oh that's right, last night.

He's as close to me as he has ever been. I can feel it. He's waiting for me to prove that I mean it and he'll take me with him. If Mother could see what kind of man he is and how he treats me, her laughter this morning would be replaced by real approval.

There's so much more to say, but it will have to wait. It's time to get dressed and order some breakfast. If tonight is as challenging as last night was, I can hardly afford to skip a meal. Looking at their picture sitting by the bedside, I can't stop smiling; such a nice day with my two parents standing in front of the Eifel Tower. Of course, that was years ago and I was so young when I took it. I wonder if those people would even recognize me today.

21.

Departure

Loneliness is the last emotion Dalton expected to feel in the morning. Opening his eyes, he pulls his covers close around him to fend off the chill. He looks around the room hoping to see something that his brain has already told him is impossible. It is jarring to experience the passion and wonder that he has shared the last few evenings with Sienna, only to wake up again and again in a cold, empty bed. Closing his eyes again, he tries to resurrect a few precious images, but all that he can see is the inside of his eyelids.

It's different now, he thinks. All of the time that we have been touching and connecting, experiencing each other in that nearly but not quite completely sexual way, I never felt like this the next day. Up till now it has been easy to accept the pleasure and live with the limits and then get up and focus on school and friends knowing that there would be the friendship, the conversation and the warmth to go to sleep to. It's as if going that next step to the more intimate has brought the whole relationship into some kind of crystalline focus. The unfairness of so much joy followed by this hollow gut emptiness is almost unbearable. 'I wouldn't trade a moment of these dream times for any amount of money', he thinks, 'I wouldn't erase a second, but getting used to this ache the next day will be a challenge'.

Pushing up from the bed, Dalton looks out the window, trying to catch up with the day. The weather seems just as unhappy, as hard gray clouds pass by, distributing a few miserly snowflakes over the frozen ground. The flakes sit in separate patches of brushy grass for a brief moment before evaporating into the air. A cardinal, who missed the email announcing plans for the winter migration so many weeks ago, sits on a branch just outside. The bird is the lone splash of color in a landscape of grays and dull browns. From his perch in bed, Dalton wonders what might have kept the silly thing from taking flight.

Taking flight! Dalton realizes that he is down to mere hours before he will board the plane and start his new life in Paris. Okay, not exactly Paris straight off, there is the stop at JFK in New York and a three hour layover, but then on to Paris. He braces himself against the chill and dashes for the bathroom with a last look at his lonely friend outside. The apartment is now down to hotel room essentials. Toiletries on the sink stand waiting to be used and packed. His travelling outfit hangs nearby. The handle to the shower door is cold to the touch and the water seems to be noncommittal about warming. Finally, the water is livable and as he settles under the flowing stream, he has time to give his thoughts a last free run.

While the nights have been a tapestry of colors and sounds that seemed so much to embody the essence of physical pleasure, the days have been a flurry of more mundane and yet somehow still exciting tasks. Skip was more than happy to help empty the contents of Dalton's apartment, a large portion of them finding a new home in Jonny's place. The remainder was carted back to Dad's garage along with the dark blue Mustang. Sherry even came by to give him a hand in cleaning up. Dalton smiles as he thinks of how much this woman has enriched his father's life. It is certainly something Dad deserves.

The rest of the morning passes in an instant. Shaving and dressing are followed by packing and a walk to the local pancake house for a last serving of their wonderful strawberry filled crepes; a fitting appetizer for a flight to France. Back at the apartment, Dalton uses his cell to arrange a cab to the airport. He checks his pockets for the twentieth time to make sure his wallet and passport are in place.

The cabdriver honks outside and sits comfortably as Dalton carts his luggage to the curb. The man is gracious enough to pop the trunk latch, and allow his new fare the privilege of dumping the cases inside. Not wanting to disturb the man from the comfort of his warm vehicle or in any way delay their departure, Dalton manages closing the trunk lid himself. It is apparent that he will be delivered to the airport by a recent lottery winner who has decided to continue working his day job. Dalton does his best to hide his chagrin, knowing that only one as fortunate as his driver could appreciate the size of the gratuity that will be forthcoming.

Sitting in the cab, there is time to say goodbye to this town that has become his home. The ride takes him past the remnants of the Lane Theater where he and Laurie had had their first actual date. The building has a "For Sale" sign in the ticket window and the marquee has a few pits and missing lights. It is a sad and crumbling monument to their brief relationship. The traffic around him moves with an utter, oblivious lack of concern for the sad state of the once proud movie house.

Now it's on to the highway and lots more cars glinting in the sun as the taxi moves past them at breakneck speed. Finally, the high arched entranceways to the main concourse are in sight. The moment of truth is at hand. The cabbie is feeling comfortable, safe in the knowledge that the all-important trunk lid switch is at his disposal, but Dalton has had a lot of time to think this through. He knows that the driver knows that an infraction took place when there was not so much as an offer to load the luggage. The vehicle pulls to the gates for departures and comes to a stop. The click of the trunk lid is as yet unheard. Dalton remains seated knowing that the cab cannot remain in this spot for too long without drawing undue attention.

"We're here," the driver says, not pulling the handle on the still running meter.

"I know."

A look of malice mixed with surprise spreads across the driver's face. Dalton makes no move for his wallet or the door.

"In about 10 seconds," he says, "I am going to get out of this cab and leave the exact amount of the fare sitting on the seat here. I have a couple of hours to kill, so I will have lots of time to make a phone call to your company describing the diligence of your service. If you don't open the trunk, you can leave with my bags, but that would be a mistake. I think it is called theft. On the other hand, should you get off your ass and remove the bags from the trunk; there may still be some shred of your tip left."

The driver considers his passenger's words. He continues to glare through the rearview mirror. After a few seconds, and with a show of great reluctance, stops the meter, unlatches the trunk, opens the door and moves with a shuffling and overplayed effort to the rear of the cab. However, once inside the trunk he handles everything with extreme gentleness and moves the cases to the curb.

"Thanks," Dalton says as he offers the man a twenty.

The cab driver looks at the bill with surprise, pocketing it quickly and then to his customer flashing the first smile of the day. "Thank *you*, sir!"

"You never know, do you?" Dalton replies with a sly grin as he turns and walks away.

In the last second before he enters the terminal Dalton turns back for a last look around. He looks up into the sky for no particular reason, but is rewarded with something he knows he has never seen before; half a dozen birds flying up so high that they barely register as more than dots. They swoop and glide, ascending to heights that maybe even they had never dreamed of before this moment.

'I'm flying to Paris,' Dalton thinks, amazed at the very idea. Caught up in the glamour of leaving the country and embarking on a new career has helped to offset the many new features that have become part of the air traveler's routine. First, there was the line to navigate before a stern-faced security officer took a few moments to check his ticket and look over his passport. Then there was the removal of shoes and belts and his laptop from its comfortable, cushioned case in preparation for the scanning machine along with his own scanning. Still, the ordeal is over soon enough and he can make his way to the gate. His flight is on time, at least according to the displays, and while he still has over ninety minutes to kill, he is too excited to eat or even read the paper. Thankfully the smells of the food court are just far enough away to leave his jumpy stomach alone.

The lights and the sounds of the people passing keep his mind just occupied enough. He thinks of the pleasant older woman at the ticket counter when he first arrived. As he placed his luggage on the conveyor, she smiled and began processing his ticket.

"Welcome to Lambert Saint Louis International Airport Mr. Hunter, the transit is all arranged and paid for. Here is a first class boarding pass to JFK in New York as well as another for the connection to Paris. The New York flight will be departing from Gate C2. They will call you when boarding begins. You have your passport with you, I assume?" There was something very kind, almost maternal in the way she asked.

"It's right here. Once I get to the Gate, is there any place to get something to eat or drink while I am waiting?"

"There's a café right across from the seating area and a bar a little further down." The agent looks down at the ticket. She smiles knowingly.

"Will you be staying in Paris a while?"

Dalton was happy to make a little casual conversation.

"I don't know how long I'll be there. I am starting a new job there and it may include some travel. Thanks a lot." He took the ticket folder that was offered and secured it in his laptop pouch, smiling as he left.

The agent calls out to him. "Have a pleasant flight and...Good luck. Follow the concourse that way and you'll see the signs."

Dalton nods and heads in the direction indicated.

"Gate C2, gate C2; okay, it's that way. Oh Sienna, I wish you could be here to see me off, or better yet, to get on the plane and go with me. Isn't that the way it is in all the romantic films?"

Sitting in the waiting area as people come and go, most with trailing cases skipping along on their little wheels, he has time to think about the night before. The early afternoon sky is dotted with scudding, puffy clouds, and the noise of the passersby offers a soft white background in which to let his mind wander.

It occurs to him that he missed something different that happened last night in the pleasure and excitement of the moment. After their lovemaking, Sienna smiled, held him close for a while and eventually fell asleep in his arms. The feeling of her hair tickling his cheek, and the wonder of her breathing slow and even was only now beginning to really register. There was just enough light in the room to make out the constellations of freckles arrayed across her shoulders and down her back. Even though he was only now recognizing that she had never slept in any dream before, he was all the more amazed by the rare and generous gift she had shared with him.

The memory of those moments is hard to shake. In the hustle and bustle of the waiting area, few people notice the young man with the glazed expression, but Dalton soon finds something of interest to pass the time. A tall, very pretty young girl with caramel colored skin walks up to a traveler sitting nearby. She looks up at the man with a child's curiosity and starts a conversation. Her mother is sitting beside the girl and is giving her a little freedom as they await their flight.

"What's your name?" she asks directly, her head tilted just a little to one side as if trying to determine something specific about the man. He is sitting with a beaten leather jacket, and wool slacks. His hair is sparse on the sides and nearly gone on top. As if to offset the loss, he wears a mustache and beard with more gray than black.

"Paul," he responds, not seeming to mind at all the child's directness. "What's yours?" he continues.

"Kamryn," she says with a slight smile, apparently pleased at meeting an old friend so far from home. She walks away for a little while apparently requiring time to digest his response.

When she returns to continue the conversation, Dalton is fascinated by the exchange and he notices that a few others have become interested as well.

"Where are you going?" Her questions have the subtlety of a courtroom cross examination.

"I am heading to Charlotte, and from there to Richmond, Virginia."

"What time is your flight?" Kamryn is focused solely on her new friend.

"My plane is supposed to board in forty five minutes. Where are you going?"

She looks to her mother for support and finally responds, "We're going to Raleigh, North Carolina. Our plane is leaving soon."

The two continue chatting quietly for a while. She is completely focused on everything the man says. When he is finished, Kamryn notices the woman sitting next to Paul. Without missing a beat, she asks, "How old are you?" to which the woman replies, "How old do you think I am?"

Kamryn looks the woman up and down and decides.

"Twenty-one," she answers in a tone that suggests the matter is settled.

"Absolutely," the woman responds happily though she is clearly more than a few years older than that. "Actually, I am fifty-three," she admits after a few seconds.

Kamryn turns to Paul asking "and how old are you?" to which he replies, "fifty-seven next week, and how old are you Kamryn?"

"Five and a half," she answers.

Once again the girl walks away to think things over, but the questions still remain. So once again she is back to continue her friendly inquisition.

Looking from the lady to her new friend Paul, she asks "Are you two married?"

The woman decides to field this one. "No sweetheart, we have never met."

Evidently this makes the woman less interesting, so she turns back to her new friend.

"How come you don't have any hair on your head?"

"Do you really want to know?"

"Yes"

"It's because I have three kids and they drive me crazy." This elicits more than a few knowing nods from some of the folks now sharing this airport moment.

"Of course it's also," the man continues, "because I have been around since the dinosaurs."

"You have not. They would have eaten you." Kamryn is obviously expert in the realm of pre-history; something she shares with all her peers.

"I would have hidden in the bushes."

Kamryn however, is not so easily put off.

"Wouldn't matter," she declares with a knowing look. "See, I'm a T Rex." She does a very convincing portrayal of the legendary beast, quickly turning her head from side to side, her arms poised forward and down. "I spot you even in the bushes and if you run, I just eat you."

"C'mon Kamryn, it's time to get on our plane." Kamryn's mother holds out her hand and the girl turns obediently but not before giving Paul a kind wave goodbye. Suddenly, the girl is gone and it seems unimaginably quiet and a little like what a beach must feel when all of the people pack their baskets and head to their cars; the sandcastles gone, the footsteps erased by the surf. Everyone returns to their own thoughts.

Eventually the call for boarding begins. Dalton's first class status allows him entry to the plane right after the call for families with small children and those who might need assistance boarding. The shadow just away from the passage to the plane shimmers as Sienna looks on. She is desperate to get his attention.

"Dalton, I wish I were going with you. I'm here. I'm right here," she says with desperation.

Dalton stops for a second as if he has heard her. He scans his surroundings, looking for what he knows is not there. As he looks, there is no Sienna. Shaking himself, he moves on. Sienna follows, trying to get his attention again.

"I know you heard me, even if it was just for a second. I'm here Dalton. I want to say goodbye."
Sienna stops and watches Dalton go on. Unlike a flesh and blood girl who would be limited to seeing him off and no more, she knows that she will be with him at the other end of the flight. She will see him later tonight when he gets where he is going.

"I'll be with you soon. I'll see you in your dreams."

Dalton hands his ticket to the attendant who scans and returns it. He walks into the passenger corridor. He can't shake the feeling that he has missed something. He looks out at the seating area once more. There are people there, but not the one he hoped to see. He turns and boards the plane.

22.

Sienna: Dalton shares his croissant

Life in Paris has far exceeded anything Dalton or I might have imagined. We have settled into a very pleasant, very small apartment in the 17'th Arrondissement, not far from Marcel's studios. The pace during the day is frantic. He is working like a demon, but he is picking up things so fast that it won't be long before he is doing location shoots. Marcel is already finding projects that take advantage of his new pupil's unique eye, while telling anyone who will listen how much of it is a result of his tutelage. When Marcel isn't taking credit for his protégé's success, he is introducing him all over as the next great shooter. I love the way Dalton takes it all in stride, knowing that this opportunity is one of a kind. The list of meetings, studio shoots, lunches, dinners, outdoor shoots, and parties to attend is almost endless. By the time he comes home, he is often too tired speak. He barely manages to shed his clothing before falling haphazardly into our bed.

    Even though he is working an unbelievable number of hours, the magic of our dream times continues. Every evening he takes me to new places that he has discovered during his day. One time we visited a nearby café and sampled such wonderfully fresh croissants and rich coffee sitting together at an outside table as if it were the brightest of mornings, with just the slightest hint of warm pink in the sky. The breeze was delicious and the light was everything I always heard Parisian light would be. Not exactly what anyone in the real world would experience in mid-January, but that's exactly what our dreams are for. Another time we talked for hours as the evening rain poured outside a fine Bistro. Apparently it can rain in dreams. The red wine offered by the waiter was beyond description, and the Beef was served with a sauce that was so light and enchanting that it brought tears to my eyes. As I dabbed and shook my head, a man playing violin nodded as if to say that my reaction was as perfect as the food itself. We have strolled by the Seine and walked through the galleries of the Louvre.

 Now that April has arrived the views we imagined have paled in comparison. The buds on the trees and sounds of the birds have restored some of the charm that the romantic in me missed when viewing the modern streets crowded with cars and heavily laden with signs and people. No matter how much the city has stepped into the twenty-first century, Paris is still Paris. The signature Eifel tower looms like a stage backdrop on steroids. There are songs and poetry that attempt to describe the light here and all I can say is how woefully short they all fall from the reality.

 Our nights run together like a continuous honeymoon, and Dalton could not be more mine if I were waiting for him all day. Of course, if I was really there, he would be way too tired and have almost no time for these wonderful hours we spend together and I would be like a prisoner in that apartment. It's such a blessing that his dreams allow us to go all out and yet his body and mine are getting their rest. While I have to admit that my impression of the place is based entirely on Dalton's perception, I still have little doubt how much smaller it would be if I had to live there all day. Dalton says that he can reach his arms out and practically touch the walls on either side of our living room.

The neighboring district includes Montmartre which climbs to the top of a large hill. At its summit is the amazing Sacre-Coeur basilica. We have walked the narrow cobbled streets as if the place belonged only to us. We have held hands and looked at the wares of the street artists and kissed outside the fabled Moulin-Rouge. Dalton takes pictures which only we can see and share. They go into an album that he keeps locked in his memory.

Outside the window, the late afternoon sun is just beginning to turn the clouds into a symphony of color. I time my arrival so that I appear to be sitting and waiting when he enters the dream. I take a seat in the kitchen which is visible to the doorway where he enters. I am wearing the simple black sheath dress that Dalton finds both sophisticated and sexy. Even though we meet in his dreams, Dalton has decided that this acting out of his arrival home helps the illusion that we are living a 'normal' life. It is a thin veneer, but I understand why he wants it this way.

When the door springs open, there is an excitement in his eyes that is surely the precursor of some important news. It does not take any gift of telepathy to figure out what the news might be. That first location gig, the mark of his ascendance has been granted.

"Where?" I ask without waiting for him to start.
"How do you know?"
"It's written all over you face. So where?"

"There's a new Latin American wave coming into fashion this year. Marcel wants me to do a whole Cole Porter – Night and Day thing – Latin style. We're going to Puerto Limon, Costa Rica. He wants me to make it raw and native; very steamy. He says that it is a new place for a shoot. He is sending a few girls who will be getting their first shot, so that we can all have fun and learn to do it together. He is sending an experienced set coordinator, to keep things moving, but I will have final say on all things as far as design is concerned."

"So when do you and Marcel plan to go?"

"Huh? Oh, when I said we, you thought I meant Marcel. I meant you and I. We are going to Costa Rica and the great thing is, in our dreams, it will only be as hot and sticky as we let it be."

Dalton is still standing in the doorway, and I rush to him and pull him inside, leaving the door open to appreciate the lovely Parisian skyline for as long as it takes our lips to find each other. A soft breeze picks lightly at the loose strands of my hair and the sound of someone playing a concertina is just close enough to be heard. When we finally come up for air there is no need for words, and so we go outside and sit together on the front steps. The evening lamps come on as if on cue which I guess you could say they did.

"When will you board the plane?" I ask as we sit quietly side by side.

"Marcel wants me to get down there in a couple of days. The shoot will begin as soon as the coordinator and I have mapped out all of the details." Dalton smiles with a look of contentment that has less to do with pride than with his honest desire to excel at his craft. I love the way he commits to things and how little his newfound success impresses him.

We celebrate at a nightclub that features dinner and dancing. After the meal, we move to the dance floor to a pounding electric beat. The bodies of the others surrounding us are furnished by a recent memory, and make the evening so real and so heavenly. There are colored lights and the sounds of shouted conversations jostle us like the currents of an approaching thunderstorm.

"I can't get enough of you," he says while we are dancing. His voice is soft and whispered into my ear as we finally move to a slow song. "Every moment during the day when I am working, there is so much to do, and sometimes I feel so maxed out, but even at those times I know you're not there. All day long it's like I am starving for oxygen. Do you know what I mean?"

His look is one of such longing and need, that it is physically painful to me.

"It's not the sex," he continues. "You know that part is wonderful. Even on nights when the things we do together seem to happen so quickly and the morning comes before I am ready, even on nights when every detail is everything I could hope for, the day begins and there are so many hours until I can be with you again. I know that this life is not so different than people who live in real time. If you were here during the day, would I see you even as much as I do now? Probably not, but it is the details that are killing me. That plane ride alone that you should be with me to enjoy. So many little things…"

I pull him as close as I can, trying to make up for his sense of longing with my sheer physical closeness. His arms wrap around me with an almost desperate intensity and the sweetness of touch counters the sadness; counters it but does not relieve it.

"Nothing would make me happier than to be with you every second of every day, though you would probably tire of my company much sooner that way." My joke falls flatter than the dance floor we are gliding over.

"I cannot be everything you would like. I can give you this much and little more. We have had so many good times and so many conversations. You have all of my love and you have that in a way that maybe no other man has ever had love. You know beyond words how I feel. If I could give you more, you wouldn't need to ask."

"I know, I know," He responds and his eyes draw me in now as tightly as his arms just did. "I am not ungrateful. I am so fortunate, and if there is anything approaching perfection in life, this is already pretty damn near it."

Instantly the dance floor dissolves and we find ourselves casually sitting on the front step. The rest of the night's dream is spent hand in hand with the early evening sky making an encore performance. Dalton has taken the lead on this. We talk and talk about the years that have led us to this place and this time. My body longs for the intimacy of our coupling, but for tonight, my head resting on his shoulder, I am satisfied as this is all the contact he needs.

23.

Dalton: My life is a dream, and yet…

How time flies. A little less than a year ago I was boarding a plane for my new life; and now look at me. Marcel said we'd have fun and he certainly has been true to his word. The lifestyle is everything Amanda Purcell promised. I have shared a meal with so many interesting people. Great food and interesting conversation seem to be a constant part of my life. The travel has been amazing and I'd be lying if I said that I haven't learned to enjoy the attention and the recognition. Certainly there are downsides to the minor form of celebrity status that I've achieved, but all in all it's been a blast.

The phone calls from Dad and Sherry are a pleasant link to the day to day life that I have left a continent away. Once he got over the surprise that I am making so much money in such a glamorous profession, Dad tried to remind me to keep my options open as anything that happens so easily might just as easily be gone. He doesn't fool me though. Sherry told me last week how he goes around to all of his friends bragging on his now famous son. The best part though is the conversations we have together, all three of us. We have become more than friends, we've become a family. I think about how pleased Mom would have been to see the man that Dad has become.

Looking out at the Paris skyline, I can see the first hopeful buds on the trees. The March air is sharp but showing a shy, early inclination towards warmth. People are roaming the streets in optimistically light jackets. A few hardy souls are even sitting around tables at the outdoor cafes. The color and the movement form a kaleidoscopic mosaic that would normally have me running for my camera, but today I am content just to watch everything from the balcony of my new apartment. It is located in the seventh arrondissement, nearer to the Eiffel Tower. It is the so-called upper class district and it fits my new lifestyle. I have a closet full of nice clothes, a special fridge stocked with a few nice bottles of wine and a sporty little Lexus in the garage. Still, Sienna never lets me get too full of myself, reminding me that all this stuff, and all the money, and even the people are not as important as staying true to the work, and the person who makes the work possible. She's right, but I don't see any harm in enjoying a few tokens of success.

  Airports and Hotels have become my second home. First class seats and incredible suites make my time away from the apartment very comfortable. Still, there have been more than a few times when I've felt lonely. In the beginning, the feeling of jumping into the air on a huge jet was so exciting; I couldn't even consider going to sleep. Looking at the clouds from above with their varied snowy patterns, seeing the endless variety of landforms or ocean views kept me watching for each new sight. Just recently, I thought of a way to make the flights better. I realized that if I allowed myself to fall asleep on the flight, then Sienna could be on the plane seated next to me. Sometimes it's hard when I wake up and realize that she isn't really there, but mostly it has made travelling better.

I have worked in a variety of locations all over the world. I have already visited islands that seem to glow with an Eden-like perfection. European streets have stood with their old world grandeur just waiting for the chance to fill my lens. It hardly seems necessary to mention the models, certainly some of the most beautiful men and women God has ever imagined. My sense of light and shadow continues to be my calling card, and I have found some new subtle ways to make the work mine. It is a life most people can only imagine or dream of. For me though, there are still some drawbacks. With everything that I have to be thankful for, it almost feels criminal to raise any complaint, but there are things in even the most amazing life that can be challenges, I guess.

It wasn't very far into my first shoot in Costa Rica that the difficult part of my new life made itself known to me. Her name was Raschelle. She was tall, brunette and as beautiful as any woman I had yet met. Just about the first minute that she started posing, it was clear that she found me attractive. At first I tried to dismiss it as her doing a little extra for the camera. The other women were smiling and making love to the camera as well, but Raschelle was different. When I tried to pretend that it was all in my mind, she decided to make things clear. During one of the breaks, she strode right up to me, kissed me forcefully on the mouth and whispered a few things she thought we might try. I know, I know, sounds like a wonderful situation, what could possibly be the problem?

First of all, there was the business side of things. Marcel had made it clear that what I did on location was my own concern, but to be careful about involvements with the models because it only took one bad situation that ended up in the press to do a number on the shooter's career and the model's career as well. He said that most of the girls understood what was at stake, but he repeated his caution.

The more difficult part of the problem was Sienna of course. Being as attuned to me as she is, it took her almost no time at all to sense what had happened. The fact that I had put the girl off with a story about a long distance relationship didn't faze Sienna at all.

"She didn't buy your story, you know. She will be coming at you twice as hard tomorrow. Maybe you should take her up on the offer."

"How do you know that? I asked, trying to ignore that last comment.

"Put it down to woman's intuition." Sienna looked at me square in the eyes. There was no hint of jealousy, hurt or anger. She could have won at professional poker with that expression.

"Is that who you think I am that I would want that? I love you."

In that moment inside our dream space Sienna kept the look pointed at me like a blue hot laser. The truth is that I am flesh and blood and male and I didn't want to have to apologize for either fact. Raschelle was gorgeous and her offer was powerful enough to melt steel. I did the best I could to fend off that first advance, but the worrisome part was that this was just the first instance of a battle I would be forced to fight again and again. Worse yet, from that first time, I learned something unbelievable. When a woman has her heart set on something, the idea of playing fair goes right out the window. I found that out the very next day. The other girls seemed to know what was going on, because they couldn't help but giggle every time a new wardrobe mishap took place for the suddenly clothing afflicted Raschelle. Somehow the tie on a bikini top suddenly came undone. Or there was the wind that blew her skirt to reveal the inconceivably forgotten undergarment. Each time something happened she looked at me with a hard to describe mixture of innocence and challenge. When that day's shoot was over, she invited me to have a drink with her, and I accepted, hoping to reach an understanding.

"I think we could have a lot of fun," Raschelle purred, as we sat together sipping our frosty Piña coladas with the pieces of grapefruit and their charming little paper umbrellas. She was dressed with the slightest edge of the provocative. Her floral blouse was all pinks and violets revealing just the smallest amount of smooth cleavage. Her cream colored skirt hugged her hips and ended just above the knee where her incredibly tanned and toned legs moved southward to a simple gold ankle bracelet and expensive leather sandals. Her subtle, sexy scent was angling toward me purposefully; on a mission. She smiled directly as awaited my reply.

"There's someone in my life," I replied quietly, keeping my eyes on my drink.

"I don't want to own you, or ruin anything. She or he would never have to know."

"Whoever it is, I would know I cheated and that's enough."

"Dalton, one look at me will tell you that I can have pretty much any guy I want, so if your no is a true "no", I won't even be thinking about it once I walk away. I will tell you that no matter what your voice is telling me, your eyes are saying something a little different, which is the only reason I haven't already left." She brought her hand to my face and gently nudged my gaze to meet hers. "I can do things with this body that you will remember for a very long time."

I held her eye contact steadily and used my hand to bring her hand to my lips for a light kiss.

"Okay," she replied and stood up and walked away. It was impossible to ignore the message in her body's movement as she left.

This was only one of the three ways that this scenario played out. Girl finds me attractive, girl makes her play, I put her off as gently as possible and no harm done. I call this one the soft sell. Not all of the girls that I encounter are models and not all of the plays go this easily. A few of the girls are more insistent and they are all gorgeous. In these cases, they would do everything they could to get my attention. When that failed they would punish me by disrupting the shoot to make me and everyone else miserable. This one I call the hard sell with a vengeance. Finally, there are girls who just can't take no for an answer. They're so intent on the conquest that they begin telling everyone that it has happened between us when it hasn't. I call this one fantasy land. In the past eight months since I started doing these assignments, each of these situations has occurred at least once and the soft sell more than that.

I don't know what Sienna thinks about these encounters. She seems neither grateful for my loyalty nor upset by the constant attention. I have tried to get her to talk about it, but she gets that look again, and that pretty much ends the discussion. I yell that it isn't my fault and she responds with a very quiet smile and a few words that say she knows this is true. There are times I think she is pulling away from me, but then we're alone in the dark and her words and her touch are just as powerful and just as real as ever.

The trouble is that I have begun to look at the future and wonder how all of this can possibly continue. I think of the things we can never do. I think of the parties with friends we can never have; the announcement of the engagement with a diamond ring, and the excitement that Sienna would feel as she shares the news with friends. There is the intricate planning of a wedding and the purchase of the perfect gown. Certainly, we could create a dream version of the wedding ceremony with Dad and Sherry and everyone. There could be a honeymoon taking place in some lovely, now familiar exotic location. Neither of us is willing to even consider such an elaborate lie. Then there is the day to day life. The common things like shopping and groceries and arguments and making up that seem so unlikely in our current situation. I wonder whether she or I are prepared to live a life without children. I can tell that Sienna is just as troubled as I am by all of these thoughts.

In our dream place, all of these things are possible, even having children. There is nothing different in the magic I used as a child to make the nighttime into day than there is to make a whole series of events happen, and we would both remember them as if they had happened. But just as I told Raschelle that I would know cheating regardless if the other party never did, I recognize this for the same kind of cheating. It is a delusion. Maybe even a dangerous one. None of my friends or family would ever share in any of this. From my father's perspective, his son would be a single, lonely man. I don't want to let go, and neither does she, but we are both conflicted about the future. I know now what Sienna meant when she said that maybe I should accept Raschelle's offer. She was offering us a convenient way to end this; a little painful, but in the long run, perhaps more healthy. She didn't mean it then and she doesn't now, but the thinking goes on.

In a novel, as I look to the skyline, I should see the approach of dark warning clouds that speak of impending trials. In this reality, the sky is clear and cloudless and the Parisian sunshine is warming my face.

There is one more part to this that I feel guilty about. As powerful and real as all of my feelings towards Sienna are, there is still a small voice that keeps telling me that the whole thing is my imagination. Waking up every morning is when that voice is the loudest. Night after night we make love and give ourselves to each other so completely. It is the stuff of fantasy. It is what any loving couple would wish for. That moment of release is so intense and joyful and pleasurable that it is almost beyond life. We are so in sync and so connected and the fire is quenched in exactly the right way. There are now flights together and tours of the many locations where I am shooting. The problem is that these experiences are all in my mind. They happen and they make me happy, but I am still flesh and blood. In the morning, my body reminds me that whatever I dreamed about had nothing to do with my physical self. There are needs that must be met and there is no Sienna to help me with them. It is not a large price, but it is there. I can't decide if the small voice has honest concern for my sanity, or is just trying to push me like a little cartoon devil on my shoulder to do something that will satisfy my physical itch. It is Sunday and I am between assignments for a couple of days. Tomorrow I will go into the studio and meet with Marcel to discuss the last trip, do some editing and look over the plans for upcoming assignments. Today I am going to find some new place that Sienna and I can visit in my dreams. I will play the travel agent again and look for something that allows us to keep my imagination alive. I will take pictures and experience it all myself so we can relive it together. For now, it is all I know how to do.

24.

Fashion, detection and conversation

February in New York has been a rainy affair and today has proven no exception. This night however, such dreary and mundane conditions are completely impermissible. Tonight is for the stars. The clouds have parted like curtains in a theater or the sliding drapes of a dressing room. Points of light in the sky flicker on the breath of passing breezes. Streetlamps and lit windows reflect off the wet, black road surface and shine like makeshift galaxies. Intermittent lowercase lightning bolts, the reckless evidence of media-based assassins, stab the air and bounce off the droplets of water sliding down the sides of long black cars. Each one parades in turn, depositing its passengers in their glowing finery. The next one, a Limousine carrying a fashion mogul just arrived from Paris, pulls up to the Hotel Excalibur in Manhattan. The paparazzi resume their efforts to turn the night into a fireworks-like cascade of light. The nearest photographer scans the face of the first person to emerge from the car as the door opens. It's a handsome face with thick, stylish dark brown hair. He takes just one more look as the young man stands to his full height. 'A good looking guy,' the photographer thinks, "shame he's a nobody.' Dalton Hunter senses the man's lack of regard and smiles as the man's eyes widen when Marcel Arden and Melisande, the latest blonde Amazonian supermodel follow close behind. Dalton is wearing a simple tailored tux in sharp contrast to the Elton John flashiness that Marcel is sporting. It is the night of the closing festivities for New York Fashion Week. In seconds the other paparazzi close in.

"Marcel! Melisande! Turn here! Look this way!" They scream and call; gull-like and just as annoying, just as relentless.

The pair turns and poses, displaying the requisite red carpet smiles. Dalton walks ahead. He shouts over his shoulder. The other men with the cameras look him over briefly and not finding anyone recognizable, ignore him as unimportant.

"Marcel, I'll see you inside," he calls over his shoulder, just as happy not to be in the sights of his distant cousins in the press.

Marcel makes a quick break from the barrage of attention to reply before turning the manufactured smile back to the throng. "Run along now Dalton, but you'll have your turn soon enough."

Dalton doubts that he will ever be that recognizable. In the time it takes to walk from the car to the hotel lobby, fleeting images of the last few moments in Paris with Sienna, boarding the plane for New York and sharing the flight with her play in his mind like a familiar slideshow. He flashes forward to the arrivals gate and the ride to the hotel alone. There was time for a quick call to Dad and Sherry and another to Skip before he lay down for a quick nap so that Sienna could welcome him back to the states properly. His new life in France awaits his return, but his old life, or as much as this night could in any way mimic his old life, seems strangely comfortable. He shakes his head to clear it, knowing that Marcel will expect him to be focused and ready for anything.

Sardines in a can are afforded more room than those guests filling the hotel lobby hoping for a glimpse of a star or model. Dalton parts this sea and makes his way through the throng toward the Ballroom. They let him go making the same mistake as the professionals outside. The star of the night is passing untouched before them. Tomorrow they will all swear they saw him. There are a series of doorways leading into the ballroom. On either end heavy mahogany doors remain closed, with a single central set that are open with a guard allowing only the most privileged to enter. Dalton presents his credentials to the man who masks his surprise quickly and allows the newcomer to go through.

Small clusters of the fashion elite stand near the still virgin table settings with their napkins primly folded and their florals freshly arranged and untouched. Chandeliers spread a cultured glow over the scene. Dalton's easy gait comes to a complete astounded end as he enters the hall. His stop is so sudden that a few of the close onlookers can hardly help but notice. A couple of those follow his gaze to the posters and make a calculated connection between the man and his work. Half a dozen oversized posters seven feet tall hang from the ceiling, three on each side of the cavernous room. Each one of them displaying Dalton's latest model poses. His signature lighting and mood are obvious.

Regaining his poise, he continues making his way inside just as the remaining doors are opened and the balance of the attendees flood in. The damage is done in a matter of seconds. Whispers make their way through the now growing crowd; electric current in search of a spotlight. The celebrities, the near-celebrities, and the models are gathered in groups with newly acquired flutes of Champagne being distributed by the formally dressed and highly efficient wait staff. More and more, heads are turned up, captivated by the images. While Dalton is taking it all in, he is tapped on the back.

"You like?" Marcel oozes charm and a little extra of his latest signature cologne.

"It is unbelievable Marcel, I'm...I'm speechless."

"You deserve it, my friend," Marcel replies, enjoying his young protégé's amazement. "You have worked hard and the results are beyond amazing. I promise you, before the night is over, people will not only know your name, they'll be telling everyone that it was they who discovered you."

"Marcel, I will never forget this. It truly is the most generous thing I have ever seen."

Marcel responds, completely straight faced.

"There's only one thing that I wish."

"What's that?" Dalton asks, a look of concern crossing his face.

"I'd be a lot happier if you were gay." Marcel finds his own humor uproariously funny and Dalton allows his friend a minute to enjoy himself.

"Marcel, for as much as you have in your life, I am happy to say that even you can't have everything."

"Come with me for a second." An all-business expression has returned and Dalton is more than happy to follow.

Marcel leads Dalton to a group standing near one of his pictures.

Dalton, I'd like to introduce you to Michael Kors and Tim Gunn of 'Project Runway'. Michael, where's Heidi?"

Dalton answers with a polite "It's nice to meet you." At the same time Michael leans over and answers Marcel confidentially which elicits a booming laugh from Marcel.

"By the way Michael, Tim; the pictures you are trying so hard not to admire were done by my friend Dalton here. He is the next big thing. If you were at all smart, you'd find a way to feature him in that show of yours."

"Try not to embarrass me any more than absolutely necessary, will you?" Dalton says with a quick jab at Marcel's ribs.

"Your work is exceptional," Tim Gunn says sincerely. Michael Kors nods his agreement as he sips his champagne and looks around.

"Thanks, that means a lot coming from the two of you." Dalton is beginning to feel a bit uncomfortable at the attention and Marcel is kind enough to notice.

"All right, enough! Go find something to play with."

Dalton nods and moves on. His thoughts turn to Sienna. The festivities are yet another reminder of the real life that has eluded them for the past two years. He catches up to a tall gowned waiter making her way through the crowd serving more chilled champagne. Dalton grabs a flute and takes a sip.

The news of who is responsible for the pictures has made its way around the ballroom. People are pulling out their cell phones to Google the new name. A short distance away from this new star, a young woman with blonde hair is intrigued by the handsome newcomer. She pulls her blackberry and contacts a friend. Dalton makes his way to a buffet situated along a far wall and carelessly piles a few things on a plate. A short distance away is another array of tables; mostly empty. An older gentleman is seated by himself. He has a careless, disheveled look with a smile to match. Dalton decides this will be a secure spot to eat and perhaps the perfect companion to help him hide away from the attention and the stares. He could have chosen an empty table, but thinks that there might be some safety in numbers.

"Hi, mind if I join you?" he asks cautiously.

"Not at all, make yourself comfortable. Are you the one everybody is talking about?" The man seems at ease and accommodating.

"I guess so, my pictures are hanging there." Dalton gestures to indicate his posters.

"They're very good, you have talent. You're with Marcel?

"Yes," Dalton answers as he relaxes. A friendly conversation ensues as the two men get to know each other.

Meanwhile, the blonde with the Blackberry ends her call and loads a plate of her own. She comes back and finds a seat within visual range of Dalton, appraising him with studied intention. She takes a bite absently when her ring tone goes off.

"So, what did you find out? Uh huh, very interesting. He's working for Marcel? Well, I will tell you one thing, I haven't seen this kind of buzz for a while. And there's something else. He's not only really good, he's absolutely delicious."

Dalton is unaware of the attention the blonde has directed toward him, but the stranger seems to have noticed. He watches the woman for a few minutes before turning back to the conversation. He wonders if her interest is based on the young man's apparent good looks, or if she has more in mind. There is something about her that brings to mind something sleek and dark with fins and long sharp teeth.

"You're fairly new to the business, aren't you? I mean, I don't think I've seen you at one of these before."

Dalton is surprised by how relaxed he is with this man. It is almost as if they share some secret.

"I've been working assignments for Marcel Arden, mostly location shoots and some stuff at his studio."

The stranger hesitates before continuing. It is rare to come across someone so open and genuine at one of these gatherings. He catches a glimpse of his own younger self and speaks when he feels his assessment is correct.

"You seem like a nice enough guy…"

"How can you tell?"

"Just about every person here would love to be getting the attention you are getting tonight. They'd be preening for all the cameras, but you, you're different. You really don't care. You're just as happy to avoid the spotlight, sharing this lavish meal with an old geezer like me. Mind if I give you some advice?"

"Well, I don't know about the geezer part," Dalton responded with a smile," but you're right, I'm not a big fan of the spotlight. As for the advice, there's never any harm in listening."

The predatory blonde is still feasting on Dalton as heartily as she is on her saucy Chicken dish. Her fork attacks the food in one hand while she balances the phone in the other.

"He could be just what I am looking for. How about our other project, any progress there? Fine, keep me informed. Yes, I meant what I said, when you have the items we're talking about, we can discuss your role in the project. Great, get to it then and we'll talk soon."

The blonde ends the call and enjoys one last satisfying visual nibble of the good looking guy across from her before rising and grabbing her expensive purse. It has not escaped her attention that while she has been checking out the younger man, the older one has been observing her and not in a particularly friendly way. She flashes him a smile that shows her total disregard for his opinion and begins to make her way through the crowd. Just for fun she adds a little extra spice to the rhythm of her hips just as a taunt. The stranger is completely unimpressed. His gaze returns to this interesting young man and offers his thoughts.

"For what it's worth, most of the people in this business are very talented and they're good people. It is easy to get caught up in the glamour, but at the end of the day, it's mostly about making a living, doing quality work, and living a particular lifestyle."

"So far, it sounds pretty good." Dalton senses that this man has had his share of the glamour and the work.

"All in all it is. The tricky part is not getting too caught up in the star shine. Personalities will clash and so will ambitions. Some of these folks will squeeze you dry, and toss you when they've used you up. From what I hear, Marcel is not like that, but I guarantee that if you lose your edge, even he won't have much patience. The key is you. You can't go wrong if you stick with who you are. It sounds trite. The truth often does. Well, I'm off," he says as he gets up and grabs a camera bag from a hidden spot behind his chair. Dalton wonders if he should know this man.

"What's your name, sir?"

"No names please; it's not important. Just remember what I said."

Dalton stands to say goodbye. "I will and I really appreciate the advice. I mean it. He looks down to work on his dinner and when he looks back up the stranger is gone.

25.

Fishing in the Big Apple

Samantha Choice grabs a hand towel to wipe the mist from the mirror and opens the bathroom door to let the fog cloud of steam escape. Violet is waiting in the bedroom somewhere, ready to do her hair and makeup, but she can wait. She will wait, Samantha thinks, that's what I pay her to do. As the mirror clears, she allows herself the pleasure of examining her reflection. Her blue eyes meet themselves and then travel down over her full, high, but not overly sharp cheekbones. Her nostrils flare briefly as her vision continues southward. Her tongue appears briefly as she flicks over her slightly parted, shapely lips. She wonders if other beautiful women get as much sheer enjoyment out of looking at themselves as she does. She checks the door to see whether Violet is in sight, and when she finds no sign, she allows her bath towel to drop away slowly.

'God, I am at my absolute peak,' she thinks. She wonders whether at this moment, this very second, she might not be about as perfect as she is ever likely to be. This is not the first time this particular thought has come to her, but it always erases any memory of the time before, so it seems completely original right now. She reaches down to retrieve the towel from the cool, white marble floor. Even the reflection of her legs, hips and breasts in the shiny surface fills her with delight. She continues caressing herself as she dries the few remaining droplets, slowly finding her way back to upright. Reaching for the light caramel colored, silk panties hanging nearby, she closes her eyes so that she can focus on the feel of them as they pass her ankles and knees and eventually caress her thighs. It seems almost a shame to wrap her two best friends in the matching, luxuriant brassiere, lovely though it is, but it is time for work and there are sacrifices that must be made. Still, when she thinks about the low cut, scoop neck blouse that she has chosen for today's activities, it seems like a small enough price to pay. There will still be plenty on display regardless of the lavish, designer undergarments. She smiles at herself and just manages to push away the impulse to blow a kiss, and it is a good thing. Violet has just stationed herself by the door and is wearing a look that indicates that she might have witnessed a bit of this self-indulgence not only today but more than once before.

"Come on Violet, let's get to work." Samantha gets a quick burst of pleasure as she sees the effort her almost former employee makes to undo the momentary lapse of discretion and replace it with a more suitable neutral expression. It would never do to have to find someone with all of Violet's particular talents just when she is starting her most important projects; the one personal and the other one professional.

Closing her eyes again, Samantha wraps herself in the peripheral sensations of first the hot iron, then the soft brush working their magic. Vi will assure that each and every luscious strand has its own place in the waterfall of her tresses. When the last stroke has completed, Sam opens her eyes briefly to inspect the results. Satisfied, she gives a barely noticeable nod and the work transitions to completing the perfection of her face. Her skin is nearly flawless, but that doesn't mean she should settle for 'nearly'. Finally, all preparations completed, she slides into her finery and excuses Violet as she makes her way out of her room.

    The cab ride is the lone time of the day when there is peace. Gently sipping the iced latte that is the next task on Violet's daily list, Samantha lets the cool fluid complete her awakening. Occasionally, Samantha will allow the vibrating colors and churning outside sounds to penetrate her yellow cocoon. Today there is a need for quiet. Not one for meditation or reflective thought, Samantha happily clears her mind of everything and enjoys the complete silence.

    Upon arrival, she sweeps from the street, through the doors, and into the offices of Choice Publications, Incorporated. Her soft peach suit jacket with the metallic gold buttons is opened to reveal the cream colored top with the heavenly neckline. Her skin, February tanned at the finest salon makes a perfect backdrop for the string of opulent pearls that end in a large pearl enhancer. Her skirt is fashionable though business length; not quite as much leg showing as she would prefer. Approaching the glass doors, her reflection confirms Violet's influence, as not one hair is out of place and her make-up is stunning.

    A handful of forceful, athletic strides and she is inside the elevator. She ignores the piercing glances of the two executives standing to each side and catches her breath while remembering the juicy young man at the other night's New York Fashion Week Banquet. Finally, the elevator stops and she winks at the older of the two men and departs. Her arrival creates a flurry of activity, most of it the result of her underlings fleeing for safe cover. Still, as she moves through the floor, two male observers trade appreciative stares. She lets them have their visual fill of her, having little interest in small men. Her lack of interest only spurs their feeble imaginings.

"Mmmm, Samantha Choice," says admirer number one, an account executive whose desk is as small as his hope for advancement.

"Oh yeah, she's choice all right." Admirer number two is a friend from marketing who has just stopped by to trade a few factually strained adventures from the past weekend over a cup of coffee. He was in the middle of one such tale when the sight of Miss Choice stopped them both mid-sentence.

"There's just one problem," number two continued.

"Oh yeah, what would that be?" Number one asks as he watches with fascination the receding view of the gorgeous woman.

"That choice could get you fired at the very least, and twisted in some very painful knots at the worst." The idea of being twisted in knots by the likes of her is something number two might not be completely opposed to regardless of his expressed opinion.

"I'm sure you're right, but still…" Number one looks once more, but she has already disappeared amidst the flurry of executives looking for a way to appear incredibly busy. They both look for that one last sight before shrugging and getting back to work. Tall tales would have to continue at some later time. With the beehive disrupted, their morning conversation is just a bit too obvious.

Samantha passes her secretary on the way to her father's office. The girl is loaded down with sketches and papers, and looks frazzled already though the clock has yet to reach nine am.

"Ms. Choice, I have the designs for the Bombay layout."

Samantha waves her flustered admin away and continues without slowing at all.

"Later Jasmine dear, right now I have to see Daddy."

The secretary recognizes the tone and peels off without a word. Samantha makes her way to her father's office, brushing off his secretary's attempt to announce her. The young woman makes a token effort to keep the Boss's daughter from going through unannounced, but gives up without too much fuss. She touches the buzzer that lets him know that someone is coming in, and it serves its purpose as he has just enough time to close out the sports website with the previous night's hoops scores that he has been examining.

Tony Choice wears a bemused expression as his daughter barges in. He rises from his desk to meet her. His office is a paneled affair with a large portrait of himself exuding sincerity. There are no windows and the light is subdued. Tony is a powerfully built man, not quite as wide as a wrestler or muscular as a body builder, but imposing nonetheless. Samantha gets her piercing blue eyes from her father. His face is smooth, but not soft. In fact there is nothing soft about him. In contrast to the somewhat generous rendering that includes a kind-hearted smile, Tony's normal expression stays in a narrow range between a challenging scowl and a more dangerous angry glare. Occasionally, he finds a smile when his daughter comes in with news that includes some financial gain. That smile is not to be seen at the moment.

"Sam, I've asked you before to let Tracy buzz me before you come in. I could be doing something important…"

Samantha is not fazed by her father's bluster. "Dad, this couldn't wait. Besides, if Tracy is at her desk, she can hardly be in here taking dictation, can she?"

Tony shakes his head and does his best to ignore the implied meaning, but his reaction shows that his daughter has struck a bit close to home. His sarcasm is a weak defense.

"Fine! So what earth shattering news do you have for me this week? Did the fashion Gods decree that skirt lengths are going back to twelve inches above the knee again?"

Samantha is used to her father's bluster, and pays it little attention. She makes a mental note to bring up Tracy in the future whenever an argument is not going well.

"I found him Dad. This is the guy that is going to turn *Fashion Expose* into the leading publication in its market. Dalton Hunter is the best photographer I have ever seen and we need him working for us right now."

"Who is Dalton Hunter?" Tony's change in tone is dramatic. His ability to turn on a dime, especially when losing an argument is one of the foundations of his success.

"Who is Dalton Hunter? Dad, you should have seen this guy's work at the banquet Saturday night. It was indescribable; dark, moody and yet comforting and enticing all at once. Dad, there were these posters, huge posters, hanging around the ballroom. They were all his. As soon as people saw them, the buzz was like nothing I've ever seen. His name went around the place like wildfire."

Tony Choice knows his daughter enough to know that her raptures are not solely based on this guy's talent. He takes a seat at his desk to assess her more carefully.

"So your interest in this guy is purely professional, right?"

Samantha groans and takes a seat in front of her father's desk. Just thinking about Dalton sends a thrill through her body. Her tone changes almost as quickly as her father's mood, going suddenly girlish.

"Daddy, if you must know, the guy was absolutely gorgeous. I have a few things in mind for him…and me."

Tony chuckles. "Fine, fine, you know what you're doing; well usually at least. Just make sure he's worth it."

"Actually, that's the reason I came in to see you." Samantha sits a little straighter in her chair and prepares for the real discussion. Wrapping Daddy around her little finger is a piece of cake for anything but this.

"That sounds ominous. We're talking dollars now, are we?"

"I'm going to have to go beyond budget a little for this one, she answers carefully. She meets her father's gaze blue eyes to blue eyes.

"How much beyond budget?" he asks with a suspicious tone.

"The offer has to be at least One-Twenty."

"As in a hundred and twenty… thousand? Have you lost your…"

Just as quickly as Tony's calm had returned, discussion of a salary in this neighborhood destroys it.

"Dad, dad, I'm telling you, this guy is the fashion equivalent of Stieglitz or Ansel Adams. He's stellar. Besides, he's getting six figures from Marcel, so it has to be a little bit more than just my obvious charms to snare him."

"Fine, but One-Twenty?" Tony has no idea who the people his daughter has named are, so he focuses on the negotiations. After all, he can't be expected to know the names of all her employees, can he?

"Look if things go the way I hope they will, and you know how rarely things don't go…"

"Right," Tony nodded, acknowledging that his daughter's track record has earned her a bit of latitude.

"You could think of it as an early wedding present."

Tony Choice loves his daughter almost as much as he loves Choice Publications, Incorporated. If he could get her married, perhaps she would calm down just a bit. He does the mental calculation in a tenth of a second and it is decided.

"I'll sign off, but I want to see a huge damn sparkling rock on your finger within three months. It had better be huge since I will essentially be buying it." His smile returns at the thought of his daughter in a white dress.

"You'll see." Samantha rises with a twinkle in her eyes. She basks in the feeling of winning a money argument with her father. She rises and starts to leave.

"Oh Sam, tell me one more thing."

"Anything, oh loving father." Her expression becomes wary as she faces him awaiting whatever is to come.

"How are you doing with our other project?" Samantha relaxes as she realizes she has won completely.

"*My* Project is moving ahead just fine. I will let you know as soon as the pieces are in place."

Samantha leaves with a catlike grin. It is a grin that has enchanted Tony Choice since Sam was about six. He shakes his head and touches the intercom.

"Tracy, could you come in and bring your steno pad?"

Samantha stifles a laugh as she passes Tracy and sees the girl pulling a steno pad from her desk drawer. She doubts there will be any more written on those pages when the girl returns than there is now. Heading back to her office, her gait is relaxed and her attitude contented. It is a plush, spacious place, which she insisted when it was being designed have exactly one more square foot than her father's. Of course, she had to be dependent on the designer to assure that her demand was met as she has no idea how anyone would calculate square footage in the first place. She lands in her chair and waves Jasmine away as the secretary drops the stack of designs she was carrying earlier on a nearby table. It is a brighter room than Tony's with a large expanse of windows looking out onto downtown Manhattan. She picks up the phone and dials a number, humming to herself as she looks out the window.

Jasmine Orza has seen the way people come and go working for Samantha Choice. She has kept her job by working long hours and creating the impression with her boss of being irreplaceable. That all works, she knows, until the first time some item is forgotten; some deadline is missed. When she started, she thought about listening in to her boss's phone conversations but didn't know how it might be done. Still, she decided, there must be a way that I can keep up with what is going on that won't get me fired. The answer came to her when she was watching an old spy movie on cable. The hero had all kinds of electronic things that he could use for listening in on conversations. If I had some kind of bug close to Samantha's phone, she thought, I could keep up with her plans and look almost telepathic in the process. Of course, there was still the question of where she might obtain such an item and how to make it work, and there was the further difficulty that electronic stuff was almost a complete mystery to her. Anything more complicated than plugging something in to an electrical outlet is pretty much beyond her. She finally remembered her neighbor Steve, who was some kind of network guy, whatever that is, down at the cable company. He was single and kind of geeky, but Jasmine figured he might be useful for what she had in mind.

  He was easily persuaded to purchase what was needed and he installed it within a few minutes one rainy Saturday. Jasmine wasn't sure that he did it right; she could only hear Samantha's side of the conversation. Still it was better than nothing. His work and a promise to forget everything had come at a rather steep price, but he was sweet in a puppy dog kind of way and so grateful for that one time that he wasn't at all surprised when she told him that there would not be a second.

The fact that her boss had rushed first to Tony's office and then back to her own was quite telling. It was just for this kind of event that her little gadget came in so handy. She opened a desk drawer and flicked the switch. It was wired to her desktop and allowed her to listen in with a set of earphones. She used these same earphones for listening to music occasionally, so there was nothing very strange or noticeable about it. She smiled as Samantha's voice could be heard so clearly.

"Hi, it's me. Hang on a sec; I want you to check something out for me. You know one of Marcel's little friends, don't you? Can you get in touch with them and find out where his new star goes for lunch? And yes, I do think that you know everybody."

Jasmine listens and takes notes as the silence indicates that whoever her boss is talking to is now responding. It's obvious who Marcel is and the new star probably refers to the photographer who made such a big splash at New York Fashion Week. It isn't long before her boss's voice is heard once more.

"Yes, that's the one. I need to know where he will be eating today. I'm planning an ambush. No, not that kind of ambush; don't be evil."

Jasmine can almost hear the laughter at the other end of the line, the pause is that brief.

"I have a strong feeling about this one. Of course, I've said that before, but this feels different. He's right and promising and just about as tasty a man as I have ever seen."

Interesting, the admin thought. She hadn't given much thought to Samantha as a woman. When she did think of her at all, the description usually started with a capitalized letter 'B'. To think of her actively considering some guy was a completely new concept. Jasmine had to shake herself for fear of losing the direction of the conversation.

"Are you jealous?"

Jasmine wonders who could possibly be on the other end of the line.

"Good, you needn't be. This is the show horse. He's the Ben in my Bennifer, the Donald to my Ivana. Only in this case, I see to it that I am the one everyone is looking at. You know how I feel about the spotlight, there's no point in it unless it's pointing at me."

The silence lasts a bit longer this time, and Jasmine is beginning to wonder if the call was as important as she expected. Then it gets interesting.

"So, have you got our plan in place yet?"

'Finally!' Jasmine's pen is poised for what comes next.

"Good, good. I agree; this would be a perfect time to finalize our agreement. Here's what I am prepared to offer. The title would be VP in charge of design with a salary of Two Fifty, all the standard benefits, with stock options and bonuses to accrue after year three."

Jackpot, the admin decided. Outwardly she is still quietly taking notes; inside she is doing a dance not likely to be approved by the folks back home.

"What do you mean it's not enough?"

The pen stops in mid stroke. Who is this person, she wonders for a second time.

"Oh, for a minute I thought you were looking for more dollars. What kind of additional benefits did you have in mind?"

The next response brings a wicked laugh.

"Somehow I had no idea that you were so naughty. I tell you what. You get me the info I need today, and let me know when our project will be ready. While you're doing that, I will consider your proposal. What do you mean, the first part's done? So you IM'd your contact and he got back with an answer? Your efficiency could be an enticement. Give me the details."

Jasmine can practically see Samantha picking up her blackberry and typing in some info.

"Greenwich Village, how quaint? Dom's Deli around twelve? Intersection of Bank and Bleeker streets; I've got it. Listen babe, it's been delightful, and I promise to give you an answer to your…idea, soon. I take it that the rest of the package is satisfactory?"

Jasmine can feel that the conversation is winding down. She will have to start trying to figure out who the person on the other end of the call is as this looks to be important.

"Don't threaten; I said I would consider it." Samantha's voice is razor edged now. She gets that from her father and has used it to put senior executives in their place.

"Right, I will talk to you soon. You know what still needs to be done," Samantha says with finality.

As the boss hangs up the phone, her admin hits the stop button on her bugging device and closes her desk drawer.

Samantha looks at the clock and does a mental calculation of how soon she will need to leave to start things rolling. She goes to the table with the designs and looks through them. "No, no this will never do," she says thinking out loud. "Jasmine dear, these are all wrong," she calls out in a voice that might be heard blocks away. Jasmine peeks in timidly.

"Come in precious, I'm not going to bite today. Get me the idiot who put this together. It's his head I'll be chomping on."

Jasmine takes away the offending documents and Samantha picks up another stack of papers, once more checking the clock.

26.

Baiting the hook in designer shoes

Dom's Deli does not look like much to Samantha as she approaches the place. Certainly it is not on a par with her normal lunchtime venues. Still, the large sidewalk is clean along the entire block of shops and restaurants, and the window is remarkably smudge-free. The deli is a couple of doors from the corner. Peering through the glass, she can see a counter stretching from the front on the left toward the back of the shop. The center of the shop has a few free standing racks and some shelving to separate the people ordering to-go sandwiches and lunch meats, from the booths and tables arranged for the sit-down trade.

    Sam checks her watch. It is five minutes to twelve and Dalton has yet to arrive. There is one booth left unoccupied and it is close enough to the front, second in line in fact. She decides to alter her plan to suit the situation, striding in right past the Please wait to be seated sign. She eases out of her coat and has a quick internal debate on whether to drop it on the seat or hang it on the less than pristine hook beside the chair. The hook option wins by a slim margin and Samantha takes a seat facing toward the entrance.

    The hostess notices the woman's arrival. Another pampered and entitled New Yorker is her appraisal. She shrugs as she decides that no harm is done.

    Samantha watches idly as the woman delivers a pair of table settings consisting of a fork and knife wrapped in a cheap paper napkin as well as a menu. She walks away without a word. Samantha sets her purse on the hard bench by her side and safely near the wall. 'At least the table is clean,' she thinks, just as Dalton appears. She trains her eyes on the menu before her, quickly making her selections from the limited options as her prey stands at the head of the sit-down row and surveys the area. His expression droops as he realizes no tables are available. Samantha continues looking down for another heartbeat, trying to appear inconspicuous. She times her smile perfectly to catch his attention.

"A bit crowded today, isn't it?" Her tone is innocent with just the slightest tint of suggestive invitation.

Of course, Samantha has no idea how crowded it normally gets.

"Promise me," she continues, "that you're not an axe murderer or a corporate lawyer, and I will be happy to share this booth."

Dalton is both surprised and pleased. Judging from the woman's expensive clothing, this is not a place she visits often. Still, she is very attractive, and he hates eating alone, or at Marcel's studio. The woman looks vaguely familiar, but Dalton thinks that's just his imagination. He offers an appreciative smile and makes his way to the seat opposite her.

"I'm neither. This is very kind." He sheds his coat, and Sam cannot help but notice that it is nearly as expensive as her own.

"Not at all; make yourself comfortable. I have already made my choice, would you like to check out the menu?"

"No thanks, I've been eating here pretty often the past few days. I practically have that thing memorized." Dalton likes this place because it reminds him of a Deli back home; the same knocked about appearance and tangy aromas. Plus, it has the advantage of being very close to the Hotel. He can't help but wonder why a woman who can clearly afford better has decided to lunch here.

Samantha is satisfied by the nature of their shared smiles; an acceptable beginning. Her satisfaction is short-lived.

The waitress arrives, very blonde, very fresh faced, wearing a greeting smile. She focuses all her attention on Dalton.

"Can I help you?" she asks, almost breathless.

"I'll have a lean Roast Beef on rye with some Cole slaw and a cup of coffee."

The girl scampers away without asking what Samantha might have.

Dalton notices the cool expression of his lunch partner and realizes something is amiss.

"Haven't you already ordered?"

Samantha shakes her head in the negative.

"That's strange. They're usually very friendly here."

Dalton waves to the waitress.

"Miss, my new friend here has not yet ordered."

"I'm sorry Ma'am, can I help you?"

Normally Samantha would tear a waiter's hide off for such incompetence, but looking to get Dalton's approval, she resists the temptation. At this point Sienna appears to be sitting in the booth behind Dalton.

"That's okay dear, it's very crowded. I'm sure you just missed me. I'll have the Chicken Salad on a bed of greens and a coffee."

Dalton is impressed by the woman's obvious warmth. The waitress is not so easily fooled and makes a face behind the woman's back as she walks away. Sienna laughs to herself as she witnesses the exchange.

"Some people would not have been that nice. I'm glad you were. It's easy to forget how hard some people have to work to make a living."

Samantha smiles while she fights back her temptation to argue the point. A person in the service trade, she feels, should be prepared to do what is required to make all of their customers happy. Instead she continues to play to her new interest. Good guys want their women to be all sweetness and light.

"You're so right. I was saying just about the very same thing to a friend of mine only last week. Speaking of work, what do you do?"

"I'm a photographer. Mostly fashion layouts with the occasional location shoot. I'm Dalton, by the way, Dalton Hunter."

"How interesting…I'm Samantha."

"What do you do?"

The waitress brings a tray bearing the plates of food and the cups of coffee for both customers. She adds a bowl with creamers in little plastic containers. These few moments of dismal service give Samantha a chance to think about the question. She does not want to seem too obvious about just happening to be at this location at this moment. There will be time for that later. They both begin to eat as they continue their conversation.

"I work in an office." Samantha offers what passes for a genuine smile and Dalton has no reason to doubt the woman's sincerity.

"Ah, so you know about hard work. How's your lunch, by the way?" He takes a modest bite of his sandwich as Samantha risks a second bite of hers.

"The chicken salad is just right, thanks. How's the sandwich?"

"Just as lean as advertised."

Samantha smiles to herself. He's a nice guy, she thinks, but not all that perceptive.

"I hope you won't think I'm prying, but your work sounds very glamorous. Have you met anyone famous?" She worries that her small talk sounds a little like movie dialogue, but her dining companion seems to take it at face value.

"I have photographed a couple of models." Dalton has learned a few things from his experiences with the models on location. He immediately changes his tone. "Listening to me, you might think I'm a big shot. Really, it's no big deal."

"Celebrity doesn't impress you?"

"Don't get me wrong, I have met some incredibly talented people. Still, if you have seen them before their make-up goes on, you realize that they're just people. Beautiful and sexy and all, but they put their bikinis on the same way as anyone else; one leg at a time."

"Okay, point taken; then what does impress you?" I might as well do a little interviewing while I am at it, she thinks.

The waitress comes by and tops off Dalton's half empty cup, but somehow misses the empty one standing across from his. Dalton waits till the girl is finished before answering. He doesn't notice the waitress' continuing lack of attention to his lunch companion. The companion, on the other hand, has to work very hard to avoid letting the girl's know what's what.

"I've seen places that most people dream about. Places with glamour as you say, situated right next to people living in the most difficult circumstances. When I think about the lives of those people, the dignity they maintain in the face of adversity…"

Dalton stops as Samantha shakes her head smiling.

"Well that clinches it. You certainly aren't from this city."

"Do I strike you as small town then?"

The honest answer will never do, so she continues feeding the boy what he expects.

"Not exactly, I find your idealism refreshing. People here can get a bit jaded."

Dalton looks at Samantha to see if she is serious. Their eyes lock for a moment and they smile together. Sienna rolls her eyes. There is something about this woman that Sienna doesn't trust. For almost a full minute nothing is spoken. Dalton looks at his watch.

"You're not leaving are you? You haven't finished your lunch."

"No, I just remembered something a friend once told me. She said that if there was a sudden break in conversation and everything got quiet you should check your watch and it would either be twenty minutes after the hour or twenty before."

Sienna smiles gently, thinking how charming this little idea is.

"So what time is it?"

"Twelve twenty."

Samantha thinks this is one of the dumber things she has ever heard. Her own smile, however, never flickers.

"How very interesting. Dalton, I didn't tell you the exact truth earlier. When you work in this town, you never know who you might meet or what they might be after. Now that I see that you are a genuinely nice guy, I feel comfortable telling you what I really do. I am a magazine editor; a fashion magazine as it happens. I hope you'll forgive me for not being completely honest."

Samantha radiates warmth and sincerity, and Dalton is so charmed, he gives no thought to the coincidence of the woman's profession and his being so aligned. His earlier thoughts of her looking familiar are also forgotten. Sienna, on the other hand, is adding two and two very easily.

The waitress returns and tops off Dalton's cup again, and as he turns to thank the girl, Samantha takes the opportunity to send the girl a withering glare, which results in getting her own cup refilled at which time Samantha smiles as if nothing has happened.

"Knowing how you spend your life hopping to exotic locales and such, can I take it that there is no lady love pining away for you back home?"

"Not exactly, what about you? Do busy fashion editors have time for a love life? I can't imagine you have any trouble filling your social calendar."

Samantha sits taller in her seat, giving Dalton every chance to inspect the merchandise, but he maintains eye contact and refrains from taking the bait. She finds his lack of attention somehow disappointing, but shakes it off and answers him.

"Let's see, to answer in order, they do, I don't, and yet there is nobody special for me at the moment, just in case you're interested."

Dalton blushes. Their lunches being finished at this point, Dalton signals for the waitress. The girl brings the check and leaves it on the table. Dalton reaches for it, but Samantha grabs it first.

"What are you doing?"

"I invited you to join me, remember? That makes you my guest. Besides, I have an expense account."

"I don't know..."

"Well, if you're insistent on paying, you'll just have to ask me out on a date. It seems pretty clear that you find my company acceptable, and you are probably starting to realize that I find you…mildly attractive."

Dalton grins at the obvious flirtation. He's enjoying the girl's obvious interest.

"Sounds like a plan. How do I reach you?"

"Do you have to get back to work?" An image of a quick side trip to the nearby Sheraton flits through her mind. It is short lived.

"Unfortunately, I do."

"Truth be told, so do I." Covering her mild disappointment is the easiest hide of the day.

Samantha pulls a card from a case in her purse and hands it to Dalton. Dalton pockets it without a look. She then tosses a couple of twenties which will make for a fairly substantial tip, but the guy does not appear to notice her generosity.

Sienna sees Dalton's interest clearly, in spite of sitting behind him. It has nothing to do with the currency.

"Oh Dalton, please be careful. This one's not for you. Can't you see the teeth?"

"Thanks, I'll be in touch." Dalton starts to rise as Samantha does. The length of her body and her obvious charms are difficult to ignore. Dalton displays a bit of gallantry, assisting his new acquaintance with her coat before grabbing for his own. Samantha talks softly as they head out onto the sidewalk. It is a typically cool February day with a high sun obviously sleeping on the job.

"I'll be waiting. My secretary won't allow any other calls through until I hear from you. If you don't want me to be fired for not doing my job, you'll call me very soon."

Dalton responds laughing. "Don't worry, I'll call right away. Unemployment is high enough."

Sienna fades as they exchange goodbyes and walk in opposite directions. Samantha waits until Dalton is distant and lost in the crowd before hailing a taxi. She toys with her necklace as she remembers the entire encounter. He is not really her type, but he could be more acceptable with some slow encouragement and intervention.

Almost as soon as Samantha returns to the office, the phone rings.

"Dalton, thank you for helping me keep me job. Now, where are we going on Saturday?"

"Actually, I was hoping you might have some ideas."

Samantha loads her voice with as much kittenish appeal as she can. "I get lots of ideas, Mr. Hunter. However, as we've just met, it might be a bit early to discuss any of those. Now that I think about it, one thing has occurred to me."

"What's that?" There's something exciting, provocative and just the littlest bit dangerous about this woman that Dalton finds almost irresistible.
Samantha laughs to herself at how easily the conversation is led.

"Now that you've saved my job, perhaps you let me offer you one…"

"A job? But you don't know anything about me."

"Feminine intuition, Dalton. You're a fashion photographer and I am an editor for a solid fashion publication. I think it was destiny that our paths crossed this morning, and I never turn my back on destiny. What do you think? The role would be similar to what you described; some studio work and a bit of location shooting."

"This is very flattering, but I would hate to leave Marcel in the…"

"Marcel? That wouldn't be Marcel Ardan would it?"

"Yes."

"Dalton, Marcel and I go way back. Look, come in and talk to my boss since he would have to interview you and make the decision. If it doesn't feel right, you can walk away with no hard feelings. We can be friends in either case, but Dalton…"

Dalton waits for Samantha to go on.

"Dalton, if you do take the job you'll have a place here in the city, and I would be close by. It could be the start of something quite lovely."

Dalton smiles as he considers the possibility. Perhaps it is time to reconsider the real girl idea.

"You have my card. Why don't you stop by my office in the morning and let me introduce you to the boss?"

"Sure thing, Samantha, I'll see you then…and thanks."

Samantha hangs up the phone. Everything is working out and her smile is ravenous.

27.

Samantha: I have a dream

Pink rimmed clouds sit lazily on the horizon. The sky is a shade of blue that only wealthy people can afford. I am lying on my stomach, sunning myself on the aft deck of the SS Tahitian Monarch watching the foaming wake of the ship trailing away. Other than a little more swaying motion over the waves than the brochure promised, the late morning is perfect; warm with a soothing breeze. I am feeling so relaxed that I have decided not to file a complaint.

Suddenly, the glamour of the day is broken by the sound of alarms going off on deck after deck. Hundreds of passengers flood out from the gangways screaming and searching for the life boats. This commotion is absolutely unacceptable. I look around casually, and slowly rise from my lounge, mindless of my bikini top which remains on the chair. I roll the hair band from my wrist and carefully pull my hair into a ponytail then bend to grab the expensive Dolce Gabana bag that sits on the deck. After all, it was a present from Daddy. Besides, it has my sun block.

I can't be bothered with the details of whatever the tragedy is that has the boat's passengers in such a panic. Still, it does seem prudent to get to the front of whatever line is forming. As if in response to my need, four muscle bound crew surround me and keep the panic stricken mob at bay while guiding me to the only lifeboat. I walk proudly, confidently to the waiting rowboat; my tits swaying slowly, perfectly as I go. I allow the two closest crewmen to assist me as I climb in. One of them speaks, saying please watch your step Miss Choice. The sound is slow and thick as syrup. As the rowboat is lowered into the choppy waves, I sit unmoved by the masses at the rail. My lifeboat eases away from the side of the ship and the four crewmen salute, but I just slide my sunglasses down from their perch atop my head and lay back to catch a few more rays. From my peripheral vision, I barely notice as the ship slides beneath the water. It was a nice boat. 'Thank goodness that's over,' I think, 'that awful shrieking was starting to give me a headache.' Now that it's quiet, I remember the iPod in my purse. I would grab it, but the effort does not seem worth it at the moment; perhaps later. My boat carries me toward the horizon. It appears to know where it is going and knows that I will make no effort to propel it. I have more important things to do.

  The warmth of the sun on my body is soothing. Now the lifeboat is rocking a bit as it moves over the waves. Are you kidding me? Just as the thought emerges, the rocking stops instantly. After a time I hear the sound of birds flying overhead. Their racket is mildly annoying, but it would seem to suggest that land is nearby. The sun has already passed the highest point in the sky. Soon there is a different noise. It is way off, barely audible, but it sounds like drums and perhaps just the faintest hint of native voices. Little by little, it grows louder, though never enough to be truly irritating. The waves get stronger as the lifeboat approaches the shore. Once again, the rocking starts matching the rhythm of the drums. I sigh and lift my sunglasses, sending a fierce glare at the bow of the boat and the ride is smoothed once more. The voices and the drums are louder. It appears to be some kind of song. The voices are joyful and they enfold me like a cocoon; comforting as the sun.

Eventually, the lifeboat comes upon the beach. A large contingent of island dwellers has come out from the overgrowth to meet me. Their skin bright after the recent escape from shadow; greens and violets move to coppers and golds. Every man is huge, healthy and handsome; their dark bodies, the color of warm chocolate, glisten with sweat. They wear necklaces of polished green gems and little else; simple loincloths. The women are lovely with long, dark, lustrous black hair adorned with crowns of flowers. They are wearing flowing skirts in colorful floral patterns and the same necklaces. Their unclothed breasts stand out proudly, but I can't help but smile. No woman has a set anywhere near as glorious as mine and they all seem to know it. An older woman, still very beautiful, approaches and lifts a crown of white flowers, placing it gently on my head. I bow slightly to accept her gift with a gracious smile and she slips back.

Two men, large even by the standards of the people I see, arrive carrying a litter. It is made of bamboo and has a nice cloth hood to keep me dry should it rain. They lower it enough to allow me to take a seat during which time all of the people, now my people, bow their heads. I am taken through a winding jungle path to a clearing some distance away. All the while it is the opposite of a parade as I move but it appears the people are passing and bowing. Once in a while a child tosses a flower to me. When the litter stops, I stand once more. To my right and left there are huge chests of jewels and pearls and coins, full to overflowing. In front of me is a tall golden throne with soft red cushions.

    Once I take my rightful seat, the feasting begins. Large trays of fruit are laid at my feet. There are trays with chicken and goat and bowls with sauces that have the most enticing aromas. I merely point this way and that and someone loads my dish. Once I have sampled a few of the many delicacies and expressed my satisfaction, the people begin to do the same. All this time there is singing and dancing. Beautiful children are brought before me, smiling and cheerful.

    The feast goes on and on. I sway to the rhythm once I have sated my appetite. The dish disappears. Darkness descends and a fire is lit, along with many torches surrounding the clearing. Large jugs are brought full of a fermented fruit drink which is delicious. I drink in the sweet nectar and the liquid burns just a little on the way down. Suddenly the music and dancing are more powerful as the rhythm begins to pound. It is brutal and insatiable. A few of the men are eyeing me boldly. Their faces are marbled with deepening shadows and flickering firelight. Even more amazing is the way some of the women seem to be doing the same. There are hundreds of shiny eyes peering from the darkness beneath the trees. I am aware of a slowly rising ball of heat at my core. The drink is more powerful than I could ever have imagined. One by one the people approach me, hands reaching out to touch me and I am surrounded but not fearful. My feet leave the ground and I am carried along by a cushion of human activity. I am borne to a shelter that I only have moments to notice before I am inside. Once there I am gently lowered to a bed of feathers and leaves covered by soft fabric. The touching continues long after I am stretched out, and goes on and on for many hours.

    The fire of the drink and the warmth of the air and the heat of those surrounding me reach a crescendo that has me rising higher and higher. I am flame; no, not exactly flame. I am the sun; again no. I am a supernova; closer, but still no. I am a burning black hole at the center of the universe. Everything is revolving and spinning; all surrounding me. The stars exist to sing me love songs. Light bends to my will. The darkness exists only to satisfy my need to shine.

    My eyes open; time to get a shower and get ready for work.

28.

Sienna: A day at the beach

She is relentless and he is slowly floating away. I can see him being pulled into her inescapable gravity and I feel so helpless. I saw her in his memories of the New York Fashion Week Banquet. Then she was at it again in that Deli, like she would ever go into a place like that by accident. God, she's so transparent, but Dalton is too trusting and kind to see her for what she is. I have to give her credit. She is beautiful and very smart. She is drawing him in a little at a time.

Still, he opens his world to me. He's generous that way. Today is not the first time that he has opened his dream place to me. Even while he is out in the world, the sum of our two minds together makes someplace that I can escape to. On my own, my sleep has dreams in it; at least I think it does. We've become so connected that it's hard for me to be sure where I start and he leaves off. Those dreams, whatever they are, wherever they happen, don't have any of this magic; his magic. I'm pretty sure that the part of me that is me is not asleep when I enter his dreams now.

Alone as I look around this room, his room, I sense his aroma and the feel of his absence. It is the room of his youth. Through all of the moves, from college to foreign lands, to the hotel rooms that we have shared vicariously, this place has become my touchstone; a way to connect with the core of who we are and what we have been. I look through his closet, so different than those he fills now with all of the expensive clothing and paraphernalia of his profession. I am back there. I touch one of his old shirts, blue with longs sleeves. The cuff has a stain from his days preparing dinner for himself and his dad. A tray of film rolls sits on his dresser. I imagine their sweet images stored inside and the thought penetrates me like the collage of our days together. I move away. I am not ready to say goodbye.

 Today I've packed a small bag with a towel and some snacks and a bottle of water. I'll lie on the towel. It's hard to say what I need with the snacks or the drink since I know I won't get hungry or thirsty. When I open the door from his old room, I am suddenly in a long hallway. First are the doors to his Paris apartments, then his New York hotel room. Looking far down the hall there are other doors that I do not recognize. Perhaps they hold secrets to Dalton's future. If they do, I am not brave enough to face those answers now. I find the door I desire, a familiar one from a tropical hotel we stayed at during a blissful shoot. I open it. The sky is a shade of blue that only people truly in love ever get to see. The beach is right there. In either direction the sand is smooth, imprinted only with the markings left by the ocean breeze. I step out in a skimpy bikini the color of early sunset; warm cream with hints of pinks and oranges. There's nobody here and I could just as easily wear nothing. If he was with me now, perhaps I could be that open. Alone, it just seems…pointless.

 I didn't pack lotion or lug an umbrella. There's nothing to worry about under this sun; his sun. His sun will turn my skin the loveliest shade of bronze with no fear of outraged freckles. It will be warm enough that I can feel the breeze, but never so much that even a single bead of sweat will be raised. The waves roll in with a rhythmic roar. It's almost like the whole place has a pulse. The water has a clarity and depth that people like that Samantha see on lots of islands that most people don't even know the names of. I have to admit that Dalton's travels have made me more familiar with some of those places. Foam from the breakers makes a lacy pattern connecting each wave with the next. The blue sky overhead reaches down and down until it makes the gentlest contact with the horizon. Just for fun a gull passes by crying a greeting. He'll be back at some point.

    He'll be back. Even in this space of quiet, not quite lonely comfort, the thought occurs. I push it away along with one or two strands of flyaway hair that tickle my cheek. I set my towel on the sand alongside my beach bag and settle cross legged on it. Distraction appears in the shape of a small lime green and white spotted butterfly that darts over the sand like musical notes on a piece of sheet music. I briefly hold its reflection on the wet beach where the water has just retreated. The distraction is short lived. The beach itself is less familiar. I recognize it not as a specific place. It is not part of a particular destination or time. It is tied to a feeling that I knew on so many exotic locations with Dalton. Sitting on the beach triggers my sense of wonder. Grains of sand and the endless arrival of wave after wave offer some hint of meaning. I wish they would just come out with it already, but apparently they have decided to keep their own counsel for the present. The gull flies higher.

Now there is a shadow. A single cloud hides my sun for a moment. I know her name, though I won't let the sound of it break into my thoughts. I wish it away; the cloud and the sound. I do get it, you know. I can't ask him to discard his place in the world. Even as I wrap myself into this dream, it's an escape, not an address. All the love in the world feels artificial when you wake up alone. We've had the most amazing expanse of one night stands that fill calendar after calendar. The nights are singular feasts from which we awaken satisfied but still hungry. That would not be so bad except for the unalterable wait until the next meal.

A series of performers entertain, having been flown in at no particular expense. A school of dolphin plays in the waves nearby. I can count at least six in all. They dive toward me like surfers through the breakers. One rides a wave parallel to the beach as if to shoot the curl. Two laughing children, both about seven years of age stop close to me and build a castle in the sand. They look familiar. Then they roar with pleasure as they knock it down and scamper away. I never give a thought to their missing parents. A crab scrambles by on his way to the water, turning sideways to notice me, but never stopping. A boat sits on the knife edge where the water meets the sky, skating slowly past. An airplane flies past, almost too high to be much of anything more than sound. Dalton walks by magically from my right to my left. He is tanned and fit. I only see the back of his head but I know it is him. He stares out to the horizon and never notices me. A few seconds later he passes again walking in the same direction. This time Samantha is on his arm totally engrossed in his every word. He looks at me this time, smiling and leaves with a faint shrug. Dalton passes a last time, again from just right to just left. This time someone else is beside him. It takes me a moment to realize that the incredibly happy woman on his arm is me. Just as they start to move out of sight I look from his arm to me with an urgent pleading expression.

    My rest lasts an entire afternoon. Thoughts and memories fill me more than the drink and snack which I consume out of habit. The question sits on the beach like a hungry bird. Occasionally it looks my way hoping for a crumb of an answer. It's time to go back. Gathering my things doesn't take much effort and I stand a little longer drinking it all in. It feels a lot like a last time, though it probably is not. The question nods goodbye.

    Once inside, I walk back through the hallway of doors. None of them are locked, but there are some I know to avoid. Some have a light on that shines through the gap under the door near the floor. Others have sounds, tawdry and loud. Behind one in particular I hear the sound of a woman's bleach blonde laughter. It sounds too expensive to have been purchased in a box. It grates on me like highly polished nails on a blackboard.

    I have to rest. He'll be done work soon and it will be no time at all before he's here. There are words to say, but not like this. I change my clothes in the magical way and gather myself to go out of here for a little while.

29.

Heart to heart

Darkness interrupted by the singular glow of the digital alarm clock, hours progress in front of him with steely determination. It has been years since Dalton has experienced such an effort to descend into sleep. He seems unable to find comfort attacked as he has been by the times of tossing and turning and the continuing parade of numbers. When his body finally relents and his eyes actually close, he is surprised to see that his dream finds him still in the same hotel room bed and not one of his bedrooms more aligned with the history he has shared with Sienna.

Instantly, he is moved to the spacious bathroom. Examining his face as has not done in some time; he cannot help but notice the sadness at the corners of his eyes. Somewhere along the edge of his mind Dalton knows what is delaying Sienna's arrival, but he is doing his best to ignore that knowledge. 'It's a good face,' he thinks, 'blue eyes set an acceptable distance apart, a straight not over large nose, and lips not overly thin or thick. Not a pretty face by the standards of the male models I have met, but strong with what some would call character; however questionable that character feels now.

'Yes,' he continues, 'there are imperfections in both the face and the man. My cheekbones are not particularly strong and the stubble on the chin fails to give the sensual effect it does for others.' The stubble disappears. 'Still, the imperfections of my face suit me and they certainly haven't hurt me with the women I have met.' The thought brings other thoughts and images, especially the images of his new acquaintance Samantha, and his lips curl up in spite of himself. Momentary satisfaction brings a wall-sized wave of guilt. Dalton knows that there is a reckoning coming. It is one he is not prepared to face now, so he moves from the mirror to a comfortable chair. Now he is holding a glass of Aussie Malbec that he tried when he was there last year.

Just as he is about to give up on her, Sienna appears from the shadows. Her face is as pretty as ever, but the usual smile has been replaced by something deep and sad. There is the unmistakable sparkle of recent tears that stabs at him sharply. 'This is my fault,' he thinks, 'and she deserves so much better.'

"Sienna, where have you been?" His tone is filled with regret.

"I'm here Dalton. Sorry, I had some thinking to do." She returns his look with one of her own, not accusing, but just a subtle question.

"Is everything okay?"

"I feel like I'm losing you," she replies looking away as tears reappear. "It's been coming on for some time, but it seemed to hit me particularly hard today."

Dalton knows that Sienna is connected to him through his dreams. Knowing this, he does his best to bury what he's been feeling about Samantha.

"Have I done something wrong?"

Dalton feels guilty about his recent lunchtime encounter with Samantha and all the thoughts he's been entertaining since then. It's the same conflict they have both been wrestling with for a while, become more and more obvious since he started this profession. No matter how wonderful the nights and dreams are, being alone all day and missing out on so many of the activities both important and mundane has taken a toll. Sienna wipes her eyes and approaches Dalton slowly, her pretty face glowing with affection.

"You are the most important part of my life, do you know that? You are my life. I can hardly remember a time when we weren't together. Do you have any idea how hard it would be for me if I lost you?"

"It's the same for me." Dalton knows as the words come out that they ring shockingly hollow.

"Is it Dalton? I don't know, but I had the strangest feeling that you were going away from me today."

Dalton realizes again that there are times when Sienna seems to know about things that happened during his day. The paranoid part of him wonders if this confirms his worry that Sienna is nothing more than a delusion. The guilty part of him knows that it is unfair to Sienna to keep secrets from her.

"You can't, you know."

"Can't what?"

"You can't keep secrets from me. I am inside your head while you are asleep. I know your thoughts as soon as you have them. I know how you worry that I am not real, but you should know better. Delusions don't feel as real as this."

Sienna comes over and touches him. The spark is still there. Dalton rises and faces her.

"In the end though, it all comes down to what you believe. In life, it always does. If I were the workings of a single night, maybe you could mark me down to some bad mac and cheese. Dalton, think about it, if I am a delusion, then I must be the most persistent one in history. There's something else. I know about your lunch with Samantha."
'There', she thought, 'at least I've hinted at my ability to be aware of his daytime actions'.

"I was just about to tell you."

"I know that too, and I am not upset. You have been wrestling with this more and more. I am what I am, Dalton. But whatever I am, I live here. When you're here, there is love and warmth and so many good things. But I can't go with you to a show or share a night with you when you are applauded for your remarkable work. I can't…" Sienna starts to cry.

"Sienna, don't. I'm sorry. I'm sorry. I'm sorry." Dalton pulls her into his arms repeating the apology into her ear over and over; each time a little softer till it fades.

"I can't give you a home or a child. Don't you think I know that? There is a world out there. You deserve all of those things; all the things that make life worth something."

Dalton closes his embrace even more tightly around her and rests his head against hers, smelling the warmth of her hair and skin.

"There's something else I know. I know that Samantha is not what you think, whatever you think of whatever this is. The life I described, the house, the child or children, all of it, could never happen with her."

Dalton pulls away. His reaction is strong and Sienna is prepared for it. He pulls away but she follows closely until he stops her from reaching out to him again. Once again she is on the verge of tears, but Dalton's anger holds him in place.

"You don't know her. How could you? You don't know everything. Oh God, I must be going crazy." Dalton stops and turns away. He knows that Sienna has only ever been everything he could ever ask for. First a friend, and then a lover, with no other thought than making him happy. Just thinking about the things they've shared softens the hard corners of his mouth. He regrets the harsh tone of a few seconds before and turns to apologize.

Suddenly, like an uninvited guest, an image of Samantha invades his thoughts. She is polished and shiny, edgy and beautiful in a way that he finds nearly impossible to ignore. He pushes the vision of her away with a force of will that almost makes him gasp.

"I know this. I know you. Dalton, there are lots of women I would gladly step aside for if it would make you happy. As hard as it would be, I will even step aside for this one, but I want to ask you one thing, why her?"

Dalton tries to step closer, hoping to avoid a response that is hardly that clear to him and can only make things worse, but Sienna puts her hands up to keep him distant.

"Answer the question, Dalton."

"I can't"

Sienna falls into the hotel bed and starts crying, her shoulders heaving as her whole body caves into misery.

Seeing her now, lying there in the bed fills him with remorse. Even with her hair tousled and her clothing slightly disheveled, she is the most beautiful woman he has ever seen. Her beauty is not similar to the way that the models are beautiful, or the way that Samantha is, but something more real and approachable. It strikes him hard that she feels real and looks real, but is locked into a small portion of his mind; of his life.

"Hurting you would be the worst thing I could ever imagine. You said it yourself. There is a world out there. I wish you were out there with me, but you're not. If you were with me, you'd never have to worry about me. There'd be no one else."

"I do know that."

"I'm trying to figure this out. I want our time to mean everything, but then I wake up. You're mine for eight hours a night. Well, most nights. I probably sleep more than any adult I know. The problem is there are a whole lot of hours after that."

Dalton sits next to Sienna on the bed. He softly strokes her back and pushes away her lovely red hair. Her tears go away and the streaks on her face are replaced by soft, dry, glowing skin. After a few minutes she sits up and faces him again. She takes his hands into hers before she speaks.

"If you want me to leave, I will understand."

"It sounds so selfish, but not tonight, Sienna, not tonight."

It would be so easy to pull her closer to me, Dalton thinks, as her arms surround him. He pushes away any thoughts of easy physical intimacy, choosing instead to allow himself to sink into the comfort of her. He turns within her arms and rests against her. Her long, sensitive fingers stroke his cheek as they both look out the window. The comfort of her caress is tangled with the comfort of a now familiar old friend; the bright disk of the glowing full moon hangs before him and clears his mind of anything else but this moment.

30.

Decisions decisions

His wallet slides easily back into his jacket pocket after handing the cabbie several bills for the fare and a generous tip. Dalton is rewarded with an equally generous smile. There is nothing left to do but grab his camera case and open the door. He steadies himself against the stiff breeze that is working on that door like a sail. The sun is out there somewhere in the cloudless February morning sky based on the brightness above, but it is barely noticeable in the canyon-like pass between the many towers that define this part of Manhattan. The tidal wall of early morning pedestrians squeeze Dalton against the side of the cab, at least until the vehicle speeds away. He manages to maintain his balance and hikes the camera case strap as he looks for a break in the flow of urban natives rushing by with eyes locked frontwards.

So many stories on the sidewalk make Dalton wish he had his camera in a more ready state and a bit more time to use it. Dozens of nearly identical businessmen rush by in suits and ties. A more varied group of women are visible, the younger ones in jeans and scoop neck tops sporting something sparkling from nose or lips or both. The older ones are decorated in dresses and jackets. Their vibrant pinks, greens and saffron yellows speak of a wish for a spring that has not quite arrived. A man with a slight limp is dressed in mechanic's garb, the name tag visible on the wrinkled navy jacket. His face is adorned with a black eye that looks pretty recent.

As he makes the short scramble through the crowded sidewalk, Dalton has a fleeting meditation on the scars that people carry; the visible ones like this man's and the other ones that are hidden. 'How can we measure where the real pain lies?' he wonders, just before he forces his way into one of the revolving doors that allow entrance to the Choice building.

Once inside, Dalton is impressed by the high ceilings and marble floors. It is not a new building, but the lobby has a gloss to it and an aroma of money. There are trees and potted plants scattered here and there as well as some comfortable chairs for those awaiting an invitation upward. He checks his watch as he makes his way to the security station. It is just a few minutes to eight. As he gets to the desk, a friendly, silver-haired black woman wearing a white blouse, navy skirt and a badge smiles and welcomes him.

"Good morning. Can I help you?"

Dalton pulls the heavy vellum business card from his suit pocket. It is the one that Samantha offered him at the deli the day before. Now for the first time he takes the time to inspect the embossed bold type on its cream-colored face. He almost chuckles as he reads the last name. Though friendly, their conversation had never gotten around to formal introductions. He asks the guard to see Samantha Choice. She asks Dalton to sign the register and calls up to her office as he does. After a short conversation, the woman hangs up the phone and returns her attention to the good looking young man.

"She's on the thirtieth floor. You can go on up," the guard says as she hands him a visitors tag. Her smile appears genuine as it lasts for a few seconds past the exchange.

"Thanks."

It is a short walk to the bank of elevators and he is surprised to find that there is no one else entering when the next one arrives. Evidently, mornings start very early for the workers here. As the doors close, Dalton lets out a little chuckle and grins at his reflection in the chrome covered elevator door.

"So, Miss Samantha Choice of Choice Publications, you're just a poor little, hardworking magazine editor. What a tough life you must have."

Stepping out of the elevator he sees the long aisle and the rows of low walled cubicles like a miniature city. Samantha strolls toward him with her confident gait and a sly expression. She pulls up to him as they meet face to face.

"You're here. I'm so glad. I know you've seen who I am, I hope you can..."

"If you were about to say you're sorry, forget it. Riding up in the elevator I realized that you are the same person I had lunch with yesterday. We had a very nice conversation."

Samantha looks at Dalton as if trying to determine if he is playing with her until it becomes clear that he is serious. A stray thought runs through her mind that she should turn and walk away as fast as possible. The truth is that he's far too serious for her, but then her eyes focus again and she can only see how absolutely gorgeous he is, and everything else gets immediately pushed aside. She slowly wills her lips into a glowing smile.

"What an incredibly sweet man you are. I can't wait for you to meet my father."

Samantha leads and Dalton follows, enjoying the view and the occasional over the shoulder glance. They stride past the admin whose eyes widen slightly at the man following her boss's daughter.

Dalton sits in a chair in front of the desk as Tony takes his seat behind it.

Samantha takes a position off to the side and turns to Dalton.

"Can I get anyone anything?" Samantha offers.

Tony smiles as he watches his daughter's obvious attraction played out before him. Dalton answers her request with a slight shake of the head while maintaining a professional focus on his potential employer.

"No thanks Honey, I'm sure Mr. Hunter would like to get on with it as much as I would."

Samantha leaves the room while making sure that her smile is turned full blast on Dalton. His response is brief before he starts to speak.

"Samantha mentioned the possibility of a position with her magazine. I told her I was open to listening. I hope you understand."

Tony meets Dalton's eyes with a look that expresses confirmation. His response is just as succinct.

"She told me that when she discussed a possible opportunity here, you didn't know she was my daughter. Is that true?"

"Yes sir."

"I'm happy to hear it. Look, I don't run my business by appeasing the whims of my daughter. After she mentioned your name, I did some quick checking. You are no doubt a talented photographer, and everything I have heard is positive. That being said, I need to hear from you why I should hire you. You've come in here to listen to an offer. Well my friend, I'm sitting here ready to listen to a pitch. Sell me and the job is yours."

Dalton never flinches as the challenge is made. He can see where Samantha gets her no-holds barred attitude.

"I'm sure I should be flattered that I am being given the opportunity to make that pitch. There are probably a thousand guys on the street right now that would pay money or give up arms and legs to be sitting where I am now, but to be frank, my situation is a bit different. Those guys didn't get the reception I got a few days ago. They don't have an offer from your daughter, and most of all, they don't have a job in hand that is already hugely satisfying and financially rewarding. There is only one reason to hire me. In spite of my loyalty to Marcel, and my satisfaction with what I have, I am sitting here with you now. Maybe it's all about your daughter. Maybe I love New York. Whatever it is, I am here. The question is now, what are you going to do about it?"

Tony lets what he has just heard settle for a minute. He locks his eyes with the young man in a visual version of arm wrestling. A slow grin appears. The kid is either that good or has a pretty good sized set; maybe both. He nods to Samantha who is waiting just by the door. She returns with a delighted grin.

"That was quick."

"Sam, you know that I trust my gut with things like this."

Turning back to the young photographer, he continues. "Dalton, I want you to know that everything my daughter told me about you is true, and believe me, I am not easily impressed." Tony Choice rises from behind his desk and reaches out to shake Dalton's hand.

"Samantha, make the offer. I will leave the two of you to work out the details. Welcome aboard Dalton"

Tony leaves the conference room and as he turns, he shoots an expression to his daughter that she is now on the hook and had better make good. She returns his look with one of her own that completes the bargain.

"Wow, I've almost never seen him like that. You just have to accept. Come on; let's find you a nice office."

"I'm pretty sure I'll accept, but I should probably see your offer first."

"Can't blame a girl for trying, can you? I have the offer at my desk"

They walk to her office. Samantha pulls an envelope from the top of her desk and hands it to Dalton. He opens it and glances at the piece of paper inside.

Dalton looks at her with surprise.

"Is this the best you can…"

Samantha is stunned until she realizes that his expression has changed.

"Sorry, I couldn't resist. I accept."

Samantha shakes her head as if to clear the earlier thought about turning away. Perhaps her instincts had been right after all. The guy has some spirit.

"Okay then," she says. "Let's go."

Samantha leads Dalton a short distance and shows him an office. It had been a bit of an ordeal to clear the previous tenant out and get the place cleaned up in so short a time. There had been a bit of screaming involved. It now is clear that the challenge was worth it. Dalton notices the large window looking out on the street where he arrived and it is high enough to let in a fair amount of sun. He also could hardly help but notice the pretty young secretary sitting right outside.

"Well, what do you think?" Samantha queries, knowing that it has to be better than Dalton expected.

"This is my office?"

Samantha stands near enough to Dalton that he can feel rather than smell her fragrance. Her warmth is a bit distracting, so he tries to focus on other things. He surveys the room a bit more closely. There is a desk and a chair that looks reasonably comfortable though he will probably spend less time in it than in the darkroom or off on location.

"This is great."

"I think you'll like the location. After all, I'm right next door. By the way, when it's just you and me, call me Sam. All my best friends do."
She turns Dalton toward her until they are practically nose to nose.

"Hmm," he replies softly, "This could be fun."

"I think so. So, what about that date? I seem to remember that you owe me a meal."

Dalton's eyes lock on Samantha's. A kiss in this situation would hardly be appropriate, so he pulls back for just a little breathing space.

"What are you doing Friday night?"

"Let's see, this is Tuesday, right? That means I will be on my fourth date with Dalton Hunter that night."

He laughs and Samantha surprises him with a quick kiss and an even quicker departure. Dalton takes off his jacket and drapes it on the back of his new chair. Reaching for the phone, He picks up the receiver and dials Marcel's number.

"Hey Marcel, I have something to tell you..."

A high pitched snicker comes through the line.

"I guess you do. It's okay Dalton, I already got the word. Your new employer called me with the news. Look Dalton, don't feel bad. You've been a wonderful asset, and I'm sorry to see you go. Whatever you do, be happy. You deserve it my friend."

Dalton had been dreading this conversation, while knowing in his heart that his friend would let him go with this kind of generosity.

"Marcel, I will never listen to another bad word about you."

"Dalton, there's only one thing that I ever found wrong with you."

Dalton shakes his head in amusement as he replies with the straight line that his friend is expecting.

"What would that be?"

"You're still not Gay."

Dalton smiles as the connection ends with a click. The intercom buzzes and the work day begins.

31.

A recipe for success

Reaching from the floor to the ceiling, extensive sheets of glass open out from the expensive, modern living room. The penthouse apartment has an almost unrivaled view. The horizon below is heavily dominated by the forest of high rise buildings with their rich, punch card like arrangement of lit and unlit windows. The city-saturated sky above reveals few stars, but the blinking of jets and helicopters overhead is fair compensation. It is a room that should be featured in Architectural Digest. Spare and tasteful, the furnishings feature large oriental rugs that subdivide the space into more manageable places for conversation or drinks. Shelves are lit with just a few mementos from trips to exotic places; a Lalique vase in one corner, an exotic tribal mask in another. The recessed lighting accents the high gloss finish of the walls and spotlights the modest framed Renoir, a present from her father.

 There are moments divided by long intervals when Samantha has the inclination to appreciate the cityscape outside. Tonight is not one of those nights. Folding her arms behind her, Samantha undoes her bra. Her Pineider alligator briefcase was quickly dropped on the chair as soon as she walked in. The doors were locked and the chandelier in the entrance way properly dimmed. The balance of the lighting did not faze her as she removed her blouse and dropped it to the floor in a manner not strictly approved by Vera Wang. On the way to the bedroom, the bra makes the next part of a cookie crumb trail. Finally, she works on the zipper of her skirt and it falls away easily. The door to her room is ajar and the drapes are fully open as she guides the light switch upward. Clicking the wall mounted IPod receiver, it responds with her favorite playlist. She shrugs out of her four inch heels and her stockings swaying to Coldplay's 'Paradise'. When she looks in the direction of her bathroom, she stops. It has been a long day, though on balance, more rewarding than most. Her desk is calling to her and she cannot resist. She removes her jewelry carefully and lays it on the dresser. She ignores the effort involved in closing her drapes and sits casually at her desk, opening the laptop there as she does. As it boots up, there is time to reflect on the day's events.

    Daddy's performance was Oscar worthy. He could have milked it a bit more, but Dalton didn't seem to notice, or maybe he really did make the grade. With Daddy, it isn't always that easy to tell. Samantha could kick herself for forgetting about that little bitch that ended up as Dalton's secretary. There were just so many details she could take care of in one morning. The girl is way too good looking. A moment of consideration recognizes that replacing the slut will be way too obvious, so it will have to be left as is until it will seem less so. After a few more keyboard clicks she is logged in.

    Samantha pages through her email, quickly jettisoning the mundane and the unimportant. She fires off a terse reply to the first really important one. Sometimes she wonders how she surrounded herself with so much incompetence. She is in too good a mood to let the question simmer and prepares to open the next email when she hears the Instant Message tone. The message box flashes and the internet assisted conversation starts.

> TRNC185
> Sam, I have good news.
>
> SAMCHOICENO1
> What?
>
> TRNC185
> I know you wanted designs from Ivan himself, but we both know how tricky stealing those would be.
> After all, they don't call him 'Ivan the Terrible' for nothing.
>
> SAMCHOICENO1
> Thought you said this was good news?
>
> TRNC185
> Have an alternate plan that I think will deliver the same results.

Samantha is not sure how she feels about a deviation from her carefully considered plan, but she continues typing, willing herself to keep an open mind.

> SAMCHOICENO1
> Go on Terry.
>
> TRNC185
> A few months ago a package arrived from Prague. It contained a whole season's worth of designs from a student living there. Sam, they were good. Ivan told the poor kid she had no talent and should think about sewing rather than design.
>
> SAMCHOICENO1
> That bastard! So there are these designs by a talented newcomer who has been told they're horrible and Ivan doesn't want them.
>
> TRNC185
> You got it. I think the asshole felt threatened. He didn't want a protégé who might at some point outshine him. The box is just sitting there. I

will have to time it right, but I think I can get you the sketches. Then we can do the handoff.

Samantha stops typing, grabbing a pencil and tapping it on her desk as she thinks. She takes a moment to enjoy the feeling of the air moving against her naked breasts, while her brain considers what she has heard. Her toes relax and stir against the plush carpet beneath them.

>TRNC185
>Sam?

The music pulses and untangles her thoughts. Paradise indeed!

>TRNC185
>Sam?

She continues to ignore the repeated entries looking for a response as she stands and stretches for a few moments. She shakes her head from side to side and loosens the clips holding her hair. She finally takes a moment to notice the lights of the city, and the planes in the sky. As good as the day has been to this point; it appears to have taken an even better turn. The music agrees: *Para-Para-Paradise*.

>TRNC185
>Sam?

Now she is just ignoring her friend for the sheer amusement value, giggling just a little and spinning once on her toes before returning to her seat. She counts slowly to five and finally responds as if she has not noticed all the comments from the other end.

>SAMCHOICENO1

Hold on a sec. I'm thinking. Here's what we'll do. We steal the drawings, but meanwhile, find this kid. What's the kid's name, by the way?

TRNC185
Anna.

SAMCHOICENO1
I like it. We could do something with that. A logo: "A N - N A". I'm thinking mirror images with sexy models; really high gloss.

TRNC185
I love it. First we hire the girl, and then we have rights to her drawings minimizing the whole theft thing. Then we do the ads, dark and steamy.

SAMCHOICENO1
You got it. Find her. Offer her some ridiculous sum with a five year contract. Make it so low she'll have to commute from Idaho. Then when we open, introduce her and make sure that Ivan is there to see it.

TRNC185
You're so bad.

SAMCHOICENO1
I have my moments. Let me know when you have the girl. For God's sake, don't let anyone know. Get me the drawings as soon as you can. If they are as good as you say we're golden. I expect you to find a way to go to Prague and take care of the details yourself.

TRNC185
Maybe this would be a good time to finalize terms.

SAMCHOICENO1
I thought we already discussed this. The title would be VP in charge of design with a salary of Two Fifty.

TRNC185
That's not good enough, I want more.

SAMCHOICENO1
But this is what we talked about as far as money and position.

TRNC185
The money's fine and the title suit me. It's the position, or should we say, the positions "sss" with an "s" that I would like to discuss. I think you can see that I am already providing value.

SAMCHOICENO1
So Is this a non-negotiable item?

TRNC185
Yes.

SAMCHOICENO1
Y does this mean so much to U?

TRNC185
Sam, I've had a thing for you since we were kids in school together.

SAMCHOICENO1
Terry, you know I am working on Dalton for a serious relationship, right?

TRNC185
I don't care. I'm not after the whole meal. I just want dessert.

SAMCHOICENO1
Fine, send me the designs. Then go to Prague and lock up Anna. Do all that to my satisfaction, and I will guarantee yours. Gotta go, I have a hot date.

TRNC185
ALL RIGHT! Have fun sweets. Bye.

Samantha closes her laptop and heads to her bathroom. There is time for a quick shower. Finally she frees herself from the confinement of her pretty silken panties. She is humming as she does.

32.

Dalton: A taste of real

Whenever I really need the weather to cooperate, I am usually pretty lucky. On some of the highest pressure shoots when real money was on the line, the day would almost always be perfect. Today is no exception. There are a number of high clouds and the sun is playing hide and seek behind them. Still, for a New York day in mid-February, it is reasonably mild. Precisely the weather you'd want for the surprise I have planned.

The morning started with an effort at getting settled into my office. I introduced myself to Jennifer, my secretary. Considering what I already knew about Samantha, the girl was surprisingly attractive. Once the preliminaries were completed, I spent the rest of the morning trying to figure out what Samantha and I could do for our second date. The first had taken place last night.

My first thought was a picnic in the park. I imagined the birds singing, the buds out everywhere, the sun shining; and then I realized what a mess it would be. I doubt if the grass has come up enough. When I gave it a bit more thought I had to chuckle. There we are on a cozy blanket near some large trees with just enough privacy, a basket filled with an upscale lunch and a good bottle of champagne and two crystal flutes. A great picture until you think about Samantha's designer shoes coated with a nice sloppy layer of mud. Samantha is hardly a sit on the grass kind of girl. Even if she could be persuaded, I think we need to continue with something a good bit more elegant.

    I thought about doing the fancy restaurant lunch, but where could I take her that she hasn't been hundreds of times and what's so special about that anyway? Besides, we had dinner at a nice place last night. For a first date it made sense to me to let her pick and she chose her current favorite. When the idea for today's date finally came to me it was so Samantha Choice that I couldn't stop smiling. God knows, I need to make this one count after last night. The meal was fine and I splurged for a bottle of Sauvignon Blanc that I had tasted back in Paris. Samantha was impressed by the selection, and even more so when she sampled it. It complemented the Lobster perfectly with a touch that was not too light and boasted a delicate finish. Our conversation started with a bit of talk about the places we had each seen and the people we had met. I was surprised by how easy it was; talking to her. The dinner continued with brandy and finished with a very subtle Crème Brûlée for dessert. The back and forth between us flowed as easy as the wine and as full of flavor as the food.

    After dinner, we asked the cab driver to slow drive through the Village and that gave us more time to talk. It was early enough that plenty of shops and restaurants were still open and the city presented itself to us like a Broadway play on opening night. It was everything we could have wanted. We even shared a little friendly lip-lock in the taxi as we headed for her place. I have to admit that between the pleasant buzz from the alcohol and the encouragement coming from her distinctive perfume, I knew it would not take much convincing to allow things to go forward with Sam. I had a pretty good idea what she was expecting, but even as stimulated as I was, I knew I had to fight to hold back. With the two of us working together, and this being our first date, I didn't want to push things too fast. She was pleasant enough as I walked her to the elevator and the kiss we shared there was thrilling. She was really doing her best to test my resistance. When I told her that we both had a busy day in the morning, she accepted it gracefully, but as I turned to go, there was just the slightest flash of real disappointment in her eyes. It was gone almost as quickly as it appeared, but it was impossible to miss.

    Today's surprise has got to be that much more special. I am hoping that it will be enough since there is no way I want to rush into a physical relationship. When our day is over, I will share my thoughts on how I see this thing going forward. It's important that she know that I take us seriously enough that I don't want to jeopardize it by rushing things. With my arrangements set, I go down to the lobby and flag a Yellow. I offer the guy a little cash up front to make it worth his while to stick around.

The same guard is seated at her station as I reenter the building. She calls out to me and smiles as I walk by. I am a little impressed that she remembers my name. With the taxi stationed out front and the meter running, I hope I can get Samantha interested without too much delay. Otherwise the cab fare combined with the cost of the surprise could end up being very steep. As the elevator arrives on the thirtieth floor, I am again struck by the level of activity and energy that sizzle all around. Heading to Samantha's office for the first time today, I put on my best expression, a mixture of casual and cool with just a hint of mischief. My knock on the door catches Samantha in a fortunate moment reviewing some copy for the next month's issue.

"Knock, knock, anybody home?"

Samantha's expression goes from intense concentration to luscious delight in a heartbeat.

"Well Dalton, it's about time. What's up?"

Once again, I see what looks like a cloudy thought cross her face and then just as quickly vanish. I'm pretty sure she is thinking about the way last night ended. It's hard to forget the way her body was pressed against mine as we waited for her elevator. Her mouth was inviting me in a way that went beyond anything words could express. Her hands wrapped behind my neck as if to claim me. My parting words echo in my mind and seem less than adequate even to me.

"Well, it's almost lunchtime. I was wondering if you had any plans."

"From the look on your face, it appears that you do."

Actually, I do. I'm sorry I cut the evening a bit short last night, but I had to get settled in at the new hotel. By the way, you didn't need to set me up in a Suite at the New York Palace. I thought if you weren't busy, I'd do my best to make it up to you now."

Samantha's smile begins to glow like a lamp with a dimmer switch that has been moved slowly to its highest setting. I can see that she already senses that this will not be a typical lunch at a restaurant. Her eyebrow is raised as she focuses a playful, wary expression my way.

"What do you have in mind for me, Mr. Hunter?"

"You'll see, but we should get going. I have a taxi waiting. It's pretty sunny out there, but there's still a little bit of chill in the air. I recommend the jacket," I say, gesturing toward her coat rack.

"I'll take your recommendation under advisement," she replies as she grabs her fur lined jacket and carries it under her right arm. Once we are past the door to her office she pulls me close with her left hand and angles her body against me in a way that makes it impossible for me to ignore the full display of her cleavage. Noticing that I am noticing fuels Sam's smile to an even higher intensity. She stays up close while we the walk through the offices, down the elevator and all the way to the street making sure that I am fully aware of her soft nearness and her intense gaze. The negotiations are underway.

Having already briefed the driver of the desired destination, I close the door to the taxi once Samantha is seated and make my way to the other side. As soon as I am seated and the door is closed, the driver begins pulling away from the curb. Samantha wastes no time regaining the close and incredibly sexy position beside me. I experience a little guilt as I realize how tangible this feels. She smiles up at me quizzically.

"How mysterious you are. I don't suppose you'll tell me where we're going?"

"Nope." I am having fun matching her curiosity with a bit of inscrutability. Not satisfied to just sit and patiently await our arrival, she tries a different tack.

"From the direction we're heading, it's not the theatre district. I don't suppose you'd give me a hint?"

"Not a chance."

"A walk in Central Park?"

"With you in those shoes? I don't think so," I answer shaking my head, though this makes me wonder again if the picnic thing might be a good option for another day.

Samantha is obviously not used to being kept in the dark and her mood turns a little sulky as the cab makes its way through streets of traffic and pedestrians. Little by little the city ebbs away. Thankfully, the ride is not too long and from her expression as we arrive, I can see that the surprise has exceeded her expectations. The view through the windshield is filled from side to side with a very imposing ninety foot yacht. It is white and gleaming in the mid-day sun. She leans even closer and plants a quick kiss on my cheek as a thank you.

"Your ship awaits your majesty."

I exit the cab and hold the door for Samantha who takes my hand and stands gracefully. The cabbie smiles gratefully at the new bills I have offered for the fare. It includes an additional gratuity beyond what I gave him when I flagged him down. Samantha is visibly impressed.

"Very stylish, Dalton, what's next?"

"We'll have lunch and a quick cruise around the harbor for starters. If you're okay with spending the rest of the day with me, we can have supper too."

A smile and barely perceptible nod are all the agreement I need and we begin ascending the gangway. The captain greets us as we board and directs us to the stern as crewmen loosen the moorings and prepare for departure. The luncheon is readied by a waiter in dress whites who stands smartly and guides us to the table. The settings are gold-rimmed platters, golden dinnerware and gold trimmed goblets and glassware all magnificent against the embossed patterned, heavy linen tablecloth. The sunlight darts among the splendor and I invite Samantha to take a seat. A quick breeze encourages her to don the jacket she has been carrying. I hold it as she places one arm after another inside the sleeves, but she stops short of blocking the view it might otherwise hide. I hold her chair and move it in as she makes herself comfortable. She looks happy and very much in her element. Apparently, my choice is inspired. I feel great as I take my place next to her. The arrangement suits as we are both able to enjoy the view.

I point toward the bow of the yacht, to the cabin ahead of us as we get comfortable.

"There's a table inside for later."

Samantha turns to look and then glances back at me with an expression I cannot quite penetrate.
The waiter places a stand for the wine I ordered near the table and offers me the first taste. It is an elegant Chardonnay from the California Russian River Valley. It has a stirring bouquet and has just the right palate and finish that the meal will require. I nod and he fills my glass and repeats the process for Samantha. She raises the glass to her lips slowly and responds agreeably to the choice.

"Mm, we're eating on deck, I see. The table is quite elegant." Samantha addresses the waiter.

"What's on the menu?"

The waiter responds to the question with no hesitation.

"Lunch will be served right away. We have Caesar salad, Surf and Turf featuring Lobster and Filet Mignon, Scalloped Potatoes, and tender baby corn. For desert we have your choice of New York Cheesecake with fresh strawberries or Crème Caramel."

He moves away, but quickly returns with warm rolls and soft, sweet cream butter. Sam picks up a roll and bites into it hungrily.

It is quiet for a few minutes as Samantha feasts on her roll and we both enjoy the passing skyline. New York smiles down on the river as the wake of the yacht rushes out. The blue sky folds over the rippling water and makes me wish my camera was handy. The roll now completely devoured, Sam seems to be eyeing me with a similar though more sensual hunger. She looks away, a little guilty at being caught in such a flagrant stare. When her eyes return, her lips are parted and ready for conversation.

"Did you always want to be a fashion photographer?"

"Actually, I thought I'd do more artistic stuff, but I am happy with this life; especially now."

"The fashion world does have its advantages, but sometimes I think about how nice it would be to live like normal people."

"Really? I mean, could you see yourself giving up all the glamour? You seem so at home."

"I have lots of nice things, Dalton. I have an expensive apartment, beautiful clothes and a lifestyle that most people envy. If you told me that some guy would offer me the whole suburban package, you know, the house with the white picket fence, well..."

Samantha's eyes probe into mine with singular intent.

"Obviously, it would have to be the right guy."

It is so easy to lose myself in those eyes, but then the spell is broken as the waiter begins to serve our lunch. I take a sip of wine and look out over the water. The food nearby smells amazing and the conversation lags for a little while as we start on the salads. Before the lunch is over, we both agree that a full day on the yacht is absolutely required.

Later, after a day of sailing out on the Atlantic, enjoying the sunshine and conversation, we end up in the cabin. The sky is darkening and there is a reddish glow over the New York skyline. The boat is making its way back to port. Samantha and I are sitting in the lounge next to the dining area. The sounds of the staff preparing the setting for dinner make a nice backdrop to our conversation. Up until now it has been comparing notes on the ways our paths have been different and the ways they are similar. Now Samantha is leaning toward me with a very come hither expression.

"There's a rumor that these boats have all kinds of amenities, including bedrooms. Care to take me below?"

It is the conversation I have been expecting, but that doesn't make it any easier. Oh well, here we go. I think I'll try for evasion.

"I would Samantha, but it's a work night and I don't want to have to explain to your father why his little girl was late for work tomorrow."

"I just thought we could do a little exploring," she says, her eyes lit with an obvious and mischievous intent.

So much for the evasive plan, guess it's time to lay the cards on the table.

"Can I be straight with you?"

"Absolutely, fire away."

"It's been a long time since I've wanted to be involved with someone. Don't think for a minute that I haven't had a few ideas like the ones I think you're having, but we both know what will happen if we get started. I don't think we could be happy with a quick few minutes of boat rocking."

Samantha giggles uncharacteristically; suddenly unguarded.

"I'm pretty sure this boat is a bit too big for us to create any steadiness issues."

She misreads my serious expression and tries for a different solution, her eyes targeting mine with a laser-like intensity.

"We could go back to my place. It has the benefit of being very close to our offices..."

"Samantha, the thing is, I can see something long term building between us and I don't want to rush it. Believe me, I am not some perfect guy, and saying good night is going to be excruciating..."

"Then don't..."

Samantha places her hands on my shoulders. Her lips are short inches away and her fragrance is making a retreat difficult. I could almost give in. From my last reserve, I find the will to speak.

"Sam, let's take our time. I promise you, building up to this will make the ultimate outcome that much sweeter."

"I have to say that I never figured you for the old fashioned type. It's charming."

She turns away, looking less than charmed. When she looks back, she has made a decision.

"You'll have to at least give me a down payment."

With that she brings her lips close to mine, but waits and lets me start the kiss. When I finally pull back, her satisfied expression is apparent.

"You drive a hard bargain sir. I promise to behave until you tell me the time is right. That is, as long as I can expect a few more of those in the meantime."

I don't hesitate; I go in for a more extensive mouth to mouth that is as deep and full of longing as I have ever experienced in my daytime life. The waiter calls and we begin to rise and approach the table.

"There, a down payment for tomorrow and I promise a few more when I take you back to your place."

The dinner passes in a blur of eating and kissing to the point that I can barely remember my name much less what has been served. The crew stood with expected formal style as we departed. When the taxi finally pulls to a stop outside Samantha's building, I have more that fulfilled my promise. Our good night kissing gets one last go-round when I see her to the door. I look at her meaningfully and go back to the cab without another word. From the surprisingly contented look on Sam's face as I pull away, it seems clear that the evening has ended much more to her liking.

33.

Day and Night

Daydreaming is not something that Samantha Choice indulges in very often, but after the activities of the previous night, concentrating on work has been a challenge. True, the end was hardly different than the end of the evening before, but there was definitely a difference in Dalton's response. One more evening like that should certainly get the boy into a more agreeable, more agitated state.

The weather has returned to a more normal February routine, raindrops spattering the windows, blocking the view. Taking a few minutes to reflect on the highs and lows of the previous night, she is far away when her assistant enters flashing her usual ultra-efficient demeanor and carrying a large parcel.

"Ms. Choice, The mail room just sent this up."

"Thanks Jazz, put it on the table there."

Jasmine moves forward as instructed. At times like this her assistant has a tendency to wear a pleasant expression more indicative of a friend than an employee. There are even times when Samantha finds this acceptable. This is not one of those times.

"It's large but not too heavy."

Jasmine stands awaiting instructions, and barely hiding her curiosity.

Samantha knows that this is one package her assistant must not see. She hardens her tone to back the girl away quickly.

"That'll be all for now, Jasmine. Close the door behind you please."

Jasmine responds with her customary professional nod and exits as instructed. She goes quickly to her desk to monitor any outbound calls her boss might make.

Ripping the tape away, Sam retrieves the book of designs from the box that her partner Terry has sent. She sits and carefully pages through and her smile is electric. There are brilliant little dresses that look as easy to slip out of as to wear. They have Party Girl written all over them. Then there are the blouses; low cut but staying on the right side of inappropriate. The slacks are sleek with a little blingy attitude. The girl has even included some nice jackets and coats. Done right, these designs would pull top dollar. Ivan should be ashamed of himself; no talent indeed! All in all, the plan is coming together. Terry is right; the work is just what she hoped for and a very nice start for a small fashion house.

Too excited to remain seated, Sam picks up her Blackberry and walks back to the window.

"Hey, it's me. Listen carefully. I want you on a plane to Prague yesterday. I mean it. The book is great. Get Anna under contract. Tell her we will produce and market her designs. Her name will be on the label ANNA for Samantha Fashions. I will text the salary schedule to you. Now don't waste a minute. You know what's on the line here, and no, I have not forgotten our arrangement. Now scoot."

Samantha closes the connection, tosses her phone gently and moves to a nearby cabinet where she inserts the book and locks it carefully before returning to her desk chair. She drops into it with abandon and lifts her arms up.

"Yes!"

Jasmine quits her listening gizmo filled with disappointment. Whatever that box contains is important, and she doubts she will have any chance to discover the contents. That doesn't mean that she will give up trying. The intercom buzzes interrupting her thoughts.

"Jasmine dear, could you come in her and dispose of this box. On her way out an unexpected treasure comes in the form of a shipping label that has come loose as the box was opened. Peeling it back, she notes the name of the original addressee. It belongs to Ivan the Terrible.

Dalton slips off his shoes and drops into his bed like a stone. The day has been filled with the kind of details he never had to worry about before, planning sessions for the next month's issue and arrangements for his next shoot. There were details to work out as far as studio space when he works in town. With nothing in house since the magazine has only dealt with freelancers up until now, he will check to see if the building has something that can be reconfigured without too much expense. The new job will feature less travel which he will miss, and less excitement which he definitely will not.

He also spent part of the day looking at ads for apartments and was not surprised when the costs were practically atmospheric. Thankfully he has a couple weeks before he has to leave the comfort of this suite and the expense account that goes with it. He pulls himself to a sitting position and reaches for the phone on the nightstand, thinking to dial room service.

The food at the hotel is first class with all of the right sauces and elegant touches that might be expected. Still, there is something to be said for a meal that's a bit more ordinary. There are plenty of nearby restaurants including more than a few recognizable chains, but none of them had much appeal as he returned to the hotel. He was just too tired to go anywhere else today. Besides, they lacked the flavor he was craving, something special, something home cooked. The thought of home cooking gets Dalton thinking of his dad and how long it has been since they have spoken. He returns the hotel phone to its cradle and pulls his cell instead, dialing quickly.

"Hey Dad, how are you?"

The voice on the other end is buoyant, and every bit as satisfying to a hunger Dalton hadn't even recognized as a burger from his father's grill would be.

"Sherry, come in here. Dalton's on the phone. C'mon hurry. I'll put you on speaker. What's up son?"

Just hearing their voices melts away much of the tension and fatigue he was feeling just a moment before. He eases back against the pillows propped against the headboard and gets comfortable.

"Actually Dad, there's been a lot going on. I'm still here in New York. I've left Marcel and have started working for a magazine here."

"Won't you miss Paris and all the gorgeous girls?"

Dalton smiles at the thought that this is his father's first reaction. Sherry jumps on it quickly.

"Hush Don, the only thing that counts is that Dalton is happy."

"I know, I know," he replies. "You are happy with this, aren't you?"

"Well Dad, I am sure you know that it was hard for me to leave Marcel. I learned a lot from him. The travel and the models and the freedom were excellent. The new gig is not bad, it's a pretty substantial fashion magazine, and I will still be in the studio shooting some pretty hot women."

"Sounds great Dalton, I am sure you will continue to be just as successful."

Sherry's voice is a bit lower, but she echoes his father's sentiments.

There is a voice inside Dalton's head urging him to share the equally important news that he has become involved with Samantha. He knows that this is something that both his father and Sherry will be happy to hear about. Don has made no secret of the fact that he is concerned about his son's 'long lonely road' as he calls it. Still, he holds back, instead describing the nice suite he is staying in currently and some details about the new job.

Sherry speaks up briefly at a momentary lull in the conversation.

"Dalton, I have a few chores to finish in the kitchen. I will give you and your dad a chance to catch up."

The connection is silent for a few moments. Dalton is hesitant to continue.

Don's voice is quiet and calm. The sound wraps around Dalton like a warm blanket. He has come to depend on that calm when he feels uncertain as he does now.

"Son, you seem, I don't know, a little preoccupied I guess. Is there something else you wanted to tell me?"

"Dad, I have a question that may seem kind of crazy to you. It's kind of a hypothetical thing. Do you want to hear it?"

"Go ahead, hit me with it."

"Okay, say there's this guy. Let's say his name is Joe. Joe has this girlfriend that he has just started seeing. Let's call her Amy. He thinks she might be the real thing…"

"Dalton! Are you trying to tell me…"

"Hold on Dad, there's a bit more."

"Oh, okay. Is there something wrong with the girl or something? You know we trust your judgment, right?"

"No it's not that, well not exactly, but there's more to the question."

Dalton waits as his father seems to calm for the momentary excitement.

"Okay, so we have Joe and his new girlfriend. What else?"

"Okay, so let's say that Joe has this other girlfriend, let's call her Brenda…"

Don's excitement ratchets up once more.

"Holy heck Dalton, are you trying to tell me that you have more than one? You sure are making up for lost…"

"Dad, for the moment let's just say that this is hypothetical."

Dalton slowly lays out the scenario for his father, trying to calmly describe all of Samantha's obvious charms, the fact that they are working together and that they have been out a couple of times and there are real feelings beginning to happen between them. He then describes Sienna. He speaks in glowing terms focusing first on her heart, her sensitivity, the way she makes him feel strong and capable. And then, before the question can be asked, he goes to great lengths to express just how gorgeous she is.

"It sounds like a perfect situation. What's the problem? It seems like all you, I mean Joe has to do is figure out which of these women will make him happiest."

Dalton stares at the wall thinking about how simple it seems, how simple it should be.

"Yeah, you would think so, wouldn't you? There is only one other detail."

"What's that?"

"The girl that Joe has known forever, the one he grew up with, she's just in his head."

Don is silent for a moment.

"Are you saying that she's an imaginary friend, like kids sometimes have?"

Dalton knows what his father must be thinking and cannot bear the guilt that this will cause.

"Let's just say that the girl in his head is an ideal. A vision of what the woman he would love to be with should be."

There is silence for more than a couple of seconds as Don gathers his thoughts and prepares his answer.

"Well Dalton, if you're asking my advice, let me start with this. You know how much I loved your mom. I am happy that Sherry stepped away so that I can say this to you about her as well. They were and are wonderful women. I have been very lucky. But Dalton, neither woman could be defined as ideal. I'm certainly not an ideal man, and as great as you have been, neither are you. If you look for perfection, you will end up a very lonely boy."

"I know."

"So at the end of all this, is there an Amy?"

"I knew I couldn't fool you Dad. I should never have tried. Her name is Samantha."

"Can I share the news?"

"Sure." Dalton feels the tiredness returning as Don calls Sherry back. He lies quietly and lets their excitement cascade out of the cell phone speaker until it finally winds down. After a while, he makes his apologies as he mentions his long day and the fact that he has yet to eat. They share their goodbyes and extract a promise from him to call again soon. He quickly agrees. Then he calls room service and orders an overpriced burger and a soft drink. He gets up to wash his face and the cool water brings him back to something like awake. Later he answers the tap at the door. The waiter sets the table by the bed at his request. Dalton has a couple of bites before fatigue overtakes him and he lets himself fall back onto the pillows.

Sienna emerges slower than usual from the shadow of Dalton's hotel room. This moment has been approaching like a freight train and now appears inevitable. Dalton looks up from his bed anxiously; his dream sleep is as troubled as his real sleep.

"Hey Sea, I was afraid you weren't coming tonight."

The sadness on her beautiful face is nearly enough to pull tears from his eyes. Dalton looks at her in a way that he has not done in way too long. Her cheekbones have become more defined and that makes the scattering of freckles now seem sexy and grown-up rather than the girlish feature they had always seemed. Her blue eyes have become somehow larger and more intense. That might also be attributed to her sorrow. In fact, as he looks closer, he can hardly miss the shadows under them or the way her face seems a bit drawn. Even the way her clothes hang slightly seem to indicate how hard the current situation is for Sienna.

"I almost didn't. In the end, I knew that was wrong. Whatever happens next, I owed it to you to come to you tonight and talk."

Sienna's eyes meet his as she comes closer. The red from the tears she has already shed is more apparent.

"It's Samantha, isn't it?"

"I don't want to talk about her yet. There's something else."

"What?"

"Your father can't help you with this."

"What do you mean?"

"I've told you before; you can't hide things from me. I can hear the memories of your conversation with him. What you told him, it isn't quite accurate, is it?"

Dalton looks up at Sienna, feeling remorseful and sad. He shakes his head slowly.

"No. I wanted his help, but in the end there wasn't a way to make him understand."

Sienna responds with a knowing glance that warms nearly to a smile. Then with thoughts of Samantha, her expression fades.

"You were right before. It is about Samantha, but not for the reason you might think. I don't care about the sex. How long have the two of you been dating now?"

"We're not having sex."

Sienna smiles a little more, partly because she is relieved, partly because this is beside the point.

"Then it's not about the sex you are not having. How long?"

"We just started since I took the new job."

Sienna focuses on Dalton's eyes. She hates the questions that are about to roll over them, but knows that she has no choice.

"It's different this time, isn't it?"

"I guess so. We work together and she is amazing. She has all this energy and confidence. When we're alone, she looks at me almost like you do."

Dalton stops. He begins to understand where this is headed. A decision is racing toward him like a steamroller.

Sienna's tone turns cooler.

"Tell me something, just how do you see this working out? You work and play with her all day and into the night and then what? You keep me in your head for special occasions? Am I to be your weekend plaything?"

"Sienna stop, you know I don't think of you that way."

Sienna freezes at the pain in her lover's eyes. Slowly she turns away. She can barely get the words out, but she feels she must.

"Dalton, the problem is I don't feel like you're doing much thinking at all. Can you honestly tell me that Samantha Choice is the one?"

Dalton hesitates, not wanting to hurt his friend; his love.

"Sea, I have tried and tried, you know I have. How many times have we had this conversation? I touch you and the feeling is electric, but I still wake up alone. The dream has been the one constant in my life and I can't imagine living without you, but I want more. I want us to have fights about how we decorate our home, or what restaurant we want to eat out at, or even how many children we want. I can no longer deny that those things are important."

Sienna walks toward the window, a fresh set of tears emerging as she looks out at the bright lights of New York.

"I've been with you through all your relationships. Childhood friends you danced with and girls who wanted much more. If Samantha was anything like the others, I would try to figure out how to go on, and I would be happy. Samantha Choice is not who you think she is."

Dalton's emotions begin to slip away from him. Anger begins to seep in riding the crest of hurt and frustration he has tried so hard to contain.

"What do you want from me?"

Sienna turns to Dalton with a look of loss that would normally pierce any feelings of irritation he felt, but tonight his response is hard and stubborn. She feels it like a slap and shakes her head slowly.

"Nothing. I came to tell you that I can't be a part of this anymore. She's going to hurt you. Either that or she'll turn you into someone I don't recognize. In any case, I can't watch and I can't stay."

"Then I guess you'll have to go. Of all the things we shared, I never expected... jealousy."

Dalton hears his own words echo in his ears and suddenly realizes what he is saying. He is aghast at his own cruelty. Sienna moves toward the shadow. She begins to disappear.

"Sienna stop! I didn't mean..."

Sienna looks back at him. She is trying to capture this moment in her mind; a goodbye look.

"I love you Dalton. Wherever you are, whatever happens, never forget that I absolutely loved you. I hope you will find what you are looking for."

She looks at him and on a whim, blows him a last passionate kiss. She disappears and even the shadow is gone.

"Fine! Leave me. I can't believe I ever thought you were real!"

Dalton bolts upright from his bed. He is awake and blinking. The alarm clock displays 2:13. He sits there feeling an emptiness that he can barely contain.

34.

Bowing the A

Nothing is the same, Dalton thinks sitting at his desk in his still new office. It feels as if he has awakened to find the sun rising in the west or Sunday following Monday. His working hours have been busy, while the nights have been a parade of endless minutes interrupted occasionally by fitful, dreamless sleep. Samantha listened patiently as Dalton begged off any further dates for the week. Trying to explain Saturday and Sunday had been a challenge, but he had finally come up with the excuse that apartment hunting was something he needed to address. He accepted a referral from Samantha for a real estate agent named Lindsay who had been very helpful. Lindsay was as sparkly in her wardrobe and jewelry as the places she presented. He was certain that as soon as their efforts completed late Sunday evening, Lindsay was on the phone with Sam detailing all of their progress.

There had not been much for Lindsay to report. He had neither the time nor the skills required to manage a fixer-upper. He had seen one and when he had caught his breath after the asking price had been revealed, he laughed and they left. They saw a couple more that were within a reasonable distance of the office. Dalton had been careful with his money if not miserly. Still the first one that was even near a price he could imagine paying was less studio and more broom closet. Lindsay had taken him to a couple others in the area that were meant to bring him back to reality, but while they were much more in line with what he wanted size-wise, the prices had reached super orbital. Lindsay had barely concealed a sneer as she suggested that he could always find something nice outside Manhattan. Debating the location versus price issue, Dalton replied with a question of whether she could "lower herself" sufficiently to assist him with that plan. She recovered quickly and they set an appointment for the coming weekend to start scouring the boroughs.

  On Monday, Sam was cooler accepting his apology and the explanation that he had so much to do in getting settled into the new job. As a woman who works well into the evening most days, Dalton figured that she could hardly complain about a similar commitment from him, at least that is how he justified the arrangement to himself. She finally capitulated, telling him to spend the time getting whatever he had to do done, but to be prepared to make it up to her with interest on Friday night.

As each hour passed, the activities and tasks he scheduled managed to fill the time, but were less effective in distracting the miserable thoughts that bounced off one another like the balls in a lotto drawing. Dalton understood that it was normal to feel the sense of loss after everything that had happened. He also knew that given a bit of time he could put his feelings for Sienna away in a box in the back of his brain. The trouble as he saw it was that instead of the joy he knew he should be feeling for the start of things with Samantha, all he felt was sad. Worse, it was Thursday afternoon and he only had the hours between now and tomorrow night to erect a happy mindset over the chasm that remained where his dreams once stood. On top of that challenge was the necessity of planning another breathtaking outing for the two of them. The concept of making up with interest was not exactly a cute little expression where a woman like Samantha was concerned.

A bit of inspiration hit him suddenly. He had heard that Strauss's 'Der Rosenkavalier' was opening at the Metropolitan Opera tomorrow night. The thought of a cultural evening seemed perfectly suited to sooth Samantha's ruffled feathers. An opera where the libretto revolved around a lover's triangle seemed like appropriate punishment. It took only a few minutes to get online and arrange the tickets. Most of the seats were already sold, but two seats in the Parterre section close to the stage were available and Dalton reserved them quickly.

The next step was to arrange something out of the ordinary to wear. He had often thought of purchasing a Tuxedo, but had always put it off as an unnecessary extravagance. Now there would be no time to go quite that far. He settled for calling a rental shop. In order to get something fitted in time, he needed to rush right out and placed the order. Thankfully, the shop was not too far and they had the perfect garment with little need for alteration. He would pick it up during lunch the next day. While he was out he stopped at a florist to arrange a delivery that would arrive at Samantha's office the next day in the early afternoon. A tall, elegant and properly over the top arrangement of golden Freesias and White Lilies in a jet black vase seemed like a sweet little flourish.

Finally, the proper after show night spot was required. He called Marcel for a recommendation, and his friend was eager to display the depth and breadth of his cultural expertise. Marcel went all out not only suggesting a spot that had a waiting list measured in months, but actually making the arrangements at a place called Oliver's. Afterwards, he related how he had tapped into a wealth of connections and his own celebrity to quickly produce the preferred table. Dalton lost no time expressing the proper amount of gratitude, and was rewarded with his friend's familiar disappointment at his not being gay. He hung up with the first smile that had passed his lips in almost a week.

    The thought of the opera got his creative side thinking. The light and shadows of a stage production fit so neatly with his photographic style. It seemed like just the right tone to set as he started his first project for the magazine. He opened a sketchbook and scribbled a few ideas to propose to Samantha during the next planning session. As he worked, his sadness began to retreat. It was hardly gone, but it began to ache in a more manageable way.

    It occurred to him that an evening such as this was something that he could hardly spring on his new girlfriend as a surprise. Samantha would need to arrange whatever she would wear just as he had, though she no doubt had a closet full of the right apparel, most with the tags still in place. The few steps to her office brought a bright welcoming smile in response.

    "Well, if it isn't the long stranger," she cracked.

    "Hey, I know I have been pretty busy this week, but I have come to make amends." Dalton returned Samantha's smile with the closest approximation he could deliver.

"Have you decided how you are going to make this long absence up to me?"

Actually, I have. That's why I'm here."

"Fire away then."

"Well, I think you'll agree that I have a knack for delivering on surprises, so while I won't give the entire agenda away, let me just say that you will need to have something formal available for tomorrow; something with flair. You might even want to spend some time getting properly fussy about your hair and stuff."

"Dalton, you have such a way with words," she replied almost girlishly. "What time do the festivities begin?"

"Dinner will be late, but you will need to be ready by about seven."

Rising from behind her desk, she walked to him with purpose, accenting her movements and targeting his eyes with hers. A new distinctive fragrance found its way to him a split second before she did. Dalton closed his eyes and let it and her wrap him up. Her mouth was eager as she arrived, and he responded without hesitation. When she had explored every possible combination of their lips and tongues, she finally relented; her smile ferocious, her body still pressed firmly against his.

"I will need a few details," she purred.

"Yes," Dalton agreed. "I was thinking we could leave right from the office, grab a quick appetizer at the club down the street and then start the date from there."

Samantha pulled away while keeping her eyes tightly on him.

"Men, when will they ever understand the efforts that a woman must undergo to prepare for such an evening?" she sighed with added dramatic gusto.

Dalton smiled sympathetically. "You're right of course. Okay, revision one point one will include me coming to your place with the appropriate transport, and we can then get the early snack before commencing with the festivities."

"I like Revision one point one. I will sign off on that."

"How early will you leave to begin your transformation?"

"My last meeting ends at two. I will head out right after that. Why?"

"Oh, no reason, I was just curious."

Samantha's expression was clearly in the 'I don't believe you for a minute' category, but she withheld further comment and made her way back to the desk.

Dalton was glad that the arrangements for the flowers were early enough that he wouldn't have to change the delivery. He winked quickly and went back to work.

Now that everything was set, the rest of his day passed without event, he enjoyed a light dinner and went to sleep in a mood that seemed to resemble tranquil. There still was no hint of a dream, at least none he could remember, but the restless intervals disappeared for an evening at least.

The sun struggles to find an opening in a sky littered with small puffy clouds. Carrying the suit bag that holds the tux he hastily picked up on the way, Dalton pushes into the Choice building. He is virtually carried along by the sea of humanity as eager to get started as he is. A late email the day before had indicated that the space he needed for his studio could be arranged within the building on a lower floor. He contacted the property manager and then stopped the elevator so that he could see it. It wasn't perfect, but when the man agreed to get a crew in over the weekend to make all of the adjustments that Dalton requested, another detail was sorted out.

Dalton's Secretary Jennifer was sitting at her desk and accepted the signed paperwork from the building manager with a nod and a smile. There was no time to chat if everything on the day's schedule were to be completed. Setting the suit bag on the coat rack, Dalton flinched as the phone rang. Already it seemed the fates were conspiring against him. However, the call was thankfully brief. Lindsay had a lead on an apartment that had just come on the market that was merely high-priced. It was located near enough to be workable and Dalton had the distinct impression that there was something odd in the price the agent related, but he agreed to give it a look the next day and quickly hung up. With everything else on his plate, whatever suspicions he held were quickly displaced. The rest of the morning passed quickly and a favorable number of items were checked off the to-do list. With a good number of items still remaining, he asked Jennifer to arrange his lunch order and continued to work.

The buzz of the intercom arrived at the expected time, and an anxious Samantha asked him to come to her office as he finished the last bite of his sandwich. Dalton agreed but responded with no hint of excitement. He walked into Samantha's office with a neutral expression to find her waiting and watching him with a look of absolute awe. Her hands were softly touching the soft petals of the arrangement. A slow sly smile crossed his face.

"They're so beautiful," she whispered. "I had to cancel my last meeting just so I could tell you." Samantha seemed genuinely touched. Her blue eyes glistened just a little. "This is an awfully good down payment, Dalton."

"I'm glad you like them," Dalton said, leaning against the door and feeling relaxation flow into his body in a way he had not believed possible the day before.

"Like them? They're amazing and so are you." Samantha's expression suddenly brightens as she has a thought.

"Close the door," she urges quietly. As he complies, she crosses the room and leans against him, brushing her lips against his neck and on up to his ear.

"There are a few ways that I would love to show my appreciation for this lovely gesture, and the only reason I am restraining that inclination is that once we got started, it would probably interfere with whatever delicious plans you have for the rest of the evening. That being said, I think you should expect a more serious demonstration as this evening ends, okay?"

The combination of the pleasure he feels with this beautiful woman draped so intimately against him, and the thought that the real girl had finally arrived, made the response seem easy and natural.

"Sounds like a plan to me." He looks deeply into Samantha's eyes with a growing anticipation that arouses more than a little surprise from her. Stretching as he pushes away from the door, he pulls her closer and follows with a kiss that Samantha finds almost overwhelming. When he releases her, he is convinced that she staggers just the littlest bit before righting herself.

"Sam, you should probably get going. I'm sure there's a whole army of folks waiting to pamper and polish you for tonight's outing."

Thinking to herself that this is hardly the same guy she has been so busy pursuing, Samantha's smile evolves into an expression much deeper and more serious; her feelings as close to real pleasure as any she has ever known. She shakes her head, a quick chuckle escaping. "It's not fair," she says, mostly to herself. Dalton lets the comment pass, but maintains a lock on her eyes as she gathers her things and prepares to leave. Just as she reaches the door, she touches his hand lightly and passes as he opens the way.

The time passes quickly as the day's end arrives, and logging off his desktop, Dalton locks his office and changes into his tux. Jennifer alerts him to the arrival of his Limo, and his departure is followed by more than a few admiring glances, including both Jennifer and Jasmine. The two share a look of lusty agreement before turning back to their work.

The Friday evening traffic is considerable. As the day progressed, the sky filled with heavier clouds and has turned sharply chilly. The cloud cover has made it dark enough that streetlamps have come up and shop signs are glowing. A few cars and an armada of taxis race in each direction. There is plenty of time to get the quick bite and still make the show, but he calls Sam from the Limo to make sure she is nearly ready as he approaches her building. She meets him at the door wearing a tight, floor length couture gown. It's a shade of red wine and accents every graceful curve as well as leaving her shoulders bare, with a clear view of the diamond laden necklace draped from her neck. He assists her with her mink wrap and takes her arm as they leave her apartment and head for the elevator.

Conversation flows freely; a short interlude covering work related topics followed by more general things. The appetizers at the restaurant bar are just filling enough to avert hunger pains during the second act and the wine fills them with the right glow. The ride to the theater is long enough to enjoy a little, quick lip lock and then a rush inside and up the long, ornate staircase in search of their seats. The woman at the door takes their tickets, hands each of them a program and steals an admiring glance at Samantha. The timing for each step of their progress has been extraordinary and they have just gotten comfortably seated when the house lights dim and the show begins.

Intermission arrives and nice red wine in plastic cups is the only awkward item in an otherwise tasteful night to this point. A few shared comments on the merits of the production trigger memories of other shows they have each seen. Samantha is quick to add how thrilled she is by Dalton's surprise. She adds that she has always been a huge fan of the Opera. To herself, she smiles, thinking how nice it is to actually be telling him something that is true for a change. She tries to probe for some hint of their dinner plans, but Dalton resists and is saved by the blinking lights indicating the curtain up for the second act.

The cast steps back from a final curtain call as applause rains down from every tier of the multi-level Opera house. Dalton and Samantha walk together closely as the crowd slowly files out. There is no rush now and Dalton contacts the limo to assure that the car is nearby as they depart the theater. A light rain has begun and they rush between the drops to the hastily opened door and the warmth inside. They are laughing and breathless when Dalton mentions the name of their next stop. Samantha's eyes widen in response. She had been to Oliver's once a while back, and she is not only surprised that Dalton has heard of the place, but somehow gotten a reservation at the well-known eatery with the a-list clientele and the ultra a-list menu.

The place is everything Dalton could have hoped for as Samantha is so clearly in her element here. More than one person recognizes her and she pauses for a quick comment on the way to their table. The waiter is suitably haughty and raises an eyebrow when the couple declines an appetizer. They get back on his good side when Dalton allows Samantha to choose an expensive bottle of wine.

"You really know how to show a girl a good time, sir," she starts. "I'm very impressed."

"Well, since I seem to be doing so well, I think I will stay on a roll and ask you to choose our entrees. How's that sound?"

"Wonderful. How do you feel about Duck?"

Samantha reaches into her small night purse to recover her Blackberry, which she had thoughtfully turned off during the performance. A slight frown crosses her face briefly as it comes to life. She tries to cover it, but not before Dalton notices.

"You look troubled. Is something wrong?"

"It's a text message. It's fine. I will catch up later. Let's just enjoy the evening."

Oliver's delivers in a way that even an experienced traveler like Dalton with a wealth of Paris experience in his pocket finds amazing. The only flaw in the otherwise amazing meal is the occasional glance that Samantha directs at the purse on the seat beside her. Whatever it is, she is having trouble ignoring it. When the last plates are cleared, the waiter brings menus with a heavenly list of deserts, but Samantha shakes her head, and he walks away. The conversation ebbs and the couple sit quietly sipping their wine. Finally the check is brought and dealt with and they make their way out.

The light rain continues. As the car approaches, Samantha's Blackberry rings and she pulls the phone to answer.

"Just a minute, okay Dalton?"

"Sure."

The limo driver takes up a position near the entrance to supply an umbrella's shelter for the short run to the car. The short call finished, Samantha deposits her cell and they all walk toward the car. Just as they reach the door, Samantha turns to Dalton with a look that does not bode well for the evening's prospects.

"I know what I told you earlier," says Samantha with obvious regret, "but the truth is that something has come up which I must deal with right away. I want you to know that this evening has been absolutely wonderful and it breaks my heart that it won't continue as I had imagined. Would you be a dear and let me take the limo?"

Dalton can see that there is real misery in Samantha's eyes. It is easy to give in to a generous impulse.

"Sure, I'll be fine. Call me when you get back to your place."

The kiss she offers is warm and sweet, ending with a whispered thank you. The car drives away and Dalton makes his way back to the club to call for a cab. His relief at not having to face the prospect of the sexual encounter that was all but inevitable is at odds with a feeling that maybe that ending would have been much preferable to this one.

35.

Samantha: I raise the baton

Raindrops splatter against the window as the limo pulls away. The sight of Dalton standing there getting wet, tears at my heart more than I might have expected, but the call from Terry was one I could not continue with Dalton in the car. The Blackberry is quickly back in hand and Terry's voice is showing signs of the stress I heard a few minutes ago. It's time to exert some of my management expertise.

"Okay Terry, slow down and give me everything from the beginning."

The glare of the lights passing, reflect and bounce against the puddles and the droplets on the car window, making a frenetic, rock and roll light show background as I travel home.

Terry takes a second to breathe and then responds.

"All right, you know that I set it up so that Anna would meet me at the airport hotel today. As soon as I arrived in Prague this morning, I got settled at the airport hotel. Then I made my way to the hotel restaurant and ordered some coffee while I waited. I waited and waited and then waited some more, but Anna never showed. Finally I got a car and made my way to her house. When I went there, her mother answered the door and told me that Anna was out. I asked the mother where her daughter was, but she either did not understand or wouldn't answer. I know that I made it clear to Anna that I would be here today. I can't imagine where the bitch could have gone off to, but I am worried that Ivan has somehow gotten wind of our plans and beaten us to the punch!"

I take a minute to catch my breath and restore some order to my frantic brain.

"What time did you set for the meet this morning?"

"We were supposed to meet at 10:30." Terry is trying to seem professional, but I am disappointed by the frantic tone. I may have to take some time to decide whether I can partner with someone who is so easily flustered.

"And were you on time?"

Terry does not miss my insinuation of blame and responds with a caustic tone.

"Samantha, I did this one by the book. The plane landed at 7, I got through luggage and customs by 8:30 and was set up in my room by 9:30. There's no way I could have missed her."

"Don't get snippy; I am just trying to think this through." I am surprised at how calm I am. Normally, I would be all over Terry for this screw-up. Perhaps I am still feeling the effects of my romantic evening. Thoughts of Dalton's touch, his mouth on mine invade for a moment; only to be pushed away with fierce effort.

I close my eyes to let the next question find its way up into my consciousness. The car is quiet except for the steady tap of raindrops on the roof. The chill of the night has eased and I stretch out while trying not to notice the empty seat beside me. I can still imagine a trace of Dalton's cologne in the air from our earlier drive. He really had me going tonight. It is only a second before clarity returns and my eyes are open.

"What kind of background checking did you do?"

"I did the standard list: friends and family, marital status, financials, education, references…"

"How old is Anna?"

"She's twenty three."

"Boyfriend?"

"Not that I know…oh, you know, I think she *may* have mentioned something…"

"All right, here's what you're going to do. First, contact your friends at Ivan's to see if there's any indication that he knows anything. If he does, we'll have to come up with something else, but I am betting that this has more to do with Anna on a personal level. If I am right, get in touch with her friends. One of them is bound to know, especially if it's some romantic thing. Play up the opportunity and I am sure you'll get everything you need in a heartbeat."

"Yeah Sam, I'll get on that immediately. Sorry that I got so worked up. I'm sure you're right."

The connection ends and I deposit the blackberry back in my purse as I consider the implications of this fiasco on what should have been an extraordinary night. One thing has become clear; I am going to have to see this thing through myself. Some part of me knows that this project is not to be shared with Dalton, at least not yet. I am not sure why I feel this way, but I never question my instincts.

Still, there are parts of my body that are not particularly happy right this minute and I don't think they will be satisfied with the promise of some future delight; not now. I tap on the window and give the driver a new destination which is thankfully close and promises a hotel room full of potential amusements. The car soon makes a turn in a different direction as I gather my make-up for a refresh.

With the evening's plans steered toward more pleasurable pursuits, I try to decide how to manage the next few weeks. I'll have to keep the Dalton campaign separated from my designs for Anna. It occurs to me that he has already given me the perfect solution. I can use his reticence toward jumping in the sack to allow things to move at a more leisurely pace while I button up the new designer. The way I figure it, both things should be handled in a month or so, six weeks at the most. By then Dalton will be ready for some companionship and I will certainly be happy to oblige. Meanwhile, if I have to make the occasional physical accommodation to feed my appetites, I will just have to be careful to keep them away from prying eyes.

My Blackberry rings and I push up on my elbows to see a clock that has no business displaying 3:49 am. Brushing a few stray strands of hair away from my eyes, I grab the phone and answer with clear disgust.

"Yeah?"

The voice on the other end of the line is ecstatic in a way that only Terry's voice can be.

"I found her friend. She told me where Anna is. It's a bit out of the way, but I am heading there now. The friend is with me and will help me to find the place."

"Do you have any idea what time it is here?" The idea of strangling Terry or at very least jettisoning the whole partner plan is getting more attractive by the minute.

"What? Oh, sorry Sam. I figured this was important enough that you would want to know."

"I'll want to know when you have the bitch on a jet in the seat beside yours. Until then, give me updates via text or email during *my* business hours."

"Okay Sam. We are on our way. Anna's friend Milada will certainly make the time in the car less tiresome."

Rising from the bed to stretch my achy body and still my growing agitation, I walk a few steps before I respond. Even now, keeping my anger at bay is less of a struggle than it might usually be.

"Listen, I expect one hundred percent concentration on the task at hand, is that clear? You lose focus for so much as a second and I will know, and everything we discussed will be forgotten. You understand? I mean everything."

The line goes deadly silent for a count of five before Terry answers. When the response finally arrives, the tone is much more serious and abashed.

"I understand."

"Good." Having made myself clear, I feel inclined to be a bit generous to inspire the right amount of diligence. "Look, find Anna. You do that and I don't care if you ease your boredom with Milada or Anna or both. Just get the job done."

Sensing that I have calmed down and that any further comment might swing things back in the wrong direction, Terry very wisely says nothing more and the connection ends.

I make my way to the bathroom and take a look at my smeared make-up and red-rimmed eyes. A splash of cool water helps a little, but not as much as a bit more sack time will. Closing the light, I cross back to the bed and quickly find my place beneath the sheets that have cooled in my absence. The coolness is short lived however, as a pair of very eager hands find their way to some very sensitive spots. Whatever-his-name-is is making his impatience felt as he moves in close behind me. I turn to him and smile as I look forward to an early breakfast.

I orchestrated the next several weeks every bit as masterfully as the conductor at 'Der Rosenkavalier' handled the orchestra at the Met. It took a bit longer than I hoped with details like arranging Anna's visa complicating things. Still, the conversation with Dalton expressed just the right amount of newfound awareness. It ended with the announcement that one of the reasons our evening ended so early was my reluctance to challenge his idea of saving sex until the time is right. When I told him that there was no other way that that incredible night could have ended, his agreement was quick and certain. It was easy to sense the disappointment in his tone. My own was a close echo muted only by the activities that have kept me satisfied at the same hotel room five or six nights a week.

To make the time pass as acceptably for Dalton as for me, I offered a list of date type activities for us to pursue. We did the hand-holding thing through Central

Park more than once. The first time ended with a picnic which was fine except for my muddy, ruined Manolo Blahniks. The next was a little better when Dalton took me out on a cute little rowboat which honestly was a fun if a tad PG. At one point, Dalton asked if everything was okay. I answered that everything was fine. His expression indicated that he was having trouble accepting my answer, but I started asking about his efforts in locating an apartment and he was easily distracted. He mentioned the place that I had quietly offered to put some money toward to make Lindsay's price more palatable. Dalton said that he had made an offer and was waiting for a response. Day by day, week by week, the time has passed.

    Terry is scheduled to return with Anna in a few days. I can finally say goodbye to my hotel nights and get things back on track with Dalton.

36.

Romantic daybreak

Renaissance Indigo shines out in big red glowing letters above the street as a crowd lines up outside the stylish eatery. Samantha makes her usual entrance, thoughtlessly striding past the queue and speaking to the Maître D as several nearby sets of eyes glare impatiently. Dalton hurries to keep up and tries not to notice the reactions on the faces closest to him. He realizes that it's beside the point that Sam has a reservation, though she probably even got that at the last minute, effectively shoving her way to the front of the line. It is the attitude she projects that she absolutely is entitled to her privileged status. As he approaches the tuxedoed gentleman already engaged in conversation with Samantha, they both turn to him and he returns a smile just as negotiations have been resolved, and soon they are on their way to a table.

    In his life as a fashion photographer, he has lived with a certain amount of celebrity though he has never thought of himself in that way. There were a whole host of parties with people who lived in that world. He had worked with Marcel, who traveled those paths with the skill of an alpine goat in a tight mountain pass. For himself, he had enjoyed some of the perks. Travelling to exotic places and meeting so many interesting people had been the best part of the adventure. The glitter and glamour paled in comparison to doing the kind of work he could be proud of. It would be easy to attribute Samantha's attitude to a combination of the city she lives in and being Tony

Choice's daughter. The glare of the neon lights, the constant attention of the paparazzi coupled with being the offspring of a well-connected, fabulously wealthy publisher would challenge just about anyone. In the back of his mind though, a whisper he could almost ignore pointed to so many he had met in similar circumstances who had not given in to the self-assured, nearly haughty attitude that his new girlfriend wore as extravagantly as her latest gown.

    As the Maître D leads the way to a more secluded part of the restaurant, Dalton cannot help noticing the jealous glances of the men and women they pass. The women's jealousy, he suspects, is aimed at the spectacular array of diamonds on Samantha's necklace. It is the same one she wore to their opera evening several weeks ago. The men's jealousy is even easier. Most of their appreciative attention probably pairs with a fantasy of replacing Dalton as this beautiful woman's escort. The balance is a less challenging admiration of Samantha's broadcast splendor. Not that the men were hurting for picturesque companions or that the women were hurting for jewels or fine attire. There is an interesting mix of obvious gawking paired with feigned indifference that follows the pair all the way to their table.

    After so many weeks of constant proximity with days of meetings and working lunches followed by scattered evenings and weekends, Dalton had convinced himself that the total package he had always dreamed of was just within his grasp. Samantha's new attitude toward sexual activity had been a little surprising, but he had convinced himself that they were working slowly toward the kind of intimacy that might be sustainable. So much so that his jacket pocket was weighted with a substantial gift box that was intended to demonstrate his desire for the sustained part. It might have been the late onset of spring, but now that it had arrived alongside the turn of the calendar to May, he had suggested an evening of reconnection. Insisting that the selection for the evening's outing be Samantha's, she had chosen a place that he had to admit had the right flair for his purposes.

Arriving at the table, Dalton helps Samantha into her seat before taking his own opposite her. The Maître D hands each a menu and adds a heavily bound wine list to Dalton.

"Your waiter will join you presently," the man states evenly before turning crisply away.

The room is lit for intimacy. There is a small lamp in the center of the table and it is splashing bits of light dramatically on them both. Dalton notices the lighting as it works on each of their neighbors. He makes a mental note to consider this effect in a future photo session. There is a quiet moment as they attend to their heavy linen napkins. The glassware sparkles, begging to be filled with some bubbling distillation. The combination of the atmosphere and the evening's intent spur Dalton to get things started.

"You look amazing, Samantha," he starts, hoping for smooth and a little nonchalant.

"Why thank you sir." Samantha's reply is as polished as ever. Sam notices that Dalton seems nervous. She chose the restaurant fully expecting that this would be the "big" night. She decides to help keep the conversation flowing while he works up the nerve.

"I've been going through the layouts for the coming issue and your images are just stunning. Your first issue was proof enough that I was right about you. These next designs are nothing short of breathtaking."

Dalton responds to the praise with a gentle nod.

"The truth is I'm having a blast. You have some truly gifted people working for you, and they make my job pretty simple."

"You're being way too modest. With no disrespect to my people, who *are* talented, your photographs have brought a whole new energy to the place. I think it goes without saying that you've brought a new energy to my life away from work as well."

Dalton composes himself for what he has planned. The moment has arrived much sooner and more naturally than he would have expected.

"These past several weeks have been very intense for me." Dalton thinks as he says these words that they are a bit of overstatement but as he composes himself to continue, the waiter brings the menus, interrupting Dalton's speech. Dalton opens the wine list and the waiter nods approvingly as Dalton indicates his choice.

"As I was saying, the past few weeks have been so..."

A different waiter interrupts Dalton with goblets of water and a tray of warm rolls wrapped in a fancy napkin. Samantha starts smiling as Dalton tries to be patient with the interfering staff.

"So, the past few weeks have been as wonderful as any in my..."

The first waiter returns, sweeping in with the wine Dalton has chosen as well as the standing wine bucket. Samantha can no longer hold back her laughter as Dalton tries not to glare at the man. Slowly, he begins to lighten up and his laughter is quiet and eases his mounting tension. The waiter pours a sample of wine that Dalton examines, sniffs and eventually brings to his lips. Dalton nods acceptance and the waiter completes the pour as Dalton eyes the man intensely. The waiter looks confused, but eventually departs. Dalton opens his mouth to start again, but Samantha places a finger to her lips.

"It seems clear to me that you're happy and I'm glad. The past few weeks have been everything I could have hoped for. You've made me happy. Why don't we enjoy our dinner and leave any new business for dessert?"

Samantha's smile is irresistible. He is more than willing to postpone what they both seem to understand is coming. When the waiter makes his next appearance, the meal is ordered and Dalton has already begun to relax. When the entrees are served, conversation turns to more mundane thoughts.

"Lindsay tells me that you are still looking for a place. May I ask why?"

"Well, much as I like the accommodations at the hotel, you know that I've been trying to find something near the office that will suit me. I never expected to be there this long. The magazine has been generous with the expense, but I hate taking advantage."

"I thought you had the one nearby pretty much decided. Actually though, while I am hardly worried about the expense, there's a better alternative than the hotel or the place that Lindsay found; one that appears to have completely escaped your attention."

"And that is?"

Samantha can see that Dalton is being sincere and honest as always. She finds his straight laced ways a little boring, but does her best to overlook them as he has so much talent, and is so easy on the eyes. He is her perfect accessory. Deciding that his seriousness will never do, she adopts a teasing tone in response.

"For such a serious man, you can be awfully silly."

Dalton is perplexed by her words and her tone. He works to keep his tone light in view of the evening's ultimate goal.

"How so?"

Samantha can see that Dalton has not understood that her words were meant as lighthearted jest. She reaches across the table for his hand before continuing.

"Honey, I have a beautiful apartment with more than enough space for the two of us. You could move in any time you want."

Samantha's smile burns away his hurt and he grabs her hand.

"Okay, but tell me something," he replies.

"Anything you ask, lover."

"You have to know that I am never going to feel comfortable living in your place. Would you consider moving to some place new that could be ours?"

"Tell you what; you move in this weekend. Try the place out for a while. If you really can't feel comfortable there we can start looking for a place together right away."

'The Salmon is a little off tonight,' Samantha thinks as she takes another bite. Considering Dalton's words, it takes less than a second to reject the idea of moving out of her penthouse condo. Leaving that brilliant view and upper echelon location is absolutely out of the question. Still, she understands that a guy like Dalton wants to feel like he is part of the equation. She figures that she has a better than even chance of convincing Dalton to stay put once he's moved in. She is even willing to consider making a little extra effort to make the amenities extra accommodating. Reaching for her wine, she smiles as Dalton sits, evidently considering her proposal.

The dishes are cleared and the waiter comes back with dessert menus. Dalton's eyes make it clear that he should go away and await a signal. The man departs at once. Dalton reaches into his jacket and pulls out the gift box. Samantha smiles, but her reaction is not so much excitement as the feeling of satisfaction derived from a plan come to fruition. Dalton quickly opens the box and removes the jewelry box from within. He places it before Sam and gently urges the top open so that the ring faces her.

"Samantha Choice, I have been looking for the perfect woman all my life. Beautiful, intelligent, accomplished, you're everything a man could hope for. I didn't expect to find you here, but if you'll have me, I'll do my best to be your perfect man. Marry me?"

Now that the moment has arrived, Samantha takes a moment to let her victory spread its warmth through her. She takes the box in her hands and takes a closer look. Setting the ring back on the table, she returns her attention to Dalton and answers with as much passion as she can muster.

"Yes Dalton. I will marry you. I have never wanted anything as much as I want to be your wife. Would you care to…?" She indicates her waiting finger and he slides the ring in place. The two raise their glasses and Dalton nods to the waiter who brings the dessert menus. A brief thought runs through his mind. He wonders at the low-key reaction that Samantha has displayed and measures it against the emotional reaction he feels certain Sienna would have shown. He knows this is unfair to both women and dismisses the thought.

The drive to Samantha's place is filled with the kind of newly-engaged activities that erase any worries Dalton might have had about Samantha's lack of enthusiasm. She leads Dalton into her apartment, switches on the lights and stays by the door; locking it as he enters. Dalton takes a few steps into the living room before he is spun around and newly attacked by Samantha; her kisses stunning and insatiable. Dalton can barely catch his breath as he responds equally. Samantha pulls back for a second, her expression a mix of pleasure and anticipation.

"Well that's more like it. All this time; I knew you were holding out on me."

"I wasn't exactly holding out. It was more like building the excitement."

"You're quite the builder. Perhaps you should go into construction."

Samantha's hands are placed firmly around Dalton's neck as her body strains close to his.

"I could wear a hard hat or something."

Samantha starts the kissing again, running past the quick chuckling reaction to fulfill the urgency of her growing need.

"Yeah, something," she agrees as she welds her mouth to his. Slowly she begins unbuttoning his shirt. She will enjoy the view in a minute, but his tongue and lips are all she needs for now.

Finally, with a small nod of approval, she turns to allow Dalton access to the zipper in the back of her gown. He pulls her close first and kisses her neck and shoulders.

"I love you. Oh... I ...love... you," Samantha purrs breathlessly. Quickly, the gown is undone and strewn on the floor. Samantha steps away and leads Dalton by the hand toward the hallway where the bedrooms are located. He has a moment to notice the kitchen through an archway as she pulls him along. Samantha kisses Dalton again as they arrive at her bedroom door.

"Mm, I love you."

Just as she opens the door, the phone rings. The mood is suspended, hanging in midair. Without skipping a beat, Samantha takes control.

"Damn. Sorry honey. Dalton, could you please go to the kitchen and grab the bottle of wine on the counter and a couple of glasses while I get rid of whoever this is."

Encouraging him with a last kiss, she opens the door.

"I promise I won't be long."

Samantha runs to the phone on her night stand. It sits in a part of the room away from the door that she has left half open. She sounds annoyed as she answers, the urgency of her need pushed away as she focuses on the call.

"Hello? Who is this? Oh, hi Terrence."

Dalton turns and heads for the kitchen. The male name does not make an impression; he is unfazed by it. He goes through the arched doorway to a spotless kitchen that not only looks clean, but unused. He looks around and finds the bottle and the glasses as requested. He hesitates to head back to the bedroom, trying to give Samantha time to finish her call.

Samantha figures she can take a few minutes to deal with the call, trusting Dalton's reserve to keep him away for at least that long.

"How was the flight from Prague? Your room at the Plaza is already booked."

Samantha remembers to check the door as her associate answers. Terry has found a way back into her good graces by completing the task without needing any more babysitting. Turning back to look out the window, she is filled with the splendor of the night outside and the sparkle of the ring inside.

"The flight was fine. Is it okay to get a room there for Anna?" Terry responds.

"Sure, why the fuck not? I can't see anything wrong with showing her a little American glamour before we shove her into the salt mine. How soon will you get there? She understands the arrangements?"

Samantha tilts her wrist this way and that noting the brilliance with some satisfaction. She nods gently as Terry confirms a few details.

"She will have her own label," Samantha agrees, "with both of our names and she will dedicate her original drawings for our first collection, right? Do you think she has what it takes to lead something like this? Yes, I know you will be guiding her, and I have confidence in your skills."

Dalton can wait no longer, so he heads back to Samantha's bedroom with opened bottle and glasses in hand. As he approaches the doorway, the sound of Samantha's voice slows him.

"Don't worry about the drawings; I have them in a safe place. The one place nobody would ever look. Of course I know that until we have Anna's Press conference, the designs are technically stolen. That's why I needed you to get your butt back here. Once we do the media tour, Ivan won't dare challenge me as he would have to explain what he did. This is the beginning of our house, Samantha Choice, Ltd."

Dalton is being drawn into the conversation in spite of his best efforts to give Samantha her space. On one hand, her intention to start a new design company is her business. On the other hand, with their relationship moving steadily toward tonight's developments, it seems hard to understand that she would have kept something so big to herself. And he could not help but hear the part about something stolen.

"He doesn't know."

To Dalton's ears, this reference shows Samantha's clear intent to keep her plans from him.

"Yes he did. He asked me tonight. It was a very acceptable rock, though to be honest, it was a bit smaller than I expected."

Dalton's expression darkens as he begins to understand the full import of his new fiancée's words. Samantha glances quickly toward the half open door before she continues, lowering her voice though not quite enough. Dalton continues to hear her from the hall.

"As soon as I have a little fun, I'll tell D that I have to go out for a little bit to visit a sick friend. It's almost true, isn't it Terrence? I mean, you wouldn't be offended if I called you sick, would you?"

Samantha laughs a bit louder than she means to...

"You are a naughty thing..."

Samantha looks up to see Dalton entering the room. She realizes that she has lost track of time at the very least.

"Umm, Terry, I'll have to get back to you."

Samantha hangs up the phone, and walks toward Dalton. He shakes his head and she stops.

"I won't even ask who you were talking to." He nods in the direction of the phone she has just abandoned.

"I hope you don't think that conversation meant anything. Whatever you heard, it's not what you think. Terry is a business associate and a friend, nothing more."

Dalton's smile makes it clear that her words are not making a dent.

"Did I ever mean anything at all to you?"

Samantha takes a step toward Dalton, sensing an opportunity to turn this around. Her tone is all sweetness.

"Oh honey, of course you did, you do. You just have to let me explain what..."

"Stop. Just be honest for once."

Samantha is surprised by Dalton's intensity.

"Dalton, you're a good looking guy. You're talented and people like you. You are the kind of guy that everyone wants to be close to, and I thought that you and I could be like one of those incredible couples, the kind that are always on the cover of US magazine or People. I know I am not bad to look at and I have a few good qualities. I'm not bad in bed for one thing. I thought we could have a little fun."

"Fun! Did you actually say fun?"

Samantha sees Dalton's attack as unjustified and responds with an attack of her own.

"You know Dalton, while we're talking about qualities, we might mention that you are a little bit self-righteous."

Dalton starts to turn.

"I'll keep that in mind."

Samantha is not used to being treated like this, and her anger reflects it.

"Where do you think you're going, you asshole? I can find a dozen more like you on any street corner. You think because you can take a few pictures, that makes you something special? Well you're not. You're average."

Dalton shakes his head as if he has just awakened from some kind of trance.

"Samantha, just remember that it was you who pursued me. Oh and by the way, you can keep that acceptable little rock. I'm sure it will come in handy as a re-gift."

Samantha's shouts follow Dalton down the hall.

"Get back here. I'm not finished with you. If you leave this apartment, you'll regret it. I will personally make sure that you never work in this city again. Do you hear me?"

Dalton closes the door behind him as he walks out.

"Well do you, do you hear me? Ooooooh!"

Samantha has heard the door close. Even the fact that it didn't slam is enraging. Yet after a few seconds her eyes close. Controlling her breathing and attending to the few streaks from her tears with the back of her right hand, she looks almost as radiant as before. Refreshed, she heads for the bathroom depositing Dalton's ring on her dresser. Just before she enters, she starts to hum.

37.

Checking in and checking out

Not only does the door to his suite creak in a way he had not noticed before, it seems harder to push open as well. Dalton switches on the nearby light and drops the packet with the magnetic keys in his pocket. His face in the mirrored glass closet doors looks more tired than unhappy now. He tosses his jacket on a nearby chair and opens the closet, grabbing his suitcases. He begins collecting his things for a morning departure. It would have been clear even without the screaming farewell that Samantha's interest in keeping him around after tonight's events will be less than zero.

With a numb, mindless effort, the bulk of the preparations are completed. There are a couple of bags near the door, and a remaining one open on a stand, only waiting for the last essentials to be packed in the morning. Making his way to the large window that fills the whole wall, he can't help but notice how the lights of the city have become cold and distant. The sky is a dark clouded stain, and Dalton finally admits his despair as he pulls the curtains together.

The memory of the past couple hours is filled with a landscape of savage noise and a commotion of battling color. As soon as he found himself on the street, Dalton weighed the idea of a speedy delivery back to his hotel by cab. He dismissed this at once. He needed the punishment of the traffic sounds. In a symphony of discordance from alto to bass they called out. "Idiot!" He craved the people shouting to music from inside the watering holes he passed as he made his way on foot. They were shouting at him. "Idiot!" The flashing signs and the constellation of lit windows that seemed so poetic previously, suddenly warped into a single accusing message. "Idiot!" All of it fit like a well-deserved, itchy sweater.

Pulling his jacket closer he looked down to avoid the wind, noting how it tugged and pushed at little bits of colored paper, perhaps the remnants of streamers from a recent party. There were scraps of newsprint and other less recognizable items. Their impossibly elfin dance at his feet pulled him slowly away from his anger and guilt. What was left inside him was a lot like what he saw on the ground.

As the memory fades, Dalton walks away from the windows and ends up sinking to the bed. It is all he can do to stay upright as the events of the evening pull at him like some vicious undertow. The realization of how many excuses he has made for Samantha chokes him. He is amazed at how ready he was to accept her arrogance and her pretty words. The final blow is his selection of Samantha over Sienna because she was real. Real is not a word he can easily associate with the screaming, angry witch whose voice carried down the hall and all the way to her elevator. Dalton grunts with an effort as he lifts himself from the bed. He moves to the desk and opens his laptop.

In the shadowed corner of the room, Sienna fades into watchful appearance though not in Dalton's line of sight. She is nearly inconsolable as she takes in her Love's dismay. The fact that this result was all but inevitable doesn't make it any less heartbreaking. She swipes at a tear as she watches. Dalton is buying a train ticket online. He pulls his wallet and carefully types his credit card information. The display shows a one-way ticket to Philadelphia departing Penn Station at 12:00 noon. Sienna eyes widen as she is finally able to connect to the information on the screen. Sienna takes a last quick look at Dalton before fading away.

Dalton removes his tie and flips it on top of the jacket. He lets his shoes fall to the floor as he finally settles into bed, too tired to finish undressing. He turns off the lamp on the nightstand and tries to sleep. He squeezes his eyes shut, but to no avail. The glow of the hotel alarm clock punishes him for his many mistakes. Some part of him knows that Sienna is gone, but he doesn't want to give in. For the first time in a long time he falls asleep to have an ordinary dream. Instead of Sienna in his hotel room, there are a series of faces, Caitlyn and Laurie, Professor Purcell and Samantha, all of them laughing. Dalton awakens again. There will be no sleep tonight. He stares at the ceiling.

"Sienna, you were right, please come back," he whispers. "I'll make you a deal right now. Come back and I'll never complain again about only having the nights. I would trade all the days I could have with anyone else just to have the nights with you."

Samantha Choice approaches the front door of the Plaza hotel as she continues a conversation on her blackberry. The hard light of the street lamps bounces off her sunglasses and the collar of her light jacket is up to fend off the evening breeze. All things considered, her mood is upbeat as she makes an atypically quiet entrance to the hotel.

"Look Dad, you know I can take care of myself. Do I wish things had worked out differently? Of course I do. Still, I have a little surprise all set up, and Mr. Dalton Hunter is going to be very sorry he let me down like that. Hold on a sec..."

Samantha goes to the front desk and catches the eye of a clerk there. She glances as discreetly as possible to make sure that there are no paparazzi nearby.

"The Royal Terrace Suite, please."

"Here's your key, Ms. Choice. Your guest arrived a little while ago. Have a pleasant stay," the desk clerk offers smiling.

Samantha removes her sunglasses and fires a withering glance at the young man behind the desk and he is immediately chastised. She is not happy to have been recognized.

"Sorry Ms. Choice, obviously this hotel considers the privacy of our guests as paramount."

"See that you remember that," she growls. She walks away, and reaches the elevator before she allows the smile that she has been holding back to find its place along her lips. One of the privileges of rank is the right to flay those of inferior birth for the pure amusement of it. She remembers her father on hold on her Blackberry and raises it back to speaking level.

"Dad, I have to get going. I'm late and I have to put the finishing touches on my plan. I will tell you all about it tomorrow. Yes, you'll meet Terry as well."

Sam dials a new number and listens but gets no answer. She shakes her head as she enters the elevator. Soon she emerges and walks toward the suite. Slotting the key and removing it she enters.

"Terry, where are you?" She strips off the jacket and tosses the sunglasses and her purse on the bed. Then she goes to the bar and adds a couple cubes of ice to a glass before pouring a couple of shots worth of bourbon over them. As she takes the first relaxing sip, the sound of the shower becomes obvious. Taking a quick gulp, she sets the glass on the nearest night stand, lets the warmth of the drink work its magic and then slowly begins to unbutton her blouse. She opens the bathroom door and calls in.

"Terrence, don't you dare get all lathered up before I get in there, you hear me?"

She closes the door behind her and the room is empty except for the sounds of splashing water and Sam's easy laughter.

Light slowly filters into Dalton's consciousness. Sleep must have overtaken him somewhere in the lowest hours he thinks, as he adjusts to whatever this new reality is. Rising from the bed, he makes his way to the window. It seems like a good idea to see what kind of weather will be present at the beginning of the rest of his life. Pushing the curtains aside, the sky has a stripe of golden blue on the horizon with a fairly heavy cloudbank above. A feature captures his eye and he goes running for his camera trying to capture it before the heavens transit to some other countenance. A single ray of light pierces the cloud and strikes a nearby building. Cityscapes don't normally interest Dalton, but this light seems indicative of something that he can almost define. It has something to do with Sienna. A second after the shot is taken, the cloud closes; the ray is gone.

Dalton puts his gear away and begins the morning's preparations. Breakfast is a minimalist affair with a cup of coffee and an English muffin. A call to Marcel is unsuccessful as it is already well into his friend's workday morning. There will be time to confer later. There is little chance of going back, as Marcel reluctantly replaced him a month after he left. Still, he might have some ideas.

Checking out from the suite brings the day's agenda to sharper focus. When Dalton exits the elevator on his way to his office, the plan is to clean out his desk and make a quick escape. What happens next is a bit more than he is prepared to face. His secretary Jennifer calls to him as he walks by.

"Mr. Hunter, you are expected in Mr. Choice's office right away." She has a sympathetic look on her face and appears to be capturing a last glance.

"Thanks, I'll go there right now."

Dalton enters Tony's office. His now former employer is scowling openly.

"Come with me. I'm afraid Samantha has discovered your little secret," Tony remarks with hostile intent.

Dalton is puzzled by the remark, but remains silent. He follows Tony to his office where Samantha stands by an open cabinet with a victorious grin. She pulls out the book of designs from Ivan's studio. Dalton has no clue what the package contains, but understands that this is Samantha's lever to break their contract.

"What is that?"

"Don't play dumb, Dalton," she answers. "These are the designs from Ivan's Rusland Studio that he received from a very talented student. They were stolen recently and now we find them in your locker. It's shocking."

Samantha is playing the victim to the hilt, even managing a couple genuine tears to make the picture complete. Tony has the sense of where this is headed and backs his daughter's plan for the moment.

"This is pretty surprising, Dalton. You really had me fooled with that straight arrow act. As you know, we have a very solid morals clause in our contract. Choice Publications has an outstanding reputation in this city. This could be a huge black mark against that reputation. Is there anything you want to say?"

Dalton replies with icy calm. "I don't think so."

Samantha approaches her almost fiancé with her typical deliberation. She pulls the ring that she received last night and places it carefully in Dalton's outstretched hand. This is more for her father's benefit than because she has any hesitation about keeping the ring. She wants her father to believe she was all set to marry Dalton before she made the 'startling' discovery.

"There's no way I can keep this now." Quietly, so that only Dalton can hear her, she adds a last remark without a trace of sarcasm.

"You break my heart."

Tony watches the exchange and knows his daughter's moves well enough not to be fooled by her calculated performance. Even if that were not the case, a little conversation with Sienna's girl Jasmine has made this whole production even more transparent. He is more than willing to let his daughter have her way and he certainly won't reveal his source as she might have other uses in the foreseeable future. That being said, Samantha may have need of some fatherly assistance.

"Dalton, here is how this works. You agree to a voided contract and also to leave the city, and we keep the whole thing under wraps. You get to stay out of jail, and my company gets to avoid a huge publicity nightmare. Agreed?"

"Agreed, I'll start packing my things."

"Come Sam, you and I have a few things to discuss."

Tony leaves the room and Samantha follows, turning back for one last look. She is sad for a fleeting second as she considers what she has lost.

"Goodbye Dalton... and good luck."

Once they are a safe distance from the Dalton's office, Tony turns to his daughter with a withering glance.

"All right, suppose you tell me what I just witnessed."

"What do you mean?" Samantha replies innocently.

"Sweetheart, you're my daughter and you know I will always back you. Still, don't talk to me like I'm an idiot. That boy did not steal anything. Now you're going to tell me who did."

Tony's tone makes it very clear that he will not stand for anything less than the truth. The easy decision is just to come clean, at least mostly.

"Dad, Terry and I have worked out the plan for starting up Samantha Choice, Ltd. Terry got a hold of some designs that were literally lying around Ivan's studio. He had no intention of using them and Terry managed to make them disappear. We have contacted the young designer who created them and she will be working for us. As a matter of fact, Terry has her set up at the Plaza as we speak. Her name is Anna and she was a student in Prague."

Tony listens carefully and then raises his hand to stop his daughter. He takes a seat at his desk.

"Wait a minute; you have to explain something to me. A couple months back you were all excited about this Dalton. He was the love of your life or some such thing. Now you discard him and wrap him up in this nonsense about stealing designs."

Samantha takes a breath and looks her father right in the eye.

"Dalton's a talented guy, but there was something about him. I never would have guessed it, but maybe I should have. You know what they say about the really good looking ones..."

"Are you trying to tell me that Dalton's gay? If that's the case, why did he give you the rock that you returned to him?"

"Who knows? Maybe he hasn't come to grips with it and thought getting married would, you know... keep his secret."

Tony looks at his daughter skeptically. He doesn't buy this hastily conceived story, but doesn't know that he cares enough to challenge it.

"Then the whole thing with Dalton stealing the designs..."

"...Gets us out of the contract with him and provides us a story if things get hairy with Ivan. Actually, I don't expect Ivan to be any problem as soon as we announce Anna. We can do that in a couple of days. He probably won't challenge us as he would have to explain the stuff he wrote to the girl and why he still kept the designs.

Tony's expression starts at annoyed and quickly evolves to exasperated.

"This could get messy, Sam. I thought your plan was to open your own studio. I never thought it would involve stolen designs and foreign nationals. I'm not squeamish or all that worried about morals as you know, but your idea to frame Dalton is absolutely stupid. If there are problems with Ivan, it would not only remove the guarantee of Dalton's silence, it might also open us to other problems."

Samantha trusts her father's judgment without question. His concern has obviously identified something she has not considered.

"Like what?

"Like the fact that Dalton has a very prominent ally in Marcel or had you forgotten? You trash Dalton and Marcel is more than a little likely to take exception. He isn't the kind of person your magazine would want to upset, much less your new house."

Tony sees that his daughter is thinking this through and is accepting his wisdom for a change. He continues a bit calmer.

"Okay, so here's what you're going to do. Get the press in tomorrow. Get Anna out for a makeover right away. I'm sure you'll want her to be very presentable. You will give her a good, a legitimate contract so that nobody can ask any questions, and so that you look like the girl's patron saint. That keeps Ivan looking bad by comparison and Dalton stays out of the picture completely, understand?"

"But Dad, what about my profits?"

"The profits will come. They just won't come as fast. Let that be a lesson. You take shortcuts; you end up paying in the long run."

Dalton completes the task of emptying his desk. His next step will be to gather a few personal items from the almost completed studio. His packed suitcases are in safe keeping with the friendly guard at the security desk who was dismayed to hear about his sudden departure. He carries the loaded box out to the reception area. Once there, he sets it down to say goodbye to the receptionist. As he stands there, the elevator doors part and a tall, fashionable black woman with strong cheekbones and exotic eyes walks in. Her voice is cool and professional as she addresses the girl at the reception desk.

"Hi, my name is Terry Griffin. I'm here to see Samantha Choice."

"Yes Ms. Griffin, I will let her know you're here."

Dalton approaches the woman. His expression is quizzical. A sudden revelation bursts like a ray of light through the clouds. He continues brightly.

"Miss Griffin, how are you?"

"Hello, do I know you?" She responds warily.

"We have a mutual friend. I'm Dalton."

"Of course, I should have known; how do you do?" She replies offering her hand.

Dalton grasps it coolly and answers her with a smile and a shrug before turning back to recover his belongings.

Terry's expression widens marginally.

"You're leaving?" she asks, as if Samantha had not given her the whole story while toweling off from their shared shower.

"Actually, yes. It seems it's time to move on."

"Well, it was nice to have met you." Terry responds with feigned sincerity.

"My pleasure, I'm sure."

Dalton pauses by the door as he opens it and turns back to Terry.

"Terry... That wouldn't be like... Terrence, would it?"

The flash in Terry's eyes answers before she regains her calm. She turns to the receptionist without reply. It is enough of an answer. Dalton smiles and walks out.

The receptionist has followed the exchange with mild curiosity but the last words that Dalton spoke are too irresistible to be ignored.

"If you don't mind my asking, what did Dalton mean by that?"

Terry sniffs before answering.

"I'm sure I haven't the slightest idea. Will Samantha be along soon?" Terry shoots the girl a look that invites no further discussion.

"She's in a meeting with Mr. Choice. She should not be much longer, Ms. Griffin."

Samantha leaves her father's office having barely contained her anger at his pontification. It was a bitter pill. The fact that he was right about everything only made the pill that much harder to swallow. She walks past Dalton's office and is only mildly surprised that he has cleaned out and cleared out so quickly. Jennifer, Dalton's secretary until a few minutes ago, is seated at her desk trying to look busy. Samantha knows that she will have to sort the girl out, but feels less than equal to the task at the moment. There are plenty of other issues that require her attention, but needing a little while to absorb all of the morning's losses, she closes her door to make it clear to the ubiquitous Jasmine that she is not in the mood for any interruptions.

Staring out the window, Sam tries to gain some perspective on the events of the past twelve hours or so. The heavier cloud bank that threatened earlier has been replaced by a sky full of smaller white clouds. She has almost convinced herself that the loss of Dalton is no big deal, though a voice deep inside is not buying this line of reasoning in the least. She shakes her head to clear the image of his face as he accepted her litany of accusations without a trace of bitterness. Her mood runs warm and cold along with the lights and shadows being cast by the passing clouds.

The intercom buzzes and pulls her attention back to the here and now.

"Yes Jasmine, what is it?"

"Sorry to interrupt, Ms. Choice, but Terry Griffin is waiting to see you."

"Thanks Jasmine, go ahead and have her sent in." Samantha rises to meet Terry. 'It will be good to get to work,' she thinks, and goes over to open her door. As she reaches for the door handle a little tickle at the corner of her left eye causes her to stop and wipe at it. She is surprised to find the spot wet. 'A tear? Unbelievable!' It's so startling that all she can do is laugh as she greets her partner in crime.

The walk from Choice Publications Penn Station is long enough to clear Dalton's thoughts as he comes to terms with his situation. Dalton combined the box full of office possessions into his suitcases. The larger one has wheels and allows the smaller though still large second one to sit on top. The weight of his luggage, a suit bag and his camera bag is like a feather compared to the weight of his thoughts. Something is nagging at him but he can't quite put his finger on it. Knowing that the best way to block the thought is to try to force it, he focuses instead on the many possible next moves. His reputation as a photographer has risen in the past few months. There are certainly plenty of suitors who will offer top dollar right now. At the same time, perhaps he can take advantage of this crossroads to reconsider the path of photographer as artist. In this moment of reflection the sun breaks once more from behind a small cloud and while it is nothing like the image he saw earlier, it reminds him of that earlier stunning single ray of light. The flash is concurrent with the thought that he was trying to resolve moments ago. It had something to do with Terrence. He will have to give it a bit more room to breathe. Meanwhile, the symbolism of the light is too strong to be ignored and for the first time ever, a different method of expression is campaigning to be engaged; just a few words that might someday be heard by a visitor to his dreams.

> *My single Ray of Light*
> *Bursts from the shadows and illuminates with*
> *Wisdom and wit*
> *Scared for so long, but not since you*
> *Beauty defined but dismissed*
> *Forgive my blindness and*
> *Take my bargain*
> *Accept this weathered heart once more*

The few blocks remaining between his current location and his destination feel increasingly daunting as the weight of his luggage and camera gear begin to make their presence known. A cab is easily hailed from the multitude of available yellow vehicles and Dalton rests as the cabbie heads toward Penn Station.

38.

Penn Station

Arrivals and departures are listed on huge signs with spinning time and location markers that sound like the loud clicking of old fashioned typewriter keys as they change. Passengers gather under them awaiting the one notice that has a personal meaning. People pass by, streaming in all directions like schools of exotic fish. Dalton is seated in a waiting area. There are plenty of attractive women to keep him visually occupied during what's left of his wait. Professional women in spring time colors and light jackets hurry to whatever important event that lies next on their busy schedules trading floor space with mothers in bright floral dresses pushing carriages or holding tight to the shy charges walking at their sides. College girls with knowing looks, appraising eyes and tight uniform jeans challenge for his attention.

 The station is an architectural labyrinth with so many vistas. The entrance that the cab pulled up to had an impressive overhang and shared features with Madison Square Garden. It was so impressive that it got Dalton to thinking. Since there remained a good couple of hours until his departure, he found a locker for his smaller suitcase and took some time to explore. After all, it might be a while before another opportunity came along to see the place again. There are long halls with thick round columns, some painted and some metallic. A cavernous area presents steel arches that seem to reach miles into the air. Ticket counters abound with lines of customers. He found more than a few items to capture in the deep, cavernous recesses of his camera lens.

After he completes his tour, he reclaims his luggage from the locker and finds a seat. As the movement continues, Dalton begins to see less and less, letting his mind wander to his last moments with Sienna. With closed eyes, she is here beside him making the hard plastic as comfortable as his father's recliner. For a precious moment he can feel her warmth through his shirt and the tingle of his arm where it grazes along hers. He can almost believe she is here. His throat tightens as he opens his eyes and sees with his heart what his brain can't ignore. He is alone.

For a moment he considers leaving the station to grab a quick bite and waste some of the remaining time. The problem is that he has no appetite. Dalton releases a sigh and continues to await the moment to board the train. Finally, the speaker roars a barely understandable alert that the departure of the train to Philadelphia is forthcoming. He gathers his things and follows the crowds to the train. As he walks past his gate to the platform, there is a movement in a nearby shadow. However, this shadow is different in a subtle way. As if Dalton senses the presence, he stops suddenly and looks around, but Sienna is nowhere to be seen. Shrugging off the feeling, he continues.

The area near the tracks is a jungle of exposed steel, concrete and dim lighting. There are patterns of tile on the floors and a mix of tiled mosaics alongside more modern ads for decoration. The walkways are remarkable clean, but crowded and the push of people encourages a speedy departure. As he nears the train, a conductor sees the number of bags he is carrying and calls to him.

"Can I offer assistance, sir?"

Dalton is so impressed by the uncommonly generous gesture that he smiles and nods immediately.

"Thanks. That would help."

The conductor takes the wheeled bag from Dalton and moves steadily toward the train. Dalton follows still looking around as if he has missed something. At first, he looks across to the next platform. There are lots of people there, but nobody with the red hair and freckled smile he seeks. He has the feeling that whatever he is missing is much closer but while the feeling is strong, he still sees nothing. The conductor is ready to load the bags aboard. Dalton stops one last time to look around. 'Where *are* you, Sienna?' he thinks to himself.

The conductor looks on patiently as the younger man's indecision stretches on for several seconds.

"It's time to board the train sir."

From the shadow, a pretty red-haired woman finally emerges from between the steel columns. She calls softly.

"Dalton, don't leave yet."

Dalton looks around to see what his ears have barely heard. She steps closer. Dalton's eyes widen as he realizes it is Sienna. The conductor can hardly take his eyes off the new arrival, confirming with vigor the reality of what Dalton wants so desperately to believe.

"Sir, will you be boarding now?" the conductor asks without ending his appraisal of the pretty young woman.

"I'm afraid I'll need my bags back. It doesn't look like I'll be going anywhere."

With a quick nod, he turns and presents the recently loaded luggage. Presenting a warm smile along with the bags, he offers a nearly silent, gracious wish.

"Good Luck."

Dalton thanks the man quickly and walks toward Sienna as if he is in a trance. It's almost as if he is in a dream state rather than fully awake. He loads the suit bag over the handle of the suitcases and approaches her.

"All these years, no matter how happy, no matter how much I believed, a part of me still wondered if I was crazy. How? Where did you..."

Sienna smiles with damp eyes as she reaches up to touch Dalton with her own hands for the first time.

"I've been looking for you for a long time. I finally caught up."

"How long have you known?"

Sienna hesitates before she answers, forcing her quiet response through the powerful emotions racing through her.

"There were things I felt, but it was only recently, the past few years, that I began to put it together. When I did, I set out to find you."

They pause briefly. Their eyes lock as their bodies begin to accept the new reality. Dalton drops his things finally, and pulls Sienna closer; his hands grasping her arms gently.

"You were right about Samantha." Dalton added with and apologetic expression.

"I was so jealous. I could hardly breathe. I wanted to stop things, but I also knew you had a right to the kind of life you were asking for. I could have come to you a bit sooner..."

"Why didn't you?"

"Dalton, I was so afraid. I wanted a life with you, but..."

"But…"

Sienna rests her head against Dalton's strong shoulder and lowers her eyes as she struggles to find the right words.

The train starts to pull away. Sienna is waiting for the noise to return to the normal din of the station so she can answer. While the two are close together, a flash of insight hits Dalton. With all of the other things competing for his attention, his brain has come to a clear place regarding Terrence and he knows now what he should do next. Finally, the echo has retreated to a level where she can be heard and she responds.

"What if it wasn't the same? What if being together didn't match everything we'd had in your dreams? When I saw how Samantha deceived you, it became clear. I had nothing to lose. I had to know. I can't believe I was ever worried. Right here, right now, this is everything I ever dreamed of."

Dalton takes his hand to gently lift Sienna's chin until her eyes meet his once more.

"I still don't understand. What are you? I mean, how did you get into my dreams?"

"The easiest way I know how to explain this is to tell you a story. Want to hear it?" The beginnings of a grin light her face from the inside.

Dalton smiles as he runs his fingers through Sienna's fine red hair.

"Go ahead, tell me a story."

"Once upon a time there was a small girl. She lived in China with her two successful parents. They were entrepreneurs, expanding their holdings around the world. The little girl spent most days alone or in the company of a governess who spoke only a few words of English and the governess's daughter who was not particularly friendly. The little girl spoke only a few words of Chinese. In her loneliness she reached out with her mind..."

39.

Sienna: Once upon a time…

Standing in an isolated and hilly, wooded area to the west of Shanghai, is a large house with a roofline that looks a little like a skirt that has been blown up by the wind at each corner. It was a seasonably cool day in February. On one side there were rice paddies where there will be workers when the warmer weather returns. On the other side is a Koi pond surrounded by rocks of all sizes. I was sitting at a window, looking past the pond, watching a shiny black car driving over a rough road getting smaller and smaller. Through the dust coming off the back of the car, I could see the houses of the village in the distance. It's all I can do to keep from running outside and chasing the car, but the rain-filled clouds are starting to get darker. When the car finally disappeared over the hill, I stayed at the window trying not to cry. My parents would be gone for several days.

"Sit, sit, sit," instructs my governess finally. I hesitated for a moment, hanging on to the last image of the departing car before I turned away from the window. The sitting room was warmed by a fireplace with a steady, soothing blaze. The furnishings included a sofa and a pair of arm chairs that my parents brought to this place. They are worn from travel, but clean and surprisingly comfortable. The sofa is perpendicular to the fireplace and forms a triangular arrangement with the chairs.

My governess is sitting on the sofa. She is not old and not young. She has a few gray hairs in her dark black hair that falls halfway down her back in a single braid. She does not speak much English, but her brown eyes are kind and she never raises her voice even when I am being difficult. I take a seat on the chair to her left and pick up the book I discarded when saying goodbye to my Mom and Dad.

    The other chair is occupied by Liang, my governess's daughter. Liang is twelve and speaks very good English when she is of a mind to. Sadly, she is not of a mind to very often owing principally to the 5 years difference in our ages. I try to pay attention to the words on the page where I left off, but they are just sitting there paying no particular attention to me. I close the book and place it down on the seat beside me. I look over toward Liang, but while her eyes are pointed in my direction, I appear to have gone invisible again. My governess appears to have noticed her daughter's behavior. She rises with a soft look.

    "Have tea now?"

    My internationally acceptable nod sets her on her way to the kitchen. I look once more at her daughter, hoping for any response.

    "I like your mother, Liang. She is very nice."

    Liang adopts her customary bored expression while making a rather large show of picking up her magazine. She is clearly not in the mood for conversation. She turns the pages slowly and lets her eyes float just above them when she thinks I am not looking. Taking a last stab at the silence I meet her eyes with a question.

    "What will breakfast be, I wonder?"

When there is still no answer, I sigh loudly and lean back in my chair, closing my eyes and letting my mind float up and away. In quiet, lonely moments it feels good to float out into the world. I often float above the ground, above the sea or even the mountains, leaving the confining room behind. I don't float when my mom and dad are around, but that still leaves a lot of time when I am by myself.

I can feel Liang's eyes on me as I start to go, even without opening my eyes. She is peering from behind her book, watching me as my eyes are closed yet obviously not asleep.

I can't remember how old I was when I first started floating. At first I found the view from the sky a bit scary, but little by little I found that I could float higher and higher and see the ground fading away as I moved slowly over the land and eventually over the trees. Something is different today. I feel a pull. It's almost like I am a little ball bearing and there is a huge magnet grabbing at me from far away. The land begins to move more and more quickly below me. The sky in front of me is brilliant blue blur that is still quite bright. My travel is silent and I feel just the slightest movement of the air past me. After what seems like a long time, the land is behind me and is replaced by an endless expanse of water. Waves tumble and crash, often topped by whitening foam. Suddenly the sky opens as the clouds are left behind. It gets progressively darker. At one point I looked behind me and saw a sky that began to glow in shades of pink. I can hear rather than see a ship below me, the engines straining as it pushes through the cresting breakers. The sea becomes more of a featureless blur. It feels like I'm in a bubble with gloom below and gloom above. After the longest time I am back over land. High mountains topped with snow are followed by endless stretches of nothing at all. It is the beginning of evening. It won't be long until there are myriad points of light above and all around. Then it is too dark to see much, but now and again there are bright patches of light arranged in checkered patterns. In all this time I stay completely warm as if the most important part of me is still curled up in front of the fire.

    Just as suddenly as it started, the movement stops. I am standing in a darkened room. I slowly become aware of the sound of a young boy crying. Seeing his face, I know one thing for certain. I am a long way from China. I look around at the bare walls and the few boxes on the floor. They seem to indicate that the boy has just moved in or will soon move out.

    I begin to adjust to the darkness. Without touching the wall switch, I turn the lights on and somehow I begin to see that where I am right now has a magic that I instinctively understand. The boy's sadness tears at me and I know immediately that I have travelled all this way to comfort him.

    "Hey sleepyhead, wake up..."
Later I awoke from my travels to find Liang watching me, a curious expression on her face.

    "Where were you?" she asks with an attitude of dark suspicion.

    "What do you mean?"

"You were speaking to someone in English. It seemed like they were responding, or were you just pretending?"

It was so wonderful to have Liang speaking to me, even though I knew that she would stop just as suddenly once her curiosity is satisfied. I couldn't care at that moment if my next words sounded crazy.

"I met someone. They were dreaming and I spoke with them."

"I see. So this was a mystical experience then." She looks anything but convinced. I ignore her tone and answer as if she has been drawn in to my encounter.

"I guess so, but it certainly felt very real."

Suddenly, Liang turns to stare out the window. I can't help but notice that she has not responded with another challenging question, but replies with a strained quiet manner. She turns back to me with a totally different manner. Sympathy and something like jealousy are on her face now.

"The best mystical experiences do. Who did you speak with?"

"A very nice, very lonely boy; his name is Dalton. At first he didn't seem to like it that I was there. Then he realized that I wasn't there to hurt him and he changed."

"Ah, this is serious."

"Is it?" I sit waiting for my now talkative companion to continue.

"There is a proverb. It says 'If a string has one end, then it has another end'. I think that this day, you may have found your other end. Be not afraid of growing slowly; be afraid only of standing still. You must reach out again and again, until the string is run out or broken."

"That's beautiful, Liang. I can do that, but he thinks I'm a dream. In my heart, I know he's real. He's very far away, but I think I will always know how to find him. This could be so wonderful; this could also hurt very badly. Do you think I should do this?"

"Better do it than wish it done."

Suddenly I jump up from my chair to run over to Liang and hug her before she can stop me. She sits quietly with my arms around her, not returning the embrace, but not shrugging it away either.

"Thank you Liang, I will never forget how kind you were to me today."

"Tell him something for me. You will know when the time is right. Tell him that I said you are 'Meng Zhong Ging Ren', the girl of his dreams; the love in his nights. Perhaps it will be enough."

"I will."

Liang turns back to Sienna. Her look is worldly and a little forlorn.

"In my world, I will marry one who is chosen or one who is considered acceptable. In your world, girls get to choose. But perhaps in your case, you are more like me than I thought. Perhaps for you, the choice has also been made. I hope whoever has chosen for you, has done a good job of it."

40.

Sealed with a kiss

People race past as Dalton listens to Sienna's story. He is barely aware of them and awaits her next sentence patiently. For Sienna, the images from that day so long ago have produced such strong emotions that she is nearly overwhelmed. The walls of the station feel suffocating and close. Dalton senses her discomfort and leans in to pull her close. She accepts the comfort for a moment before pulling back to continue.

"Liang spoke to me once in a while after that, but only on that day did she find me interesting. My loneliness returned even stronger afterwards as I realized that she and I would not be friends and that she was as lonely, maybe more so, than me."

"I'm sorry."

"Well, it was a long time ago. Funny thing is; she ended up in California. She got a scholarship, left China behind and eventually married for love."

Dalton waits a few seconds to see if anything more is forthcoming. When he realizes that Sienna has finished her story, he asks the question that has been on his mind since he was seven years old.

"Okay, I get that you were lonely and I was lonely and something happened. My question is what happened?"

Sienna thinks for a moment, trying to come up with an explanation that makes any more sense now than at any of the other thousands of times she has tried to come to some understanding.

"The closest thing I can think of is mental telepathy. Something allowed my mind to link with yours; specifically with yours."

"Have you ever been able to link with anyone else? Have you tried?"

"I have tried, not because I wanted to feel what I did with you, but just to see what this thing really is."

"And?"

"Nothing. I couldn't make any connection. I think about that morning as I flew over the sea and I arrived at one very specific location. As I said, it seemed like I was being drawn to you. I have tried so many times to figure out how we happened. I don't know how and I don't know why. Maybe Liang was right; maybe it was mystical. Or maybe it was destiny."

Dalton tries to make sense of what he has now heard. There is no answer, at least not one that gives any feeling of completion. He struggles for a minute to deal with the idea that he may not ever know how Sienna came to him and in that precise second, the clarity arrives. Sienna did come to him. How or why is so much less important than the ultimate fact that she had indeed come to him on that night so long ago. The smile that lights in his eyes is so strong, so stirring, that Sienna cannot help but be curious.

"What are you smiling about?"

"It's so simple really. You found me... twice. I can't even imagine what my life would be if you hadn't."

With the surge of commuters pushing past, Dalton starts to realize how warm the platform is. It feels as if he might suffocate if he doesn't get to the fresh air immediately. Dalton grabs his suitcases and gear with one hand while urgently leading Sienna out of the building. Sienna is startled by the sudden change of attitude, but is unable to catch Dalton's attention. He sets a frantic pace as if he cannot stand another second in the crowded station. Sienna struggles to keep up and calls to him with an expression of concern, as if her lover has suddenly lost his senses. The two crash out into the bright sunshine of New York spring, nearly colliding with a passing pedestrian. As soon as Dalton finds them both in the clear, he only hesitates a second before he begins to kiss her. Sienna responds enthusiastically. The kiss is strong and deep, lips and tongues engaged fully, but then something even more dramatic and thrilling begins. It feels a little like the spread of warmth they experienced so many times in the past. They are connected. Much like the dreams, they are both aware of each other's memories, hopes and feelings. They continue to kiss while the magic spreads. No longer needing to speak, they communicate via thought. Dalton starts down the street looking for the next available cab.

'Dalton wait! Where are we going? I doubt that we can stay in New York,' Sienna shares.

'That's not gonna be a problem. I have plenty of money and even if I didn't, I am sure I can find another job. I can work right here or maybe I will start working on my artistic career.'

He smiles over his shoulder as Sienna learns everything Dalton has surmised.

'Hang on a minute,' Sienna cries as she does her best to assimilate all the new information. Dalton's smile gets even brighter, feeling as if the world has been lifted from his shoulders. They are joined in a partnership in a way that a marriage certificate could never do, not that he has any problem going forward with that step. When they are once more face to face, her questions have already faded. 'So there's no reason to worry about Samantha Choice. What you learned about Terry will keep her from being a problem.'

'That's it exactly. I know who Terry Griffin is and who she works for. I also know some very juicy details that Sam will be happy to keep quiet.'

Sienna begins to laugh as she realizes how little she has to worry about.

'So where *are* we going?'

'We're going to check back into my hotel. It was a long night and it's been a pretty long morning. I'm tired.'

Finally flagging a cab, the two take a moment to load Dalton's baggage into the trunk opened with no hesitation by the cabbie. Dalton holds the door as Sienna slides in. He follows closely and pulls her to him. 'God, you feel so good.'

"The Waldorf, please," Dalton says as direction to the cab driver.

Taking a moment to breathe Sienna in, her aroma is different than what he has known from his dreams, but with the new connection, even more satisfying. A new thought occurs. He looks at her with something like parental concern as the cab pulls away.

'You look very tired too. Don't you feel tired?' The long vowels of the word 'feel' are extended almost to the breaking point. Sienna understands immediately the message he is guiding her way. Her smile opens like the sun suddenly emerging from a bank of heavy cloud. Just as quickly she her eyes droop and her body relaxes against him as if she might fall over. Dalton loves how quickly she has adjusted to their new communication.

'I think you're right. I can hardly keep my eyes open. I'm exhausted.' A giggle slips from her mouth just as Dalton joins his to it. Sienna misses the sounds of their voices and decides to return to speaking.

"Better get me back to your hotel room right away."

Dalton stops suddenly.

"Uh oh."

The sudden change in Dalton's expression pulls Sienna up straight.

"What's wrong?"

"Well you know what this means, don't you?"

Sienna shakes her head, 'no'.

"There were all those nights we were together, those nights in my dreams?"

A look of understanding begins to show on Sienna's face.

"You can't be worried that it won't be as good in real life, can you?"

"Not at all, we'll be wonderful. It's only, now we'll have to be careful."

Sienna takes Dalton's hand in hers and squeezes it gently.

"No we won't, Dalton. No we won't."